The Broken Ones

Also by Stephen M. Irwin

The Dead Path

The Broken Ones

a novel

Stephen M. Irwin

DOUBLEDAY *New York London Toronto Sydney Auckland*

Copyright © 2011 by Stephen M. Irwin

All rights reserved. Published in the United States by Doubleday,
a division of Random House, Inc., New York,
and in Canada by Random House of Canada Limited, Toronto.

www.doubleday.com

Originally published in slightly different form in paperback in Australia by Hachette Australia, an imprint of Hachette Australia Pty Limited, Sydney, in 2011.

DOUBLEDAY and the portrayal of an anchor with a dolphin are registered trademarks of Random House, Inc.

Book design by Maria Carella
Title page photograph by Josef Kubicek/Vetta/Getty Images
Jacket design by Michael J. Windsor

Library of Congress Cataloging-in-Publication Data
Irwin, Stephen M.
  The broken ones : a novel / Stephen M. Irwin. — 1st ed.
    p. cm.
I. Title.
PR9619.4.I79B76 2012
823'.92—dc23   2011039733

ISBN 978-0-385-53465-9

MANUFACTURED IN THE UNITED STATES OF AMERICA

10 9 8 7 6 5 4 3 2 1

First American Edition

For Kitty.

The key to it all.

They haunt me—her lutes and her forests;
No beauty on earth I see
But shadowed with that dream recalls
Her loveliness to me:
Still eyes look coldly upon me,
Cold voices whisper and say—
"He is crazed with the spell of far Arabia,
They have stolen his wits away."

WALTER DE LA MARE, "Arabia"

The Broken Ones

Prologue

From page 1, *The Argus,*
September 10

EDITORIAL
Three Years on—Still No Answers

The ability of humankind to emerge from calamity into better times has manifested again and again throughout our history. The plague-ridden and religiously extreme Middle Ages birthed the Renaissance, the opening of the world by sail, and the Enlightenment's bright lights of science. Last century's appalling World Wars, with their unprecedented casualties, spurred discoveries that have yielded extraordinary peacetime benefits: penicillin, rockets, and jet travel. It remains, however, difficult to imagine what reward could come from the dark event that occurred three years ago today, the repercussions of which continue to be felt by each of us, in every corner of the globe.

On that Wednesday—commonly known as Gray Wednesday in the West, Black Wednesday in Russia, and the innocuous Day of Change in the People's Republic of China—few of us could have predicted how different our world would be today, three years on. None of us could have been expected to; no single event has so definitively tied psychological harm to economic depression and technological failure. The hallmarks of disaster, though, were instantly apparent: at just after 10:00 GMT, the earth's poles switched. Every compass in the world swung 180 degrees, and two hundred and sixteen passenger jets either collided or simply fell from the skies, with their navigation systems fatally flummoxed. No one knows how many smaller aircraft also fell, but estimates range between seven and sixteen thousand. Almost all post–Cold War satellites met a similar fate, with their onboard computing systems instantly and simultaneously failing, plunging global telecommunications into a new age of darkness from which we have only barely begun to recover. Few civilian organizations—indeed, few governments—have been able to launch new satellites because of the economic despair that now seems so deeply entrenched that many are regarding it as the new status quo.

We still tell our children that the sun rises in the east and Santa Claus lives at the North Pole, but we all know that north is south and the world is upside down in so many ways. The state of the global economy is dire. Unemployment here remains at 21 percent; in the UK, the USA, and Germany, it is closer to 25 percent. Japan, which was still recovering from nuclear disaster when Gray Wednesday occurred, is worse still, with unemployment at around 30 percent and rising. We don't know what is occurring everywhere; Saudi Arabia, Pakistan, Serbia are among the countries that have sealed their borders. But in those nations which are still attempting to participate in world trade, it is not just their blue-collar industries that have been decimated by depression and suicide: all sectors of all industries were hit hard by Gray Wednesday. The lack of a reliable workforce in the mining sector has resulted in coal shortages and power outages. Oil companies have suffered similarly, resulting in a rapid escalation in the prices of crude oil and refined fuels like gasoline and diesel. Most manufacturing industries have reported significant downturns as a result of erratic supplies of material, power, and workers. Crop and livestock industries are, if anything, even worse off; the rice, tea, coffee, cocoa, and rubber industries have all shrunk enormously in scale, and the resultant explosion in commodities prices has escalated inflation in countries too numerous to mention. With the sharp collapse in the value of legal tender, people everywhere have turned to older-fashioned means of exchange. Black markets have burgeoned, and almost everyone now uses barter at least a little and sometimes exclusively, further reducing governments' tax incomes. Poorer governments mean poorly paid government workers and a commensurate vulnerability to bribery. The conviction last month of the federal agriculture minister for contempt of Parliament is the tip of a large iceberg. As companies collapse and their surviving contemporaries scramble to fill the voids, graft and blackmail are becoming well-honed tools in all sectors of business.

The challenges to national economies have been worsened by a dramatic shift in global weather patterns in the past thirty-six months. Rainfall patterns have changed on all continents, and average temperatures have swung by up to seven degrees Fahrenheit: summer heats are rising, and the past three winters in the Northern Hemisphere have been the coldest on record. Climatologists speculate that the cause of this was the switching of the poles, but detailed research may take decades to conduct and unravel. Some people are not prepared to wait that long: in Turkey two years ago, and in South Korea last month, members of religious sects committed suicide on a massive scale—four thousand lives in total. Death on a smaller, more murderous scale occurred in January, when four men and a woman drove a bus packed with explosives through the main gate to the Large Hadron Collider, near Geneva: the explosion killed them and twenty-three staff members.

Nothing, however, has ameliorated the situation that Gray Wednesday has left us in. The federal Commission of Inquiry drags on, now under its second commissioner and still with no tangible results. Government-funded and private policy institutes have made innumerable recommendations to help preserve liquidity and protect jobs, but none have made any inroads toward finding a solution. Our country is not alone; the rest of the world is just as baffled. Our guests that arrived on September 10 three years ago seem fixed to stay; the psychological impact of their arrival may have to be judged by future generations. In the meantime, our economies run flat and our stomachs get emptier. The question remains: Where is the silver lining? Where, in short, is the hope?

Chapter 1

A boy emerged from the deep shadows under a dripping doorway awning, a cautious mollusk venturing from its shell. He was sixteen or so, his face a small, pale triangle above dark clothes, eyes hidden by dark lank hair and gloom. When he saw Oscar's car, he retreated into darkness.

Inside the tired sedan, Oscar Mariani gripped the wheel unhappily. Dusk: the hour when Delete addicts and street prostitutes rose to score or hook. The car's engine kept the repainted police cruiser's interior warm, and the windows were lightly fogged. Rain tapped on the roof, the sound muffled by the sagging hood lining. It was not a muscular downpour but a constant, weeping drizzle barely more substantial than mist. Oscar wondered if this rain would ever stop. It would ease, certainly, then a foggy morning might open onto a rare day of sunshine, then an inevitable storm . . . and another week of this god-awful wet.

He'd parked on the cruddy street opposite the mouth of a lane so narrow it was almost an alley. Halfway down it, the red and blue lights of patrol cars intruded, slicing through the drizzle, reflecting off the dull eyes of windows and turning the droplets of water on his sedan's windows into startling instants of sapphire and blood. Somewhere down there, dogs barked.

Oscar reached for the door handle and stopped to look at the man staring back at him in the rearview mirror. The stubble on his thin face badly needed either taming with a razor or grooming into a beard. Under thick coppery hair, his tall forehead was beginning to wrinkle as thirty faded and forty loomed. But it was his own stare that held him: gray, wide-set eyes that one woman long ago had called beautiful and another much more recently had called disturbed. Now they just looked exhausted.

Down the alley, figures crossing in front of the turning emergency lights cast long, insect shadows with scissor legs and swollen heads. Another polished white police car, glistening with raindrops, rolled around the corner near Oscar and turned down the alley to join the others. By its headlights, he could see a woman in a yellow raincoat hunched under an eave near the collection of squad cars. Neve was here already.

Oscar sighed and pulled on his waxed cotton motorcycle jacket, patched in several places but warm and blessed with lots of pockets, all full. From the seat beside him he took his black hat—a wide-brimmed squat thing with all the style of a dropped towel—and pulled it low onto his head. It was ugly, but it kept the rain off.

And the rain was cold; it whispered shyly on Oscar's shoulders and hat as he put the car key in the door and gave it an arcane series of twists until it caught and locked. He headed toward the flashing lights.

Old townhouses crowded in on both sides of the alley; their small back courtyards were separated from the garbage-strewn thorough-fare by a continuous fence that was an alternating patchwork of graf-fitied brick, graffitied timber, graffitied metal, and barbed wire. Despite the steady rain, the air smelled of burned things and urine. Three white patrol cruisers stood out like pearls in a coal hopper; in front of them were a Scenes of Crime van and an unmarked patrol car. Onlookers had gathered under awnings and in doorways: gray-faced people loosely hunched in tired clothes, smoking silently and watching with the atten-tion of seagulls observing picnickers, wondering what might be left behind.

"Where have you been?" Neve asked.

Neve de Rossa was more than ten years younger than Oscar. He was tall and she was petite; the top of her head barely reached his shoulders. Her blonde hair was wet and plastered flat, its peltlike sheen reflecting the emergency lights. Her face and shoulders were taut, as if she were in a ceaseless flinch, always anticipating a blow.

"Doing my face," Oscar replied. "I like to look good when I meet real cops."

Neve grimaced at his rusty stubble and stepped from cover, arms tight about herself.

"Cold?" he asked.

"Need to pee."

At a sheet-metal gate stood a uniformed constable in a clean blue slick, watching them approach from under his visor. From behind him came the loud barking of the dogs.

"You could have gone in without me," Oscar said.

Neve's cheeks, already pink, reddened a little more. "You're the ranking officer."

Oscar said nothing. He knew very well why she didn't go in alone. There wasn't much pride in announcing their unit. Over the past three years, Oscar's original small team of officers and public servants had dwindled, each quietly transferring away and rarely replaced. He'd become so used to the regular hemorrhage of faces that when Neve joined his unit over a year ago he'd treated her with frosty detachment, expecting her any day to realize her error and leave. For some reason, she hadn't. Now it was just him and her.

They showed their identifications to the constable, who didn't bother suppressing a smirk. The metal gate squealed as Oscar pushed it open, and the dogs redoubled their barking.

The tiny yard was all mud. Puddles of dark water reflected the glum light from the townhouse's kitchen window. Two dogs were frenzied shadows in the corner of the yard, straining in savage arcs against their heavy chains. Rain and evening had made their coats black, but their teeth shone a striking white. Their loud, brutal barks sent primal shock waves into Oscar's gut. The air was dense with the reek of dog shit.

Up a short rise of concrete stairs, the back door was open; within was a huddle of crisp blue uniforms. Silent lightning flashed behind them. Oscar coughed. The detective in the doorway turned; she had a scarred chin and unblinking eyes. Oscar tried to recall her name. She regarded him and Neve coolly, then said loudly, "Barelies."

Oscar's lips tightened. The nickname still rankled. Three years ago, when the Nine-Ten Investigation Unit was created, some wag thought "Nine-Ten" sounded enough like "Nineteen" that everyone soon began calling his unit the Barely Legals, an epithet thought doubly amusing because it also connoted a lack of law-enforcement power, which, like all good jokes, was at least half true.

The kitchen was so small that a man could touch opposite walls with outstretched arms—but not now in the crush of pressed blue trousers, shining blue raincoats, and gray wool suits. Oscar instinctively pushed through first, making room for Neve. She shrugged off his help. The ceiling was high and stained by decades of smoke and hot grease. The fridge was the yellow of an old tooth. A single bare bulb glowed feebly from the end of a perished rubber cord. The furniture looked salvaged. A figure lay on the floor, obscured by the forest of blue and gray torsos and legs. Flash: another photograph.

"Detectives Mariani and de Rossa."

A hush fell, and the ranks parted to let a tall officer stride into the kitchen. Haig's iron-gray mustache was neatly trimmed, and his visor was the polished black of a cavalry horse's hoof. On each shoulder epaulette was bright "birdshit"—three silver diamonds and a gold crest.

"Inspector Haig," Oscar said, glancing around the room at the blue uniforms crowded around the single body. "Outnumbered?"

Haig's smile was like a split in ice. "This one's homicide. Clean and clear. Save yourself and"—he nodded at Neve—"the young lady trouble."

Oscar shrugged and waited.

Haig's wide jaw tightened. "Ian?"

"Done," said the police photographer, scurrying aside.

The dead man lay in a puddle of blood that was seeping away through the join between two curled sheets of old linoleum. His once white dressing gown was stained in a dozen places with vibrant red rosettes of blood. He lay in a flamboyant pose, legs akimbo, an arm above his head, his surprised face turned half to the light above. One eye was a blank stare, the other a collapsed, leaking sac. The hem of his robe had ridden up a fat thigh to reveal pale flesh so streaked with veins it looked like a side of marbled beef. One stubbled cheek gaped open in a strange new mouth, a slit rimmed with blood. His neck, hands, arms, and buttocks had all been stabbed. Some of the wounds still leaked. In the blood sat two upturned dog bowls forever out of the dead man's reach, their ground-meat contents turning rufous as they absorbed his liquid.

"Darryl Ambrocio Tambassis." Haig hardly had to raise his voice to be heard above the dogs outside. "Forty-one, unemployed. Still warm. Around thirty stab wounds."

Oscar looked at the dead man's hands; the nearest lay curled like a pale crab, and there were three clear stab wounds in its puffy flesh.

"Did you find the weapons?" asked Oscar.

"The knife is already en route for testing," Haig said. He hesitated. "Weapons?"

"The wounds on his hands are two different profiles," Oscar said. "One type has two sharp edges, the other only one. Two knives."

Oscar felt every eye in the room on him. The air seemed statically charged.

Haig's smile turned even colder. "Shouldn't you be interviewing your suspect, Detective? You've only got"—Haig checked his watch—"eleven minutes."

"Thirty," corrected Oscar. The deeply flawed legislation allowed him thirty minutes at the scene with the suspect.

Haig shook his head and pointed his large, well-manicured thumb at Neve. "She's been here twenty already."

"I was outside!" Neve protested.

"Neve," Oscar said quietly.

Neve returned a glare, but bit down on her words. Oscar looked at Haig. "Suspect?"

"Wife," Haig replied. He motioned for his officers and the others to allow Oscar and Neve deeper into the house. "Ten minutes," he said, and turned away.

Oscar stepped into the gloomy hallway. As he glanced back he was pleased to see uniformed cops grumbling as they dropped to hands and knees, looking for the second knife.

———

The rest of the townhouse was as narrow and murky as the kitchen. Its ceilings were disproportionately high, there were too few lights, and the lack of furniture let footsteps echo dolefully. Yet another uniformed officer leaned against the hallway wall. When he saw Oscar and Neve, he wordlessly pushed himself off the wall and led the detectives through a door into a small sitting room. It was piled high with urban detritus: a rusted walking machine; cardboard cartons overflowing with shabby Christmas decorations and moth-eaten clothes; magazines on dog breeding, dog nutrition, dog fighting. The single window was a small rectangle of cobweb gray, unwashed in years and hunched on a sill dusted with the husks of dead flies. Rain pattered on the glass. A single bulb hung by a rubber cord the color of dirty bone, its glow hardly stronger than a few candles would make. Junk had been pushed aside to make space for a card table at which sat a young detective constable in a trim single-breasted suit, trying to read a newspaper by the weak light. Opposite him sat a string-thin, middle-aged woman whose hands were knitting themselves in worried knots. Another door was set in the far wall.

"Barelies," said the officer in the doorway.

The seated detective looked up from his newspaper. "Seriously? You're still bothering?"

Oscar waited.

The uniformed officer left. The young detective sighed and held out his hand for their IDs.

"Oh, come on," Neve said.

Oscar squeezed her shoulder. She made a disgusted sound and handed over her badge. Oscar passed across his. The young detective made a show of inspecting them and handed them back. Oscar noticed the lad was already developing a paunch.

"Bazley, isn't it?" Oscar asked. "Haig teaching you manners?"

Bazley ignored him and turned to the thin woman. "Mrs. Tambassis?" She seemed to flinch at the mention of her name. "Detective Sergeant Marina and Detective Constable de Rossi here—"

"Mariani," Neve corrected, "and de Rossa."

"—are with the Nine-Ten Investigation Unit. Due to the nature of your statements to arresting officers, these detectives have been summoned." His voice slid down into the monotone of rote learning. "They are vested with full rights and powers to interview you, and anything you say to them can be used as evidence at trial. Should you wish not to answer their questions here, you have the right to a formal interview in a state police facility, courthouse, or location nominated by a justice of the peace with or without representation by a practicing solicitor. Do you understand?"

Oscar watched the thin woman's eyes dart about nervously. They fixed for a moment on a blank patch of wall near the other door, then slid off it as if they'd met something oily and unpleasant. She nodded once.

Bazley looked at Oscar and glanced meaningfully at his watch.

"We know," Oscar said.

Bazley picked up his paper and sauntered from the room.

Oscar removed his wet hat and wiped his hands on his trousers. "Mrs. Tambassis? May we sit?"

Seen closer, Mrs. Tambassis was not middle-aged but a hard-worn thirty or thirty-two. She licked her lips, then nodded again. Oscar and Neve sat. Oscar placed a small digital recorder on the tabletop and slid it toward the woman; she stared at it as if it were a new and dangerous breed of insect. He switched the recorder on and a red light, small as a pinprick of blood, glowed on its side. The woman's eyes followed a worried triangular path—recorder, Oscar, Neve, recorder, Oscar, Neve— then dropped to watch her own nervously weaving fingers. The room was silent except for the muffled barking of the dogs.

"Aren't you going to ask me anything?" she said.

Oscar gave Neve an almost imperceptible nod.

"Mrs. Tambassis," Neve began, "you killed your husband this evening. You took two knives from your kitchen and while he was carrying bowls of food for his dogs you stabbed him. Many, many times."

Mrs. Tambassis watched her hands. "*His* dogs," she said quietly.

"You called the police?" Neve asked.

The woman nodded. "My phone's out of credit, but the cops are a free call."

"And when they came and asked you what happened, what did you tell them?"

The woman looked up. Her skin seemed as thin as wax paper; the bags under her eyes were puffy and gray. "You know. You're here."

Oscar could see that the front of the woman's dress was flecked with blood; a long spittle of red was crusting dry on her neck.

"Mrs. Tambassis," Neve continued, "can you tell us why you killed your husband?"

The woman's eyes darted from the tape recorder to the empty wall, then back to the little red light.

"I didn't think it was him I was stabbing," she said. "I thought I was stabbing him." She jabbed her finger at the blank wall.

"Who, Mrs. Tambassis?"

"*Him.* My uncle. Uncle Robert." She spat the name like a sour thing and stared at the empty wall with scared, angry eyes.

The small room fell silent for a long moment. Even the dogs were momentarily quiet, and the only sound was the sad whisper of rain.

Oscar spoke: "We don't see anyone where you're pointing, Mrs. Tambassis."

"Of course you don't." She looked at Oscar as if he were a fool. "He's dead."

Oscar could see that the woman was very pale. Her pulse thumped in the artery on the side of her neck. Shock's setting in, he thought. The hammering knowledge that she'd taken another person's life would soon shut down her thought processes, and they'd get nothing from her.

"Mrs. Tambassis," Oscar said carefully. "If it was your uncle's ghost that you attacked, why is your husband dead?"

The woman glared at him. "He must have stood in front of Darryl just as I went for him, didn't he?"

"And you've seen him before today?" he asked. "Your dead uncle?"

Her eyes narrowed, wary of a trick question. "I've seen him since we all started seeing them."

"Which was?" Neve asked.

"You know very well."

"Tell us anyway."

"You know this!" the woman cried. "Years! Since Gray Wednesday. Jesus . . ."

Neve glanced at Oscar. Time was running out.

"Why did you attack your uncle?"

The woman stared at the table for so long that Oscar thought the stunning curtain of shock had closed already. Then she spoke again. "Because he's always here. You know what they're like. Always standing there, staring. Wherever I am, there he is, watching me. Yes!" she accused the empty wall, lips curled in disgust. "He's there when I sleep, there when I wake up. When I eat, when I shop, when I p-piss. My fucking filthy shadow . . ." She looked at Oscar, tears welling in her eyes. Her voice dropped to a dry whisper. "You know what they're like. The dead bastard has stolen my life."

Oscar felt the back of his neck turn cold.

"Let me get this straight, Mrs. Tambassis," he said. "Your dead uncle has been tormenting you—"

"Yes," the woman nodded. "Tormenting, yes."

"Driving you mad."

"Mad." She nodded quicker, eyes bright.

"Making your life unlivable."

"A living hell, exactly!"

"For years."

"Years! Three years!"

"Then why did you wait until this evening to attack him?"

The woman blinked like someone who'd just missed a step on a staircase, surprised and suddenly afraid of a fall. Oscar knew this was the critical point, the terminator moment that separated truth from lie, or a well-planned lie from a spontaneous one.

"Had you attacked this vision of your uncle before?"

The woman's eyes flicked between Oscar and Neve.

"Yes," she decided.

"How?" Oscar asked. "Fists? Threw something?"

"Threw something," she agreed. "A glass."

"And what happened?"

"Well, it broke, didn't it? On the wall."

"It went through him?"

"Some detective."

He kept his voice low and reasonable. "Then why did you attack him this evening with knives?"

The woman's tongue emerged again, a cautious snake from its hole, testing the air and finding it fraught. Her eyes found the red light of the recorder; she forced herself to look at a spot on the floor and said nothing.

Oscar said, "And why did you wait until your husband had both hands occupied holding dog bowls?"

Silence settled heavily over the room. Neve glanced at Oscar. Her expression betrayed nothing, but a small gleam of triumph lit her eyes. Oscar knew that Neve held little love for people who murdered their spouses.

"Mrs. Tambassis," Oscar continued. "What do you know about Clause Seventeen of the Personal Sightings Act, also known as the Nine-Ten Act or the September Ten Act?"

The woman licked her lips again. A sheen of tight panic closed over her face. "I know what everyone knows. If you, if you kill someone and you say you were told to do it by"—she nodded harder, as if to say, *You know what I mean*—"by the dead, you won't go to jail."

"Which is just what you say, isn't it, Mrs. Tambassis?" Oscar asked. "You say a ghost made you kill your husband."

Her hands twisted like fighting insects.

"Do you know, Mrs. Tambassis," Oscar continued, "how many homicides we attend where the suspect invokes Clause Seventeen? It's become very popular. There are even people—some of them are street lawyers, some of them are just off the street—who for a few dollars will tell a person exactly what to say to the police about Clause Seventeen, should they happen to commit a serious crime. Like arson or homicide. Did you know that?"

The woman kept staring at the floor and shook her head. "I don't have a few dollars," she whispered.

That I believe, Oscar thought.

The woman's narrow lips worked as her mind tried to concoct a way out. But it wasn't coming, and fresh tears of fear and frustration welled in her overbright eyes.

"I don't . . ."

"If there is a problem with your story, Mrs. Tambassis, it's not too late to change it."

The woman looked at him. Her cheeks trembled, and her whole body had started to shake.

Beside him, Neve radiated energy. Oscar nodded to her.

Neve spoke clearly. "If you were attacking the ghost of your uncle, Mrs. Tambassis, why didn't you stop when you realized it was your husband? Why did you continue to stab him more than thirty times?"

The woman's eyes were wide and glossed with tears. Her face worked like the front of a building whose foundations had just been detonated. She glanced over at the empty patch of wall.

"Fuck you!" She spat not at Oscar or Neve but at the empty wall. "Fuck *you*!"

The dogs barked louder. The handle of the second door rattled softly, and the door opened a crack.

"Mummy?"

In the open doorway Oscar glimpsed the pale curve of a little girl's face. Haig had made no mention of a child.

The thin woman's breath seemed to catch in her throat. With great effort, she wiped her cheeks and forced lightness into her voice and said, "Go back to your room, Button. Mummy's nearly done."

The door began to close.

"Wait," Oscar said. The door stopped moving. The pale hint of face hovered in the shadows behind it. Oscar turned to the woman. "Your daughter?"

Tears finally broke from the woman's eyes and rolled down her ashen cheeks. "You don't need to see her." She looked at Neve, pleading. "Don't."

Neve stared back evenly.

"Come in please, honey," Oscar said to the girl behind the door. "It's okay."

The door creaked wider, and a small girl stepped sheepishly into the dimly lit room. She was barely taller than a toddler, but her face could have been a five- or an eight-year-old's. It was hard to tell, because huge scars distorted one entire side of her small face, pinching in one eye and lifting one side of her mouth into an ugly sneer. One nostril was far too large where part of her nose had been torn away. The disfiguring scars, still fresh, crawled down her neck like pink lizards. Oscar felt his stomach tighten. The girl had been savaged, and it wasn't hard to guess how. The dogs were still barking.

Oscar looked again at Neve. She was watching him, and he knew what she was thinking. *And now we have motive.* Oscar knew he should have been thrilled. Instead, he felt hollow and tired.

"Mummy shouted," the little girl said quietly. Her "sh" sound came out like a whispered hush. "I want to see Mummy."

"Of course you do, sweetheart," said Oscar, and he smiled. He was out of practice and hoped the expression didn't look as beastly as it felt.

The girl moved quickly across the room and slid like a shadow behind her mother. The woman didn't know where to look—she chose to stare at the digital recorder on the tabletop. The main door opened, and Bazley looked in. "One minute."

"Then get out," Oscar said.

Bazley slammed the door shut.

Oscar looked at the woman. Her daughter's hand had crept around her waist and was clutching it tightly.

"Mrs. Tambassis?" The woman's wet eyes slowly met Oscar's. "Did your husband's dogs do that to your daughter?" The woman's brow became a mire of furrows, and tears rolled.down her cheeks. "Why didn't you press charges?"

The woman lifted her chin. Her soft voice was full of contempt. "I did," she said. "They didn't stick."

Oscar switched off the digital recorder.

"Oscar," Neve said. "What are you doing?"

Oscar ignored her and instead leaned toward the woman, speaking low and quickly. "You hold to your story. You went for your uncle. I'll sign off on that, and under—"

"Oh, Oscar!" snapped Neve. "What the hell!"

"—Clause Seventeen you should only be charged with involuntary manslaughter and get home detention and court-appointed counseling. Okay?"

The woman stared at him for a long moment, then nodded.

"Oscar!" hissed Neve.

Oscar dropped the recorder into one of his many pockets. He opened the nearest door and called for Bazley. He arrived, carrying a red folder. "Well?"

Oscar said, "We're done."

"We're not!" Neve said.

"We're signing her Seventeen," he finished.

"Oscar!"

Bazley held out the folder, amused. "Jesus, Mariani, why not get a rubber stamp—"

Suddenly, there was a meaty slap, and Bazley's eyes widened. Oscar was surprised at how whip-fast his own hands had moved, one slapping and grabbing a handful of stomach skin and twisting hard, the other restraining the young man's wrist. He was surprised, too, at how angry the comment had made him. Something to think about.

His voice was mild, though. "Detective *Sergeant* Mariani. Not Jesus. Maybe the facial hair threw you."

Bazley was pale. "You're a crazy f—"

Oscar squeezed tighter, pain cutting off the detective constable's words.

"I'm going," Neve said, fed up.

Oscar released his grip and Bazley skittered backward, clutching his belly. He kicked halfheartedly at Oscar. "Loser," he hissed.

Although it was whispered, the word smarted. Oscar signed the form, threw the folder down beside the young detective, and went after Neve.

———

He edged past the dogs to the gate and down into the lane. The rain was heavier, and the sky was dark gray. Night was settling fast and the surrounding buildings were black cliffs. A shining hearse was now parked outside the fence and two undertakers in suits were lifting the murdered man's covered body into its back. Half of the police officers had left; only two squad cars remained. Neve hadn't waited—she was already stumping up the alley. Oscar sighed. He'd let her cool down; in ten minutes, she'd be fine again

"A shame." The voice was edged brightly with good humor.

Oscar looked around. Haig idled out of the metal gate, hands in pockets. Very few inspectors left their offices for the shitty streets. Haig seemed to relish it. He was also the only inspector Oscar knew who preferred a uniform to a suit.

"How's that?" Oscar said.

"Well, I thought you had one there." Haig reached into his jacket for a small tin box of cigarillos. "Clear motive. No lawyer. A story that was, let's face it, uninventive at best."

Haig shielded the cigarillo from the rain with his cap brim as he lit it, then, almost as an afterthought, held the tin out. The smell of good tobacco made Oscar's mouth water. He shook his head. Haig was not a man to be indebted to.

"Why wasn't Tambassis prosecuted when his dogs ripped that little girl's face off?" Oscar asked.

Haig returned the cigarillo tin to his pocket and exhaled blue smoke. "Who knows? Record keeping has gone to hell in the last few years. He must have slipped through the cracks."

Oscar knew how those cracks were greased. Another reason Haig liked to arrive in person.

"You gave Bazley pause for thought," Haig said.

"No respect for rank."

Haig looked Oscar up and down. "Coming from you, that's quite rich." He took one more puff, then threw the hardly smoked cigarillo into the fast-flowing gutter water. Oscar couldn't help but watch longingly as the precious cylinder fizzed and floated away.

"Bazley is young," Haig continued. "He doesn't understand why an officer would poison his own career to save a criminal."

Oscar met Haig's stare. "But I'm sure he's learning how to fast-track his career by becoming one."

Haig's eyes were chips of blue ice. The soles of Oscar's feet prickled, like he'd just stepped to the edge of a chasm. Then Haig turned, unlocked his cruiser, and slid into the driver's seat. He took off his spotless cap, revealing a healthy pink scalp under closely cropped slate-gray hair. "Poor Mariani. Trying to lead the lost to safety with his little broken compass." Haig's car started with a purr, nothing like the asthmatic wheeze of Oscar's sedan. He looked again at Oscar and smiled. "Touch one of my officers again, you might just disappear."

Haig closed his door. A moment later, the white cruiser slipped like a pale shark up the narrow street. Oscar felt eyes watching him and turned. The female detective with the scarred chin stood beside the metal gate. Kace was her name, Oscar remembered. She watched him with mild curiosity. He wasn't flattered; she'd regarded the stabbed corpse of Darryl Tambassis wearing the same expression.

"I hear they're shutting you down," she said.

"I heard that, too," he replied. He'd been hearing it for two years. He nodded at the graffitied fence. "What about the dogs?"

"We'll find someone to take care of them."

As if her curiosity were now satisfied, Kace looked away. Oscar noticed a graffito on the fence. It had been spray-painted through a stencil: it showed a cartoon ghost wearing a crown at a jaunty angle. Its grin was friendly, but instead of eyes it had dark, empty sockets. The jolly spirit was in intimate congress between the legs of a buxom woman whose own eyes were wide either in heavenly ecstasy or abject terror. The caption read, "Ghosts Fucking Rule."

Suddenly, from behind the fence came four cracker snaps of gunshots. Oscar jumped. Kace watched him, smiling coolly. The dogs had finally stopped barking.

———

Neve was waiting near his car, her arms shoved deep into her pockets. Rain slicked her hair down onto the shoulders of her jacket. She was trying not to shiver.

"We need to buy you an umbrella," Oscar said.

"I have an umbrella." Her jaw was tight. "What we need is a prosecution."

Oscar unlocked the passenger door, then his own. The air inside the car was cold now, and their breaths condensed into fragile drifts of fog.

"We had her, Oscar. Neatly painted into a corner." He'd expected Neve to have calmed; instead, her words were clipped razor sharp. "She couldn't afford a lawyer. Ten more seconds, she'd have cracked. We had her."

Oscar looked down the alley. The last police cruiser's red taillights came on, and they disappeared down the narrow thoroughfare. He threw his hat on the backseat. "What good would it have done? We prosecute her for murder, she ends up in a cell with six other women, and that little girl loses her mother."

Neve nodded impatiently, as if she'd heard it all before. "Yeah, yeah. One less victim clogging up an overloaded system. But she stabbed him in the *eye*. She *did* murder him."

"I thought you Catholics didn't believe in divorce."

It was a bad joke, and badly timed. Neve stared out the windshield, almost vibrating with tension. Oscar couldn't recall ever seeing her quite so wound up. In the street, shadows were detaching from shadows. More rough trade coming out now: hookers and rent boys, black marketeers and thieves. Oscar put the key in the ignition; the starter motor ground dismally before the engine coughed and caught. "We're fine. When did they convict Dixon? Week and a half back?"

Neve looked at him. "Dixon was five weeks ago."

Oscar covered his surprise by pretending to adjust his seat belt. Had it really been five weeks?

He felt Neve still watching him. "I know why you do it," she said.

"That's enough," he said quietly.

"Letting these fucking criminals walk won't undo what you did three years ago."

"*Enough.*"

Neve wrapped her arms tighter around herself and stared at nothing. Oscar put the exhausted sedan into gear and eased out into the street. As he turned the wheel, his headlights picked out the young man who'd been watching him when he arrived. As Oscar drove closer, the boy took a shy half step back into the alcove. Ignore the dismal shit, Oscar thought. But he couldn't help himself. After he'd passed the doorway, he glanced through the smeared window at the boy. Reflections of Oscar's headlights fluttered over the youth's pale face like white wings: a brief touch, then gone.

Oscar pressed hard on the accelerator, keen to flee the whores, junkies, scarred children, and the dead.

———

How nice not to smell smoke. No matter how much he hated returning to headquarters, there was always the one upside of filtered air. Coming here was like a respite in a clean-scrubbed oasis. Even the hospitals suffered rolling blackouts, but here in City Station the air was warm and cleansed of the harsh smoke tang that, over the past three years, had burrowed its way into almost every room, every brick, every piece of clothing, every pore. People burned anything to cook and heat, although most didn't have a proper wood-burning stove, so many ended up accidentally torching their houses and themselves.

He tried to engage Neve in small talk as they wended between the empty cubicles of the Industrial Relations Branch to his so-called department's so-called office, but she remained silent. They reached a tiny corner desk adjacent to the emergency exit: two chairs, one old computer, a cluster of cell-phone chargers, and a hat stand Oscar had brought from home. There had once been a laminated sign that proclaimed the cubicle the Nine-Ten Investigation Unit, but one day the sign had simply vanished, leaving only four blue gobbets of Blu-Tack. The next day, even the Blu-Tack had disappeared. He hung his wet hat on the stand and switched on the computer. Its cooling fans clattered dispiritedly.

He turned to Neve. "Listen—"

"Back in a minute."

He watched her walk toward the far corridor, which led to the toilets. He sat. His in-tray held his payslip and an interoffice envelope, the kind scrawled with the names of previous recipients and sealed with string looped between two buttons. Oscar ignored them and typed a brief report of the Tambassis interview. With every word, he grew angrier. Haig and Neve were both right: Tambassis had strong motive, a piss-weak story, no lawyer. An easy conviction. There were few people whose minds had not been twisted when the ghosts appeared on Gray Wednesday. Many couldn't cope with their new, ghastly shadows; hospitalizations for self-harm erupted, and psychiatrists and telephone helplines were overwhelmed. In the short time it took to understand that the ghosts weren't leaving, suicide rates skyrocketed. And many began taking others' lives. Violence and murder cases soared, and courtrooms became jammed with perpetrators who claimed that their ghosts "drove them to it." There were stories of ghosts leading people to lost brooches and buried tins of money, so why not to murder? Clause Seventeen had been included in the Personal Sightings Act to exonerate people whose mental health had been genuinely fried by the appearance of the dead. At first, the courts had loved the clause: it was the perfect pressure valve for a justice system on the brink of explosion. But there lay the curse of Clause Seventeen—since nobody can see any ghost but the one that haunts him, if a suspect stuck firm to his story, who could argue that his specter *didn't* drive him to kill? Courts and cops alike soon realized that blaming the dead was becoming the blanket excuse for murder and units like the Barelies were hastily created. It was Oscar's job to sort the psychologically traumatized from the rat cunning. Yet here he was, signing another get-out-of-jail-free card. Not doing his job. He clicked Print.

As the old Epson in the middle of the office wheezed into life, he felt eyes on the back of his neck and turned. The shadows near the stationery cabinets were deep; the outer corridor was dark. He was alone. The printer clacked loudly and paper began to hum through the machine. Oscar turned again to his desk, and leaned back in his chair. He had discovered that if he angled and twisted just so, he got a glimpse of buildings, and so could tell his father without lying that his office had city views. True, there wasn't much to see; the skyscrapers were almost all dark spires, and only the occasional streetlamp worked. In the distance, near the Captain Cook Bridge, the glass flanks of a distant high-rise flickered an angry, wasp-wound red. Fire. Oscar waited for his cell phone to ring, but it slumbered in his pocket. Nine-Ten calls were becoming rare. Some uniformed cops simply skipped the protocol of calling the Barelies to a crime scene even if the suspect pleaded Clause Seventeen, and received no reprimand. Oscar wondered if he should have removed himself the day the sign disappeared.

"On your feet, Mariani!"

The thunderous yell at his shoulder made Oscar jump.

Jon Gest was as big as his voice was deep. He was like some huge Victorian-era engine made flesh: a heavily cast machine of wide catenaries and lumpen mass, capable of grinding rock or pistoning tonnage without fatigue. Unstoppable. He was grinning.

"Jumpy bastard. Guilty thoughts?"

"About why your wife keeps calling, begging to be satisfied by a real man."

Jon's grin faltered, and he sat heavily in Neve's chair—it sagged precariously under his nineteen stone. "It's true. Leonie knows." He shook his head and ran his fingers through his hair. "My heart hasn't been in the marriage since my true love rejected me." He grabbed Oscar with hands the size of hams and planted a wet kiss on his cheek. "Love me, Oscar! Love me back!"

Oscar pushed his friend away and wiped his face. "Idiot."

"No woman wants you. You're wound up tighter than an eight-day clock. I'd be surprised if you could convince your one-eyed baldie to puke, let alone make a kitty shriek." Jon chuckled and began hunting through Oscar's desk drawer, flipping aside bulldog clips and spent batteries. "Where are they?"

Oscar reached into the lowest drawer, pulled out a half roll of peppermints, and threw them to Jon. "So why the visit? Bored? DCP burning the midnight oil?"

Jon worked for the Department of Civic Prosecutions. When he and Oscar had been reassigned from Ethical Standards, they'd been split up: Jon—with a law degree—was slid down and across to DCP. Oscar—with half an undergraduate degree in philosophy and three semesters in horticultural studies—slid even further to this tiny desk without a sign. Judging by Jon's unpatched jacket and reasonably new shoes, he was doing okay.

"Nope." Jon chewed. "Looking for you."

"Aren't you lucky?"

"*Au contraire, mon ami.* Detective work. I *detected* that you were here. And speaking of here: here."

He handed Oscar a folded sheet of paper.

"What is it?"

Jon suppressed a smile and nodded for Oscar to open it. In Jon's handwriting were a name and two phone numbers.

"And this is?"

"A job." Jon smiled openly. "Friend of a friend told me. Cushy position, ranger service in the state forests up north. Decent super, sick pay, no stress, simple. Applications have closed, but my mate's mate reckons they're still open to hearing from the right person." He nudged Oscar with a prodigious shoulder.

Oscar stared at the paper as if it were a curiosity from another century, the purpose of which wasn't quite clear.

Jon leaned forward, excited. "It's plant shit, your kind of stuff. You know, like your precious damn fruit trees but on a big scale. Easy work. I mean, the pay's not great, but nothing runs on money anymore anyway, right?"

Oscar nodded. "What about Neve?"

"Neve's smart. She'll be fine."

Oscar looked at the phone numbers a moment longer, then up at Jon.

"Couldn't get me anything in DCP?"

Jon's expression faltered.

"Oscar." He sat back in his chair. "Man, sometimes . . . I just don't know."

"Haig threatened me tonight," Oscar said.

Jon sighed. "Here we go."

"Oh, come on, Jon. *Haig.* Would you want to leave the service with him still here?" Even to his own ears, Oscar's voice sounded childish and petulant, but he couldn't stop himself. "We had him."

"We didn't have him," Jon said. His voice gained a hard edge. "We half-had him. Maybe quarter-had him. Then we totally lost him. I don't want to go over all this again. Good Christ. He's an *inspector.* He won."

"He tried to have you killed."

Jon shook his head, exasperated by a subject that had long ago become boring. "Look, one: I don't believe that—"

"Stabbed."

"—and two: so what? I'm here. If he did try, he failed. And now we're out of Ethical Standards and we're no threat to him. We're safe. Isn't that enough? I'm not saying the slate's clean, but Christ, does it matter anymore? It's a whole new world now. Everything's different, everyone's got grief. You especially, man, I know. But, seriously, you gotta move on." He tapped the note with one solid finger and stood. To Oscar it felt like a wave lifting beside him. "I thought this was a way to help with that."

The door at the far side of the silent office opened. Neve entered, adjusting her holster and straightening her shirt. She saw Oscar and Jon, lifted her chin, and headed over.

Jon looked down at Oscar unhappily. "Leonie's birthday party. Sunday. Sevenish." Before Oscar could speak, the big man was on his way out, greeting Neve in passing. "Detective de Rossa, looking beautiful."

"Sergeant Gest, looking married."

Jon grinned and ambled out of the office.

Neve arrived at the desk. Her face was dry, but she'd missed a tiny patch where her mascara had run. The lights in the bathrooms weren't good. Oscar congratulated himself: he'd let a murderer walk free, physically assaulted one of Haig's detectives, pissed off his best friend, and made his partner cry. As Mrs. Tambassis had said: some detective.

"It's late, and we don't get overtime." Neve's words were clipped.

"We're done," Oscar said. "Could you just grab that from the printer?"

While she was gone, he opened the interoffice envelope. Inside was a memo from the deputy commissioner. The budget review of State Crime Command, scheduled for next quarter, was being brought forward to next week. One telling sentence was highlighted in yellow: "All units must provide a two-page (max) summary of operations during the last financial year (i.e., arrests, charges laid, prosecutions), including person hours per."

Oscar felt his mouth go dry. Unemployment was running at twenty-five percent; state-funded institutions were acting like desperate field surgeons, cutting off useless limbs, and the police service was hacking with fervor. Budgets ran on statistics, and the Barelies' statistics were less than favorable. As Neve had pointed out, they hadn't brought in a prosecution in weeks.

And whose fault was that?

Jon must have caught wind of the advance review and had begun hunting about for a safety net for his former partner. Instead of gratitude, another flurry of dumb anger sloshed about inside Oscar. He didn't need saving.

"What's that?" Neve nodded at the memo.

Oscar folded the paper. "Reminder not to use the east elevators after nine."

She held out his printed report on the Tambassis interview. Oscar could see that her hand was trembling. "I don't feel comfortable signing this."

He nodded wearily. "I didn't ask you to."

Oscar signed it, put it in the interoffice envelope, addressed it to the attention of Inspector Moechtar, and put it in the out-tray.

"I'll drive you home," he said. "And, listen—"

He looked around. She'd already left.

———

It was payday, so Oscar found a working ATM watched over by a uniformed security guard who wore a new pistol in a polished leather holster. Oscar keyed in his PIN, did a quick calculation, then emptied all but the fortnightly mortgage repayment from the account.

The traffic was thin, so it took only half an hour to reach his destination. At red lights on the way, he riffled through the banknotes, setting aside enough for gas, food, and the small tips and tiny bribes that kept this new world spinning. He put the remaining cash in a plain envelope.

He pulled into a street lined with bare-limbed liquidambar trees, their twigged fingers poking at the rain. He parked in front of an unremarkable, boxlike house on stilts; the glow from a kerosene lamp warmed one window, but it was not inviting. Oscar left the engine running, went to the mailbox, and slid the envelope in—it made a pitiful slap as it hit the bottom. As he turned, he saw movement in the yellow-lit window. A dark figure stood there looking down at him. Oscar felt his heart beat a bit faster. The figure watched him a moment longer, then slid the curtain shut.

Oscar felt relieved to drive away. As he did every time.

———

A quarter of an hour later, he stopped the car in front of a metal shutter door that was rusted and covered with graffiti. The garage was at the side of what was once a tapas restaurant but was now—like so many thousands of buildings—a boarded-up shell. Oscar rented the garage from the former restaurateur because his own tiny house a few hundred yards away had no off-street parking. He unlocked and lifted the shutter. The metallic clatter was loud in the empty street, and he looked around to see if the noise had attracted anyone. The street remained still, no movement other than the steady tumble of drops and the slosh of black water in gutters. He drove the car inside, dropped the shutter, and clicked the brass padlock shut. He pulled his hat hard over his head, shoved his hands into his pockets, and strode out onto a footpath that was cracked and overgrown with lush weeds.

The roads were empty of traffic, but not empty of cars: both sides were lined with vehicles, some of them festooned with faded bouquets of parking tickets. Most had smashed windows, a few were no more that burned shells, all of them had been stripped of wheels, seats, mirrors—anything that could be removed in haste and peddled. Sump boxes were cracked open and their oil drained for use in lamps. Driving was a luxury few outside the Heights could afford. Half the cars in the city—half the cars around the world, Oscar supposed—had been dented or crashed on Gray Wednesday. His own car had gained a dent in the front. Oscar drew down another shutter on that memory.

Rain tapped on his hat and waxed jacket. Voices ahead in the dark.

The Church of St. Brigid stood as dark and imposing as a castle, with pointed spires and tall windows as narrow and deep as arrow slits. Those stained-glass windows were now boarded over with warped and spray-painted plyboard. The church grounds commanded a sweeping view: the city's skyscrapers punched up into the low sky a half mile away, and the surrounding suburbs were a patchwork of blacks and grays, sprinkled with weak yellow stars of kerosene lamps. Once, Oscar had been pleased to live so close to the city; now he felt he was in some kind of shackled dance with it. As he passed a low brick wall, he saw a fire burning inside an old washing-machine tub between the church's brick buttresses. Flames hissed as drops fell from under the eaves. The wet air carried the unmistakable, acidic smell of Delete—a cheap hallucinogen made from solvents found in correction fluid and cooked in basement drug labs. The firelight cast tall shadows over the church's brick flanks, heavily spray-painted with tags, grotesque faces and roughly drawn sex organs. Feet shuffled in the shadows.

"Ciggy, mate?"

Oscar couldn't tell if the voice was male or female; it was as rough as boot heels on husks. A figure detached from the darkness behind the dancing flames. "Cigarette? Tea? Greek for a tea bag."

Oscar heard a muffled sound of metal and fabric, something being unzipped. Or unsheathed.

He drew his pistol and held it in clear view.

"'Kay, okay." The shadow retreated.

His street was steep, and he walked slowly so as not to slip on wet leaves that would never be swept. Houses were dark and close together. His own was a slim, pretty timber worker's cottage that sat expectantly on a skirt of white battens, as if tonight might be the night Oscar would finally clean and paint her. He unlocked the front door and was about to call out that he was home, and felt foolish. Old habits. His keys slipped from his grasp and hit the wood floor with a clatter. As he bent to retrieve them, a dark shadow slipped silently behind him, shoving against his calves and tripping his feet. His mind yelled in a sudden panic—he put out one hand to stop himself from falling and his other arm fumbled for his gun. The shadow then did a loop and came back to rub itself against his arms and legs. It let out a gravelly mew.

"Sissy." Oscar got up, the pain in his knees making him feel old. "Idiot."

The cat looked at him archly, as if to say, "Idiot? Who was the one who fell down?" His purr sent deep vibrations up Oscar's legs for a moment, then the cat sauntered with a strange, crablike gait into the dark kitchen. A less milquetoasty cat was difficult to imagine: Sisyphus was unnaturally large, and his coat was a battleground of ashy-gray fur and hairless patches of scarred skin. One ear was ripped at its edges, the other was half gone, and he walked as if his spine had been permanently redirected. He checked his food bowl and let out a disappointed growl. Oscar took off his coat and lit the hurricane lamp; the cat's pupils became large orange orbs.

Oscar squatted on the tiled hearth in front of the fireplace, slipped his fingers into two almost invisible holes, and pulled out the false brick panel. Behind were three shelves: on the bottommost were two boxes of cat food. It seemed no time since there had been dozens, bought before the big supermarket on LaTrobe Terrace went out of business. That was nearly two years ago. When these biscuits ran out, Sissy would have to start eating leftovers.

While he squatted, Oscar took quick inventory of the other two shelves. A depleting carton of condom boxes, a few blister packs of genuine Viagra tablets, three cardboard boxes of tea bags in sealed sachets, several cartons of foul-smelling Jilu cigarettes, and one of infinitely more valuable Camels. With the global labor shortage, anything made, picked, tapped, or sorted by hand had become horrendously expensive. Beneath the smokes, some bars of French soap, 9-mm. cartridges, and one and a half cartons of LP propane canisters. Behind those, his real treasures: salt, pepper, paprika, olive oil, and a bottle of French Bordeaux that he was saving for an occasion that warranted French Bordeaux. He closed the cache and filled Sissy's bowl. The cat wolfed his food.

Oscar set a saucepan of water on the gas ring, and it began to tick as it heated. He opened the kitchen window. Rain dripped steadily from the awning above the window like strings of dirty glass beads. Somewhere out in the night, a fusillade of gunshots rolled off the wind. A few moments later, a single shot, then silence. Closer, two doors down, a small weasel-headed dog named either Terry or Derek yapped for the ten thousandth time, and a deep-voiced woman yelled for Terry/Derek to shut the Christless fuck up. Oscar filled a glass with water and poured it onto the soil of the potted oregano on the windowsill he was trying to coax back to life after a fortnight of leaden, leaking skies. Below, in the yard, the rain tutted in the leaves of his lime and lemon trees, and a cold breeze ruffled the stands of rosemary and basil and the overgrown patch of lawn grass. The world turned from black to silver for a moment as lightning, getting closer, stabbed at the TV towers on the hunch of hills to the west. A moment later came a rumble of thunder.

Oscar checked the water and stripped off his damp clothes, shivering. The fingers of cold air on his skin raised goose bumps, and forgotten blood stirred in his groin. It was just neglect, he knew; like the house, the organs were waiting impatiently for attention. Two fumbling affairs since the divorce, both mercifully brief and both truncated by sensible women who saw past whatever little rough charm he had left into an empty future. He felt idiotic and desperate. He searched the dark houses surrounding in the vain hope that a window would illuminate for him, revealing a shapely silhouette.

Knowing he shouldn't, Oscar pulled open the kitchen drawer and found the piece of paper he'd tried a hundred times to throw away. Sissy watched from the floor, and his eyes narrowed as if in disapproval. Oscar found a phone with signal and dialed.

A click as the phone was answered.

"Hello?" She sounded tired. "Hello?"

In the background, Oscar heard a man's voice. Then crying. An infant: a hungry newborn.

"Hello?" Sabine repeated. Her voice changed—quieter, harder. "Hello?"

He hung up. His penis had lulled to a sleeping pendulum. The first year, there had been reasons to call Sabine—the separation, the divorce, division of assets. The second year, fewer excuses, the odd checks to see if the other was attending a mutual friend's party and to negotiate around awkward meetings. After her remarriage, there had been no cause to call. They'd loved each other once, then their marriage became a bicycle pedaled on one side only—still a bicycle, but dangerous. Finally, the acknowledgment that they had to get off before they both crashed. He'd bought out her half of the mortgage and kept the house. Why had he fought so hard for it? The house was a museum from which all valuable exhibits had been removed, a leaky-roofed symbol of the foolish hope that things could be reversed, that time could go backward, that accidents could be undone.

Sissy startled Oscar, jumping onto the kitchen bench, to the windowsill, and out into the night. The water was boiling now. Down the street, Terry/Derek barked again. Oscar yelled, "Keep your bloody dog quiet!"

Lightning split the sky again, turning night briefly to ghost-white day. Below, under the bare persimmon tree, stood the boy. His pale triangular face stared up at Oscar, as it had for the past three years. On Gray Wednesday, everyone on earth suddenly found himself with a ghost at his side. Many people became haunted by someone they knew: a dead father, a dead grandmother, a creditor, a friend, an enemy. Neve got her mother. Mrs. Tambassis got a lecherous uncle. Sabine got her baby sister, dead thirty years; Jon got a cousin killed by meningitis. Oscar was haunted by a stranger: this boy he didn't recognize. Under the black, skeletal branches, rain passed through the dead boy as if he were smoke. The boy shuffled shyly, as if unwilling to advance or unable to retreat. After a moment, he tentatively raised a hand as if in greeting.

Lightning flashed again, and Oscar could see the pits where the boy's eyes should be—like finger holes poked into wet, dark sand. Lidless and shifting and worming.

"Go to hell," Oscar whispered.

The boy's hand wavered.

"Go to hell," Oscar repeated, and closed the window. He pulled down the shade and took his bathwater off the stove.

Chapter **2**

Three years earlier

S abine was blocking the hallway.

"Tell me you're not serious," she said.

In his mind, Oscar was already sliding past her, out to the car, racing along city streets to the alley.

"Yeah, I am," he said, gently taking her forearm. "I have to go. We can talk later—"

She slapped his hand away, and he blinked. She'd never hit him before. It was like reaching into a box of cereal and pulling out a wasp. Her usually pretty face was pulled as tight as a balloon over a fist.

"You want me to cancel the weekend," she said. The word "cancel" made her snarl.

"I have to go, Sab."

"No!" She slammed her hand against the wall, and the prints hanging there rattled in their frames. "You *always* have to go. You *always* have something."

He didn't have time for this. He took hold of her arm again. "Jon's waiting for me."

"*I'm* waiting for you!" She grabbed his arm hard and rose on her toes, yelling into his face, "I'm *always* waiting! Waiting for this shift to end so we can eat a cold dinner, or that surveillance to end so we can have a civilized fucking Saturday together, or some other fucking investigation to finish so we can have a holiday!"

Sabine was the chief financial officer of a charitable trust whose board included some of the state's most notorious prima donnas— a former Olympian, a dance doyen, a Man Booker winner, several media-hungry entrepreneurs. She had to deal weekly with their fits of pique and bizarre demands, yet Oscar had never heard her lose her temper. Nothing like this. "It's one weekend, Sab. We're just postponing."

"It's 'tomorrow syndrome,' Oscar. It never comes! This weekend was the one we postponed a month ago—and that one was postponed from fucking April!" She spat the last word out.

He knew she was right, but it didn't stop the burners under the nasty brew in his gut turning up to full.

"It's my job, Sabine. You knew when we—"

"When we started going out blah-de-blah, I don't care! It's not a job, it's a life! It's *our* life, and it sucks! You're either at work or you're writing a work report or you're home and making calls about work. Why do you need to work this hard? Look at you."

He gritted his teeth. "I'm trying to get—"

"You're getting fat! You've got no time to exercise, you've always got a cold. I can't remember the last time you got me off; Christ knows what you're doing for yourself."

He glanced at his watch. It was five to nine. He was due to meet Jon and the new informant at nine. She saw him check the time.

"Oh, for fuck's sake." She sagged away from him, shaking her head.

"It's Haig, Sabine."

"Haig, fucking Haig, fucking Haig! What about me?"

He pushed her aside and strode out the front door, slamming it hard behind him.

————

He drove too fast, running orange lights, the speedometer nudging eighty. His heart hammered in his chest, pushing angry blood uselessly behind his eyes, into his forearms. But inside he was cold. It didn't matter. What mattered was Haig. What mattered was that finally, after a nine-month investigation that had been teetering on the brink of exhaustion, he and Jon had found someone willing to go on the record about Geoffrey Haig.

Rumors that Haig was on the take had been rife long before Oscar joined Conduct and Ethical Standards, but there seemed no live soul willing to give a hair of evidence against him. Rumors spread like a virus, infecting the body then keen to jump further. When the media began implying that Haig, then head of the state's Organized Crime

Group, was turning a blind eye to certain criminal actions in return for who-knew-what, the commissioner ordered Ethical Standards to investigate. It took Oscar and Jon six months of delicate cozening to uncover a picture as old as time: steal a little, go to jail; steal it all and become king. And Haig was king. A very wily monarch who chose his vassals carefully. These were men and women who were in equal turns smart and intimidating, and who all knew the drill: if you're caught, don't squeal, because squealers vanish. Three informants and one cop had disappeared in the preceding two years. Nothing—*nothing*—was ever found of them. No one knew if they'd been paid off or put down. Well, that wasn't true. Some people knew, but they were smart or scared or rich enough to say nothing.

Oscar had pushed for permission to bug Haig's home and cell phone. Rather than put another officer at any risk of retribution, he had planted the bugs himself. But Haig's conversations and telephone calls were benign to the point of stultifying: kids' swimming lessons, roof repairs, chats with his elderly mother. Perhaps Haig knew that his home was monitored, or perhaps he was naturally suspicious and played it smart. His finances were even more benign, but behind the trust accounts was a Gordian knot of investments that curled in on themselves, offering teasing glimpses of blandly named banks in the Channel Island Bailiwicks and the Cayman Islands.

The break had come with Jon receiving a call from an aggrieved narc. He hadn't been paid properly, and one of Haig's people had put the word out that he couldn't be trusted. He was angry, and willing to go on the record. He wanted to meet Jon and Oscar somewhere private, to sound them out. And now Oscar was running ten minutes late.

The main street running north through Fortitude Valley was four lanes wide; two were jammed with nighttime traffic and two packed tightly with the parked cars of patrons visiting Chinese restaurants, massage parlors, tattoo parlors, pubs, nightclubs, strip clubs—a colorful tinsel world of shadow, blinking lights, mirrored glass, and fake gold. Oscar steered his car into a side road where the lights were fewer and the shadows deeper, and then into a back street where there were hardly any lights at all. He knew the alley the informant had chosen. It was a smart choice: a spot behind a bar frequented by Chinese Australians, older men who liked to gamble and knew how to keep secrets. In daylight hours, the alley was choked with delivery vans stocking cold rooms with bok choy, Tsingtao beer, and slaughtered poultry; at night, it was empty except for the raucous hum of a dozen massive fans in heat-exchange units. Impossible to bug.

Oscar saw Jon's Ford sedan; by training and habit he parked a good ninety feet or so distant. He locked the car and walked quickly. Spring had arrived, but the air was still and cold. Gutters smelled of cabbage and spoiling fish. Oscar's footsteps echoed off brick buildings. He checked his phone; no messages, no missed calls. From the mouth of the alley came the filtered hubbub of men's voices inside the building, and the electric hum of cooling fans. The alley was barely ten feet wide, a canyon of darkness.

"Jon?" Oscar called.

No answer. He reached into his suit pocket and found a thin pencil flashlight. He flicked on its beam.

A large rat scurried from a hole in the lid of an industrial Dumpster. Ahead, a row of washing machine–size boxes that rattled, blowing fetid air around the alley. On the cold asphalt between two Oscar could see a dark lump of clothing, a motionless crescent of face, a pale hand.

He ran.

———

"That's it?"

The General Duties senior constable who'd been first on the scene after Oscar's call looked up from his notepad.

Oscar nodded. "That's it."

The officer closed his notepad.

"I'll need a copy of your report," Oscar said. "And Scenes of Crime's when they're done."

"No problem." The senior constable stood. "Good luck."

He left Oscar alone in the Emergency Department cubicle. Three bays down, a child wailed. Burned, Oscar had gathered from the whispers of nurses; flannel pajamas and a bar heater. He stared at the floor of the empty cubicle. Jon's bed had been wheeled away to the operating theater more than an hour earlier. No one had come yet to mop up the spatters of blood. He was amazed that his partner had any left to spill; the alley had seemed awash with it. Eight stab wounds.

"But nothing vital," the paramedic had said as they bounced along in the back of the ambulance. Jon's shirt was open, and his bearlike chest was a patchwork of adhesive bandages. His head was wrapped in white gauze. "He's lucky."

Oscar's phone rang shrilly. He checked the screen. Sabine. He stared at it a moment, then rejected the call.

————

It was two in the morning, and the alley now glowed like a strip-light in a darkroom, almost too bright to look at. To Oscar, it seemed smaller, plainer, unmysterious. Scenes of Crime officers in blue overalls prowled the gutters, emptied the industrial bins, dusted broken bottles, photographed every square inch. The senior officer came up to Oscar, shaking his head. No weapon, no prints. Oscar paced and watched. Men and women in blue uniforms entered and exited the bars and clubs nearby. He waited another two hours, and learned nothing.

————

It was after four, and kookaburras were laughing in the dawn. Sabine rolled toward him as he slipped into bed. Her arms closed around him. He wondered if it was out of love or habit.

"Your inspector rang," she said. "Told me."

"Sorry. I got caught up."

"Poor Jon."

Then she rolled away.

When he rose at nine, she'd already left for work.

————

Oscar was allowed in at lunchtime. Jon was pale but awake; tubes and hoses ran in and out of him, and a clear plastic oxygen mask covered his nose and mouth. Leonie held his large hand. Oscar had first met her the week that he and Jon were partnered in Ethical Standards. She was as petite as Jon was big. Where his footfalls shook rooms, she moved with fairy-fine steps. He bellowed; she giggled silently. They were perfect opposites, and always seemed genuinely delighted to see Oscar and Sabine. Seeing him now, Leonie rose, kissed Jon's cheek, squeezed Oscar on the arm, and left the partners alone.

Jon lifted his big face to look at Oscar and forced a smile. It made Oscar feel like crying.

"I'm so sorry," Oscar said.

Jon shook his head, and the lines on his monitor danced.

"Was it your narc?" Oscar asked.

Jon lifted a finger with a VO_2 monitor attached and pointed at his bandaged head. "Didn't see." His voice was a dry whisper behind the mask. "Whumped me. Wallet's gone. Left the gun." He shrugged.

Oscar nodded. The attacker wasn't likely to be the informant. Why risk an assault for a few bucks in a wallet when, as a grass, he could make hundreds or more? No. Most likely this was just another stock-standard assault and robbery. Shamefully preventable.

"I should have been there," Oscar said.

"Glad you weren't," Jon said. "Could have been both of us."

But Oscar saw the look in his eyes.

———

Oscar returned to headquarters to write his report. On his desk waited a bouquet of flowers. The card read simply, "Commiserations. G. Haig." Oscar flung them into the wastebin.

———

A week later, Oscar received two pieces of news: Jon had been released from the hospital, and the investigation into Geoffrey Haig was suspended pending "appraisal of progress." One healthy diagnosis, one a fatal one. He left his inspector's office on numb legs and marched straight down to the parking lot. The sun was low in the west as he pulled out of headquarters and steered into the heavy traffic. Everything felt fragile: the tangerine sunlight sparking off windscreens, the cool air, his career, his marriage. The whole world felt overwrought and teetering: another lingering, hard winter in the Northern Hemisphere;

more crippling earthquakes in Japan, Chile, New Zealand; bushfires and floods, cyclones and tsunamis.

He steered around a bus. Two young men in business suits crossed against the lights. Oscar leaned on the horn. One of the men raised a finger without breaking conversation. Oscar pressed hard on the accelerator and turned the wheel.

The setting sun was dazzling, striking the smears and dust inside the windshield into a wash of gold. *Commiserations. G. Haig.* Fuck him, the arrogant shit, Oscar thought. He couldn't wait until the day—

There was a boy standing in the middle of the road.

Oscar jammed his right foot on the brake pedal and wrenched the steering wheel to the left. An instinctive move, and one that he would perform over and over in his dreams. The view over the car's hood slewed away from the boy and toward the footpath. Oscar could feel the tires slip and squeal as the car hurtled too quickly toward the shadowed shop awnings above the footpath. Right in front of him, directly before the charging hood, a man and an adolescent girl were walking with their backs to the car that was about to hit them. Oscar turned the wheel again, right right right . . . but it didn't respond. The tires slid. His foot was jammed so hard on the brake that his leg shook. Then a nasty jolt and the sound of metal snapping as the front wheel hit the curb and bent in like a losing boxer's tooth. Vaguely, over the sounds of failing metal and squealing rubber, he heard people screaming. The car shuddered, its momentum slowed but still strong, and the front bumper smacked hard into the aluminum seat of a bus stop. In the dreadful slow motion of the inevitable, he saw an advertisement for a new romantic-comedy film starring two pretty American B-list actors—the shout line read, "Sometimes Nothing Fits." The car smashed the seat aside, dumping its weight on one broken wheel and jolting as the other front wheel buckled. The hood was now just a few yards from the man and the girl. Maybe then the man heard something, the grinding of metal on asphalt: he began to turn. The girl, though, did not. Oscar could see that her head was down. She carried a schoolbag over one shoulder. Her hair was tied up in a loose bun, and wisps of chestnut hair as fine as spider silk drifted at the base of her skull over a long, cream-colored neck.

Oscar's hands gripped the wheel as hard as if it were electric. The steering wheel didn't even kick as the front bumper struck the girl behind her knees. Her head turned, just a little, as if someone had called her name . . . then, as fast as the snap of a finger, the car ate her. Her spine whipped, and her descending pelvis struck the hood edge with a sound like a green twig breaking. Her head flung back and those pretty hairs blurred, then her legs, pinned under the stopping car, jerked her forward again and out of sight. But Oscar heard the crack as something broke on hard ground. The car juddered to a stop.

He unclipped his seat belt and rushed out into the cool air. He was aware of people screaming, of the sounds of traffic, of more tires squealing . . . but the thuds of his own footsteps and the tight hiss of his breaths were louder. The man who'd been walking alongside the girl, who Oscar would later learn was her father, was staring at his broken daughter, wearing a frown, as if unsure of what he was see-ing. Oscar bent to the girl half hidden under the car's sagging front. The blood was just starting to come from her in rivulets. One arm was cocked uncomfortably behind her back; the other seemed to reach forward like a relay runner's. Her face was turned to the west, and was unmarked, but a corona was growing behind her cheek on the cold footpath—a spreading crimson puddle that reflected the light. Her eyes were glazed, and one was filling red with blood. Her mouth was open in a small expression of surprise.

Oscar looked around, ready to tell someone to call an ambulance.

The street was in chaos. Some cars had rammed others, and yet more were smashing into those. A truck had struck a light pole across the street, and wires were sparking. People were pointing in all direc-tions and yelling. One woman stood stock-still in the middle of the road between screeching, sliding vehicles, staring horrified at empty space. A riderless motorcycle was spinning on its side down the middle of the road, trailing sparks. And in the sky Oscar saw a white jetliner plunging steeply to earth.

In the midst of all this, ninety feet or so down the footpath, a young man with a pale triangular face watched Oscar through eyes that were all black shadow.

Chapter 3

When Oscar drove through the main entrance, he saw only one patrol car in the wide, leaf-strewn parking lot. He parked next to the white cruiser, pulled on his hat and coat, and stepped into the cold rain.

No overhead lights illuminated the field of wet asphalt, but that wasn't surprising; these days even facilities like this had their power heavily rationed. Oscar rubbed his cold hands together. Dawn was still an hour away.

Neve was waiting near the tall chain-link fence, her cheeks flushed in the cold, wet air. Rain rumbled on her umbrella.

"How did you get here?" he asked.

"Train." She pointed out into the dark. "It's only half a click from the station."

Jesus, Oscar thought. The trains were dangerous enough in daylight hours—they seemed to draw like magnets the barely hinged who wanted a captive audience to bash, stab, or burn. At night, even uniformed cops traveled in trios and wore Kevlar vests. But Neve was different from him in lots of ways. She carried her gun loaded, for starters.

"You should have stayed in bed," he said. "I can handle this."

She said nothing. Oscar noticed that the skin under her eyes was dark, a sign of poor sleep. He felt an annoying fillip of guilt. He covered it by indicating the lone squad car. "Interesting change."

She shrugged. "Maybe Homicide hasn't arrived yet."

They avoided puddles in the potholed asphalt on their way to the pedestrian gate. Despite the steady rain, the air smelled ripe and spoiled, a thick brew of feces and rot.

Oscar pressed the intercom buzzer and waited. Cold seeped up through his shoes. He pressed again. A tin sign was clipped to the fence, exhorting caution and explaining processes—all forms and functions of earlier, more ordered days. Someone had used a marker to write across the verbiage, "Shit." Across a dark courtyard beyond the fence was a long, low building. A single light glowed behind one of the many windows.

"Hello!" Oscar shouted through the fence. "Police!"

A rectangle of matching glow appeared beside the window as a figure arrived in the open doorway. "Detective Manari?"

"Mariani," Oscar replied.

The gate latch buzzed like a dying hornet.

The sewage plant's night supervisor was thin; a cheap cigarette cantilevered from one corner of his mouth. He briefly touched hands with Oscar and Neve, then turned, picked up a stained flashlight, and led them deeper into the plant.

"Your friend is waiting for you," said the supervisor.

It took Oscar a moment to realize that the supervisor was referring not to a corpse but to the police officer who was already there.

"We're a separate department," Oscar explained.

"Aren't you detectives?" The supervisor finished his smoke and immediately lit another without breaking stride. He didn't share.

"Yes," Neve replied.

"Murders?"

"Generally."

"Then you'll love this."

The supervisor opened a final door, and they were out again in the rain. The smell struck the nostrils like a blow and wiped the back of the throat like a filthy thumb. Oscar understood why the supervisor chain-smoked. They followed his drunkenly swaying light up a set of metal stairs. When their path intersected an empty walkway, Oscar saw the supervisor glare out at a patch of darkness and curse under his breath.

Oscar shivered. "Who is yours?" he asked.

The supervisor looked back at Oscar, as if ready to tell him to fuck right off. Soon after Gray Wednesday, it became rude and intrusive to ask a stranger who his ghost is. It was as if the phantoms were dirty secrets that, if unacknowledged, might suddenly disappear as readily as they'd arrived. Of course, they had not. Oscar found the question about ghosts a useful button to press: people didn't expect it. The supervisor ran his fingers through his greasy hair, seeming to remind himself that it was a cop who'd asked, so he should answer.

"My father," he said, and snorted a sour laugh. "Cocksucker always said if I didn't pull my socks up my life wouldn't be worth shit." He aimed his flashlight into the empty corner and grinned savagely. "Yet here I am, Dad, in a world of shit, so what the fuck did you know?" The supervisor looked again at Oscar and Neve. "Don't know why we yell at them. They never talk back, do they?" He continued up the wet metal stairs. Oscar stole a glance behind him, but there was no sign of the dead boy.

A minute later they emerged on a gridwork landing; under a solitary halogen light sat a constable wearing a uniform as new and well-finished as his patrol car, smoking a cigarette. When he saw Oscar and Neve, he got to his feet.

"Barelies?" he asked. "Nine-Ten, I mean?"

Oscar nodded.

"Thank God," the constable said. "Yours." He headed for the gate, but Oscar caught him by the arm.

"Wait on. Where's Homicide?"

The constable shook his head. "I figured it's for you guys. And my shift ended an hour ago." He shook off Oscar's grip and hurried down the metal stairs. A door slammed, and he was gone.

"Luke!" the supervisor called into the surrounding dark. His voice echoed off hard concrete and metal. "Luke!" He turned to Oscar. "Hopeless shit. I don't know how you go, but all I got for staff are hopeless shits."

"I have her," Oscar said.

The supervisor looked at Neve, then nodded bitterly, as if that confirmed how some people have all the luck. He gestured for Oscar and Neve to follow him along another walkway.

"On nights I used to have two guys, but one left and never come back, so now I just got Warm Hand Luke. He's probably in the can jerking off. The rest of us need blue bombers to bar up, but Luke? He slings cheese all day long." The supervisor shook his head and started down a steel ladder. "He's a lazy fucking retard, but he sticks around because I let him keep what he finds in the secondary filter box."

Oscar tested the ladder. It wobbled but held. He descended. "Like?"

"Oh, all sortsa shit. Sometimes money, sometimes costume jewelry that might clean up. So Luke hangs around here like a bad smell." The supervisor laughed at his own joke. The sound of machinery grew louder as they went lower. "It was Luke who found her."

They reached another metal landing. The smell was so profound that Oscar's nostrils decided to surrender and accept that they were overrun. He could see Neve working hard not to retch. That was one good thing about predawn calls—no food to lose. They followed the supervisor along the gangway and around a corner, where he stopped and shined his flashlight out into space. The wavering beam picked up two enormous augers—parallel screws each three feet wide and thirty long, sitting beside each other like shotgun barrels. They were set in half-open tubes that rose at 45 degrees from some point below where Oscar and Neve stood to a concrete dam wall overhead. The massive screw on the right was turning, hypnotically rising and rising, lifting foul-smelling oily sludge up to the top holding tank. Its twin, the screw on the left, was still.

"There," the supervisor shouted, leaning out over the rail and pointing the white circle of his flashlight beam downward.

At the bottom of the left screw, the light caught pale flesh. A naked body was caught in the metal. It had been savagely sectioned by the massive helical blade and was twisted at awful, unnatural angles. Oscar felt his gut tighten; behind him, he heard Neve vomit quietly through the grille floor.

"Smoke?" he loudly asked the supervisor.

The man appraised him through slitted eyes. "A dollar."

Oscar shook his head and reached into one of his many pockets. He produced a sealed condom in a plastic wrapper. Worth more than a dollar, but Oscar simply didn't have spare cash. The supervisor inspected the date on the seal, pocketed the prophylactic, and lit a cigarette for Oscar. The cheap smoke tasted like burned soil but settled his roiling stomach.

"You'll want to get down," the supervisor shouted, opening a metal hatch and revealing another, narrower steel ladder.

The three descended to the thick concrete wall of the lower outlet tank from which emerged the twin screws and the most awful smell Oscar had ever inhaled. He offered his cigarette to Neve. She shook her head.

Three flukes of the screw blade had embedded themselves in the girl. At first glance, it looked as if she were embarrassed at being found in this awkward pose and had turned her head shyly away from spectators and into the half-tube—then Oscar saw that the blade had taken hold of her face, torn it from her skull, and stopped only after it had crushed the naked bone of her lower jaw. One leg had been severed and wrenched from its hip socket. Her torso had been split open, and one arm was gone. Steady rain had washed away much of the blood, but it could do nothing to hide a pink loop of intestine that trailed down toward the lower tank.

Oscar looked at Neve. The color had drained from her cheeks. He turned and yelled above the rumble of the other, working screw: "Her body tripped a load switch?"

The supervisor shook his head and spat into the sewage. "Her body fizzed the motor. Fucking shit thing was on its last legs. I'd been trying to run it out to the new financial year. My maintenance budget—I can hardly buy a fucking tube of white grease, let alone spring for a motor rewind. If the motor had been new, or working like number two there, the girl there would be mincemeat already—it'd chew her up like sausage. It's used to shifting slurry, nothin' solid. Auger blade hit bone, and that was that. The strain fried it."

Oscar noticed bolt holes running up the sides of the tubes.

"Shouldn't these things be covered?" he asked.

The supervisor scratched his nose. "I think they were, once."

Neve wiped her mouth and shined her light into the pit of effluent from which the augers rose. "I don't understand. Aren't there bars or a filter to catch big things in the mix before they get here?" She gestured toward the long helices.

"Absolutely," the supervisor replied, and lit another cigarette. His match flared brightly in the methane-rich air.

Oscar looked up to the landing they'd just descended from. "She didn't arrive in the sewage system. She came from up there."

Neve followed his gaze to the landing above. "Jumped?"

"Jumped," Oscar said, "or dumped."

He watched Neve, seeing how quickly she'd join the logic. She frowned and said, "If she jumped, she jumped naked. Which means she either arrived naked—pretty unlikely—or there's a pile of her clothes around here somewhere."

Oscar nodded and turned to the supervisor.

"Find any girl's clothes?"

"No, but you're welcome to look."

"Do the augers run constantly?"

"There's a cut switch in the lower tank," the supervisor replied, angling his own light. "Switches off when the effluent drops below a certain level, kinda like the water valve in your home-toilet cistern, 'cept in reverse. But most times it runs. City keeps on shitting."

Oscar looked out at the girl, then up at the landing. Rain fell on the handrail. There would be no dusting for fingerprints.

Neve said, "So if someone dumped her they didn't wait around to hear her body jam the screw."

"Or they heard it fail and took off anyway," Oscar said, and looked at the supervisor. "After the warning light went on, how long before your lad—Luke?—got out here?"

The supervisor shrugged. "Eight, ten minutes?"

Oscar looked at Neve. Ample time for anyone dumping a body to make himself scarce.

"And he was with you in the control room when the warning light went on?"

"Just him and me."

Oscar reluctantly stubbed out the last of his cigarette and indicated the motionless auger. "That thing isolated?"

The supervisor nodded.

"I'm going out." Oscar pulled on a pair of latex gloves, put his flashlight between his teeth, and crawled hand over hand across the narrow concrete edge of the outlet tank.

"How did someone get in here?" Neve shouted. "Why didn't your security stop them?"

The supervisor barked a laugh. "Love, my operating budget doesn't stretch to running security lights, let alone security guards."

"Cameras?"

"Don't have 'em. Who wants to look at crap pumping around?"

Oscar reached the body and held tight to the slick concrete with one hand while he switched on his flashlight. He guessed the girl was in her early teens. Her wet hair was brown. The auger had opened her like a dull but brutally swung butcher's cleaver, down to bone and in some places clean through. He gently touched the skin—cold. He gingerly lifted an arm; it moved with a little stiffness, dragging up at the torso. Rigor mortis was beginning to set in.

He ran the flashlight beam down the ruined body and stopped at the girl's belly.

Just above the smear of wet pubic hair, cuts had been carved into her slightly flabby flesh. Even in the shaky flashlight under steady rain, it was clear that the marking had nothing to do with the rude, machete-deep slashes the auger had inflicted. Oscar's heart thudded. Looking at the pattern was like glimpsing a snake or the sheer fall of a cliff; a deep, fundamental fear sewn into his blood warned, *This is dangerous*. The overall shape—about the size of a man's open hand—was made up of an intricate pattern of dozens of interlinked curls and lines. At the center of them was an elaborate cross, and imposed over it was a seven-pointed star.

———

Oscar pulled on his hat as he watched the two men from the funeral home extract the girl from the blades of the auger. The undertakers wore plastic overalls over their suits; they looked tired. As they lifted the torso out of the pit, the upper intestine and slick organs began to slump out. The men argued quietly, then tied a garbage bag around the open cavity.

Oscar saw how wan Neve was and sent her to scour the plant grounds for a pile of girl's clothing they both knew she wouldn't find. He'd telephoned Scenes of Crime, but there had been a triple fatality at a food cannery, so no staff was available to photograph and forensically assess the corpse in situ. Oscar returned to his car, to get his digital camera, then climbed back to the body only to discover that the battery—which had been fully charged that morning—was flat. He cursed and took pictures with the camera in his phone, a tiny thing better suited to capturing birthday cakes and beach cricket than murder victims. He wished that he'd bribed the supervisor out of his entire packet of smokes.

The undertakers laid the body on a small blue tarpaulin, and rain snapped on the plastic like tiny firecrackers. The dead girl stared up into the rain through the eye that had not been ripped away by the auger.

"Have you got a thermometer?" Oscar asked.

"For her?"

Oscar nodded. "A mercury one. A glass one."

One of the men went to the hearse and returned with a long rectal thermometer. Oscar wondered where to put it—the girl's lower torso had been badly chopped by the auger blade. He forced the thermometer down her split throat and felt unpleasant resistance as he reached the upper esophageal sphincter. He pushed harder, sticking the glass rod as deeply down her throat as he could reach. It came back just over 84 degrees. About two and a half hours had passed since the supervisor phoned the police. How long had the girl been dead before that? Another three hours? Four? It was hard to say—the combination of cold rain and evisceration was rapidly cooling the body. Oscar stood and wondered if he should wash and keep the latex gloves. He decided that was too parsimonious even for him.

Neve returned and shook her head once in reply to Oscar's unspoken question. A bit of color had returned to her cheeks. Oscar nodded to the undertakers that they could now take the body to the morgue. As they unfolded a cadaver bag from their kit, his eyes were drawn to the girl's body. Naked and broken, she looked utterly defenseless, exposed inside and out. So young. The awful marking on her belly glared like a brand. The cause of death wasn't clear, but the girl didn't carve her own belly and throw herself into spinning metal and stinking sewage. Someone had thrown her—dead or alive—into the auger. As the undertakers lifted the small body gently into the bag and zipped it shut, the nausea that had been squeezing Oscar's stomach was gone. The deep weariness that seemed to have been his constant companion for years had also vanished. In their place was something volatile and bitter. He was angry.

"Did you phone Homicide?" she asked. "We shouldn't release her till they come."

"I'm not calling Homicide. We're keeping this one."

He felt Neve's stare like a cold wind on the side of his face.

"You want to keep her," she said quietly.

"It's murder."

The undertakers lifted the cadaver bag onto a stretcher and began to carry it up the steel stairs. Oscar followed, and Neve trailed after.

"Exactly," she said. "It's murder. But it isn't a Clause Seventeen."

"You saw that thing carved on her?"

"Listen." She had to jog to keep up with him. "She's got nothing. No clothes, no ID, no *face*. No suspects. A case like this needs feet on the ground. Haig has thirty people. We're two. Giving her to Homicide is the best chance she's got. It's a case that needs their—"

"Brains?" The irritation inside him grew hotter.

"Resources. A case like this will take a month, and we don't have a month. They're going to shut us down! Oscar! We need to spend the next few weeks getting every conviction we can. We need to—"

"Bump up our stats?" Oscar asked.

He realized that Neve had stopped following. He turned and faced her, and she flinched.

"You know we do," she said. "I do. I need my job."

Oscar chewed his lip. Neve was right: this case would be a time pit. But that didn't seem to matter to him.

"Or is this just a pissing contest between you and Haig?" she said. "Because I know who's winning."

He glared at her. "You know what Haig will do? He'll glance in Missing Persons, and if there isn't an instant match she'll go on the back burner as a runaway Jane Doe, too hard to solve."

Neve's lips tightened. Oscar could see she was holding herself tight as a fist, fighting to keep her voice steady. "He'd have a point. There are ten murders a week here in the city. It's terrible, but this girl is just one more. Let's fight the fights we can win. Please, Oscar, be reasonable. Let Haig have her. If I bum out with you I'm back to Generals, and you know what the pay's like there. No one gets by without—"

She bit her lip, but he knew what she was about to say. Taking bribes.

Oscar watched the undertakers gently lift the stretcher over the last rail and out toward the parking lot. The rain grew heavier. He looked inside himself for a gracious retreat, for polite agreement; all he found was anger. A girl had been stripped, mutilated, and thrown away like so much garbage. He wanted to find who did it.

"We're keeping her," he said.

His footsteps clattered as he went down the stairs.

———

He drove, quietly blessing the rain. The weepy dawn sky dropped a cold pall over the neglect and destruction, hiding the overgrown parks and unchecked weeds, damping down the reek of uncollected rubbish dumped on unswept footpaths, filling sore-like potholes with water. The sky looked almost solid: oystershell to the west, slate to the east, cobweb curtains of rain ahead—gray on gray on gray. The city had once been quite beautiful, but three years had made such a difference.

Three long years. A long time to hold a grudge, Oscar had to admit. After hitting the girl on Gray Wednesday, Oscar took a week's personal leave. By the time he was back and Jon was out of the hospital, the investigation of Geoffrey Haig had formally ended. Haig had no doubt learned about the bug, and knew that Oscar had been inside his home. Oscar knew Haig hated him to the marrow.

"Left," Neve said, jolting Oscar back to the present.

She had a street directory open on her lap but was staring out the passenger-side window. He could feel her ire bouncing against his own, like the same poles of two magnets repelling each other. Rain fell harder, drumming on the roof like an endless exhalation. Ahead, he caught glimpses of the city, glass towers all but shrouded by the downpour. The drabness they passed was briefly relieved by a blue banner across a half-finished building: THATCH CONSTRUCTION. People were building again. Maybe there was hope.

Neve indicated a side street.

"Here. This one."

Oscar turned the wheel.

———

Lucas Purden lay on a mattress in a squat house, desperately waving pot smoke that didn't exist out of the air. He had clearly forgotten what drug he'd taken but knew he'd taken *something*, and—seeing badges— had enough capacity to know he'd better hide the fact. Purden was twenty or twenty-one. His eyes were a dull brown, and the earrings in both lobes were a dull and dirty silver. His skin was greasy. His blond hair, stained jeans, and green collared work shirt all bore an oily grime that said they hadn't been washed in weeks. And, Oscar noticed, he smelled. But then so did the whole squat. Luke was the only person in it; the other residents had cleared out the moment a police car—even a weary, unmarked sedan like Oscar's—turned into their street. They hadn't bothered to alert Luke.

Despite his theatrical flapping, Luke had forgotten that his fly was unzipped; Oscar and Neve had interrupted what was clearly enjoyable leisure time. Neve looked away from the metronome waving of his erection and knelt beside him, just out of arm's reach. She sent an unhappy glance at Oscar. He ignored it and nodded—go ahead. She sighed and turned to the grubby boy.

"Lucas Purden?" she asked.

"Guh," Purden replied. Oscar could see the boy's eyes were glazed, his pupils almost as large as small coins.

"We're here to ask you about the girl. You found a girl last night, Lucas, in the number-one auger pipe at your work."

"No." Purden nodded. "Yeah?" He shook his head. "Guh."

Neve looked at Oscar. He made a circular gesture with his finger— keep going—and began to look around. Aside from the mattress, there was a line of old school lockers against one wall, and a stereo chained to a sink pipe.

"How did you find her?" Neve asked.

Purden licked his lips and tried to look composed.

"Light. Light the pipe. *Not* light the pipe." He began to giggle and tried hard to stop it. "Light *on* the pipe. Red warning light. On the pipe. Flipped."

"What flipped?"

"We flipped!" Purden giggled more, nodding. "Flipped a coin. To go out. Me and Mister Bruce."

"Your supervisor?"

While Neve quizzed the young man about whether he saw anyone on his trip to or from the jammed auger, Oscar inspected the locker's door. On it was written, "Lukes. Dont touch. Privat!" The style was childish, and the letters' component lines and curves were shaky. Oscar looked at the boy—his hands vibrated in a slight but uncontrollable palsy. Purden hadn't made the fine scalpel cuts they'd seen on the dead girl's abdomen. Interestingly, though, there was a circular bandage stuck on the boy's neck.

"Luke, give me your locker key," Oscar said.

"Locker?"

Oscar tapped the locker, and Purden's eyebrows rose in surprise, as if he'd never noticed the six-foot metal cabinet next to his mattress.

"Five seconds, Lucas. Then you're under arrest. Four."

It took three of those four seconds for the message to sink into Purden's brain, then he fumbled quickly in his pockets. His penis flailed as he hunted for his keys. Neve picked a spot on the far wall to stare at while the ruddy member waved like a drowning man's arm.

"Here, here."

The boy passed the keys to Neve, who took them in a delicate pinch and passed them to Oscar. The locker door groaned. Inside was a damp pile of pornographic magazines with heavily worn corners, three empty bottles of roll-on deodorant, a small Vegemite jar containing only a dusting of cannabis, a glass pipe with a blackened bowl giving off the sweet chemical snap of Delete. Oscar pushed them aside and looked inside a shoebox. It held mostly junk retrieved from the bottom of the plant's filter box: a cheap silver earring, a broken watch, a foreign coin, a medal from a school's running race . . . but one thing caught his eye. A packet of Fentanyl patches. Fentanyl was a powerful painkiller—it was used in lollipops issued to combat soldiers. Quality analgesics like Fentanyl were as rare as truffles and almost as expensive, far beyond the economic reach of a slow-witted boy who worked in a sewage plant. Oscar opened the packet. Inside were a dozen sealed medicated patches just like the one on Purden's neck. A small fortune's worth.

He showed the pack to Lucas. "Where from?"

Purden's euphoria had dulled, and his eyes slid like marbles in oil. "Mine." His voice was groggy.

"How did you afford them?"

Purden licked his dry lips and smiled.

Oscar knelt beside Neve and loosened Purden's collar. Another two patches were stuck on the skin of his upper chest.

"Mine," Purden repeated, on the edge of sleep. "Come on."

Purden's half-open eyes glazed, and a snore rattled through his nostrils. His penis held bravely high.

"We've lost him," Neve said, and stood. "Maybe he found some jewelry that was actually worth something and went to town on it."

"Maybe."

"Take him in to the watch?" Neve asked.

Oscar shook his head. "He'll be raped." It was the simple truth. The watchhouse was understaffed and overcrowded. Oscar pulled out his business card and dropped it on the snoring boy's chest.

———

His car started on the third try.

"I can fill in the report," he said.

"Thank you." Her tone was curt.

"Home?"

"Church."

"Really? You don't want a shower first?"

She looked at him.

"You smell a bit," he explained. "We both do."

"It's Saturday." Her words were edged with ice chips. "It's a working bee."

He shrugged. "I'll need directions."

———

Hunched pedestrians scuttled like beetles over the wet roads, heads down. Oscar felt a little embarrassed that he'd been working with Neve for more than a year and he had no idea where she worshipped. But then he had no idea where anyone worshipped anymore; the faithful had become a rare and reclusive species. In the weeks and months immediately after Gray Wednesday, houses of worship enjoyed an enormous influx of congregants petitioning their brand of God to remove the blight of the ghosts. But when they discovered that prayer did nothing to shift their personal dead—who were, it seemed, immutable evidence of a joyless afterlife—congregations plummeted. Churches, temples, and mosques steadily emptied. It wasn't the same everywhere: in North America, Canada's Mennonites swelled in number and bulged down into the United States, rubbing heatedly against Mormonism, which had shifted and adapted and spread up to Pennsylvania and down to Tijuana; in Africa, a resurgence of animism stretched from Senegal to Mozambique; Norway had all but closed its borders, and whispers from Sweden reported mass sacrifices to Odin. But most of Europe had turned its back on gods old and new, and languished in economic depression.

Neve directed him over the river into a section of town that had gone through a strange circle of life. Before the Second World War, this area had suffered a reputation for ruffianism and black marketeering; then it became a rich larder of multiculturalism with the influx of post-war migrants; then a third shift to gentrified exclusivity; finally, after Gray Wednesday, it underwent a swift devolution to its original state. A hundred times in the past year Oscar had tried to persuade Neve to move to a safer suburb; a hundred times she had refused. He understood now that she refused to abandon it. She held hope that, one day, her suburb could be resurrected.

He slowed at the huge white Catholic church on the hill. Its grounds were a battlefield of broken bottles and garbage; its stained-glass windows were long gone, replaced with scorched and bullet-pocked boards and tin. "Not this one," she said. "We've lost this one."

She directed him through narrower streets to stop outside a tall brick fence. The brickwork was recent, and on its top course upturned broken bottles were set in mortar to deter fence-climbers. A stout, plain gate sat in a neat architrave.

Neve didn't get out. She remained silent and still for such a long moment that Oscar wondered if she was waiting for him to say something.

"Look," he began, "let's just get the autopsy—"

"You can come in," she said primly. She looked up at him. A frown rode her forehead, and her mouth was a pink knot. "If you want."

He stared at her. "In?"

Pink flushes appeared on her cheeks. "It's just a working bee. No prayer. You don't have to pray or anything."

He tried to think what this all meant. "Um . . ."

Neve looked away, embarrassed, and fumbled for the door latch. "Never mind."

He watched her go to the gate and knock, not a typical rap-rap-rap but a coded staccato tapping. A moment later, the heavy gate swung open, revealing men and women in jeans and work shirts in front of a tiny, old wooden church with scaffolding around its small spire. A young man broke into a smile when he saw Neve and kissed her chastely on the cheek. Oscar felt jealous little wings flap inside him. Stupid. Of course she'd have men interested in her. But what arrested Oscar was Neve's expression. She was smiling. He wondered if he'd ever seen her do that; it was as surprising as stumbling across a previously undiscovered portal that opened to a new and fascinating world. But then Neve seemed to remember something. She turned to glance back at Oscar, and her smile fell away to a more thoughtful, troubled look. The gate swung shut, severing the stare and returning Oscar to the filthy gloom of the street.

He put the car in gear and drove off.

Chapter 4

H e's not home."

The woman was speaking even as she inched the front door open.

"He's here." Oscar stepped onto the tiled porch. "His motorbike is up the side."

"He's sick," the woman continued. "Migraine, terrible. Not to be disturbed."

Oscar gently took Denna Lovering's shoulders, kissed both her cheeks, then entered the house. She sighed and followed. "You're thin."

"I'm fine."

"I'll get you some soup. You know where he is."

Denna pottered off through a pair of saloon doors, tut-tutting to the empty kitchen. "She has no pride in herself, she's moved in with the man, a married woman. . . ."

The Loverings' house was immaculately neat, but nothing post-dated the mid-eighties. On one wallpapered wall was a framed photograph of a younger Denna Lovering, her husband, Paz, and their two black-haired boys; around it were a dozen sepia photographs of unsmiling progenitors. In the wood-paneled dining room Oscar passed an orange velour settee, a white-painted fireplace, a china cabinet full of Lladro figurines, and a menorah on the topmost glass shelf.

Oscar took the internal stairs down to the basement door. He didn't knock.

The air in the basement was cold. The room had low ceilings and deep shadows. Old furniture was neatly stacked against walls and covered with sheets that had become gray and dusty with age. A kitchen hutch remained uncovered, and on its shelves were curios from two dozen countries: carved bowls and feathered blowpipes, bronze deities and wooden masks, painted plates and snow globes. Homemade sausages hung from ropes strung under the stairs, and their meaty smell competed with the brimstone tang of soldering flux that wafted from a workbench. Working under two angled spotlights was a late-middle-aged man, concentrating intently as he dipped the mercury silver tip of an iron into a small tin; a puff of yellow flux smoke rose, turning him into a medieval alchemist laboring over bubbling tinctures.

"You don't listen to my wife," said Paz Lovering, not looking up.

"She's not a good liar," said Oscar. "Migraine?"

"You're my fucking headache," Lovering said without malice. "Besides, who wants a wife who's a good liar? Look where it got you."

"Sabine never lied. She just didn't answer the questions I never asked."

Lovering grunted, and the soldering iron hissed as he cleaned it on a damp sponge. In different times, Paz Lovering would have been a fat man; instead, his flesh hung on his bones like forlorn sails. Paz had once been a producer on a string of current-affairs television shows including *ARClight*, a foreign-affairs program spanning hot spots from Port-au-Prince to Jerusalem. A few months before Gray Wednesday, Lovering had been caught up in a bribery scandal involving several media outlets, a former communications minister, and the police union. Oscar and Jon had been the investigating officers. The attorney general had wanted to burn away the whiff of corruption by making a loud, well-publicized case of it, and had sought to bring charges against all and sundry. Oscar knew Lovering's involvement had been incidental, and managed to shield the producer from the fracas. As a result, Lovering felt forever indebted to him . . . and the man clearly hated being obligated. Lovering wiped his hands on his jeans and ran his hand through his thinning hair in frustration.

"It wouldn't kill you to telephone, you know."

"You don't answer the phone," Oscar said.

"Exactly."

Lovering screwed a circuit board to the chassis of a DVD player. In the past three years, television had been reduced to the weather channel; a taxpayer-funded federal network that broadcast sessions of Parliament, national news, and cheaply made shows for children; a shaky commercial broadcaster rerunning ancient sitcoms; and three channels of what amounted to soft porn. The industry had died, and Lovering kept his household afloat by repairing electrical equipment. Lovering had once revealed—after several Glenlivets—that his ghost was his grandmother, a stern, unsmiling creature whose appearance had not improved with death, and who was never more than a few steps away. She was one reason that he liked the long hours at his workbench, where he could keep his back to the horrid apparition. Oscar found his own eyes probing the shadows, but there was no sign of the dead boy. He kept his distance; Oscar knew he had that to be grateful for.

"Working on the Sabbath?" he asked. "Shouldn't you be at temple?"

"The temples are all closed," Lovering replied. "And what does a bead-mumbler know about Shabbat?"

"I'm not Catholic."

"Of course you are. You're Italian."

"I'm not Italian."

"You were raised Italian." Denna descended the stairs with a tray of soup, a plate of *flódni*, and a pot of coffee. "Don't use those words, Pazel; you don't know what a person believes these days." She set the tray down and caught Oscar's eye. "And you, don't sound so ungrateful."

Lovering eyed the sweet desserts. "Great. Now he'll never want to go. We can't keep him, he's not neutered." He squinted at Oscar. "Or are you?"

Oscar ignored him and thanked Denna; she waved away the gratitude and returned up the stairs. Oscar sipped the soup and realized that he was ravenous. Was it wrong to be hungry after finding a dead girl? He ate anyway, one-handed, and pulled his phone from his pocket, activating it with a musical tinkle.

"I don't do cell phones," said Lovering, stealing a glance at the device. "Okay, I do Siemens. And old Nokias. But only for cash."

Oscar shook his head as he scrolled through the photographs. He handed Lovering the phone. On the LCD screen was a close-up of the symbol carved into the dead girl's lower abdomen. A residual chill of when he first saw those tiny, careful cuts spidered up his back.

Now Lovering was staring at the picture. "For fuck's sake," he whispered. "Dead?"

Oscar nodded. "Found this morning."

"So why are you showing me? You just want to ruin my appetite? The more for you?"

"I thought you might recognize it."

"You and thinking never got along."

"She was murdered, Paz."

"By a Jew, you reckon?"

"A man has to start somewhere."

"So why not with the Heebs? Hardly a fucking original idea." Lovering zoomed in on the star carved into the dead girl's flesh, then handed the phone back. "That's not the Magen David. Seven points, not six. Can you count? Do they let anyone into that police force of yours?"

"Not the star, the writing."

"I don't read scalpel."

"You read Hebrew."

"I fake it. It keeps the peace." Lovering poured coffee and prodded the circuit board. "You know, I need to get this finished for someone who is *paying* me to work."

Oscar shrugged, chewing cake. "Hey, I thought the executive producer of *ARClight* knew stuff. My mistake."

Lovering glared at him a long moment, then sighed and gestured for the phone. He twisted it with a careful finger, as if what was on the screen might be contagious. He adjusted his glasses, squinting. Even from a distance, Oscar could see the strange text, twisting like curls of poisonous smoke.

"I don't think it's Hebrew," Lovering said. "It's hard to read . . . but some of it is pictorial, like hieroglyphs. This—these wedgy symbols— looks like old cuneiform." He looked up at Oscar. "I'm still in touch with some of my researchers. One, she's good. She might agree to look into this."

"I'd appreciate it."

"She doesn't work for nothing," Lovering warned, and connected the phone to an old Canon printer.

"I can pay," Oscar said.

Lovering looked dubious.

Oscar's watch alarm sounded; Lucas Purden would be rousing from his Fentanyl stupor soon. Lovering printed two copies of the symbol and handed one and the phone to Oscar.

"Thanks," Oscar said. "Let me know." He went to the stairs.

"Mariani?"

Oscar turned back. Lovering was staring at the photograph.

"Yes?"

Lovering regarded the picture a moment longer, then folded it sharply and shoved it into his pocket. "Go, get gone. Leave a man to make a buck." He turned back to his workbench.

––––––––

It took twenty minutes to reach Purden's flophouse. Oscar parked in front and went inside. Again, the street had seen him coming: the squat was empty. So was the boy's locker; its door hung open. The mattress was bare. Lucas Purden was gone.

––––––––

Oscar slowed as he drove into the strange borderland between the deteriorating office buildings of downtown and the run-together alleys of Chinatown. The steady rain had driven the seediest elements from the streets. Oscar found the doorway he was looking for and parked. He knocked; no answer. In an adjoining doorway, a beggar opened one eye, appraised Oscar in a glance, then closed it again. Brave little breezes puffed snatches of mud salt from the river mangroves, piss from the gutters, and slaps of fish and cabbage from the alleys. A burned doll lay in the gutter. Oscar went back to his car to wait.

She arrived through the rain under an umbrella, an elegant, black-sailed caravel navigating polluted waters. Her name was Tanta, a name she'd chosen, Oscar was sure, because it allowed her to show her little pink tongue when introducing herself to new clients. She carried a small bag of groceries.

He stepped out of the car. "You look beautiful," he said.

She took one look at Oscar's outfit and tutted softly; her once famous tongue winked red between pearl-white teeth.

"What are we going to do with you?" she said.

"Hopeless case," he agreed, and showed her a bottle of wine he'd scrounged. "Do you have a moment?"

"Pleasure before pleasure," she replied.

Oscar followed her up stairs as narrow as a coffin to a tiny bedroom. A double bed with black satin sheets took up so much of the floor that only one person could walk crabwise around it. Oscar guessed that people didn't come up here to walk. Tanta had once worked from a penthouse apartment overlooking Southbank, until a client—a member of Parliament representing a dry and dusty western electorate—found the Lord a month or so before Gray Wednesday and decided to publicly confess his sins. Tanta, perhaps the most colorful of those misdeeds, was caught up in the orgiastic reportage. She soon found herself out of her penthouse and working from this tiny room; after Gray Wednesday, there was no going back uptown. She lit three candles.

"Bad luck, three to a match," she said. "But bad's the new good, right?"

He handed her a paper cup of wine. "Fentanyl," he said.

"No one I know uses it. Who could afford it?" She looked at Oscar and smiled. "Who did afford it?"

He told her about the now vanished Lucas Purden.

"If he's smart, he can hide anywhere."

"He's not smart."

"He gave *you* the slip." She sipped delicately. "How does a silly boy afford Fentanyl?"

"By doing something silly. Will you ask around?"

"May I ask what this is about?"

"Do you want to know?"

"Does it involve sweaty men who want their assholes fingered and cry after coming?"

"I don't think so."

"Then, God, yes."

Oscar showed Tanta the photograph Lovering had printed for him. Her full lips curled downward.

"Oh, my."

"Heard of anything like this?" he asked. "Guys into knives, into the occult?"

"Everyone carries knives, Oscar." She smiled a mild rebuke. "And everyone believes in ghosts. But I'll ask."

He reached into his wallet and pulled out his last twenty.

Tanta made a face, offended. "I think you need it more than I do."

She stood, intending to tuck the photograph down her décolletage, then thought better of it and put it in her small clutch purse.

Oscar stood. "I have to run."

He kissed her lightly on the lips because he knew she liked it. She closed her eyes, just a little, and leaned into him. He felt the bulge in her crotch against his leg. She looked down at it, then back up through heavy lashes.

"What can I say? You do things," she admitted. Her smile became more humid. "You *could* do things. Rain makes for a quiet night."

He smiled. "It's always raining."

"You're a lovely disappointment," she said, sighing.

"Years of practice."

At the door, she called to him. "Hon? Don't hold your breath. These days, secrets stay secret."

––––––––

The late-afternoon sky was so heavy with rain it drooped. Oscar parked under police headquarters and took the lift to the Industrial Relations floor. He wound his way between empty chairs and silent cubicles to his desk and sat. He soon printed the thirty or more pages required to report a death and request that the coroner approve an autopsy. Many of the blanks he filled with the same answer. Family advised of death? No. Formal identification? No. Has a criminal proceeding been commenced against any person in relation to this death? No. The one person who might have been of assistance—Lucas Purden, a boy with barely more intellect than an Irish setter—had deceived and eluded him.

He logged on to Prophet, the service's intranet. Prophet had become so unstable that officers and staff called it Loss; anyone wanting to check files without the risk of having them disappear before their eyes went to the hard copies. But for once Prophet seemed to be cooperating, and Oscar accessed the Missing Persons database. He entered the parameters of what he knew about his Jane Doe: approximate age, approximate height, hair color. Without a face, the Jane Doe was a Caucasian adolescent with brown hair and brown eyes—a quarter of a million girls across the country would fit her description. The search returned 192 possible matches: a solid week's work just to cross-reference them all. And those were just girls *reported* missing. With schools' registers in turmoil and child allowance payments terminated, there was neither stick nor carrot to entice loveless parents to register a runaway.

Oscar flipped through the files. Most included a photograph—a holiday snap, a graduation photo, a cropped family portrait—but these were all useless for identifying a corpse whose face had been torn off and shredded by industrial machinery. Prophet shuddered, rallied, and spat itself back to its index page.

Oscar logged in again, and diverted to Prophet's Violent Crimes database. Again, how to narrow it down? Five hundred homicides every year, and ten times that number of serious assaults. He confined his search to homicides involving mutilation and deprivation of liberty. Sixty-three files. Each was accompanied by the arrest photograph and charge sheet of the perpetrator. Men and women who stared at the camera with expressions that ranged from outraged surprise to exhausted relief and amused indifference. Most files included two photographs of the victim: one snap when he or she was alive—a frozen, prosaic moment at a party or laughing at the beach or proudly displaying a sports ribbon; the second was a death shot that bit at the viewer's soul. Skirts rode up or shorts pulled down, exposing limbs set at awkward angles, thighs and buttocks and rib cages black with bruises or deeply slashed or studded red with cigarette burns. Thin wrists and ankles, too often a woman's or a child's, encircled by bruises or bound with fence wire or a belt, or slashed open with wounds like tiny, screaming mouths. The dead faces never smiled.

Oscar forced himself to look at the images. Yes, some bodies had been carved into, but usually roughly and generally with words— "bitch," "cunt," "slut"—and on occasion swastikas or death's heads or crude phalluses. None, though, remotely resembled the incisions he'd seen on the girl pulled from the sewage-plant auger: cuts suggestive more of a careful watchmaker than of an enraged butcher.

Prophet spasmed again and coughed up a "system error" window. Oscar shut the program and proofread his initial report. "Flimsy" was too kind a word for it. No likely victim. No likely perpetrator. He printed it, signed triplicates, and went to Moechtar's pigeonhole. He held the papers to the slot but hesitated. Very likely he and Neve would have no chance of finding the dead girl's name, let alone her murderer's. With only two detectives and a performance review pending, the girl's body and her file would be shuffled down and on, deeper and farther into cold drawers and file drawers, until she was barely a statistic. Lost. Jon had a point: Oscar did seem hell-bent on committing career suicide, part of his self-punishment for hitting the girl on Gray Wednesday. Or was it as Neve had accused—that Oscar just wanted to keep one more bone away from Haig?

"Pull the report," he told himself. "Let Homicide have this one."

But the image of the symbol on the girl's belly was stuck in his mind. Who carved it? And *why*? Was the poor thing alive when it was done?

He pushed the folded paperwork into Moechtar's pigeonhole.

uke looked around through the evening rain, wondering whether anyone would see if he pulled it out here and had a quick wank. He told himself to wait and kept walking. But he was restless; sometimes even half an hour between flogs seemed to be an aching forever. It just wouldn't fucking go away, this hard-on. Well, it might subside for fifteen or twenty minutes after he splodged, but then: hey presto! A rabbit that pulled itself from the magician's hat. The mental image made him smile.

Besides, the erections weren't his fault, he reasoned; they were *hers*. Legs, Christ. Ass, Christ. Tits, Churrrist. As long as he didn't look at her face and see who she was, or see those twisting-socket eyes, he could imagine she was any chick. And *that* got him very hot and hard.

Luke finally stopped and turned about in a full circle, looking for people. Usually, on his way to and from work at the shit farm, he walked with one hand in his knapsack gripping a length of heavy galvanized-steel pipe, for protection. After the cops, he'd left in such a hurry that he couldn't find it.

But you got another hard pipe, doncha?

He giggled aloud this time.

No one heard. Except his mother, in that tight top and short shorts. She looked at him worriedly, disapprovingly. But she was dead and he was alive, so she could just, you know, fuck the fuck off.

Luke thought he recognized the street he was on. There weren't many buildings left on this deserted stretch. Until a few months ago, there were heaps of Delete labs around here, but then there was an explosion and a motherfucker of a fire, and the cops came and the council flattened half the street. Tall weeds and scrubby stuff were growing between the piles of sooty brick in the empty lots. There were a couple of old houses left, and nearby was an old movie theater. Luke didn't like movie theaters, but it was the only building with a doorway that was deep enough to afford just a little privacy, and the urgency of his throbbing crotch couldn't be ignored any longer. He nimbly avoided puddles and stepped under the solid marquee into the gloomy vestibule. He put his backpack down beside the nailed-shut doors, leaned against the wall, and undid his fly. He licked his palm and started.

While he stroked, he looked around. He wondered if this was the theater. When he was nine or ten, he'd sneaked away from home. Mum was with some guy, and he wanted to see that pirate movie. Mum hadn't been able to afford to take him (bitch), but he was determined to see it. Yes, he was sure this was the very same cinema. He'd spotted a family with a heap of kids and simply tagged along with them; once inside, he'd found a seat in the dark to curl on. He'd spent the first few minutes focused more on being sprung by the attendant than on the movie, but then the story and the pictures took hold. It was brilliant and exciting, even funny, right up until the scene when the big black ship came along and the pirates all became skeletons. Suddenly, the movie stopped being fun and started being scary. Very arsefuckingly scary. The ship was long and dark and almost alive, like a shark, and covered with tattered sails. And when the pirates' skin all melted away and they became skull and bone, but moving—undead and chasing and wanting—he'd had to look away before he gravy-trained his pants.

Luke realized that the memory of the movie was softening him up, so he shook his mind away and looked across at his mother. She stood on the footpath, watching him. The rain passed through her, and her hair and tight top remained forever dry. Her eyes—those horrible black nothings, like grub holes in a rotten apple—watched him and her mouth moved silently. He hated to see her face, and hated to think what she was trying to say. So he looked down at her tits instead. But the sight of her nipples through the top made him think of the dead girl's little tits. That had been fucked up, finding that girl caught in the number-one screw, chopped the way he used to chop lizards with a razor blade. His cock went slack in his hand. A waste of time. Strange. Unusual. Not to worry—he'd find a squat tonight, and there was usually some Deleted slag up for dick. Sometimes guys, too, but girls felt better. And if no one wanted it, more fool them—Mrs. Palmer and her five daughters were always ready.

As he was zipping up, it arrived.

When it emerged from the rain, a huge long black thing that growled low and rumbly, his heart thudded hard and he thought for a stupid, panicked moment it was that pirate ship, gliding across a dark sea. But then he saw the wheels and the shining black flanks and dark windows. A clean, new car in these parts was not much less unusual than a pirate ship, though, so as it slowed to a halt outside the old theater Luke slipped his hand into the backpack and remembered with an unpleasant shiver that he didn't have the pipe.

For a long moment, nothing happened, and Luke wondered if the person inside the car had noticed him at all and had simply pulled up outside the old theater by coincidence. Just as he'd convinced himself of that, the passenger-side window slid down. In the dark of evening, and with the rain, he could just make out the shape of a small elderly man with drawn-back hair.

"Young man?"

Luke was simple—couldn't pour water from a shoe with instructions on the heel, his mother used to say—but he knew the sound of men who wanted to rob and men who wanted to fuck ass, and this guy didn't sound like he needed to rob anyone and, judging by the car, could afford much cleaner ass than Luke's. Luke caught movement at the corner of his eye and glanced that way. It was only his mother. As usual, she was staring at him with those empty eyes, and again, her mouth was pleading silently.

"I wonder if we could talk some business?" the old man continued. "Do you mind?"

Maybe this guy did want some cock; there was something about him that said he was no stranger to rough stuff. That was okay, if he had the bucks to pay for it. Luke stepped out into the rain. His mother was waving wildly, her mouth working wide in a silent shout. He shooed her away like a fly.

"Okay," Luke said. "Is it just you, or your mate, too?"

He crouched to see the driver, but the man was in shadow. That made him uneasy. He told himself it was just the drug patches. Besides, he was nearly at the car now.

"My friend is certainly interested in you," the old man said, and reached into his jacket. "Take a look."

As Luke put his hands on the open windowsill to stoop and get a better look at the driver, the old man grabbed his wrists.

"What the fuck!" Luke yelled. He twisted, but the old man's grip was shockingly strong.

The driver-side door opened, and the other man stepped out. Luke recognized him, and his heart jumped like a kicked pigeon.

"Hold him," the other man said.

Luke wrenched wildly and shook off the old man's fingers. He turned to run like hell.

And slipped.

The footpath was wet and slick, and he went down. A second later, the driver was on top of him.

"I'll give it back! I'll give it back!" Luke yelled, although part of him, deep inside, knew it was far too late for that.

Something struck him on the side of the head, and the edges of the world grew very dark. Before it faded, the car's trunk swung high in the air, like a sail of that dark, dead pirate ship. And Luke screamed.

Chapter **6**

With shopkeepers unwilling or unable to commit to lease payments, shopping malls had become as quiet as mausoleums and trade had gone outdoors. The closest markets to Oscar were in Castlemaine Street. They were a collection of canvas stalls, trestle tables, and covered wheelbarrows that trimmed the western length of the football stadium like the colorful hem of a monstrous dress. Some kiosks were impressive structures with brightly embroidered flaps; others were dark little secrets with sharp-eyed minders perched outside. Most were open-fronted benches or tables displaying goods as diverse as the people who offered them: live chickens sold by old men, pornography by old women, knives by children, lightbulbs by a blind man, rifle cartridges by twin girls. Fresh herbs, bread, jars of kerosene, cooked possums hung by their tails, disposable diapers, small bottles of drinking water, large bottles of dodgy alcohol, cigarettes, shoes, haircuts, hand jobs, crematory urns.

Behind the stalls were the tents: colorful tents offered aphrodisiacs and puppet shows; darker tents rented sex and peddled curses; black tents in the shadows sold abortions. People wandered and sniffed samples and spun gun barrels and held condoms to the light and drank. Men wore suspicious scowls and scars. Women wore suspicious scowls and kohl. Children wore a circus-clown collection of patched clothes, handmade bibs, and trimmed hand-me-downs. The air was a rich swell of scents: dried spices and beeswax candles, fresh blood and old fish, honey and horseshit and sex.

The morning rain was hardly more than mist, and Oscar walked slowly, letting his eyes rove over the orange blurs of fearful chickens, the blue-red of skinned rabbits, the small tubs of ice as precious as diamonds. Oscar had spent an hour picking over fruit already turning brown, almonds as hard as horn, sugar speckled with ants, and flour shifting with weevils. But fruit could be stewed, almonds ground, flour sifted. He'd overpaid for eggs, and a knob of yellow butter had cost him two packets of Jilu. He was nearly done; all he needed now was ribbon and wrapping paper.

A flurry of fingers snatched at his legs and jacket hem, and he spun around. A flock of children, none older than eight, circled him like ducks after bread, diving and scrabbling.

"Hey, mister, what do you—"

"Hungry? Thirsty? I can—"

" . . . ever seen! Let me show you—"

" . . . cheap, just a dollar, and I'll take you to—"

Oscar shook his head and batted them away with his hat; they gave him a halfhearted last salvo, then flapped off to find an easier target. He found himself in a row of tents painted with pentagrams and eyes of Horus and signs of the zodiac. From awnings and bright-colored posts hung candelabra, charms, the painted skulls of dogs, and the severed feet of cats mounted on nickel chains. Bells rang softly in air that moved and smelled now of woodsmoke and herbs. Men and women sat behind beaded curtains, reading palms, faces, eyes, bowls of water. Those without clients called to Oscar.

"Tell your future, sir?"

"Third eye, can give you the gift of—"

"Love charms, true love here—"

"Lift your curse, sir? Rid yourself of your ghost?"

This last made Oscar hesitate. Thirty paces behind him, between the vibrantly painted stalls, stood the dead boy. Oscar looked back at the old man who called the offer.

"Really."

The old man offered a solemn smile of few teeth. "Absolutely, sir. I discovered the way."

In the months after Gray Wednesday, Oscar had quietly tried a dozen ways to exorcise himself of the dead boy. Three psychics, baptism, Taoism, celibacy (not hard, with Sabine gone), hypnosis, fasting . . . The last—and, on reflection, most desperate—attempt involved a late-night visit by a middle-aged man with wild, unwashed hair and earrings the size of dinner plates. Oscar was commanded to disrobe, lift his arms to the sky, and keep his eyes closed at all costs while the feverish man marked his naked body with a foul-smelling liquid. When Oscar noticed a new aroma emerging, he glanced down to see that the would-be exorcist had put down his paintbrush and was vigorously stimulating himself front and back. As he kicked the charlatan out of the house, Oscar acknowledged that the dead boy was here to stay.

The old man was holding open the oily flap of a tent. "Foolproof it is, sir. S'not cheap, mind."

Oscar shook his head. "Nothing worthwhile is. Wrapping paper?"

The old man wrinkled his nose at the lost sale. "Try Mother Mim." He gestured farther along.

Three stalls up, Oscar found a late-middle-aged woman, trim and healthy-looking in jeans, white shirt, and sunglasses. In a glance, he took in her wares laid on purple silk: hand mirrors; a manicure set; a collection of highlighting pens; a framed Maxfield Parrish print; rolls of sticky tape and an old green stapler; jars of homemade jam; small fired-clay totems: dolphins, zodiac figurines, the double face of Janus; a fish tank empty of water but holding sawdust, a twisted length of branch, and a dozen small brown skinks. At one end of her bench was a little brass tripod—from its apex swung a little chain with a crow's beak at the end, and beneath the beak was a metal plate engraved with a twelve-pointed star and symbols at each ray that Oscar didn't recognize. The woman turned to him.

"What can I do for you?"

"Mother Mim?" he asked.

"I am." The woman had a friendly voice. "Why the hat? It's not sunny."

"It's good for rain, too," he replied. "Why the sunglasses?"

"Same deal. Something in particular?"

"Cellophane, if you have it, or wrapping paper. The old bloke three doors up said you might have some."

Mother Mim bent beneath the counter and straightened holding a box. She reached in and produced a folded square of faded red cellophane. Oscar lifted it. Its corner was torn, it had a hole in the center, and was patched with tape.

"This is garbage."

"It's slightly used," she admitted.

"It's holier than the pope, look at it."

She leaned forward and pulled off her sunglasses. Oscar flinched. Her lids hung slack, like drapes over dark windows—there were no eyes in her sockets, and he could glimpse the purpled flesh that lined her orbits.

"Well, aren't we particular," she said, taking back the cellophane and rustling in the box.

"How did you know I wear a hat?" Oscar asked.

The woman smiled. "Same way I know there's leather under your left armpit. I can hear it." Her clever fingers searched in the box. "I pulled them out myself, in case you're wondering." She laughed. "I know, what an idiot. But I was just seeing a bit too much of my ex-husband. Still, quite a good outcome. Now I don't see him, but I see other things." On the counter she placed another square of clear, virgin cellophane and dropped onto it a length of satin ribbon. "Three dollars."

"No way."

She shrugged and lifted the cellophane away.

"Wait." He placed a length of three unopened condoms on the bench. She felt them and smiled coyly.

"An offer?"

"A trade."

"A shame."

She had a nice smile. She vanished the condoms and pushed the cellophane and ribbon toward Oscar. As he reached for them, she took his wrist. "Now. Read your fortune?"

"I can't afford it."

She didn't let him go. "A free taste. A thank-you for an easy trans-action."

The blind woman's grip was surprisingly strong. She ran a cool, dry fingertip across his palm. After a moment, she frowned and released his wrist.

"Well?" he asked.

"I'd lose the hat," she suggested.

Oscar picked up his cellophane and ribbon. "Why?"

The woman replaced her sunglasses over the empty sockets. "You need to watch the skies."

———

Under rain, the cemetery was all cold grays and dark greens. Rainwater trickled down Oscar's back and drops dripped heavily from the brim of his hat; warm water ran up his sleeves. He heard snatches of clattering, like the chatter of mechanical teeth, and could smell cut grass, soapy water, and damp soil.

The clattering stopped suddenly and was replaced by *slide-clunk, slide-clunk.*

"*Stu cazzo!*"

Oscar peered over the headstone he was washing. Alessandro Mariani was drenched. His gray hair was plastered down on his clean-shaved, wan cheeks; his arthritic knuckles looked like a row of cicada husks. He was grimly shoving at the hand mower. Oscar had tried to dissuade his father from coming out here when it was raining, but Sandro was implacable. Worse, the old man stubbornly refused to let Oscar do the mowing, insisting that his son perform the less masculine tasks of washing the grave and changing the flowers.

Sandro Mariani gave the mower another frustrated yank, and his face opened up in a surprised flare of pain. "*Pezzo di merda.*"

Oscar squeezed out the sponge, pulled himself wearily up on the black marble. After nearly five years, this fortnightly ritual had gotten no easier. If anything, it had gotten worse. Vedetta had been the leavening influence in their small family; after she succumbed to breast cancer, there was nothing to warm the cool space between father and son.

"Dad. There's grass caught in it."

Sandro either didn't hear or ignored him. "*Sta migna.*" He attacked the handle of the mower, shaking it harder and harder with every word: "*Inutile. Iarrusu. Piseddu.*"

Oscar exhaled through his teeth and walked over.

"Dad! There's a chunk of grass, here in the—"

Oscar reached for the mower, and Sandro, like a child whose toy is in peril, tried to snatch it away. Another electric jolt of pain grounded on his wrinkled face. "Leave it!" Sandro snapped. "I've got it."

"It's jammed!" Oscar said, and knelt. More cold rain ran down his back. "Just don't fucking push it while my fingers are in it, okay?"

Sandro was an unhappy passenger attached to the machine. "Don't swear here."

"You were swearing."

Oscar pulled at a thick knot of lush green paspalum lodged between the curved blade and the fixed edge. The thought of it biting into his fingers reminded him of the huge auger blade in the sewage plant. Christ, who could throw a child into that, dead or alive?

"Well?" Sandro said. "Hurry up. You want to drown?"

"Sometimes." Oscar yanked the clump free. "There."

Sandro pushed the mower. The wheels turned and the three blades whirred. He grunted, then looked down at Oscar. "What are you sitting down for? Are you finished?"

Oscar bit his tongue and went back to his mother's grave.

The men worked another quarter of an hour, saying nothing, until the flowers were set, the grave was washed clean of grass clippings, and Sandro Mariani had kissed his swollen fingers and touched them lightly to the polished marble. Rain pummeled the flowers. Oscar picked up the mower, weeding tools and bucket, and followed his father's foot-prints back to the car.

———

"Where did you get these? They're shit."

Sandro Mariani inspected the fruit and greens Oscar had brought. Oscar stood at the kitchen bench that had changed little in thirty years, making up dough for *ossa dei morti*—"bones of the dead"—sweet bis-cuits. He threw a small handful of flour over the laminate worktop and pointed to lemons, basil, and spinach.

"Those there are from my garden. Those"—he nodded at apples that were more brown than red, and a pawpaw that, like Lazarus, was three days past prime but still going—"from the markets."

"Henh," his father said, a sound that covered a thousand shades of disappointment. "No rabbit?"

"I'm not paying for rabbit. I can shoot rabbit."

"Anyone can shoot rabbit. The difference is between talking and doing."

"Well, I couldn't. I was working yesterday." Now was the moment when a father whose son had followed him into the same trade might ask, How is work? What are you doing? Anything I can do to help? But not my father, Oscar thought. Sandro Mariani didn't discuss police work at home. "I'll get you rabbit next weekend."

"For *coniglio in sugo*. So, potatoes, too."

"I'll try."

Sandro rolled his eyes as if that, right there, spelled disaster. He scowled at the dough Oscar was kneading. "And what are you trying to do with that, talk it into bed? It's not a nipple, don't tease it. *Impastilo!* Here." He nudged Oscar aside and drove his knurled fingers into the brown dough.

"You want to live my life, too?"

"No, thank you. A mouse in a fucking cattery has a better life than you."

"And yours is such a treat. All your friends lining up to visit."

Oscar went to the cupboard and got down two shot glasses, then to the pantry for the grappa. There was barely a half inch of the amber liquid.

"Where's all the booze?"

Sandro looked up a moment, then returned to the dough. "I did some drinking on Tuesday."

Oscar thought that if anyone had a right to develop an alcohol problem it was his father, but he'd never known Sandro to drink alone.

"What happened? Catch a glimpse of Mrs. Colless in her scanties?"

Mrs. Colless had lived next door for half a century and had looked sixty when Oscar was a boy. Sandro didn't smile.

"Someone died," he said.

"On Tuesday?"

Sandro pounded the dough. "Jesus, is this *Sixty Minutes*? No, he died a few weeks ago. I found out on Tuesday."

"You must have really liked him." Oscar sloshed the remaining ounce of grappa. "Or her."

"Him," Sandro said, and his face darkened. "Hated him. I hope he burned slowly."

Sandro flicked his eyes at his son, as if realizing that he'd said too much. Oscar watched. It was his chance now to do the asking. Who was he, Dad? What did he do to warrant drinking half a bottle to his demise? Was he a dirty cop? Someone you put behind bars? And what do you mean, burned? But a five-year silence felt too wide, too deep. . . . Oscar turned away and replaced the bottle in the pantry. "I'll get you some more."

Sandro nodded and began dividing the dough.

Oscar touched the camp oven over the gas ring. The metal was barely warm. He followed the gas hose under the sink and tapped the bottle.

"You're out of gas. Have you got more?"

Sandro raised his floury hands in exasperation. "What am I? Madame Tussaud?"

"That's the wax museum, Dad."

"Take your genius self downstairs and look."

————

The basement floor was covered by an inch of tea-colored water that smelled of roots and clay.

"Dad! You're flooded!" Oscar listened. "Dad!"

Above, the gramophone had started and he heard the faint strains of Al Martino singing "Spanish Eyes."

Oscar sighed, took off his shoes and socks, and looked around for where to begin the rescue. He found a pile of roof tiles and set out four short stacks, then lifted the washing machine onto them, cursing his father for keeping a contraption that was useless without electricity. An old Genoa chair was already wicking dampness up its tapestry sides; he used the last two tiles and a doorstop to lift it above the water. A timber door wedge floated like a tiny boat into the bathroom in the corner. Beside the workbench were two piles of cardboard boxes: one was a neat stack of three boxes; the other was a haphazard tower that had clearly been moved from the original pile. The bottom boxes were swelling with water. Oscar began shifting them to the workbench, looking into each as he moved it. The first box contained empty preserve jars; the next held angling magazines (though Oscar couldn't recall ever having seen his father fish) and old copies of Reader's Digest dating back to the seventies—he knew without looking that the "Increase Your Word Power" vocabulary pages would all be tabbed and marked with ballpoint pen. The bottommost box began to sag open when Oscar lifted it; he caught its dripping bottom before it dropped its innards. His mind flashed again to the dead girl's body and how it slooped when it was lifted from the auger pit. He placed it on the bench and bent to the box at the top of the neater stack—the box it seemed that Sandro had moved the others in order to find.

Oscar lifted the cardboard flap and peered inside.

Newspaper clippings. Not dozens but hundreds. Some were recent, their paper almost white; others were yellow with age. Some were large clippings with halftone photos; others were merely a byline and a paragraph of copy. Oscar lifted the top handful and leafed through them. Murder convictions, murder trials, murderers apprehended, murder victims found. Where the articles had photographs, the halftone images were of men in the backseats of police cars or paddy wagons, trying to cover their heads behind upraised arms and under jumpers. Often, the offenders sat between the same two officers: Sandro Mariani and his partner, Vic Pascoe. "Cassidy's Killer Arrested" declared one headline; "Murder Suspect Remanded" read another. A small photo surprised him, and it took a moment for Oscar to recognize himself at a press conference standing behind a former commissioner, neatly shaved and looking startlingly young in dress uniform. The last clipping he held was the one that had been on top of the rest. The paper was the color of old ivory. There was no copy text, just a headline and a photograph. It showed a long-haired man in his thirties wearing a wide-collared shirt; his face was to the sky. He was laughing as a young and vital Sandro Mariani led him away in cuffs.

"You died down there?" Sandro called. Al Martino had fallen silent. "I should throw this pasta away?"

"Coming," Oscar replied.

He replaced the clipping, then put the last boxes on the bench.

And if the waters rose that high? Well, maybe the past could wash away.

———————

He carried the gas bottle up the stairs, walking silently on bare feet. He stopped inside the doorway to the kitchen. Sandro wasn't looking at him or at the tray of bone-shaped biscuits. The old man was staring down at an empty space on the bench, smiling the beatific smile that adults reserve for their infant children.

Chapter 7

The night was cold, and lightning winked in the distant clouds to the east. From the street he could hear laughter; the balcony of the Gests' apartment glowed with the festival warmth of paper lanterns. Jon and Leonie lived in a building with river views and, enviably, a propane generator. Oscar took off his hat and pressed the buzzer. Leonie was a pianist and had been in the chamber orchestra until it folded; now she tutored from home. Oscar got the sense that she and Jon couldn't have children but he had never quite worked out how to ask. A moment later, the door opened on Leonie's smiling, pixie face. When she recognized Oscar, her smile stuttered.

"Oh dear," she said.

"Nice to see you, too."

Over her shoulder, across the crowded lounge room, Oscar saw a familiar profile. Sabine looked lovely. Asleep on her shoulder was a baby, its face a pleasantly squashed circle. Beside her was her new husband. Oscar understood.

"Jon forgot to uninvite me," he said.

Leonie sighed and opened her hands. "I'm married to an idiot. Anyway, come in."

"I'll go."

"Stay." She took his wrist and kissed him lightly. "I insist. For me. Make it my birthday present."

Oscar hesitated, then rolled his shoulders and let her guide him into the burbling room. He handed her the biscotti wrapped in cellophane. "You get these, too."

"You baked?" She looked from the sugar-dusted cookies up to Oscar. "Such a waste." He wasn't sure if Leonie meant the biscuits or him. She took his face in both her hands and turned his head toward a glittering trove of bottles. "Do me a favor? There's the bar. Drink a lot and *talk* to your ex—it'll make life easier for all of us. Now, I have some matrimonial ass-kicking to do."

She smiled prettily and slipped away between the partygoers like a forest sprite among trees.

Oscar moved carefully, keeping as much of the small crowd as possible between himself and Sabine. Snatches of conversation were idle clouds passing: "I mean, how are you supposed to straighten your hair without it?" "So I asked Gai's husband—" "The scientist?" "Her first husband was a scientist. . . ." "Another baby! How can they afford it?" "The house next door is vacant, so they bought a goat—" " . . . a gun and made him empty his pockets." "What did the police say?" "Christ, it probably *was* the police."

Oscar poured a short whiskey. Laughter like thunder shook the room. He looked up and saw Jon with a sergeant from Counterterrorism, sharing what seemed to be a bawdy joke. Jon shook his head and looked across the room and caught Oscar's eye. His eyes widened a little, and said, "Oh, fuck . . ."

Oscar raised his plastic glass.

Jon's shoulders sagged. He mouthed an apology and mimed putting a pistol in his mouth. Oscar smiled and waved it away. He pushed politely through the crowd, uncomfortable in the crush.

As he glanced at faces, Oscar noticed the tiny flicks of people's eyes. A man in deep conversation might suddenly glance at an empty patch of wall, or a woman laughing at her friend's story might catch sight of something not far away and the merriment in her eyes would die a little. How many people were in the apartment? Fifty? Sixty? Then there were sixty ghosts in here, too, standing as he was, watching, each unseen by anybody but one. The thought made him look across the room. At the far end of the crowded hallway stood the pale, dead boy. He gave Oscar a timid nod. Oscar ignored him.

He pushed past the kitchen, casting a glance inside at the caterers; one opened a new stainless-steel refrigerator to retrieve a platter. Oscar felt another bubble of jealousy rise in him. His home had neither regular power nor a fridge, let alone a new double-doored monster.

He found a corner with a window where he could pretend to inspect the view of the dark apartment buildings opposite. Outside, night and rain had turned the city into a huge and gloomy spread of black mono-liths and occasional winks of dull light. It reminded him of a cemetery he'd visited in a small town near Innsbruck on a holiday with Sabine a thousand years ago. It had been nearly Christmas, and beside dozens of the dark headstones in the small churchyard were little candles in small red lanterns. He and Sabine had held hands, walking the narrow path between the headstones, reading the names as snow drifted in silence. Those flickering, tiny lights had been placed with tenderness and care; the lights winking in the dark outside this window were loveless. The path here was a river, black and snaking. The river, Oscar thought. Why not dump the girl in the river? Six feet of chain would hold her down for weeks. Someone was so concerned that her body would be identi-fied that the best option was to destroy it in an industrial auger. Only it wasn't destroyed.

A hand touched his shoulder, and he flinched.

"I saw your biscuits in the present pile."

Sabine wore a frown that might have been angry, or confused, or concerned. Oscar thought that not knowing which after all these years must be some kind of sign. He willed his jittering heart to settle.

"Leonie won't eat them—she survives on air," he said. "But Jon likes them. Where's Lambert?"

Lambert Powter had become a councilman at twenty-eight, a deputy mayor at thirty, and Sabine's new husband at thirty-three. Oscar wondered what other conquests awaited him.

Sabine pointed with her narrow chin. "There, holding Alice."

"Alice." Oscar nodded. "Nice." *Nice?* he thought sourly. He tried to think of a more enthusiastic adjective. "Really nice," he added.

Sabine inclined her head. "We'll have to get her home soon."

"I thought babies could sleep through anything."

"We're the ones who need the sleep." Sabine watched him carefully. "So, you know, things like late-night phone calls aren't really appreciated."

Oscar felt his face grow warm, but he said nothing.

Sabine reached out, and he found himself recoiling from her hand—another sign he wished he'd learned to read a long time ago. She ran critical fingers over his bike jacket's front pockets. "Oh, Oscar, this old thing."

"I like it."

She nodded as if she knew that fact very well. "They do still make jackets. The world hasn't ended."

"I have budget priorities."

Sabine's eyes hardened.

"Are you still giving away half your wages?"

Oscar felt a familiar blister of heat rise inside him, returning as readily as the lyrics of a Christmas carol. It was as if cogs of time had slipped and they were having the same argument they'd had week after week three years ago. "Sabby, please," he said. "Give it a rest."

"You are, aren't you?"

"I can make my own decisions."

"Shitty ones," Sabine said. "I care about you, Oscar. You have to stop it."

"You know, I don't think I do."

"Yes, you *really* do. You're killing yourself over something that wasn't your fault."

"Really? Because it was my car that hit her. My hands on the wheel."

"You thought you were saving a life."

"And wasn't that rich? Because instead I ruined one."

Sabine's lips had pursed down to a tight horizon. "Were you charged? No. Were you exonerated? Yes. Do they have homes for people like her? Yes. Do they have hospitals?"

"Have you been to a public hospital lately? Or one of those homes? It's the fucking Dark Ages out there, Sab. But you live on the Heights, so you wouldn't—"

"It. Wasn't. Your. Fault." Her teeth were gritted.

"Then whose fault was it?!"

"It was an accident!"

"I put her in a *fucking wheelchair!*"

Oscar was suddenly struck by how quiet the room had become. The music had stopped, and people were staring. Other guests had edged a little away from the pretty, frowning woman and the untidy man in the patched motorcycle jacket; he and Sabine had become a little Krakatoa surrounded by a sea of nervous silence. Leonie was doing the rounds with a plate of canapés—she gave Oscar a worried smile.

Well, you asked me to talk to her, he thought.

Suddenly, the Violent Femmes began singing an old Marc Bolan song. Jon turned up the volume, and a few moments later conversations started again.

"Everything okay?"

Lambert Powter was dressed with the casual ease of a yachtsman sailing off the Hamptons, and he cradled his sleeping baby like a man born to love children. He was as tall as Oscar but had looks that would hold all his life. Where Oscar's face already felt stubbled an hour after shaving, Powter's square face was shaved so smoothly that light skated on it. Aside from the infant on his shoulder, he looked as if he had just stepped from a Ralph Lauren advertisement.

"Hi, Lambert," Oscar said brightly. "How's City Hall? Getting that pesky staff parking sorted out?"

Powter ignored him and looked down at Sabine. She gave him a twist of the head that was inscrutable to Oscar but had crystal-clear meaning for his successor. Satisfied, Powter looked up at Oscar. "Nice seeing you."

Powter carried the baby into a crowd, where two young women began to coo over her.

Oscar suddenly felt very tired. "I have to go," he said.

"Oscar." Sabine touched his arm and stared at him with an expression he could not identify. "You have to change. People who won't . . . don't make it anymore."

Chain lightning flashed in the west, strobing the outline of the building across the street. Its rooftop was almost level with the Gests' apartment. On the roof edge, directly opposite Oscar, was a child-size silhouette. The instant the thought registered in his mind, the child jumped.

"Oh, fuck," Oscar shouted. The small form became shadow as it dived in a speedy arc down toward the street.

"What?"

"A kid just jumped off that building."

"What!"

Oscar pushed through the crowd, riding a wave of rising voices. He flung the door open, ran down the corridor, and took the stairs three at a time. At the bottom, water had pooled and the air had the alkaline odor of wet concrete. He slammed down on the handle and burst out into the rain.

He ran out to the street, expecting to hear the screams of onlookers and the squeals of brakes as cars stopped to see what had struck the footpath . . . but the road was quiet. A taxi rattled by, tires hissing on the wet. The footpath across the road was in shadow.

Oscar sprinted behind the cab and across the road, eyes probing the dark asphalt of the footpath for a tiny, shattered body. Chain lightning again jolted the clouds into a moment of silver light, and details jumped forward. A trash can was stuffed to overflowing, weeds flourished in the untended garden flanking the unlit path, but no body. Darkness again. Thunder rumbled.

"Oscar?"

He turned. Jon and several guests had followed him out onto the street.

"What happened?" Jon called. "Os!"

You dreamed it, Oscar told himself. *You imagined it.*

But his racing heart said that wasn't true. He'd seen something the height of an eight-year-old child plunge from the roof. Impossible. City birds didn't come that big.

"I don't know," Oscar said. "I saw something fall from the roof up there."

"Where?" a guest asked.

"Someone said a kid jumped," another said.

Despite the rain, more guests were arriving. A crowd of a dozen or so were now milling around asking what had happened.

Oscar hunted in the dark, hoping to find something that might have fallen from the roof—a vent cowling, a box, anything. But there was nothing.

"Are you sure?" Jon asked.

Oscar looked up, squinting against the raindrops. The sky above was as black as a well. The thunder roll echoed off the canyon of buildings and died.

Guests began to trickle back indoors. "Drunk," he heard one say. Oscar felt his neck grow hot. Before long, it was just him and Jon getting drenched.

"Maybe," Jon began, "a trick of the light?"

"Yeah. Maybe."

"Lightning, I mean—" Jon's big fingers flicked in the air.

"Look, get back inside," Oscar said. "Leonie will kill me for letting you get wet."

"What, kill her biscotti dealer? No way." Jon grinned and clapped him on the shoulder. "Come back in. Get a drink."

"I think I'll head home."

Oscar saw a flash of relief in his friend's eyes.

"Well, get some rest, yeah?"

"No worries."

The big man hurried inside. Lightning flashed again, and heavy thunder rolled like mighty bones in a mightier drum. From somewhere in the concrete-sided dark came a heavy *whoosh*, then another, departing. Maybe it was wind.

Oscar strode quickly to his car. Across the road, keeping pace with him and watching the footpath, was the dead boy.

Chapter **8**

·

In daylight hours, the Industrial Relations Branch was a grating drone of bland phone calls, clattering printers, and wheezing copiers. Oscar hung his jacket and hat on the stand beside his desk and looked out the window. The rain had stopped, but the sky remained as gray as moth wings, and wind beat against the buildings. Far below on the street, a woman and a child pushed against the prevailing gust. Then someone coughed behind him.

Neve's lips were pursed tight. The frown she'd worn yesterday had returned and looked settled in to stay.

"Hi," he said. "You all right?"

"Oscar." She rocked unhappily from foot to foot, not looking into his eyes. "Listen. Yesterday, I was thinking—"

Oscar's phone rang. He held up a finger—one second— and picked up the receiver. "Mariani."

"Good, you're in."

Inspector Benjamin Moechtar had a light, democratically flat voice that elevated no syllable above its cousins. "Do you have a minute?"

Oscar could see that Neve was working to keep her arms at her sides, as if they wanted to spring loose and fly her far away.

"Yes, sir."

Moechtar asked, "Now all right?"

"I'm on my way."

Oscar hung up and looked at Neve. "What?"

Suddenly, she turned and hurried off across the Branch floor. She strode past Foley, the overweight senior sergeant currently heading IRB. Foley looked up from his computer, watched Neve's backside, then turned to Oscar and gave a connoisseur's nod of approval.

Oscar went to the elevators. He still hadn't formed an opinion about Moechtar, who'd been his commanding officer for nearly two months following the resignation of Bob Daley. Daley's wife had taken a turn and needed him at home. "Taken a turn" had later been revealed to mean "tried to poison her three grandchildren by putting pesticide in a birthday cake." When she pleaded that "the man with no head" had made her do it, Oscar had been called in to investigate. But since no deaths had occurred the offense had been bandied about in departmental no-man's-land just long enough for Daley to agree to an early, very quiet departure. Moechtar, his replacement, now headed three departments: Internal Audit, Conduct and Ethical Standards, and the Nine-Ten Investigation Unit. He'd come from Legal Services, which now had forty percent fewer full-time staff. Moechtar was a former accountant: a financial hatchet man.

At the ninth floor, Oscar strode down a hushed corridor to stop outside a dark-paneled door. He knocked.

"Come in."

Oscar entered. The carpet was business blue and impeccably clean. Two more doors ran off the office: one to a small meeting room, another to a private bathroom—a perk that made Moechtar's rank an attractive goal. Moechtar himself was seated behind his desk, a small, spare man in his late forties. His glasses, his suit, his tie, his hair were all neat and regularly proportioned. Like his speech, Moechtar's face was an instrument calibrated to range between polite interest and civil unconcern. On one paneled wall were photographs of Moechtar with various VIPs: the state premier, the New Zealand defense minister, a now dead Italian tenor. In none of the photographs was Moechtar's expression any different from the one of neutral attention that he now presented to Oscar.

"Good morning, sir," Oscar said.

Moechtar nodded and spoke evenly. "Service guidelines state that, as a detective, you are permitted to wear"—he opened a tabbed page in the manual—"'Neat business clothes, preferably suit and tie for males.'" He looked up at Oscar.

Oscar tried to recall when he last ironed his threadbare shirt and hand-patched trousers but failed. He did have a tie; it was currently holding up the drain hose of his washing machine, which itself worked only on the rare occasions that the power came on.

"Take a look at what the guidelines recommend for females," Oscar suggested.

Moechtar looked down at the manual. He read, " 'Neat business clothes, preferably business suit or jacket-pant set.' "

"Exactly. No tie," Oscar said. "Kind of discriminatory. Maybe we guys should get together and complain."

Moechtar looked up at him, wearing the expression of an entomologist observing an insect of a genus he really should know but just couldn't quite catalog.

"Take a seat, Oscar."

"I'm kind of busy."

"Please."

Oscar sat. Careful as a beekeeper, Moechtar flipped with neat fingers through the top papers of his in-tray and found the envelope that he was looking for. He handed it to Oscar.

"What is it?"

Moechtar nodded for Oscar to read. He opened it. A request for transfer. Neve had signed and dated it that morning. Oscar felt a bitter little stab in his belly.

Moechtar said, "She brought it to me. I could sign it, but I'd prefer to leave that to her supervising officer."

Oscar folded the paper and put it into a jacket pocket.

"And I read your report," Moechtar continued. "The Jane Doe at the sewage plant."

"Yes, sir."

"You kept it from Homicide."

"The attending General Duties officer thought it was a Nine-Ten case. I agree."

Moechtar nodded thoughtfully. "Homicide would like it."

Oscar felt a twitch of excited satisfaction. "Haig called you?"

"Yes, he did. Would you consider giving it over?"

"Sure." Oscar thought for a moment. "No."

Moechtar sighed like a put-upon maître d' and pulled from his in-tray a grubby-looking collection of papers. Oscar recognized the interim report he'd put in Moechtar's pigeonhole two days ago.

"I understand no one is claiming it to be a Clause Seventeen killing."

"There was no one there *to* claim it, except the body. There is evidence of mutilation that suggests an occult ritual was associated with the death."

"The symbol."

"Yes."

"So, murder, you think?"

"Yes, sir."

"Yet not for Homicide?"

"No offense, but Homicide can go get fucked."

Behind Moechtar a toilet flushed, and Oscar heard one of the doors in the back of the office open. He turned as Haig stepped out, flicking his fingers dry.

"Fucked by whom, Mariani?" Haig asked, wearing a pleasant smile. "Not you, surely. You're too busy, I hear. Paperwork, paperwork."

Haig stood at a leather chair and looked to Moechtar, who nodded. Haig sat and crossed his ankles, a man at his ease.

Oscar felt his jaw tighten.

Moechtar said, "I did tell Inspector Haig that although the case is yours I would be just as happy if you chose to devote the next few days to compiling a clear operational summary that we can make some decisions on."

Oscar frowned. He felt like a man who'd come home in the dark to discover that someone had rearranged all the furniture. "Next few days? What do you mean? What about other Clause Seventeens?"

Moechtar checked his watch and began slipping papers into a leather document wallet. "I've sent a memo out around the South-East to say the Nine-Ten Unit is offline."

"Offline this week?" Oscar felt a new possibility dawn. "Or offline for good?"

"That really depends on your operational summary," Moechtar said. "So, what to do with this." He slid Oscar's report to the middle of the desk. "As far as I'm concerned, Detective, it's your case. But since Inspector Haig, who's read your report, believes it falls under his purview it would be common decency to hand it over."

Oscar turned and watched Haig.

"I'm not commonly decent," Oscar said.

Haig's smile didn't change, but something hard sparked behind his eyes. "Well, that's no skin off my nose." He stood and walked to the door. "Just trying to help. Ben. Detective."

"Geoffrey."

"Inspector."

Haig pulled the door shut behind him. The office fell quiet for a long moment.

Moechtar picked up Oscar's report and returned it to his in-tray.

"I'm no detective, Oscar, but to me this looks like a fairly standard assault and murder of a street kid."

"There was nothing standard about her mutilation."

Moechtar nodded, not really interested. "Well, do what you will. But get me a coherent operational report by close of business Friday. I don't want a muddled collection of guesses—I want considered numbers that I can work with. Accurate paperwork is essential to the delivery of justice."

He zipped closed the document wallet, then stood and looked meaningfully at Oscar.

Oscar took the hint: the meeting was over. He stood and headed for the door, pausing only when Moechtar spoke again.

"And, Detective? Do try and look the part."

———

Oscar sat at his desk, thinking. He could still shift the case. He could hand the Jane Doe over to Homicide with his inspector's blessing, knuckle down, and bring home some solid convictions for the Barelies. The thought left him cold.

Because, as he had told Moechtar, the Jane Doe's mutilation was unusual. This was a Nine-Ten case; he was sure of it.

His phone beeped. A text message from Paz Lovering, asking if he'd like to know more about his "ugly damned symbol."

"Anyone seen de Rossa?" Oscar asked the room.

Foley was staring intently at his computer; he shrugged his spongy shoulders. "Hey, Mariani?" Foley's chair groaned as it swiveled. "Where'd you come from again? Before here?" He clicked his fat fingers.

Oscar stood and pulled on his coat. "Ethical Standards."

Foley pointed at him—gotcha—then tapped his screen. "Listen, hypothetically, if I had a . . . you in a hurry or something?"

"Kind of," Oscar said, grabbing his hat.

Foley nodded, held up fat hands. "It'll keep. Another time." He grinned. "Hey, I'm happy to slip Neve a note? Something else?"

Foley winked. Oscar ignored him and strode out to the elevators.

———

"Slow down," Lovering said. "You're not on 'Dancing with the Assholes.' Stop wiggling your feet and watch the damned road. Jesus, you're worse than Denna."

Wind buffeted the car, and the sky was undecided; clouds skidded in from the east like street thugs trying to look casual. Oscar drove across the Story Bridge and into the winding, river-hugging streets of New Farm, where apartment buildings and houses coexisted behind overgrown trees.

Gelareh Barirani had been one of Paz's researchers at *ARClight*. She was in her late fifties or older, and Oscar thought she must once have been utterly striking. Her hair was still dark, and her cheekbones high and distinct. She lived in a six-pack: a rectangular three-story block of flats—three up, three down. Hers was ground floor and boasted a tiny courtyard that smelled of mint, coriander, and climbing rose. Oscar asked her how she persuaded her herbs to flourish and her grandchildren not to destroy them, and she replied with a dozen tips. Their horticultural banter made Lovering grizzle, retreat to a corner of the courtyard, and close his eyes.

Gelareh made mint tea and pulled out the photograph Paz had printed of the symbol on the Jane Doe's belly, and a sheaf of greaseproof papers. On each sheet she had traced different elements of the sigil: on one, the star; on another, the patterned cross; on yet another, the texts with arabesque swirls, and the chopped and wedge-shaped symbols. While she poured the tea, Gelareh apologized for not having had more time to work on it.

"Your symbol is, I think, a concoction." Her voice had a lovely curl that sounded like waves and stirred up tastes of spice. "Not from one country, not from one era." She shuffled the papers. "Now, where to start?"

"Assume he knows nothing," Lovering called from outside. "I find that is the least frustrating way."

"Oh, yes, because you're so smart, Paz Lovering," she shouted back. "You who got lost in Ben Yehuda Street."

"It was busy!" Lovering looked at Oscar for sympathy. "It was crazy with tourists. Baden-Powell would have gotten lost there."

"Some Jew," Gelareh tutted, and smoothed out the first sheet of onionskin paper. On it was traced the seven-pointed star. "Okay, the heptagram. Well, seven, as you know, is the number of perfection for some religions, including some divisions of Christianity and the Kabbalah. The star of seven points is also called the Faery Star, or Elven Star. Some pagans believe it shows the four cardinal directions—north, south, east, west—as well as above, below, and inside . . . within. Some Wiccans believe it helps open the way to the realm of Faerie. Alchemists from the sixteenth century used it as a symbol of power, to denote the seven planets then known in the solar system. Oh, and the seven-pointed star is also used five times on the Australian flag." She looked at Oscar. "Patriots have been known to go too far."

"That doesn't really narrow down our list of suspects," Oscar said. "Christians, Jews, pagans, alchemists, and radical patriots. I guess I can rule out alchemists."

"I'm not finished. Older than all these was the star's use in my stomping ground." She smiled. "Mesopotamia. Five-, six-, and seven-pointed stars were all symbols associated with various gods and goddesses. They were appropriated and absorbed and amalgamated as years went by. The seven-pointed star"— she touched the tracing—"was associated with the goddesses Inanna and Ereshkigal."

"And who were they?" Oscar asked.

"Sisters. The queen of heaven and the demon goddess of chaos."

"Polar opposites."

Gelareh shrugged noncommittally and flattened out the next tracing. The cross. On paper, it looked like an elaborate plus sign, its equal-length arms filigreed at the ends but appearing almost structural with a gridwork of crisscross patterns.

"I had to guess some of the lines," Gelareh explained. "But this looks like a vévé. Or, really, a part of a vévé."

"A what?"

"See?" Lovering called. "I told you."

Gelareh ignored him. "Vévés are sigils used in vodou. You know what vodou is?"

"Voodoo? From Haiti," Oscar replied. "Spirit worship. Possession."

Gelareh wrinkled her nose. "Haitian vodou has strong roots in West

African vodun, you know? Yes, it is spirit worship, not unlike Native American and Celtic religions. The belief that spirits govern all aspects of earth and life. They live in stones, trees, animals, and they can be called upon to render assistance, to give comfort, confer favors—"

"To intervene," Oscar said.

"Exactly. If they are called correctly and given appropriate offerings. The vévé—they are like doors, or keys, or . . . hmm." She searched for the word. She looked outside to Lovering, but he was snoring lightly, the teacup on his belly. "The towers with the lights?"

"Lighthouses?" Oscar said.

She nodded. "Yes. Lighthouses to attract the Loa, the spirits. Like nasty moths." She smiled, and the paper rustled dryly under her fingers. "This looks very much like a portion, the cross portion, of the vévé used to summon Baron Samedi."

"Samedi?" Oscar asked. "French? Baron Saturday?"

"He is one of the major spirits. A Guédé, a guardian of the cross-roads between the dead and the living. But, as I say, this is only a portion of the Baron's vévé. Here."

She had a reference book tabbed, and opened to a page that showed an almost childlike drawing that looked like a cross on an altar flanked by two coffins and embellished with asterisks.

Oscar frowned. "And the vodou priests and priestesses, they cut these into their flesh?"

"Oh, no. They draw them with powder, maybe flour, even gunpowder. Like the Navajo use pollen or cornmeal. But no incisions, no."

This was raising more questions than answering them, Oscar thought. And they were only halfway through the sheets.

Gelareh flipped to the next tracing: crescents, stars, something that looked like a church spire, and other badly formed shapes that made no sense to Oscar.

"Pictograms," Gelareh explained. "Very hard to read from the photograph."

"It wasn't the best quality."

Gelareh said nothing. "Still. This glyph"—she turned the image upside down and Oscar could see that it looked like a heron or a crane—"looks very much like an Akh."

"Egyptian?"

She nodded. "The symbol of the soul. A ghost." She drew his eye down to a curl of lines that came into unpleasant focus: a skull in profile. "And this looks a little like an Aztec image. I'm not so good with Aztec. But skulls and skeletons? Very popular in ancient Central America."

Oscar remembered his and Sabine's honeymoon—October in New England and November in San Francisco. The stores there were full of pumpkins and Halloween masks. Oscar and Sabine had gone down to Garfield Square to see the Day of the Dead festival—*Dia de los Muertos*. So many skeletons. "For *La Calavera Catrina*," explained a beautiful young woman whose face was painted as a white-and-black skull. "To remind us that even the rich die."

Gelareh produced the last sheet. This was covered with dozens of lines—some straight, some curled, some ending in flourishes, some terminating in tiny stars or blunt slashes.

"These are undeniably words. But there is no single language. This one could be Bronze Age Hittite." She peered at the photograph and shrugged. "Because the instrument used and the . . . medium were so unusual, it is tricky, as you say."

"I can show you the original."

She looked up at him and shook her head. "I moved to this country so I'd see fewer bodies. Thank you, but better photographs would do. If you want me to continue, that is. Of course, it will take some time."

Gelareh looked at the floor, and an awkward silence fell.

"Oh, yes," Oscar said. He reached into his bag and produced a sealed box of loose tea. "I don't have cash. A bit embarrassing."

"No, no, this is wonderful."

"We used to have money for this—"

"And I hate to ask. Only because, you know—"

"Of course."

"—my time."

"Yes."

Another silence descended, and Oscar picked up the photograph. "What sort of a person would do this?" he asked.

Gelareh didn't speak at once. "A serious one," she said.

"A serious scholar? A serious nutter?"

Again, she hesitated, weighing her words. "I don't know. But there's work in this. I think whoever did this believed in what they were doing."

"Which was what?"

She tapped the edge of the photograph with the care someone might exercise touching a tarantula's cage. "As I said, a lighthouse. They were trying to bring something in."

The air outside had become still but charged, waiting like an indrawn breath, latent with the promise of a storm.

"So they're crazy," Oscar said.

"Do you think so? Look around you. Somewhere there's a dead person only you can see. Sitting there"—she smiled unhappily and pointed to an empty chair beneath a framed eighteenth-century pen-and-wash of a winged lion with a bearded man's head—"is someone only I can see: a man my father killed more than fifty years ago." Oscar felt the hairs on the back of his neck prickle. "It's already happened," Gelareh continued. "Things have already come in."

Outside, a breeze tugged at Lovering's gray hair, and the air began to grow cold. Somewhere an alarm clock sounded. Gelareh checked her watch.

"Will you excuse me?" She smiled apologetically, went to her bedroom, and shut the door.

Oscar looked at the traced pages. A lighthouse. A beacon.

Nonsense.

And yet in his mind flickered the memory of something falling from the building opposite Jon and Leonie's apartment. Falling . . . then flying.

He heard Lovering cough, and the teacup on his stomach rattled as he sat up. He rubbed at the stain on his shirt. The sky was now gray and dark.

Gelareh returned, dressed in a cleaner's uniform, pinning to her blouse a nametag branded with an inner-city hotel's logo. She smiled at Oscar as she collated her papers.

"If you can get me some clearer photographs, I'll continue tomorrow."

Chapter 9

n the foyer of the state mortuary, a family of a dozen Polynesians had gone to war. They took turns screaming at the sole reception clerk, demanding that he give them a body back. Two uniformed cops stood by the front door, impassively watching as if they'd seen it all a hundred times before. Oscar supposed they probably had.

He stepped behind the islanders and held up his ID to the reception clerk. The clerk, a tall Nigerian, waved him forward. Oscar pressed the ID against the glass.

"How come you talk to this moke but you won' talk to us?" demanded a young Polynesian the size of a small tractor. Oscar showed a glimpse of his holster.

"Manners?"

The islander grinned at the gun. "Fucking pigs." But he turned and ambled back to his kin, who began to tease him.

The clerk thumbed in a code to the glass security door, and Oscar stepped quickly inside; on the other side of the glass, the Polynesians' expletives and threats became the muted roar of distant surf.

He followed the clerk, who walked unhurriedly along the corridors.

Oscar looked around. Before Gray Wednesday, Forensic Services held an atmosphere of respectful quiet: morgue technicians wore paper slippers, voices were hushed, and the air had a scent of chemicalized lavender. Today, phones rang shrilly, people yelled, and the air was a languid stew of sweat and formaldehyde. Suddenly, the clerk stopped and lashed out at the empty air, making Oscar jolt.

"*Ban gane ba!*" the clerk shouted at a blank wall, pointing angrily. "*Na gaji!*"

Oscar took a careful half step back.

The clerk sent a final, angry flick at nothing, then turned to Oscar. "Sorry," he said, and gestured loosely toward a closed door up ahead, then returned the way he came.

Oscar opened the door and went inside.

The large examination room was the clouded gray of a dead tooth, and cold. An overhead gantry system for transporting bodies ran across the ceiling and through a twin set of plastic flap doors. One door was jammed open, and beyond Oscar could see barely controlled chaos in the adjoining storeroom. A technician was short-temperedly hunting through stainless-steel body drawers; each was built for single occupancy but held two or three white cadaver bags. Nearby, cool air spilled in a fog from an open cold-room door, and two more technicians in stained white coats were arguing about how to fit another body in. From somewhere came an AC/DC song, sounding thin and strangled. In the exam room proper were six stainless-steel necropsy tables, each with its own sink and U-shaped faucets. A body lay on every table, five in white plastic bags, the one on the farthest table exposed. This was a woman's body; her face had been peeled down over her chin, and a small figure in a lab coat and plastic visor was running a dumbbell-shaped Stryker saw around the crown of the exposed skull. There was a clatter as the skullcap slipped from the pathologist's gloved fingers onto the perforated tabletop.

"Shit it."

The pathologist flicked off the saw and its nasal whine hazzed down to silence. She picked up the skullcap and dropped it into the stainless-steel bucket. Oscar remembered Dianne Hyde as a woman defined by her work: quiet, even-humored, and unrushed. So when she lifted her visor Oscar was shocked to see Hyde's face taut with exhaustion.

"Oscar Mariani," she said, flicking off the Surgilux lamp. "I presume you've come to give me that bucatini recipe you've been promising?"

He surprised her by pulling the handwritten recipe from his pocket. A small smile appeared on Hyde's face—it looked bewildered and out of place.

"And where am I supposed to get Pecorino cheese?"

"You're a resourceful woman."

"I'm an old woman." She pocketed the recipe. "With a workload."

The cadaver she was working on was in her twenties. The dead woman's legs were swollen and purple; her chest and breasts were ice-white. A rope bruise on her neck rose in an inverted V under her left ear. Her fingertips were chafed, and one nail had been torn off. The young woman had changed her mind after kicking away the chair, and had clawed at the fatal rope.

"Suicide," he said.

"Suicide," Hyde agreed, and nodded at the next two cadavers. "Suicide, suicide . . ." She gestured through the flap doors to the overfilled cold rooms, raised her hands, and then let them drop helplessly by her sides. Oscar felt his stomach grow cold. So many. Was life really that bad? But then he was lucky: his ghost mostly hid himself away. Oscar had heard numberless accounts of people whose dead wouldn't leave their side. People would go to sleep at night with their dead grandfather or drowned school friend or cancered cousin an arm's length away, staring down with those worming finger-hole eyes. Waking, the first thing they saw was a death mask looking back. In every mirror, at every meal, every time they went to buy a paper or drink tea or make love to their partner, the staring dead would be there, a silent, corpselike chaperone. Could anyone blame those who couldn't cope?

"Do you have to autopsy them all?" Oscar asked.

Hyde smiled humorlessly. "Legislation, from the good old days when we only had two dozen suicides a year. Until some bright spark in Parliament puts forward a change, we have to postmortem them all. I invite you to write to your local member. So, Detective, what can I do you for?"

He handed her another slip of paper with a file number on it and produced his digital camera. This time he'd replaced the battery. "I need some better pics of a cadaver."

"Scenes of Crime?"

"Didn't get there."

Hyde rolled her eyes and gestured for Oscar to follow her to the computer at one side of the room.

"How's Sabine?" she asked as she typed in the details from his note.

"Still divorced."

Hyde grimaced. "I'm sorry. I forgot."

"I do that. It's more embarrassing when I do."

Hyde peered at the screen. "This cadaver's Tetlow's. Patrick Tetlow, he's good. Gone home sick today, but . . . oh."

She stared at the screen.

"Oh?" Oscar asked. "Oh, what?"

Hyde frowned and checked the number against the slip of paper. The corners of her mouth turned downward.

"That body's been released," she said.

"Released?" Oscar leaned to look over her shoulder. "When?"

"Today."

"Released to whom?"

Hyde tapped the screen. "Released for destruction. It's gone to the crematorium."

———

Oscar watched the speedometer's needle climb. There was little traffic on the freeway heading south out of the city. It took him less than fifteen minutes to reach the crematorium.

Business must be good. The gardens were tended, the columbaria clean, the Art Deco–style chapel locked but undamaged. The woman who met him at the front office rocked from hip to hip as she walked with arthritic slowness down plush maroon carpets past walls the color of buttermilk. She'd tried the intercom out to the cremator but got no response. "It's hard for Richard to hear the intercom over the burner," she explained. "He turned it on a few minutes ago. We only have the one body this morning."

Oscar mentally willed her to walk faster.

"If they've made a mistake, we're not responsible," the woman warned. "We get a lot of work from the government because we follow the paperwork. We do all the morgues while they're still waiting on parts for their N20; we do bodies from two hospitals. We even do the university's biotrash. One time we even had to destroy a truck full of monkeys that had died of some disease. We all had to wear these suits—"

"Can we hurry?" Oscar said.

"All I'm saying is, we just follow the paperwork."

She hauled back on a swing door and allowed Oscar into a roofed alleyway between buildings. Carpet gave way to tiles, and the scent of roses to the pungent burn of bleach. She reached another pair of swing doors and pushed them open with a stiff arm. Warm air struck Oscar's face.

"Richaaaard?" the woman bellowed.

Oscar broke into a jog. To his left was a series of stainless-steel rollers on tracks that led from an open pair of shuttered windows, inside which he could glimpse the chapel curtains. Ahead to his right was a tall stainless-steel box, eight feet high and thirteen long. The cremator's internal roar sounded like a trapped bushfire. The woman behind Oscar called again, and from around the oven's corner poked a balding head. The mortician's glasses reflected the colored lights of glowing buttons, and his pale eyes bounced from the woman to Oscar. He gave a wave.

He called, "Let me send this one in and I'll be with you."

Suddenly, there was a loud solenoidal click, the pneumatic hiss of a door opening, and the surflike roar of flames grew louder.

Oscar ran around to the front of the oven and was hit by a wave of intense heat punched out by pressurized, burning gas. Attached to the oven by two couplings below the door was a large, slab-sided gurney topped with rubberized steel rollers. On these rested a cardboard casket. The mortician's finger moved to the green button that would launch the casket into the fierce orange glow.

Oscar slammed one hand hard over the mortician's and threw his other arm over the casket. "No!"

The bald man looked down at Oscar over his glasses and pressed a red button. The hatch closed with a solid thunk, cutting off the intense heat.

He gently unplucked himself from Oscar's grip.

"That," the mortician said, "is very unsafe behavior."

———

Oscar concentrated on not letting the trolley get away from him. The wind had strengthened, threatening to yank his hat from his head. It hissed in the gum trees and blew a strange, mournful note between the low brick walls studded with brass plaques. His sedan sat in the wind like an old, whipped dog. In his pocket was the Form Six, signed by Dr. Patrick Tetlow, MBBS FRCPA. In the casket was the girl torn by the auger.

The mortician plucked at Oscar's sleeve. "You're not licensed to carry human remains."

"If I catch myself, I can issue a fine." Oscar popped his car trunk and folded down the backseat. "Give me a hand?"

The mortician helped lift the casket into the car and cleared his throat. "Maybe I should phone the mortuary?"

"You do that," Oscar replied.

"I don't like you taking our paperwork," the woman protested, hobbling to keep up. "We don't get paid unless we present the Form Six."

Oscar closed the trunk lid, locking the murdered girl's body into his car. "Why should you get paid," he said. "You didn't burn her."

He got behind the wheel.

———

At Forensic Services, he searched two laboratories, the storeroom, the tearoom, and both toilets. He found Dianne Hyde pacing on the flat roof. The stiff wind carried the raw taint of smoke. Hyde let her lab coat flap about her like mad wings while she tried to light a cigarette with an uncooperative lighter. She seemed unsurprised to see Oscar.

He found a match and cupped the flame around the tip of her cigarette. "Avoiding me?"

She didn't meet his eye. "Avoiding trouble. One gets to my age by drinking lots of water and avoiding trouble." She coughed as she inhaled.

"When did you start smoking?"

"After I looked for your dead girl's blood samples. Here we take three samples: one for testing, one for backup or further tests, and one gets locked in our evidence fridge for ten years." She inhaled and coughed. "There are no samples. So I rang Tetlow's house. Didn't care if I woke him from his sickbed. His number has been disconnected. He lives three minutes that way, so I drove over. He's gone."

Oscar felt something tighten inside him. "Gone?"

"Gone. House empty. Gone." She stubbed out her cigarette and immediately lit another, watching Oscar. "Do you think he won the lottery?"

Oscar shook his head. The remote chance that this was all just an administrative error had evaporated.

"What's going on, Oscar? Who is this girl? On second thought, don't tell me. I'm a grandmother. I'm up here because I don't want to know. I forgot you could be persistent when it took your fancy."

Oscar heard a growling croak behind him and turned. Two crows were perched on the building's cold chimney crown. Their feathers were the blue-black of wet coal; their eyes were yellow and unblinking. One of them opened its wings and swooped to land on the graveled rooftop just three feet from Oscar and cawed hungrily. He took a swing at it with one shoe. The crow croaked unhappily and flew back up to its cousin. Thoughts collided in Oscar's head like marbles. Someone had persuaded Tetlow, a good pathologist according to Hyde, to authorize an unknown cadaver's destruction before an investigation had even begun, and then pack himself up and disappear. And Oscar knew someone whose threats were an effective means of persuasion, because he followed through. But if it got out that Oscar had retrieved the cadaver, wouldn't Haig offer those same threats to Dianne Hyde?

"You saved the body?" Hyde asked. The white cigarette vibrated in her fingers.

"It's in my car."

"Lovely. Warming up nicely."

He squeezed Hyde's arm, turned, and went to the stairwell doorway. "Just play dumb. If I see anyone downstairs, I'll tell them I couldn't find you."

At the door, he glanced back. Hyde was watching him.

"Take it back, Oscar," she called. "Take it back and burn it. There's enough dying going on. One more doesn't matter."

When he entered the stairwell and closed the door behind him, he heard the breathy rush of the crows taking wing above him. The sound sent an ice-bright shiver up his spine.

Chapter 10

The horse knew it was about to be killed. Its wide eyes showed whites, and its nostrils flared; its frantic whinnying hurt Oscar's ears. Three men were trying to hold the beast secure—one held a rope around its snout, one a rope around its neck, and the third ran around with something in his hand. The horse—a strong brown mare—tried to rear so she could kick at the men, but her forelegs were hobbled, so she simply pushed up, jerking wildly; when she landed, her steel shoes sparked on the concrete. Oscar didn't want to see this, but he needed to speak to the man beside him at a galvanized-steel rail overlooking what had once been a loading bay. This new killing room smelled of ammonia, horse sweat, and blood.

"A racehorse that kept coming last." Gregos Kannis grinned. "I bet it would run like blazes now."

"People buy horse meat?" Oscar asked.

"People buy *dog* meat," Kannis replied. "A smart man sells the horse as beef and the dog as lamb. But me, I'm not so smart." The mare whinnied again and Kannis yelled to his men, "Get it down, for Christ's fucking sake, I can't hear a thing here!"

"We're trying, Mister Kannis, we're—"

The horse struck the man's thigh a glancing blow, and he yelled in pain.

Kannis shook his head. "Idiots. I've told them adrenaline makes the meat bitter." Another hoot of pain from the floor made Kannis grimace. "Excuse me, Oscar."

Oscar watched Kannis jump the rail and stride into the melee. Kannis took the pistol from the man without a rope. The mare pulled harder, and her hooves scraped against concrete wet with her own reeking urine.

"Mister Kannis, watch out!"

The mare twisted her head, pulling one man off balance, and rose on her rear legs. Kannis stepped nimbly under the rope, pointed the pistol at the animal's head, and pulled the trigger. The gun's report was not much louder than a large book dropped on the floor. The mare's momentum carried her up so she held gracefully in midair for a moment, then collapsed on the concrete. Oscar heard a horrible snap as the dead creature's skull hit the hard floor.

Kannis handed back the gun. Two of the men immediately began looping a chain around the mare's rear legs, and one went to fetch a hose. Oscar fought to keep his face from betraying how sickened he was by the terrified animal's slaughter.

"I apologize." Kannis stepped back under the rail, wiping his hands on his trousers. "Now, Oscar, are you here on business or on business? I must warn you, if it's your business, my permits are in order."

"I'm not even here," Oscar replied.

Kannis grinned. "My kind of business."

The butcher's office was a small affair constructed in the space between cold rooms. Across the plain concrete corridor was the staff entrance into the butcher storefront. From somewhere came the steady clank of a chain block and the mad wasp whine of a band saw. Kannis motioned for Oscar to sit. There were perhaps thirty framed photographs on the wall of the tiny office. Most featured Kannis on the backs of boats, holding aloft large fish. But Oscar's eyes were drawn to a photo without Kannis that was decades old, faded to blues and greens. One of the two men in the picture could have been Kannis's twin: it was his father. Oscar knew this because the man next to Kannis Senior was Sandro Mariani.

"It's been a while since I've seen you here," Kannis said. He offered a cigarette. Oscar declined. "Six months? Eight? Are you getting your father's rabbits from somewhere else?"

"I'm in a bit of a rush."

Kannis nodded inside his cocoon of smoke. "Time. The curse of the honest man, eh? So, small talk, *fft*—gone. What do you need in such a hurry?"

"Space."

"How much? For storage? For living?" Kannis's eyes widened and he tapped his nose slyly. "Ah, you finally have a mistress! I have a nice single bedroom in Albion—no view, but who wants to stare at trees when you can look at a bush?" He opened a drawer.

Oscar shook his head. "Here."

"Here what?"

"Here, behind your shop."

Kannis laughed. "You're not serious." He saw Oscar's expression and sobered. "I have no space here. Every cold room is full."

"The one nearest the steel gate has dust on the handle," Oscar said. "No one's been in or out in at least a week."

"Frozen goods," Kannis explained.

"The compressor motor's stone cold. It's empty."

Kannis sighed, leaned back in his chair, eyes never leaving Oscar.

"Why does an honest cop need a cold room?"

"Why does a dishonest butcher care?"

Kannis watched Oscar for a long moment. "A cold room like that— she's premium space."

"Dead space. I'd be doing you a favor."

"My men might get nervous knowing there's a detective swimming about the place. It might affect the quality of their work."

After seeing three men fail to humanely execute a single dumb animal, Oscar wondered what quality there was to compromise.

"I thought you liked to help your friends in the service."

"Oscar," Kannis said, smiling sadly, "you're no one's friend."

Oscar reached into his leather satchel and unwrapped the carton of Camel soft packs he'd picked up from home. He placed them on the desk. Kannis's dark eyes licked over the pristine wrapping, inspecting it for flaws and calculating its street value.

"Serious stuff."

"For a week," Oscar said. "And if we go into a second week, another two."

Where he would get another two cartons of Camels, he had no idea. But he could tell from the sparkle in Kannis's eye that he had a deal. Kannis leaned forward and offered Oscar his hand. Oscar took it and shook.

"My dad always liked your father. Said he was infuriating. 'Sandro Mariani only wants what he wants—he takes nothing for nothing and you can't change his mind.'"

"We are notoriously stupid," Oscar agreed.

Kannis stood and pulled a key off a series of hooks. "I can have it running for you tomorrow morning."

Oscar shook his head. "Now."

———

In the parking lot, Oscar pulled up Neve's number and hit Dial. The call rang through for twenty seconds, then was rejected. He put the phone in his pocket, opened his trunk, and lifted the girl's white, heartbreakingly light cadaver bag from the cardboard casket. He carried it through the gate and into the small white cold room. The air was already chilling, and his breaths condensed into ephemeral clouds under the greenish fluorescent light. He'd pulled two sets of bare galvanized-steel shelves from the walls and set them side by side in the middle of the concrete floor to form a table, then laid the cadaver bag on them. He pulled on latex gloves he'd taken from the morgue and unzipped the white plastic. A faint but foul sigh of wet hair and blood and diluted feces puffed out at him. A dribble of dark blood threatened to escape the white plastic—he hurriedly lifted up the edge to catch it.

The girl's flesh was warm, and an instinctive thrill of doubt raced up from Oscar's gut. *She's alive!* But of course she wasn't; she'd just been out of storage for hours.

In the harsh light, the savaging by the auger blade was horribly clear. Exposed, her body looked even smaller: a fragile, twisted thing, uncomfortable even in death. Her torso had been opened to the spine, and the slick gloss of organs reflected the light between broken ribs. The limbs that hadn't been hacked open or wrenched out were lightly muscled. One thigh was opened up its outside by a wound that was a canyon down into bone; the bone itself was split open like a sapling. The whole leg was at odds with the body, yanked clockwise by the wrenching metal blade. Her vaginal opening had been gouged and mangled, and another raw wound opened up across her navel; Oscar could see the cross-sectioned strata of pale skin, creamy belly fat, and red muscle. One arm had been severed at the shoulder and now rested between her legs—pooled blood had seeped up the skin and stained the hairs. In the harsh, clean light, Oscar could see faint bands of purplish skin around the girl's wrists and ankles. She'd been restrained. Torture and murder.

The girl's dank hair was shoulder-length and brown. Where her face had been torn away, the exposed pink-white skull shone like dirty china. The lower jaw had snapped and was cocked to one side in a ghastly grin. One of the girl's eyes had been punctured by the blade that had torn her face from her skull, but the other was whole. Oscar leaned close and looked into it. The cornea was flat and lifeless, turning cloudy. The pupil was a black moon in a copper sky. Hazel eyes.

He leaned back and looked at the broken body. No neat saw cut around the skull, no Y-shaped incision, no rough sutures. The girl had not been autopsied at the morgue.

He realized that he'd been avoiding looking at the wound on her belly. He took a step down the makeshift table and saw that the hairs were standing up on his arms. The cold, he told himself, but he knew that wasn't true. It was the symbol itself. It was at once fascinating and repulsive, like watching footage of an execution—hideously powerful and fundamentally sinful. Oscar forced himself to examine its component parts.

As Gelareh had noted, the star had seven long points, and each triangle had something different carved inside it. Behind the star was the cross, filled with diamondlike grids. He noticed now that each little diamond had its own symbol sliced within it. The véve. How had Gelareh described it? A lighthouse for the spirits. Was it still calling them? Oscar suddenly wanted to be out of the room. He pulled a ballpoint pen from his pocket and probed the incisions. They were almost uniformly deep, four or five millimeters. How long had this taken to carve? Thirty minutes? An hour? Had the girl been alive while the scalpel sliced hundreds of times into the skin of her belly? The pain would have been unbearable. So would the screaming. Around the véve, more arcane glyphs: skulls, birds, arrows, swordlike shapes, and two figures that looked as if they might have flames growing from them. Oscar peered closer. Flames? Or wings?

Something scratched on the roof, and Oscar felt his shoulders jerk and the flesh above his kidneys crawl. He listened.

Silence.

"Enough," he told himself. He pulled out his camera, pressed a button. The musical notes of its start-up melody were shrill in the small, quiet room. He straightened and opened the girl's broken jawbone and photographed her teeth, but even a quick look revealed no fillings. He took thirty or more photographs of her ruined body and of the symbol. He took photos from both sides. He saved her faceless skull for last. He desperately wanted to leave. Instead, he forced himself to lean in to focus on the girl's sightless eye. The sunken orb became sharp in his viewfinder, and his finger pressed the shutter button. As the flash sparked, the skull seemed to jump toward the lens.

I have opened the curtain of bone.

Oscar jolted upright, his body electric.

The words had come unbidden into his head, and were as clear as a whisper in his ear.

The girl was motionless, staring emptily at the pressed-steel ceiling. The room was filled with an awful, waiting silence.

Oscar listened. Outside, the wind moaned in metal eaves. Something, somewhere, scratched.

He realized that the camera he held was shaking with the fast, steady pulses of his racing heart.

"Idiot," he said aloud. He made himself take one last photo of the unblinking eye, then put the camera away. But the words remained in his mind like a fishhook.

I have opened the curtain of bone.

He shook the thought away and produced a fingerprint kit he'd taken from Hyde's desk. He inked the fingers of the girl's right hand and rolled each onto a cardboard blank. Her fingers were cold, but the flesh felt strangely supple. An image forced its way into his mind: her fingers twitching and opening, grabbing his own wrist in a grip shockingly strong, and drawing him down toward that skull, that broken grinning jaw, which would open wider, much wider than a human mouth could, and—

Fool! he thought, snapping at himself.

He took a step back. It was just a body; just a poor murdered girl's body. And he had a job to finish. He produced a clean card and delicately picked up the severed arm. Printing the fingers of this limb was easier, but it made his stomach convulse. He swallowed dryly and concentrated as he got the last prints down, then wiped all ten digits clean.

Finished. He leaned back and placed the loose arm beside her body. And frowned. He bent closer and gingerly touched the cold skin again. On her wrists and forearms were fine, pale hairs, but they vanished just before the elbows and then reappeared on her upper arms. It was almost as if waxing strips had been run right around both forearms. He pulled out the camera again and took another few photos.

Time, he thought, and rezipped the cadaver bag. As the plastic closed over the carved symbol, he felt relief, as if the lids of a staring eye had finally shut. He gazed at the white, tough plastic and realized that he was waiting to see if it would move, expand out with a breath or suck in with a hungry inhalation.

Idiot.

He went to the door and reached for the rubberized light switch beside it.

I have opened the curtain of bone.

He turned around. The cadaver bag was still. His breaths plumed in tiny, hurried puffs, and the hairs on the back of his neck were stiff as spears.

Oscar clenched his jaw and switched off the light, then stepped out quickly. He fumbled to put the large brass padlock through the clasp and hurried out onto the wet road.

Oscar parked outside a huge knuckle of a building. The former convent was red brick and dark windows, ugly and forbidding. The steel security gate was unlocked. He climbed a set of austere concrete stairs, then walked along the second-floor brick veranda. The open walkway looked over an asphalt courtyard that struck Oscar as strange, and it took him a moment to realize that it was because the space wasn't edged in rubbish and debris. He found the door he wanted and knocked. As he waited, he turned his back to the night sky. Suddenly, the skin over the small of his back felt cold and dreadfully exposed to silent things with sharp claws. He took a step toward the wall and knocked sharply again.

The door opened a few centimeters before a chain clacked taut. A young woman with thin lips and a boxer's jaw looked out through the gap.

Oscar showed his badge. "I'm Mariani."

The young woman's lips crushed to a tighter line.

"Who is it?" Neve's voice came from somewhere in the apartment.

"Your partner," the girl answered coldly, her eyes locked on Oscar. Her hand tightened on the door, ready to close it if Neve said to.

"It's okay, Alex," Neve called after a pause. "Let him in."

Alex hesitated, then unlatched the chain and stepped aside for Oscar. She was low-set and looked powerful enough to carry a goat up a muddy riverbank. She watched Oscar with unreserved dislike.

"Tell him to wait," Neve called from down the narrow hallway.

Alex raised her eyebrows at Oscar. He nodded and looked around.

The former nuns' quarters were compact but comfortable. Small touches gave it warmth: placemats on the old coffee table, a tiny vase holding nasturtiums, a Chinese table runner over the sideboard. By comparison, Oscar's house looked like a ransacked crypt. On the break-fast bar were three small stacks: envelopes, cover letters, and résumés.

"In here," Neve called.

Oscar looked around at Alex; she pointed permission with her solid chin.

Oscar passed through darkness toward the orange glow of a kerosene lamp; it made a billow of steam glow like smoke above a lively bonfire. Working hot water. The door was open.

"Come in." Neve's voice was clipped by the deadening steam.

Oscar entered.

She sat on the toilet lid wrapped in a towel. Her legs were bare from the thigh down. Oscar felt awkwardly drawn to look at them and fought to keep his eyes on hers. Her jaw was set and her expression was difficult to read.

"I don't like you coming to my home," she said.

"I called," he replied.

She kept watching him and said nothing. He felt a twinge of pride— she'd learned well in the past twelve months when to ask questions and when to use silence to rattle the interviewee. She was a good cop.

She pulled a damp strand of hair behind one ear, and the towel around her chest shifted a centimeter lower. Oscar didn't know where to look now, so he picked the drain grate on the floor. "Moechtar gave me your transfer request."

From the corner of his eye, he saw her muscles twitch. "I wanted to tell you this morning," she said. "But you were busy."

Oscar nodded.

"He also told me we're offline," Neve continued. "It would have been nice to hear it from my so-called partner."

"I just stole a body."

She blinked. "You what?"

He told her about the visit to Dianne Hyde, the race to the crematorium, the installation of the body in Kannis's cold room, the discovery that no postmortem had been performed—and that the dead girl had hazel eyes. By the time he finished, the steam had vanished and the bathroom was cold. Neve was staring at him.

"Do you have any idea how many parts of the Crim Code you've violated?"

"A few. Nothing serious."

She shook her head. "You have to take it back—"

"Were you listening?" he interrupted. "Someone wanted the body gone. Someone with clout enough to spook a career pathologist. If we take it back to the morgue, the same thing will happen."

She watched him warily. "What are you thinking?"

"It stinks of Haig."

"Oh, Oscar."

"Haig has a rep for making this kind of stuff happen. He wanted Moechtar to have me hand the case over to Homicide."

"Then tell Moechtar."

Oscar snorted. "He's an accountant."

"He's our boss."

"He won't care," Oscar said. "He'll take the path of least resistance and say give it to Homicide."

"Ethical Standards, then."

"They're idiots."

"Since you left."

Oscar shrugged.

Neve rubbed her face, frustrated. "So, what then? What's your grand plan?"

"Let's find out who she is, then we can go to Moechtar. Once we have her identified, we'll have a better idea of why Haig wanted her to vanish."

Neve stared at him. She wore an expression that Oscar couldn't quite pin down. It looked hurt and pitying and confused. He watched her stretch a finger up toward his arm, but before she touched it she drew back and clutched the towel tighter around herself. The skin on her legs and arms was goosepimpled.

"There is no 'we,' Oscar."

Oscar's jaw was so tight it hurt. "I need your help."

"You need help," Neve agreed, "but not from me." She looked up at him, her face set harder now. "I won't report you, Oscar, but I'm sure as hell not signing up for this Jonestown jaunt of yours." She looked down at the damp tiles. "I'm sorry."

––––––––

The sergeant on shift in the Fingerprint Bureau glared at Oscar suspiciously as he handed over the cards on which he'd rolled the dead girl's prints.

"Late," she said.

"Isn't it?"

Her stare weighed a ton. She cast a warning glare over her shoulder at him, then went to the Morpho terminal and scanned the card. She returned ten minutes later, shaking her head.

No matches.

––––––––

He returned to his office, printed blowups of the photographs he'd taken of the symbol, put them into an envelope, and drove to Gelareh Barirani's flat. He slipped them into her letter box, then headed back toward home. It was after eleven, and the moon loitered over the city. Milky light fluttered down through clouds as fine as feathers, turning the wet roads silver and casting shadows as black as ink.

Haig.

It made sense, to a point. Yes, Haig wanted the case. Yes, Haig had the connections to fast-track a cadaver's destruction and the history of intimidation that explained a public servant fleeing town on a moment's notice. But why murder a young girl? Extortion? Although Oscar had seen even the least likely people charged with the most repulsive of acts, he couldn't picture Haig involved in torture. The mutilation, that unsettling, cruel symbol, made even less sense. Haig was pragmatic, if nothing else. No. If Haig was involved, it was as a facilitator. He was working for others. But Haig wasn't charitable; he worked for a fee—either favors or cash. Neither was easy to trace.

Oscar pulled into the driveway and his headlights blared on the graffitied shutter door to his garage. He left the car running and stepped out to undo the padlock. As he stooped to kneel, something shifted in the shadows across the street, and his heart jumped to a sprint. A poinciana tree spread dark fingers over the footpath behind him, and in the shadows below it was the dead boy, his pale face hovering like a moth.

Oscar didn't want to turn away from him; the feeling of being watched was a regular itch between his shoulder blades. Even after all these years, he disliked knowing that the dead boy might be behind him. The boy was confusing. On one hand, he seemed to shun Oscar, rarely appearing in a small room with him. But outdoors and in large spaces, he was never more than twenty or so yards away, silently staring. Was he bound to Oscar, as if by an invisible lead that allowed him no farther away? When Oscar drove, he watched the windows, kidding himself that he wasn't looking for the boy. Did he fly behind the car like a ghastly banderole as Oscar drove? Or did he flicker between places, jolting from here to here to here like a face glimpsed across platforms through a speeding train? Oscar didn't know. The boy was simply there, whenever he paused at traffic lights or arrived at his destination, watching, sometimes shifting on his spectral feet as if anxious to pass on a message then flee, yet he never advanced or retreated. On the one jet flight Oscar had taken since Gray Wednesday—a trip to Melbourne for his uncle's funeral—he'd clicked his seat belt and looked up the aisle. In the alcove where the flight attendants prepared the meals stood the boy, shyly stooped, not seeming to notice when people stepped through him, watching Oscar through those empty, well-like sockets. Was he as resentful as Oscar about being shackled to a stranger? Did he blame his living, breathing anchor for his torment? It was hard to read a face from thirty paces; harder still when that face had no eyes.

Oscar slid a key into the padlock. And the boy took a step toward him. Then another.

The hairs on the back of Oscar's hands rose. In three years, the boy had never taken more than a step toward him. What if the ghost kept coming? What if he put himself in front of Oscar's face and never left, forcing him to stare forever into those socket holes where eyes should be? Would he go mad? Would he, like so many killers he had interviewed, fumble for a weapon and stab or swing or shoot, his mind snapped and screaming?

"What do you want?" Oscar said. His voice sounded as dry as old paper.

The boy took another step closer and stopped. His pale fingers opened and closed, as if in indecision.

Oscar forced himself to turn away; his heart jolted behind his ribs as he turned in the glare of the headlights and undid the padlock. When he lifted the shutter, the beams speared into the dark.

At first, he had the irrational thought that Sabine had left her purse on the garage floor. But Sabine had left a long time ago, and this was, on closer look, too misshapen to be a purse. He stepped into the cold garage, his legs throwing long spindly shadows. He stopped next to the object on the dirty concrete. It was a dog's head, resting in the very center of the garage. Its lips were drawn back in a terrified snarl. The eyes were gone, and the headlights shone in slick, purple sockets. The fur was stained magenta with blood and other fluids but had once been tàn; the muzzle was narrow and pointed, the black flesh of the nose bisected by a deep cut. It was Terry/Derek, the yapper from down Oscar's street.

He knelt and looked closer.

Flesh and tendon and blood vessels hung from the base of the dog's skull like wet streamers from a grotesque party favor. The head hadn't been severed; it had been torn from the body. And the skull itself seemed askew, all odd, lazy angles and frowning asymmetrically in on itself. Crushed, Oscar realized. It reminded him of the lizard and rat heads that Sissy would occasionally leave as gifts or trophies on the back doormat. Oscar stood and turned a slow circle. Dust rose in the beams of the headlights like tiny cold sparks. Nothing else seemed amiss. Suddenly, something clapped in the darkness, and Oscar's head jerked up. Twelve feet above the concrete floor, a bank of hopper windows lined the far wall—three large frames with flaked paint and glass caked with grime, each hinged at the center. One clattered, swinging loose in the wind. Loops of narrow chain ran from each frame to a hook set at shoulder height. The chain of the loose window dangled, unhitched.

Oscar carefully pulled the window closed and threaded a cold metal link over a hook.

He returned to the head and cautiously paced around it, searching the dust for footprints. The only ones he saw were his own. Had a person done this? No man he knew had the strength to wrench the head off a dog and crush its skull. Had the dog been caught under a truck, its jamming wheels ripping the head off?

Oscar went outside and inspected the ground under the windows. There were no telltale depressions from ladder marks. He returned inside, pulled old brochures from a box against the wall, and scooped the head off the slab; as he got another grip on it, he could feel that it was still a little warm. He took it out and dropped it in the gutter; the broken plates of bone ground together like pieces of a smashed bowl in a small, wet sack. He idled his car into the garage and drew down the shutter; it clattered as loudly as a train, then fell to a silence so profound that the click of the padlock echoed up the street. He looked around.

The skull was a lump in the gutter. The street was empty, except under the dark coral branches of the tree across the road, where the dead boy stood watching. When he caught Oscar's glance he deliberately looked up to the wispy clouds.

Lose the hat, the blind woman had said. *You need to watch the skies.*

Oscar hurried home.

————

He fed Sissy, washed, and slipped naked into bed, curled against the cold. He lay still for a long time, listening to every shift and sigh the house made. Finally, he slept.

He was walking down either a corridor or a tunnel, dark and miserably cold. The walls were stone or brick, and his steps echoed and re-echoed. He was lost. Ahead, something glowed with a strange light that was neither natural nor comforting—a greenish, rotten luminescence. He wanted to turn back, but behind was pitch darkness. He pressed on toward the glow. It came from a wall that closed off the passageway. It seemed to be made of long, narrow bricks. No; as he got closer, he saw that wasn't right. It was not a wall at all but a high, wide tapestry—a hundred feet across, and so high its top was lost in inky darkness. This curtain was woven with the bones and skulls of ten thousand people. Femurs and rib bones were the weft, and humeri and ulnae the warp. Skulls were ivory sequins. This awful drapery was the source of the sick, eldritch light—and behind it was a yawning darkness more terrible than the narrow, blind confusion he'd left behind. He knew he had to go. Then the curtain rippled. The bilious light shimmered, and he heard an unmusical tinkle, the discord of a thousand untuned pianos as bone ticked against bone. Something was on the other side. Something huge. It was coming.

He turned to flee, but his legs and arms were leaden and refused to shift. He fell to the ground, but the best he could manage was a desperate crawl, fingers and toes scrabbling for purchase on the slick rock floor. The bones clattered, a sound louder than the breaking of boulders. The air shifted as something massive moved behind him, coming closer, coming fast. He screamed in terror. Whatever had woken behind the curtain of bone shrieked in hungry delight.

Chapter 11

Winter sunlight was a bright shout, spearing down between lush green leaves and bouncing countless diamonds off frosted car windscreens.

Oscar's hands felt light on the wheel. Despite the dog's head, and despite his dreams, he had awakened feeling refreshed, and as he drove he hummed. He hadn't saved a life, but he'd saved a body from destruction. He was on the job, and it felt good.

He remembered a morning, more than twenty years ago. He'd risen quietly and padded on bare feet down the hall to the kitchen. The night before, he'd heard his father return late. Someone had raped and killed a young boy in the bayside suburbs; Sandro had been one of the detectives on the task force. Oscar had guessed they'd found another curled and voided little body. The silence that came home with Alessandro Mariani was as solid and dreadful as a corpse, so frigidly still that Oscar had heard the two words his parents had spoken from all the way across the house. "Another?" his mother had asked. "Yes," Sandro had replied. Vedetta Mariani knew her husband well enough not to ask any more. Sandro claimed he didn't bring his work home, but he did: not in words but in arctic silences where he'd stop mid-sentence to stare for long minutes at something deep in his own mind, and in his sudden bursts of white-hot anger at a drawer that wouldn't close properly or a pen that had run out of ink. Oscar would look to his mother, who would smile softly, shake her head, and remind him that Papa would be fine in a minute or two. But that night, two decades ago, the dread quiet had been so profound, and his father's sleepless pacing through the hall so untouchable, that Oscar thought the house would be frozen by sadness forever. The next morning when he'd crept to the kitchen, Oscar was shocked to find his mother at the stove frying *salsicce* and his father, dressed for work, behind her with his arms around her waist, both of them smiling as they slowly swayed to Jerry Vale turned low on the radio. After Sandro had left for work, Oscar asked his mother how his father could have forgotten last night's horrors so easily. "He hasn't forgotten," she'd replied. "But he's smart enough to know that today is not yesterday."

Oscar arrived at his destination. He parked his car and went into a white pavilion.

In the cold marble hallway hung dozens of framed black-and-white photographs. As Oscar passed, one caught his eye: the old image was of a monkey in a silk jersey and a matching cap on the back of a grinning greyhound; dog and monkey both looked oddly serene, as if the moment captured couldn't be more natural. From ahead came a metallic crack that made Oscar flinch, followed by a swelling chorus of men's voices and the harsh, rising tones of a race announcer. Oscar stepped again into brittle winter sunlight.

A low turquoise rail ran along the inside of the oval track, and a surging mass of dogs chased a mechanical lure. The announcer's words over the loudspeakers were also a swirling race: "Up the inside comes Jet Stream followed by Ragged Ace and Hardly Shaken and into the far turn as No Argument *thunnnders* up from behind. . . ."

Oscar found Teddy Gillin among the dozens of men leaning hopefully on the trackside fence. The race finished. Men tore up tickets and left the fence.

Gillin's silver hair was combed, his tie was neatly knotted, and his suit, though twenty years old, had been pressed with care. Oscar could see that Gillin's blue eyes were bloodshot but bright with intelligence. They rolled when they saw Oscar.

"No."

"I haven't even asked for anything," Oscar said.

Gillin clasped his hands behind his back as he walked back toward the pavilion. Somewhere, someone cheered, and punters shot sour glances in that direction. "Your being here is question enough, and I say, thank you but no."

Gillin's voice had rounded diction that sounded more British than Australian. Oscar loved the man. Dr. Theodore Gillin had been Oscar's general practitioner as long as he could remember. Sandro and

Vedetta Mariani had taken young Oscar to Gillin for tetanus shots, a split scalp, concussion, two broken arms, tonsillitis, mumps, and a frank (and, frankly, embarrassing) talk about nocturnal emissions. As an adult Oscar took himself to Gillin for flu shots, ingrown toenails, ear infections, and a referral for sperm-motility testing back when he and Sabine had been planning to start a family. The scales had tipped when Gillin's love of drink outweighed his cautious care for his patients and he administered a quadruple dose of diamorphine to a girl who was fortunate to live. The girl's family sued, and Gillin was struck off the medical register. He lost his wife and his house. Oscar often wondered about that drink that had tipped Gillin over the edge. Had he poured the shot knowing that this could be the one that would kill his career?

"How's your father?" Gillin asked.

"You know. Only happy when he's in a right shit of a mood." Gillin glared from under heavy white brows, and Oscar sighed. "He's fine. Apart from the arthritis."

"He still on Warfarin?"

Oscar nodded, although it was only an educated guess. Sandro Mariani liked discussing his health almost as much as he had enjoyed talking about his work.

"Make sure he keeps up his blood tests."

"They cost a fortune."

"Then find a fortune. It's your father's health, for Christ's sake. Money comes and goes; parents don't."

"That's not my experience."

They made it to the pavilion bar. Oscar ordered two Tullamore Dews, one neat, and tried not to flinch when the bartender gave the price. Oscar handed Gillin his drink.

"May misfortune follow you the rest of your life—" Gillin began.

"—and never catch up," Oscar finished.

He winced as he sipped, but the whiskey bit kindly on the way down and spread warmth through his belly. Gillin downed it as easily as tepid tea.

"You hate gambling as much as your old man does." Gillin waved to the bartender for another, then looked sidelong at Oscar. "Here for the fashion tips?"

"I need a smart doctor."

Gillin chuckled humorlessly. "Then you're two moves behind." His eyes narrowed. "You haven't got the clap, because idiots like you don't screw around. It's not heart disease, because of all the red wine you Mediterraneans drink."

"I'm not Italian."

Gillin waved that away. "So, what is it? You hooked on something? Go cold turkey, grow some balls."

"I need a postmortem."

Gillin's eyebrows rose a little. "Get a pathologist."

"I had a pathologist. Two pathologists. One has disappeared and the other is actively uninterested."

Gillin looked at Oscar for a long moment. Then he sighed and swirled his whiskey glass, inspecting the amber liquid. "I remember soon after your father brought you home. What were you, six?"

"Five."

Gillin nodded. "Small blond kid. Angry little bastard. You'd got it into your head you didn't like your new house or your new family, and you went to run away. Climbed out the second-story window, over a garage or some such?"

Oscar remembered the corrugated-iron roof of the carport outside his bedroom window. In October, the jacaranda near it was thick with panicles of purple flowers. When the breeze blew, a surreal lavender snowfall would cover the roof, which in sunlight buzzed lazily with bees. He remembered vividly running away with great success at fifteen, and the frigid distance that had developed between him and Sandro afterward, but he didn't recall this earlier incident.

"I don't remember."

"Well, you'd waited until late—at any rate, it was late when Sandro brought you to me—and you'd climbed out of your window onto the roof so you could jump to the tree, like some chimpanzee. Only you were more like some retarded chimpanzee who couldn't climb and couldn't jump. You missed by a mile and landed on your head on the grass. Half a foot to the left, Sandro said, you'd have hit concrete and split your skull like a melon. He brought you to my home surgery. You'd opened your scalp and were bleeding like it was going out of fashion. And Sandro was crying."

Oscar shook his head. He couldn't imagine Sandro Mariani's stern, soldierly face wet with tears.

"He said, 'Look after his head, Teddy. He's a smart boy. Look after his head.'" Gillin looked at Oscar. "Given that you are ignoring very strong hints from two stiff-shifters—who, unlike you, actually completed their degrees—I have to wonder if your father wasted a trip that night."

Oscar sipped. "Or whether you failed to look after my precious head."

The race caller announced the scratching of two entries from the next race. Gillin sat upright, staring out across the track.

"I'm Joe Blow, Oscar. Worse, I'm *fallen*. Any findings I made, any statements, would be *non gradus anus rodentum*. They'd be ridiculed, or worse."

"I'd keep your name off the paperwork."

Gillin shook his head. "Do you know how long it's been since I looked inside a dead person? 1970. I remember, because it was the year Hendrix died and I was wondering what they'd find inside him. Robert Johnson was my guess."

"I don't want an internal autopsy—I'm hoping we can get that later. I just want your thoughts."

For the first time, Gillin was lost for words. The men drank in silence. Around them, punters checked their watches, finished drinks, and began the shuffle back to the racetrack.

"You're right," Oscar said, finally, and put down his glass. "There probably isn't much to find, anyway."

He stood. The men shook hands.

"Who was it?" Gillin asked.

"We don't know. A young girl."

"Addict? Hooker?"

"I don't think so," Oscar replied. "Someone mutilated her and threw her into the sewer works, hoping she'd be pulped."

"Good Lord," Gillin muttered.

Oscar leaned forward. "Teddy, you nearly killed a girl. It was a mistake. But now here's a chance to help bring one back from the dead."

Gillin looked up at Oscar evenly. "Are you sure you're not doing this for exactly the same reason?"

Oscar stared.

The last of the spectators hurried past to the track. Oscar watched Gillin feel the pull of the tide. The old man drained his drink and stood. But he hesitated, troubled. "You bloody Marianis. Coming to me with your troubles."

He put his hands behind his back and began to walk away.

"Doctor?" Oscar called. "Please?"

Gillin walked another few steps, then stopped.

"Bloody Marianis."

————

At Kannis's butchery, a man Oscar recognized from his previous visit watched them for a moment, gave a comradely nod, and disappeared into the shopfront.

"Unorthodox," Gillin said.

Oscar unlocked the side gate and the cold-room padlock. As his fingers closed on the door handle, he realized that his heart was stamping, and the flesh on his arm had grown tight, as if expecting to be grabbed. But when the fluorescent blinked awake, the girl's body bag was lying small and still on the makeshift bench.

They dressed in items Oscar had purchased en route: plastic aprons, face masks, latex gloves. Gillin stared at the white bag.

"No X-ray," he said. "No internal exam. No blood tests. I hope you have low expectations."

Oscar produced a notepad. "There's always something."

They unzipped the cadaver bag, and again an exhalation of sweet early decay filled the cold air. Seeing the faceless skull, the gouges as deep as shark bites, the torn and twisted limbs, Gillin let out a hiss.

"My good Christ, this isn't a postmortem. It's a jigsaw puzzle. And that"—his breath caught in his throat when he saw the symbol carved into the pale skin—"is unusual."

The symbol seemed to stare up from the girl's belly. Even looking away from it, Oscar had the feeling it was watching. He forced himself to ignore it. "Let's just see."

Gillin held the bag like a spout while Oscar collected in a plastic bucket the dark blood that had pooled. Oscar wiped down the body with clean rags and sealed them in a Ziploc bag. Then the men worked in near-silence, speaking only to read out measurements and repeat observations. Skull circumference. Body length. Limb length. Digit count. Mild seborrhea of the scalp. Shaved underarms and lower legs. Full adult dental count, no obvious caries. Bite marks on the tongue and on the inside flap of the remaining cheek. The trauma to the face and jaw made it impossible to know whether she'd been gagged. No signs of malnourishment. No froth in the windpipe, mouth, or nostrils that would suggest drowning; no marks or burst blood vessels to suggest asphyxiation by other means. Abrasions and contusions with inflamed edges around both wrists and ankles, consistent with restraint.

"Cloth, do you think?" Gillin asked.

"No rope fibers," Oscar replied. "And none of the gouging you'd expect with hard leather or handcuffs. Yes, cloth or padded restraints, but tight."

The doctor moved down to the girl's legs, one twisted and opened to the bone, the other attached and largely undamaged. Gillin lifted the good leg and bent it at the knee.

"Dead how long?" he asked.

"Sixty hours or so."

They inspected her limbs for puncture wounds and injection marks. None.

"What do you make of this?" Oscar asked. He held up the girl's forearm and pointed to the ring of nearly hairless skin near her elbow.

Gillin touched it and grunted noncommittally.

They returned to the torso. Oscar noticed the way the doctor avoided touching the carved symbol.

"Can we tell if she was alive when that happened?" Oscar asked.

Gillin shook his head. "I can't." He leaned closer. "Genital area is severely traumatized. Impossible to determine any signs of sexual activity."

"Blood tests?" Oscar asked.

"They might tell you if she was taking oral contraceptives, or whether she had any STDs. The tox test will show if she was drugged or poisoned. Internal exam should confirm pregnancy, or . . ."

The older man's voice drifted to silence.

Gillin was frowning as he probed the slash that had bisected the girl's stomach: the deep wound that had opened her side and snapped her lower ribs.

Oscar asked, "What?"

Gillin returned to the cut across the girl's upper belly. "This penetration," he said. "Here."

Oscar leaned closer, and he felt his breath stop in his throat. He'd been so distracted by the symbol, so repulsed by it, that he hadn't paid much attention to the gouge just below the girl's navel. It was as deep as the other damage caused by the auger, but the cut was much cleaner.

"The auger blade didn't do this," Oscar whispered.

Gillin nodded in agreement. "I know you don't want to do an internal exam, but the work's half done." He leaned toward the body. "Help me."

The doctor took Oscar's gloved hands and put them under the small of the girl's back.

"Lift."

Oscar lifted the girl's lower torso. The split across her belly parted like lips, and another puff of unpleasant, meaty air wafted up.

"Hold," Gillin said.

He curled his fingers under a loop of small intestine. "How strong are you? Can you hold her with one hand?" Oscar placed his elbow on the cold steel of the makeshift table and nodded. "Give me your other hand," Gillin continued. "Take this. Now pull it up and aside. Yes. Now get your fat head out of my way."

The doctor put one hand under the girl's bladder and pulled it down. He stopped moving.

"Good Lord."

"Teddy?"

Gillin straightened, then stared for a moment at his gloved hand finger-deep in the wound. "Take a look."

He put one arm under the girl to take the weight Oscar had been carrying. Oscar leaned and looked into the raw crucible, and saw nothing but torn and cut flesh. "What am I looking for?"

"What do you see?"

"Nothing. It's all just . . . it's been cut up."

"Exactly. It's been excised. And no effort to close off the severed blood vessels."

"Forget for a second that I don't have a degree in anatomical sciences. What's been excised?"

"Her uterus, Oscar. The girl's uterus is gone."

———

An hour later, Oscar emptied the last bucket of red water down a grate and wrung out the mop. He locked the cold room and turned the temperature down. The sun was a pale disk low in the west. Gillin sat straight-backed on the footpath, sipping amber liquid from a foam cup. Oscar helped him stand, and they walked together toward his car.

As they drove in silence, Oscar thought about the girl and her rude, violent hysterectomy.

Two recent cases stood out in his memory. The first from the late nineties: a young man with a history of mental illness claimed he'd become convinced that a rival's child was gestating in his heroin-addicted girlfriend's womb. He tied her to a bed frame, did her up with a shot from the girl's stash of Aunt Hazel (he wasn't thoughtless, merely motivated), and proceeded to give her an ad hoc abortion. His lack of surgical talent, evidenced by the pool of blood in which the police found the girl, was also reflected in his clinical skill: he had, mercifully, overdosed her before his knife touched her flesh. Outcome: served five years for manslaughter, followed by a spate of arrests for property crime until his own overdose resulted in profound brain damage; at last report, he was in institutional care in Western Australia. Case two, from a few years before Gray Wednesday: a teller who had worked at a bank branch near a Catholic girls' school was laid off for breaches in protocol (read: yelling at customers). Neighbors in his apartment block complained about "out-of-hours renovations" coming from the former teller's unit, and a representative from the body corporate visited. The teller denied doing any renovations but failed to adequately disguise the smell of rot coming from within his dwelling. Police discovered twin fifteen-year-old girls, students at the Catholic school and occasional users of the bank's ATM. A witness had seen one of the girls refusing the accused's attentions. The former teller, who professed undying love for the girls, had kidnapped them but agreed to release them—after he'd performed vulvectomies so that he would have keepsakes. One girl had bled out and died; the other had survived and, chained to the bathroom vanity, had used a toothbrush glass to tap on the walls whenever she thought her captor wasn't home. Outcome: life sentence without parole. The teller had lasted less than a month in prison—long weeks, Oscar guessed, involving much physical and sexual assault—before he hanged himself.

The light of the lowering sun caught Oscar's eye as it flashed off the Ferris wheel going up in the show grounds a half mile from the city's heart. Next week was Royal National Show Day. Had the dead girl looked forward to the holiday—to laughing as she ate cotton candy and corn dogs, and screaming as she rode the Zipper? Instead, her last screams were of terror, for her life, pointless. What went through her mind while someone carved into her soft skin a hundred times? Was she drugged? Did she faint? He hoped to God so. But if she was conscious, what sort of person could have tolerated her terrified begging?

They reached Gillin's tenement building. Outside, a line of men and women sat or stood at the front steps, waiting. When the nearest recognized Gillin in the car, a ripple ran quickly through the queue. Oscar realized that Teddy may have been struck off the register, but he still had plenty of patients.

"Thank you," Oscar said.

Gillin grunted and picked his medical bag off the floor. He put his hand on the door handle but hesitated. "Catch the fellow, won't you?"

Oscar nodded.

Gillin got out and closed the car door. With his old back as straight as a yacht's mast on a calm day, he sailed toward the waiting men and women, and they rose like waterfowl to greet him. The last was a small young man who leaned like a collapsing derrick as he waited for the rest of the patients to climb the steps. The boy then hobbled up the steps with one hand on the rail; from his other arm hung an aluminum crutch by gray plastic loops.

Oscar stared as the boy disappeared from view.

Elbow crutches. Gray plastic cuffs. The hair worn from around the dead girl's forearm.

His Jane Doe had used crutches.

———

The last of the public servants were leaving the Industrial Relations floor, giving Oscar polite nods as he wound his way between them toward his desk. Neve had her back to the rest of the branch floor; she was hunched forward, her head resting on one hand and her fingers tight in her hair. Foley sat at his desk, leaning back with his hands behind his head, talking to her.

" . . . and the water's warm all year round. You can get on that white sand and just roll around. . . ." Foley raised his arms above his head, revealing sweat stains as large as dinner plates, and waggled his hips luxuriantly. "Strip right down, feel the sun on your skin. Oscar! I was just telling Detective de Rossa about 1770. Ever been?"

"No."

Neve didn't look up. Every square inch of her desk was covered with files. On top of one pile of folders was a paper cup and an empty Paracetamol blister pack. Her hand covered her eyes, but her cheeks were the unhealthy color of new cheese.

"Oh, you should go," Foley continued. "It's just so *open*. I've seen couples on the beach, uninhibited. Having sex right there on the sand. So beautiful, natural."

Oscar saw Neve shudder, and lifted the wastepaper bin in time to catch her stream of vomit.

Oscar looked back at Foley. "Go on."

Foley stared at the slosh leaking down the side of the bin. "Nah, I'm good." He stood and pulled his uniform cap on. He pointed at Oscar. "We gotta chat."

"Sure."

Foley left.

"I hate him," Neve whispered, and looked at Oscar from bleary eyes. "You missed his top tips for getting masseuses to work topless."

"I'm taking you home," he said.

She shook her head and wiped the corner of her mouth. "It's just a headache. We need to get this operational summary done." She cocked a bleary eye at him. "It's a mess, Oscar."

He recognized the names on printed labels in the files' corners. Tambassis. Dixon. A hundred others. Maybe one in seven was tabbed with a sticky note. Oscar felt a sharp pang. Was that their conviction rate? One in seven?

"Home," he said, and took her arm.

She shook him off weakly, then relented and let him help her stand. Outside, the western sky was a burned welt. People hurried head-down to buses and trains, ignoring car horns and sidestepping piles of rubbish. Opposite headquarters huddled a line of taxis.

"I saw Moechtar," Neve said, throat croaky. "He said you haven't signed my transfer."

"I forgot. I will."

She noticed a spot of blood on his sleeve. "What happened? You okay?"

He nodded—I'm fine—and led her across to the first cab in the queue. "I looked over our Jane Doe today. I think she used crutches."

"And?"

He folded her into the backseat. "I thought you didn't want anything to do with it," he said. Beneath her clothes, she felt exhausted, limp. He reached into his jacket and pulled out a cab-charge voucher.

The taxi driver saw the coupon and waved his hand as if dispelling a foul smell. "No, no! Cash."

"Cash? Sure. But first—" Oscar flipped open his badge, then reached in past the cabbie and pulled the man's license ID off the visor; the man in the photo was not the man behind the wheel. "Just let me go photocopy this—"

"Okay, okay! Fuck." The driver shook his head, as if disgusted at how venal the world was. He snatched the voucher.

Oscar looked in the backseat—Neve was already curled asleep. He gave the driver her address, and the cab rattled away into evening air that reeked of smoke.

———

Alone on the Industrial Relations floor, he logged on to Prophet.

In the Missing Persons files, Oscar counted thirty-seven teenagers around the state with physical disabilities or who'd had a leg injury at the time they vanished. Half those were boys, and of the girls he could eliminate most as too young or too old. Of the remaining six, one was Asian, one was too short, another was blonde, one was profoundly disabled and needed a wheelchair, and one was an amputee. He was down to one.

He stared at the photograph of a fourteen-year-old girl with chestnut hair cut into a quirky bob, dressed in a black T-shirt emblazoned with the street spray art of the winking ghost in congress with a buxom woman. The girl in the photograph held the handle of a forearm crutch in one hand, the gray plastic cuff out of focus around her arm. With her other hand she pointed to her T-shirt and winced comically, as if to wonder, Is this for real? Oscar supposed that, if anyone could know for certain, she now did. He looked at her name.

Penelope (Penny) Adeline Roth, daughter of Carole and Paul. Oscar reread the names. Carole and Paul Roth. Familiar, but he couldn't place them. He read on. Penny was diagnosed with cerebral palsy at age three. He gazed at her photo again. A plain but pleasant-looking girl with brazen eyes. Fun. Impudent. *Alive.* The mental jump from this cocky snapshot to the skull with a split jaw and no face was impossible.

Oscar clicked to the next page, to see who had reported Penny missing, and from where.

He didn't like the answer at all.

Chapter 12

The house had once been a filigreed gem, a Federation master-piece in the Queen Anne–revival style. Narrow, white-framed windows with tiny colored top glasses; generous gables trimmed with fretwork as delicate as a wedding cake's icing. Tall, slender columns above dark brick walls crawling with ivy; curved sunrooms topped by spires that prodded up between half a dozen tall brick chimneys. But the paint was flaking. Green-glazed edging tiles had chipped and hadn't been replaced. The peppertrees and flowering plum were overgrown and turning wild. A wisteria pergola that had once been a shaded floral walkway was now a dark, throatlike nest that promised not refuge but spiders and hidden things. Ferns conspired under windows, and the summerhouse was black shadow inside.

Elverly House easily fitted into a pattern of spiraling neglect. Since Gray Wednesday, federal and state revenues had plummeted. Key services were forced to run on budgets stretched as tight as piano wire; nonessential services lost funding altogether. Aged care, child care, and disability services received the bare minimum, and so relied almost exclusively on volunteers and private moneys, both of which were in short supply. Wards of the state brought in a small stipend. Already it was common to see the chronically disabled at train stations and bus exchanges with cups in hand, begging for coins.

Oscar's feet crunched on gravel overrun by chickweed and cobbler's pegs. A perilously leaning signpost pointed one direction to ALL DELIVERIES and the other to RECEPTION. Elverly House and its rambling grounds were starkly incongruous with the plain, tall brick faces of warehouse buildings that boxed them in, making Oscar feel as if he were miniature and walking at the bottom of a box in a diorama creation of a secret garden that had somehow been corrupted by being left too long in shadow.

He climbed a low set of granite steps to a tiled porch and pushed open the heavy door. Elverly's foyer was a study in dark wood and old brass. Thin light washed in through a stained-glass window depicting native lizards climbing a fire-wheel tree. Oscar rang the bell and listened to the chime echo down the halls.

"Hello?" he called.

No one answered. Somewhere, a child cried. Through a window, Oscar could see a boy with an overlarge head being pushed on a swing by a short, stocky woman who was also trying to prevent two other, more robust but hobbling children from fighting over what might have been a doll or a stick. Behind them stood a figure watching Oscar. The dead boy with the wormhole eyes shifted on his feet and tentatively raised a hand in greeting. Oscar felt a flash of anger. Here of all places, he thought, and struck the bell sharply again.

On the other side of the counter was a door with the word OFFICE in gold and black paint. Oscar waited a few more moments, then stepped behind the counter and tried the door handle.

The office was surprisingly cheerful. Two tall windows shined daylight on pale lemon walls. Freshly picked flowers were pleasant blinks of bright color on each of the two desks. On one wall hung a series of photographs of center directors, certificates of appreciation, and children's art in vivid colors. Crayon drawings of cows, rockets, houses, smiling boys and girls in wheelchairs, walking frames, crutches. Oscar scanned the pictures until he found a paper smudged in palm-size slashes of yellow and green. "Flowers," a caregiver had written in the corner, "by Megan M."

Against another wall were three filing cabinets. On a third wall hung two whiteboards: one was a staff roster with in/out columns and magnets in each; the other was a table showing thirty-six rooms, under each of which was written the occupant's name. Oscar found the same name—Megan M.—and went looking for the room.

———

Above the door was a fretwork breezeway, all Edwardian filigrees curving and curling around the stylized forms of two kookaburras.

The birds were beak to beak, devoid of humorous charm. The shapes wreathing around the predators arrested Oscar, reminding him of the arcane symbols carved on the dead girl's abdomen. Through the dozens of tiny sawed holes of the breezeway came what was either laughter or sobs. Oscar noted the deadlock latch above the handle. He rapped softly and opened the door.

In the corner under the single, narrow window, a girl of sixteen was fighting her young caregiver. The girl's arms batted and struck the young woman who was trying to lift her from a wheelchair; tears squeezed from eyes screwed shut against the world. She moaned, an awful calf-like holler. Oscar stared. He had not seen Megan McAuliffe since the trial three years ago, when the girl's father had wheeled her into the courtroom. Then she'd still looked something like the adolescent he'd broken under his car on Gray Wednesday. Now her flesh had lost its vigor. It was pale and soft, her hair was lank, and her once pretty face looked as puffy and wildly confused as a sick infant's. Megan lashed out with barely coordinated hands.

"Come on, Meggie," the caregiver said. "Take my hands."

The young woman was in her early twenties, with short hair and a sharp, foxlike face; she took the slaps without flinching, and her calming voice never rose. "Come on, Meggie-pie. Take my arms, we'll be done in no time."

Megan wailed louder, her mouth open wide not in pain but in some deeper misery. The cry fell over Oscar like a pall, cloying and awful. He stepped into the room on feet as heavy as stone.

"Can I—" He cleared his throat. "Can I help you?"

But the caregiver didn't hear him because Megan yowled again. Her wet eyes flashed open and rolled around savagely. They fell on Oscar, and held on him a moment—a strange, slippery stare that may have been recognition or just a momentary fascination with someone new.

The young woman followed Megan's stare to Oscar. It was like having something honed and dangerous waved at him. The young woman wore no makeup, which made her acid-green eyes look larger; her skin was lightly freckled. She tensed like a cornered bird, ready either to fly away or to spear and scratch. Oscar raised his hands, palms forward, then slowly walked to the wheelchair.

"Let me help," he offered. "I'm a police officer."

The young woman watched him a moment longer, then gave a resigned nod.

"Okay, Meggie-pie," she said, her eyes not leaving Oscar. "Here we go."

Oscar slipped his hands under Megan's armpits and felt the fine, damp hair there. He watched the caregiver for her cue.

"One, two . . . three."

They lifted. Despite her thrashings, Megan felt light. She was about the same weight as the cadaver he'd carried into Kannis's cold room. He didn't like that thought. They put her on the bed, where an adult diaper was waiting. On her back, now, Megan grinned. The caregiver ran her hands over Megan's face, and the girl suddenly giggled—a sad, oafish trilling. The caregiver turned to look at Oscar. No smile.

"You should go now."

"Listen, how is Megan doing?"

"Hello?"

The voice from the doorway made Oscar turn.

A late-middle-aged woman watched Oscar with the suspicion of a terrier that's sensed a rat. She wore sensible clothes—pants and shirt, a wood bead necklace her only concession to fashion. Her hair was up and out of the way. On one shoulder, a child of three or four slept soundly.

Oscar showed his ID. "Oscar Mariani."

The woman took the badge carefully and scrutinized it, then him: a juror's stare. "Detective Mariani. So you've finally come to visit Megan?"

Oscar felt the sharp-faced caregiver's stare on the side of his face. He shook his head.

"I'm here to talk about Penelope Roth."

———

"I reported Penny missing last Thursday."

As she'd walked Oscar along the narrow corridors to another room, the woman had introduced herself as Leslie Chalk, Elverly House's Director of Care. She moved briskly, and Oscar noticed dark circles under her eyes.

"It must be a challenge. Running a place like this," he said.

"We all have our crosses to bear, Detective." She smiled bittersweetly. "There are benefits."

They stopped outside a numbered door, and she placed the sleeping child in Oscar's arms while she reached into her pocket for a key. The child suddenly cried out in his sleep, and Oscar awkwardly patted his bottom; the child rolled a little, sucked his thumb, and dozed again. Chalk unlocked the door, swung it open, and extended her arms to take the child back.

Oscar stepped inside.

"When did you notice that Penny was missing?" he asked.

"That morning. She wasn't in her bed. We searched the building, then the grounds, then the streets."

Penny Roth's room was almost identical to Megan McAuliffe's: narrow, one window with bars. The bed was stripped and the small wardrobe hung open and empty.

"You've packed up quickly," he said. "Where are her things?"

"We sent them back to her parents. We badly need the room. We have a girl moving in this afternoon."

Oscar tested the bars. Solid. "You weren't expecting Penny back?" He looked at Chalk.

She smiled understandingly. "Detective, this isn't paradise and only a fool would pretend it is. We do what we can to keep them, which is to say we feed them and clean them and give them what physical therapy our staff are trained to deliver. But boys and girls try to leave—all the time. The grass is always greener. So when they do run off we report them straightaway, for what that's worth. But if they get it in their minds to run away again and again, there really isn't much we can do. Penny had run away from here four times in the last two years. She was getting good at it. So, sadly, no; I wasn't expecting her back."

"Penny had cerebral palsy," Oscar said.

"Do you know much about cerebral palsy?"

"No."

"It's a motor-control disease. Yes, she had to use crutches, but Penny was as smart and willful as any fourteen-year-old girl. I told you some children didn't like it here? Penny hated it. She hated Elverly, she hated most of the caregivers, but most of all she hated the people who put her here."

"Her parents."

"I expect you'll want their details?"

Oscar nodded. They stepped back out into the corridor.

"So," he said, "people are prepared to pay to keep their problem children at arm's length?"

Chalk dropped the keys. Oscar bent to pick them up. She forced a smile of thanks as she took them from him.

"They pay, Detective, but not handsomely." She relocked the door. "The world has not changed that much."

"Are you okay?" Oscar asked.

"A death in the family," Chalk replied. "Unexpected." She pocketed the keys and headed up the corridor. Oscar kept pace.

"Did Penny have any visitors on Wednesday night?" he asked.

"No. Penny had no regular visitors at all."

"Who was on shift in Penny's section?"

"Zoe. Zoe Trucek. You've already met her."

———

The young woman's green eyes had narrowed to slits. She sat on the office chair like a cat above a yardful of dogs and stared at Oscar as if he were the nearest and worst of the hounds. He guessed that she had figured his connection to Megan.

He asked, "Did you see Penelope Roth after she went to bed?"

"No."

"Did anything unusual happen through the shift? Any children sick, needing to leave their rooms?"

"No."

"Visitors? Deliveries? Unexpected phone calls?"

"No." Zoe Trucek inclined her head, eyes never leaving Oscar. "But Megan McAuliffe cried in her sleep. She does that a lot."

Oscar felt his throat tighten.

She raised her eyebrows, an invitation for more questions.

"Thank you, Zoe," Leslie Chalk said coolly.

The young woman kept her hard jade stare on Oscar a moment longer, then unfolded her thin limbs and hurried from the office. The whiteboards shook when she slammed the door.

"Sorry about the manners," Chalk said. "Beggars can't be choosers. She is actually quite wonderful with the kids."

Oscar sat for a moment, angry with himself. The taunt about Megan had been aimed and delivered with startling precision. Did Zoe Trucek hate all police, or just him? He was too wounded by the thought of Megan crying alone in her bed to think clearly, and that made him angrier.

Chalk opened a filing cabinet, found a manila folder, took it to one of the desks, and transcribed details onto a clean sheet of paper. She tore it off and held it out like a posy.

Oscar rose and took the sheet. On it was written the address and telephone number of Paul and Carole Roth.

Chapter 13

The Heights. A few square miles of high suburb, flanked on their southern boundary by the river and commanding views of the city and its fires. There were no fires on the Heights. Since the turn of the twentieth century, this suburb had been home to state premiers and surgeons, judges and property moguls. The wealth of a state seven times larger than the UK funneled into the grand homes that speckled these hillsides like Fabergé eggs set on lush green satin.

When the economic chaos caused by Gray Wednesday spread like fever through the population, a silent concordat was made by the residents of what was to become the Heights. Oscar remembered the joke Jon made the day the wall started to go up: that finally someone was putting the *real* criminals behind bars. But the wisecracks dried up as the wall grew longer and higher, and private security guards began manning the gateways and patrolling the boundaries with large dogs. The wall was electrified and the Heights were secured. The rich suburb and its wealthy owners were sealed almost in toto from the decay. Soon the city simply accepted that it had its own glistening compound where its "better" citizens lived. Similar enclaves had been created in hundreds of cities around the world, but few had been accepted as peacefully.

Naturally, the residents of the Heights were free to come and go—they still had to get to their practices and boardrooms, courthouses and surgeries. And outsiders were allowed in—the well-to-do needed their gardeners and their repairmen and their grocers and their cleaners—but identification and intention were checked at boom gates by unsmiling men in black uniforms with telltale bulges under their arms. And the police were allowed in. Oscar had visited the Heights twice for Clause Seventeens. Even the rich had their ghosts.

Oscar slowed the car as he approached the boom gate and presented his ID.

"Visiting?" asked the security guard.

"That's right."

The guard's eyes were invisible behind sunglasses. "Who are you visiting, sir?"

"Paul and Carole Roth." Oscar gave the address.

"One moment."

The guard stepped into a neat, air-conditioned guardhouse, and Oscar watched him through greenish glass an inch thick. The guard noted Oscar's license plate, then picked up a phone.

Oscar looked out the open window. On the horizon, bruise-blue clouds rolled in like wave heads. The air felt charged and fraught. He was a long way from having conclusive proof, but the tight excitement in his gut told him his Jane Doe was Penny Roth.

The guard returned and offered a printed map of the Heights; he had marked in a red twisting line from "You Are Here" at the gatehouse to the Roth household.

The boom gate rose, and Oscar drove onto the Heights and back in time.

The streets here were clean. Flawless lawns sparkled under dew. No rubbish clogged the gutters or storm-water grates. Footpaths were swept, and no weeds flourished in their cracks. Hedges were neatly trimmed. At a street café, women in pretty coats and men in Aran wool sat under gas heaters, sipping coffee, smiling and laughing. In a small park, a jogger in silvery shoes stretched, and a woman in designer jeans watched her child clamber up a colorful play fort. The houses were large, with windows that were clean and winked back sunlight; no graffiti stained their picket or brick or sandstone fences. Oscar stared as he passed a chocolaterie. His car wound its way higher.

The Roth house was a three-story Art Deco iceberg floating on a sea of emerald grass. It was a balanced whole of flat facets and sweeping curves, sparkling glass and white walls—yet it looked strangely ominous under the dark clouds that roiled overhead. Oscar lowered his window and buzzed the intercom. A woman's voice asked his name. There was an electric click, and the gates rolled silently open.

A long driveway curved between hedges up to a tall white colonnade off the house; under the carriageway were two black BMWs and a

gull-gray Bentley. Oscar parked his sedan and stepped onto a pathway
of ice-white quartz flanked by waxy green camellias. He pulled his
jacket closed against the chill air.

He'd done his share of death knocks in General Duties. Was it the
worst job in the world? He'd thought so at the time. Two in the morning, exhausted by shift work and drained by the sight of a young man
flayed by jagged windscreen glass so that he looked more like a medical
dummy, all exposed muscles and tendons, or of a woman burst like a
melon as the passenger side of her vehicle spun into a power pole with
enough force that the car folded around and through her. He spoke to
the drivers who called in the crash; he waited for Accident Investigation to arrive and measure the tire skids; he watched as firefighters
hosed oil and glass and blood off the road. Then he got into his cruiser
and found the address and, stifling yawns and burying the bad jokes
all cops needed to share in order to temporarily banish the pictures of
dead flesh from their minds, he walked along a path to a front door and
knocked and spoke and watched as a father or mother or husband or
daughter turned white.

The Roths' tiled porch was scrubbed clean, and Oscar's footsteps
rang in the vestibule. He reached for the polished brass door knocker,
but before he could touch it the door was opened by a slender Asian
woman in a trim black dress suit.

"Detective," she said. It was her voice that Oscar had heard on the
intercom. He followed the woman down a wide hallway; she knocked
once on a door.

"Thank you, Angelique," came a man's voice on the other side.

The woman nodded for Oscar to enter.

Paul Roth's home office was a stunning, round sunroom. One
semicircle was curved walls lined with shelves packed neatly with law
books: between ranks of spines was a polished headstand holding a gray
horsehair wig, and Oscar remembered at last who Paul Roth was—the
barrister appointed by Geoffrey Haig's solicitor at the final, futile stage
of Oscar's Ethical Standards investigation. The curve of bookshelves
was broken by a wide white fireplace and two tall gloss-black doors.
Opposite was a semicircle of graceful French windows that looked out
onto a courtyard enclosed by ivy-laden trellises. Oscar returned his
attention to the man seated at the desk.

Roth was dressed in striped silk pajamas and a fluffy white dressing gown. He was almost remarkable in every respect: not quite tall, not quite athletic, not quite handsome. And Oscar couldn't quite peg the man's mood; Roth looked pale and very tired. Yet he vibrated with a happy energy, and self-confidence punched out from behind designer eyeglasses that, Oscar suspected, Roth didn't need to wear. He finished writing a note, then put down his pen, stood, and fixed Oscar with a raised-chin stare—a move, Oscar decided, that was choreographed for the courtroom and perfected in a bathroom mirror. Oscar wondered if Roth would remember him.

"Detective Mariani? It's a pleasure to meet you. I'd offer to shake your hand, but I've been a bit under the weather."

Oscar nodded, his question answered.

Roth continued, "Police usually telephone."

"Is Mrs. Roth here?"

Roth didn't move. "If there's something I should know, I'd prefer to hear it before I trouble my wife."

"I'm here to talk about your daughter."

Roth's eyes narrowed a little, and he chewed the inside of his cheek. "Take a seat," he said after a pause, and went to the French doors. He opened one and cool air tumbled in. "Carole?" he called. "Carole?" The barrister looked back at Oscar, smiled as if nothing could be more normal, and stepped out onto the courtyard flagstones calling his wife's name.

Oscar watched Roth's progress between the columns and the ivy. He was heading across the lawn toward two women silhouetted against the climbing sun. One woman also wore a dressing gown that billowed about her like a loose sail and glowed in the light. Oscar guessed that was Carole Roth. One of her arms circled wildly in the sky, as if she were trying to capture invisible lightning from the air; her other arm was held by the second woman. She wore a tailored suit; her frame was slender, yet she held firmly against Carole Roth's turbulence.

Oscar went quickly to Roth's desk and let his eyes rove over the books and papers there. An address book was beside the telephone, open to the Cs. Oscar looked at it a moment, then strode back to the door he entered through and stepped into the hall.

"Angelique?" he called.

A moment later, the woman appeared from a side office.

Oscar jammed a thumb over his shoulder. "Mr. Roth just called for you from the yard. He's having some trouble with Mrs. Roth."

She licked a lower lip, smiled, and hurried up to Roth's office. "Thank you."

Oscar watched her exit through the French door, then he went deeper into the Roths' house.

The bedrooms were upstairs. It took only a minute to find the one furnished for a teenage girl. Oscar stepped inside, closed the door quietly, and looked around. It was Spartan: a single bed, neatly made; no posters, no ornaments; a school desk with just a lamp and a pencil holder; a dressing table in pink, the only obvious concession to gender. On this was a framed photograph of the same girl Oscar had seen in the Missing Persons file pointing to her GHOSTS FUCKING RULE T-shirt—only in this photograph she was younger: a ten-year-old smiling under a bob haircut. Beside her was a pretty dark-haired woman—Carole Roth. A man's hand rested on Carole's arm, but he had been cropped from the photo.

Oscar opened the dresser's top drawer. Inside, laid out with mathematical precision, was a small makeup kit, a mirror, a manicure set, and a hairbrush. He knelt to inspect the brush. Not a single hair was caught in the bristles. He lifted it by the bristles and held the handle to the light. Not a smudge of a fingerprint. He placed the brush back in the drawer and stood.

This looked like the bedroom of a child already declared dead.

The door opened behind him. "Detective?"

He turned. Angelique was in the doorway. She wasn't smiling politely now.

"This isn't the toilet," Oscar said.

"No." Her eyes were hard. "Did you want some directions?"

"It'll keep. The Roths are ready?"

"They're downstairs."

"Who was the woman with them?"

Angelique simply waited.

———

"Dead?"

Carole Roth frowned, as if trying to place a faint snatch of familiar music. Oscar could see that her face, which had been so pretty in the photograph with Penny, now looked as narrow and pale as a horse's skull. Her pupils were dilated despite the bright morning glare in the office.

"We don't know that," Oscar said. "But we'd like your help to determine whether the body we have is hers."

Paul Roth was watching Oscar carefully now. Angelique had whispered in his ear when they returned to the office, and his stare had become steely.

"Help, how?" Roth asked.

"DNA swab."

Carole Roth began giggling, and looked over at Paul. Her eyes were mirthless, almost mad. "She's dead."

"Honey," Roth began.

Carole Roth stood. "I'm going to lie down now." She banged her shins heavily into the coffee table and let out a sudden, piercing shriek. Angelique ran forward and took her arm. Carole Roth shook the woman away with a fury that was sudden and surprising. "I can make my own way," she snapped. Oscar saw a large, pearl-size drop of blood running down her shin. Passing Oscar, Carole lifted a finger toward him. "Bad news, Detective," she said with a small, grotesque smile, and stumbled away.

Oscar was alone with Roth.

"Okay," Roth said. "Tell me how this proceeds."

"Normally, we'd ask a relative to view and identify the remains. But the body is in bad shape."

"Her face," Roth said. "Because of the . . . industrial machinery?"

"Exactly. So we'd like to carry out a DNA test."

"A swab, you say."

"Or a blood test. Swab's usually fine."

Roth's gaze ticktocked between Oscar's eyes.

"It would be Carole's DNA you want. Penny is her daughter."

"Previous marriage?"

"Carole's first husband is deceased."

"You and she? No kids together?"

"After Carole's first experience, we agreed that children were not advisable."

Oscar decided he didn't like the man.

"I appreciate that your wife is under the weather right now, Mr. Roth. But we need to get that sample as soon as possible."

"I understand the urgency, and we don't want to hold up your investigation." Roth returned to the other side of his desk, tightened his dressing gown, and sat. "You can have the sample the moment you furnish a coronial request."

Oscar wasn't sure he'd heard correctly. "Pardon?"

Roth's face was an illegible blank. "You can swab my wife's mouth once you give me the appropriate request in writing, signed by a state coroner."

Oscar frowned.

"Don't you want to know if we have Penny? If she's dead or alive?"

"No, and no." Roth shrugged. "Don't looked so shocked, Detective. I'm sure you've heard from Elverly how much of a disagreeable little shit Penny is. Or was. She wanted to be anywhere she wasn't. She played up her disability. She wanted to be free of it, but she refused to do her exercises. When she visited here, she treated it like a concentration camp and us like the Gestapo, like it was her duty to escape. I don't know what sort of friends she had, but if they were anything like her I'm not surprised if she got herself into trouble."

Oscar watched the barrister.

"Which is why you shipped her off to Elverly."

"Of course. She's caused nothing but heartache to her mother and me."

Oscar nodded and stood.

"We'll get the request."

He headed to the door but hesitated. "Oh. Can I ask where you were Saturday night?"

Roth smiled coolly. "Here on the Heights, Detective Mariani. Like I say, I've been unwell. The screaming shits, if you need the detail. Any more questions?"

"Just one. Which is your car?"

Roth took a microsecond to adjust to the fresh current.

"The Seven series."

"Nice," Oscar said. "Thank you for your time."

Oscar walked down the neatly trimmed path. The wind tugged at his hair. He really did need to get it cut.

At the side of the house, the three expensive sedans lay stretched under the portico like sleek guard dogs. As Oscar approached them, he noticed a white-haired man standing at the hood of the Bentley, his hands behind his back, watching him patiently. Oscar was struck by how unnaturally slender the man was: he was almost a parody of a thin man. Then he noticed the driver's hair was not white but a blond of almost albino fairness; his face was unlined and ageless. During his second year of study for his philosophy degree, Oscar went to Europe to tread the roads walked by Frege, Voltaire, and Hobbes. But once there he was seduced from scholarship by Southern France's sunny beaches, tanned women, and elegant buildings. It was at a museum in Saint-Paul de Vence that Oscar saw a work by Giacometti: *L'Homme qui marche,* "The Walking Man." The sculpture was of a skeletally thin figure walking as purposefully as the indentured dead; disproportionately long and delicate, yet oddly strong and utterly composed. This driver reminded Oscar of it. Seeing that he had Oscar's attention, the thin man nodded, turned, and walked back through the carriageway.

Oscar followed into the striped shadows cast by the colonnade but stopped at the cars, took out his notepad, and jotted down the license plates of all three vehicles. The driver waited patiently on the other side of the portico. When Oscar pocketed his notepad, the man turned and passed through a patinated stone arch and out of sight. Oscar strolled after him.

This was a different garden again. A stand of Chinese tallow trees was a red slash dividing a rink of lawn from a smaller yard with an ornamental pond. There was no sign of the driver. Oscar continued around the house, and his eye caught a billow of black behind a lush green hedge. He walked toward it, and found the woman who'd been with Carole Roth on the lawn. Fine white fingers held her tailored gray jacket close about her neck against the wind, and her hair flew behind her like a black flag. Despite the fact that she was in shade, she was staring at the bronze markings on an old sundial.

"Ms. Chaume?" he said.

The woman looked up at him, and Oscar felt momentarily illuminated. Her eyes were a bleached aquamarine so pale that, for a moment, he thought she was blind—until those eyes moved over his with such measured precision that there was no mistaking that she saw everything very clearly. She wore no jewelry, yet her appearance suggested great wealth. The woman's skin was eggshell white, and her gray outfit made her look otherworldly, anachronistic, as if she had stepped out of a black-and-white glamour magazine from a past, politer time. The stark palette brought attention to red lips, sharply but generously carved. As he approached, she extended a hand. Closer, he could see that she wasn't petite; she was almost as tall as he was, but in proportions reserved for willowy Art Nouveau bronzes. He tried to guess her age, but her skin was flawless.

"Anne," she said. Her voice had a musical timbre; it floated lightly, birdlike. "How did you know?"

They shook hands. Her skin was dry and warm.

"Mr. Roth's address book was open on his desk, at C," Oscar said. "Yours was the only woman's name I could see on the page. It was a guess."

Her face showed no reaction.

"Are you finished inside?"

"Mr. Roth seems to think so."

She wrinkled her nose. "Good."

"You don't like Paul Roth?"

"Do you?"

"He's not my barrister."

She inclined her head. "Another guess?"

He nodded.

She smiled slowly, an expression that Oscar found more attractive than he would have liked. He took a half step back to get out of the way of it.

"Where's your driver?"

"Karl knows when to make himself scarce."

"Not much to make scarce."

She laughed; it was a pretty sound. "Karl is only slight of weight. He is invaluable. Much more than a driver."

The smile lingered on her face, and he found himself smiling back.

"He led me here, so I gather you wanted to see me, Ms. Chaume?"

She nodded. "I want to know if you're here because of Penny."

"What's it to you?"

"Carole is my friend, Detective—"

"Mariani."

"You don't look Italian."

"Surprisingly few people say that."

"Carole is my friend," she repeated. "And Penny is her daughter and she's been worried sick about her. Police like you—" Her eyes roved up and down Oscar, and he felt their passage like a physical touch. "Homicide police, I'm guessing, don't tend to arrive with good news. I want to know how to approach Carole when I go back inside."

"With a stomach pump," Oscar said. "What's she on?"

Chaume pursed her lips. "As a friend, I'd want to keep that private. But since you're a sworn officer, she calls them her 'Paul pills.' Do you think that means they're from Paul, or to cope with him?"

"Mrs. Roth doesn't look like she's coping at all."

Chaume shrugged. "As I say, she has been worried about Penny. And she didn't think Paul was sharing her concerns."

"Was she right?"

She fixed Oscar with a look that was both grave and strangely playful. "What do you think of Paul Roth, Detective Mariani?"

Oscar knew he shouldn't engage in banter with the woman, but he found himself, stupidly, unable to resist. "Paul Roth is a person of interest."

"That's your professional take. What's your personal opinion?"

"The exact opposite."

She smiled wider, showing white teeth and a delicate tongue. "There you go. But everyone is useful for something."

He watched her eyes sweep over his face. Her stare was candid, and Oscar felt the pull in his belly creep lower and warmer. To distract himself, he took out his notepad. Chaume looked at it curiously.

"Am I a person of interest, too, Detective? That's delightful. No one has found me interesting for a long time. You want to know where I was on the night in question?"

"Do I?"

"I was home."

"Alone?"

"Now we're getting personal," she tutted. "A shame."

She glanced over Oscar's shoulder. He followed her gaze. Karl was waiting near the portico. Beside him stood the dead boy. Oscar would have thought them both ghosts, had the thin man not cast a long, lean shadow. Storm clouds were racing across the sky, and a front of cold air was shoving at the trees and making them hiss like water on a skittle. Chaume's pale eyes refocused on Oscar. She regarded him for a long moment, as if trying to make a decision.

"Carole loved her daughter, Detective. And while Paul is a selfish bombast, I don't think he has murder in him. So do me one favor? Please take care in your investigation, won't you?"

She gave him one more smile, then walked away, catlike, neither hurried nor slow. Her hair blew about her head like black silk; her legs were long.

A moment later, Oscar heard the motor of the large Bentley start, and the crunch of gravel on the drive. His phone rang. It was Neve.

"Yes?"

"Where are you?"

With the image of Anne Chaume sidling away in his mind, Oscar fought the odd, guilty impulse to lie. "The Heights. Why?"

"Haig called. They found Lucas Purden."

———

The air between the buttresses beneath the bridge smelled of salty mud and wet concrete. The sky had grown as dark as evening; hard rain was only minutes away. A wide pedestrian path ran parallel with the river under the end of the bridge, and a narrow set of graffiti-slashed stairs led up to the road that the bridge emptied onto. A shifting knot of two dozen onlookers waited behind barrier tape. Uniformed police in blue knit sweaters or blue leather jackets seemed lashed to ice-white flashlight beams that scoured the path like erratic dogs. On the far side of the huddle, Detective Kace took notes while an Asian man in a Lions jersey and fishing pants nodded enthusiastically. Below the path, an embankment of large flinty rocks was a steep and slimy five-yard grade down to the dark water. Oily brown waves slapped at the rocks and gently twisted Lucas Purden's pale ankles.

Oscar found Neve waiting well away from the crowd and the uniformed police.

"The Heights?" she said. "Fancy."

He led her toward the barrier tape. "What are you doing in today? You should be home in bed. The summary report can wait."

"It's waited too long already."

They showed their IDs and pushed through. Lingering above the tang of river salt rode the leathery scent of good tobacco smoke.

Haig leaned against one of the wide concrete columns under the bridge, his blue uniform almost black in the gloom. The end of his cigarillo glowed, and his eyes twinkled red under the glossy brim of his cap.

"Mariani." Haig sounded pleased. "Go ahead, take a look. The boy's not going anywhere."

Two Scenes of Crime officers in white plastic overalls had rappelling ropes tied around their waists and were being helped up the treacherously slick rocks by stout officers on the path.

"Stay up here," Oscar said to Neve.

"Screw that," Neve replied quietly. "I'm coming."

"Gloves?" Oscar asked the first forensic tech. The man reluctantly handed over two pairs.

Oscar and Neve climbed down slowly. No one offered ropes.

Lucas Purden was on his back, as if to better admire the arching cement girders. His lids and eyeballs had been pecked away by fish, and the rest of his skin was the sickly yellow-white of beef fat that had begun to turn. Oscar flicked on his flashlight. The dead boy's fingers were pulp: splinters of pink and white bone speared through ruptured skin wadded with flesh. The legs of his pants were rolled up, and his loose ankles were bound together with large nylon cable ties. Purden's feet looked as if they'd been shortened: the heels were recognizable, but the flesh forward of them had been pulverized; broken bones protruded like snapped chopsticks from the pale, pink-gray flesh. The top of his jeans had been rolled down to his upper thighs, and his once indefatigable penis had met the same fate as his fingers and toes. His belly was swollen, and he was starting to rot.

"Oh hell," Neve whispered.

Oscar knelt awkwardly on the slippery rocks and lifted Purden's wrist. The arm flopped, unresisting. Around both wrists were contusions so deep they had eaten through skin into flesh and tendon. Oscar carefully inspected the boy's head. The face was waxy and cold, and the skin on his chin, forehead, and the tip of his nose was badly torn. Oscar gently rolled the boy's head and parted his wet hair. The back of his head had been flattened; in the middle of that plateau was a hollow the size of a toddler's fist.

"A hammer?" Neve asked.

Oscar shrugged and nodded.

"What are these welts?" She touched one of Purden's wrists. "Handcuffed?"

Oscar shined his flashlight on one of the dead boy's wrists. The light picked out a fine, stiff hair embedded in the torn skin. A rope fiber.

"His chin and nose are torn," Oscar said. "I think he was put on his stomach, a rope on each wrist pulled tight out in opposite directions, and his fingers, toes, penis were smashed until, I don't know, his killer heard what he wanted or got his jollies. Then he stoved in the back of Luke's skull."

Neve prodded the boy's tightly rounded belly.

"Three days."

Oscar nodded. "Snatched pretty soon after we interviewed him."

"Who by?"

Oscar turned off his flashlight. "By whoever paid him for information about the sewage-plant augers."

When they climbed back up, Haig was waiting. Beside him stood Kace, her notepad ready and a small, strange smile on her face.

"Isn't fishing a tonic?" Haig asked Oscar. "You know him?"

"You know we do. We interviewed him about a body found at his workplace."

Haig nodded. "I read that in your report. About the Jane Doe."

"She's not a Jane Doe anymore."

The inspector raised his eyebrows just a little, and lit another cigarillo, cupping the flame against the stiffening wind.

"Have your people got a time of death?" Oscar asked.

Haig shook out the match and tossed it over toward the river. "I invited you here to answer questions, not ask them." Oscar felt the skin of his stomach grow tight and cold. "So you were the last to see Purden alive?"

"No," Oscar replied. "That would have been his murderer."

Haig nodded slowly, then looked at Kace. She reached into a pocket and handed Oscar a small sealed evidence bag. Inside was Oscar's business card. A smooth crescent of blood had turned a coppery brown in the corner, leaching and spreading through the damp cardboard.

Kace said, "In your report you said that you returned to Purden's place of residence and he was gone." She watched Oscar, dark eyes sparkling. "So you still had questions to ask him?"

Oscar could feel heat radiate off Neve beside him. She began, "What are you suggesting?"

"Detective Kace is not suggesting anything," Haig interrupted, his voice light. "Merely wondering. Although you are desperate for a conviction."

Oscar shook his head. "I don't think you know me very well, Inspector."

"Oh, I think I do." Haig drew smoke deep into his lungs. It puffed out as he spoke. "I know when you start something you want to keep going till it's finished. With little regard for the people involved. No regard, some would say."

"This isn't my style." Oscar gestured down at Purden's body. "We both know whose style this is."

Haig said nothing.

"And I found your little present," Oscar said. "On my garage floor."

Haig leaned back as an errant flashlight beam sliced over his face. His smile was dazzling white; his eyes were glacier cold. "I don't know what you're talking about." He gestured.

Oscar handed the card back, and Kace slipped it into her pocket with a conjurer's deftness. Haig turned to his people and clapped his hands cheerfully. "All right, let's pack this up."

Haig headed toward the stairs rising to the main road. Kace closed her notebook, smiled at Oscar, and headed off into the assembly of officers. Neve turned to Oscar.

"Not good," she observed.

"Let's go," he said.

———

The storm broke. Rain smashed down on the car roof, and the windshield wipers slapped hard, failing to keep up. Oscar switched on the headlights and drove slowly, the downpour grinding the peak-hour traffic down to a crawl. He had to divert to a side street because tired uniformed police had blocked a road while firefighters sprayed foam into a burning car. In the street parallel, a construction site was a blaze of spotlights behind a gauze fence—pile drivers and diggers rammed earth and air with steel and noise. A banner read THATCH CONSTRUCTION.

Ten minutes later, they were outside the former convent where Neve lived. The rain continued its rowdy dance on the roof and hood. She didn't move to get out.

"You've ID'd the girl's body?"

"I think so."

"Where is it?"

"Kannis's."

Neve didn't hide her disgust. "That sleaze." After a long moment, she asked, "How?"

Oscar told her about Gillin's external autopsy, the violent hysterectomy, the hairless bands around the dead girl's forearms, the trip to Elverly, and the visit to the Roths.

"Paul Roth," Neve said, frowning. "You think he killed his own stepdaughter?"

"I don't know."

"Does Haig think you killed Lucas Purden?"

"I don't know."

She watched him, troubled. "If Haig had anything to do with Penny Roth's death, if he's tied up with Paul Roth, this case is dead already. Worse than dead. Dangerous."

"They don't know where the body is. I just need the coroner to authorize a DNA test of Carole Roth, and once Penny is formally ID'd I'll find a way to search Roth's house. There'll be something there, always is."

He felt rotten telling her another half-truth. If Roth was involved, he was smart enough to have already cleaned his house from basement to attic and torched any paper trail.

The rain started to ease.

Neve shifted in her seat, and said quietly, "Have you signed my transfer?"

"Yeah. It's at home," he said. It was in his pocket, unsigned.

"Tomorrow, then?" she asked.

"Sure," he said. "Go in, get an early night. You're probably exhausted after yesterday."

"What are you going to do?"

"I'm going home."

Yet another lie.

He watched her run across the street through the drizzle. He knew he should pull the transfer request out right now, sign it, and give it to her. Get her well away from this investigation, from Haig. He just couldn't picture the Barelies without her. She was good. She was nice. And while she was in the office, pounding away at the performance summary, he could stay out on the case with some tiny hope that he'd still have a job next week.

A few days. He'd talk her around.

Chapter 14

The pastries looked mummified. Oscar picked the one that felt least like wood, then squeezed chicory essence from a tube into the bottom of a foam cup and depressed the lever. A wheezy trickle of steaming water dribbled into the cup. He dropped a coin into an honesty box beside the dispenser; a man behind the counter gave him a fraternal nod. Across the cafeteria, two officers on night shift chewed automatically while they read newspapers. On the far wall was a rising arc of plaster patches, reminiscent of china wall ducks, where an officer had decided his dead brother could just stop following him around and emptied his service pistol. Two and a half years, and still the patches hadn't been painted.

Oscar sat and ate. The tough pastry forced him to chew slowly, allowing him time to think.

Perhaps Haig had not personally killed Lucas Purden, but Oscar could imagine the inspector standing in the corner of a room, asking polite questions while another swung a hammer into the boy's knuckles. Oscar found himself watching the cafeteria doorway for arrivals. He was in trouble.

The Industrial Relations floor was silent. Little puddles of light picked out the sharp edges of empty desks and the curves of chair backs. Neve had again left their desk covered with neat stacks of folders. He balanced the computer keyboard on top and filled out a Form Five, requesting a DNA sample from Carole Roth. He thought for a moment, then added Paul Roth's name to the form and clicked Print. While the old machine in the center of the empty office warmed up, he logged on to Prophet and searched for "Roth, Paul."

The system coughed, rallied, and spat out the unsatisfying answer that Oscar had expected. Roth's name was mentioned on dozens of files as defense counsel, but he had no criminal record. The only hint of besmirchment was a parking violation in 2006, left unpaid while he and Carole honeymooned in the Loire Valley. An appeal was made upon return, and all fines were paid.

Oscar exited Prophet and typed "Chaume, Anne" into the search engine and waited.

Anne Isabelle Chaume was the daughter and only child of hotelier Sidney Chaume, a man who made headlines in the early nineties when he married the much older Daphne Carter, widow and heiress to the Carter mining fortune. More headlines were made when Daphne died just two years later, succumbing to bone cancer that the press speculated Sidney Chaume must have known about. Sidney weathered the storm, comforted perhaps by his nine-figure net worth. When Sidney died five years ago, Anne inherited the entire Chaume Carter fortune, including Chislehurst, a five-acre property dominated by an imposing nineteenth-century manor regarded by many as the finest residence in the state, perched at the top of the Heights. During probate, Anne engaged the services of Paul Roth.

The search also brought up photographs of the beautiful Ms. Chaume at various gala events and fund-raisers; one photograph showed her looking almost luminescent in a bridal grown, smiling widely next to her groom, a handsome young man named Liam Moreley. Moreley had been due to inherit the Moreley yacht-building company from his father, but did not live to do so. Six years into his marriage to Anne Chaume, he contracted a parasitic infection while holidaying in Egypt and was unlucky enough to sustain organ damage that saw him fatally degenerate over the next few months. Oscar flicked through photos taken just weeks before Gray Wednesday of the funeral service at St. John's Cathedral—Anne Chaume's eyes were sparkling spots of aquamarine in a sea of black.

Oscar looked up and realized that the Industrial Relations floor was silent—the printer had long finished its work. He stood, and then stopped suddenly. The dead boy was in the corner, standing beside the stationery cabinet. Oscar stared, unnerved. This was the first time the boy had shown himself in Oscar's workplace. When the boy saw that Oscar was still watching, he nodded and raised a hand to his chest. Oscar looked away and hurried to the printer. He retrieved and signed the Form Five and went to his in-tray to look for an envelope. In the tray he found a note from Foley: "A chick named T called. Said u'd know who. Call her. Foley. PS Get a fucking secretary. PPS Need 2 pick ur brains when u have time. PPPS How's Neve?"

Oscar addressed the envelope to Moechtar, pigeonholed it, grabbed his hat and jacket and—staying well clear of the dead boy—went to the elevators.

———

While Tanta finished with a client, Oscar held off the chill by shuttling like a loom up and down the wet street. From the shadows, men and boys watched him pass, unsure what to make of him—too shabbily dressed to pickpocket, too sure-footed for a Delete addict. In confusion, they let him pass. From an alley came a mélange of smells: coal smoke, raw fish, an unusual tang of herbal incense. He paced.

Finally, Tanta's door opened and a man shouldered past Oscar and up the street. Oscar climbed the narrow stairs. Tanta was behind a gauzy curtain, washing herself in a bowl from which rose fragrant steam. She was cranky.

"That friend of yours, Foley," she said. "He's a dirty motherfucker. Doesn't know how to speak to a lady."

"That's true."

"Does he have money?"

Oscar changed the subject. "Purden's dead," he said. "He's been found. You can stop asking around."

"I heard. The river." He watched her silhouette as she toweled herself front and back. "This isn't about Purden. It's about your symbol."

She emerged, tightening a silk gown about herself. She reached into a purse hardly larger than a wallet and produced a tiny notepad. She wrote an address. "Ask for Dalmar."

———

Steel girders cantilevered into the night sky like the massive feelers of some alien craft. In the deep shadows under the stadium, dozens of dark figures shifted in the gloom—thieves, dealers, whores of all ages and flavors. Nestled not far from a bus interchange and one entrance to the tunnel city of Hades, the stadium was a dangerous place to solicit: a thorny blueberry patch within a minefield.

Oscar scanned the murky walls of the coliseum, counting the gate numbers as he passed. He found the gate number that Tanta had written on her note. He stepped cautiously into soupy darkness.

He could just make out figures ahead—men or women, boys or girls, it was impossible to say. The air was thick with the tang of Delete smoke and the milky cloy of semen.

"Hi there," said a voice. It sounded like a child's.

"Dalmar," he said.

The shapes moved. Oscar found his hand reaching inside his jacket. Then a stranger's hand took his. He tried not to jump.

"I'm Dalmar." A girl's voice.

Her hand squeezed once, then opened on his palm like a tiny bowl. Understanding, Oscar reached into a pocket and pulled out the last twenty he'd been saving. It melted away faster than a snowflake.

"Oscar," he said.

"The astronomer?"

Something clicked and rubbed. Oscar's eyes were adjusting to the minelike gloom. The girl was small, and he could see her smiling up at him as she detached a prosthetic calf and scratched her stump.

"Astronomer?" Oscar said.

"A joke, hon." The little prostitute strapped her leg back on. "You're looking for the star, right?"

"Yes."

She asked, "Do you have a car?"

———

The roads shone like black ribbon. As Oscar drove, Dalmar ate crackers from the car's glove box, speaking around mouthfuls. She hadn't always worked off the streets, she explained. But some guys like girls with quirks, so why not ride that wave? She had enjoyed long-term employ at a brothel in Spring Hill, a half mile out from the city. Not plush, but not bad—it had once been an art gallery. Dalmar had suffered a few knocks about the head as a child (hard to run away with only one leg, ha-ha) and so had wondered if the whirring sound she heard while men grinded away on her front or back or face was real or just inside her skull. So one evening, on a break between clients, she decided to trace the whirring sound, and followed it, louder and louder, down the alley adjoining the former art gallery to a room.

"It was like being caught in a fucking karaoke film clip," Dalmar explained. "All billowy curtains and shit, *whoosh-whoosh*. Pushed through. Smelled of incense and that mystic shit. There's a card table with silky shit on top, a mirror made of some shiny metal shit, maybe brass, and then more of those fucking curtains. 'Hello?' I say, and the whirring stops. The curtain opens, and there's this nice-looking bitch with her arms covered in—" She hunted for the word.

"Shit?" Oscar offered.

"Clay. Potter's clay. And an oven."

"A stove?"

"No, a clay oven."

"A kiln."

"Yeah. An oven for clay," the girl said, as if he was a cretin, and pointed him down a side street. "She made little clay things: animals, moons, stars, shit. And she had a nice little kitchen, little bed, radio. Nice."

The pottery-making fortune-teller's name, the young prostitute explained, was Florica. No more a real name than Dalmar, ha-ha. Still, she offered to read Dalmar's palm.

" 'You will meet a number of men,' she says. 'No fucking shit,' I say."

She and Florica became friends, of sorts, with Dalmar going behind the brothel to visit her on cigarette breaks. One night a few weeks ago, Dalmar visited Florica and found her agitated—"all nerves and shit"— and Dalmar followed her back through her curtains. "An' I see all this mystical stuff pinned on the walls. Sketches of stars and crosses and weird writing like fucking Korean shit. All held up with thumbtacks.

" 'Whatcha working on?' I ask her. 'A sculpture,' she says. 'Like Michelangelo?' I say. 'Mike-a-who?' she says, and then she says, 'You better go; my client's coming.' I ask if he's got money, and maybe he could come next door and ask for Dalmar, all the usual shit. But she's shooin' me out, and shuts the door behind me. She don't let me in after that. Couple nights later, I get to work, and there's no work."

"No customers?"

"No *work*. The brothel, the old gallery, Florica's place—all just a pile of ash."

"When was this?"

Dalmar thought. "Four, five weeks ago. Turn here."

Oscar steered the car down a back way as narrow as a canal. The lane was just wide enough for two cars to pass if their side mirrors kissed, and the choked baritone of his wounded exhaust rattled off the dumb faces of brick buildings. Clots of rubbish accreted against fences. His headlights reflected from tiny eyes that scurried away, taking long, pink-gray tails with them. A house with stairs disconnecting and yawning into darkness. A small tiled building, all arches and swoops of stained stucco with a refrigerator hanging out a second-floor window— thieves had found it too awkward to fit, and now its open door gaped over the rampant weeds below. A building with a cornerstone carved TURIN AUCTIONS. Beside it, a chain-link fence around a field of ash.

"Yuh-huh," Dalmar said.

Oscar parked and they both got out. The air was cold, and his skin goosepimpled. He flicked on his flashlight and shined the beam through the temporary fence. Weeks of rain had pummeled the ash of the burned building into glossy mounds of black mud; sharp, char-coaled stubs of posts thrust up from them at odd angles, like witches' teeth from diseased gums.

Dalmar sighed. "They say it was that fucking bitch's clay oven."

Oscar asked, "Did you see this client she spoke about?"

The girl shook her head. "I had to get back to work anyhows. Speaking of which"—she nudged her body against him, and the prosthesis groaned—"do you have any more money?"

"I don't. Sorry."

She nodded regretfully. "I'll take your car, then."

She swung a bottle into his head. It exploded on his skull and inside it like fireworks. Time and gravity slipped away from him and he realized that he was on the ground, with a hand rummaging through his pockets. He heard her say "Fuck!" and then a frantic, silvery jangle.

He forced himself to his knees, swaying.

In double vision, he saw that she was trying to unlock the door of the sedan, but the fickle lock had foiled her.

"Fuuuck!" she screamed again in frustration.

He pulled himself up using the fence wire and reached inside his jacket.

"Stop," he managed to whisper.

"Fuck you!" the girl spat, and threw the keys at his face. He managed to jerk his head aside, but a jagged nickel edge caught his ear and the keys clattered onto the dirty footpath. The girl ran away down the street, her uneven footsteps echoing long after she was lost in shadow.

The world spun one last time as Oscar bent to pick up his keys. He straightened and felt his scalp. Wet, but only a little. He looked around, unsure if he was checking for witnesses or vultures. Neither appeared. He saw a red blink from the corner of his eye and turned. Whatever it was had gone; the windows of the street were dark and empty.

He found a loose section of wire and pulled the rusty links upward. He crawled under, careful not to catch his tender head. No light came from the sky; the lot was a crater held close in shadow. The air smelled burned and rancid. He played the flashlight beam over the dark, slick curves that looked like beached things harpooned with burned, rotting piers. He started out across the lot. Every step was unpleasant: damp ash and wet charcoal would crunch, then his foot would sink into the squelching slurry. Dalmar had said Florica's rented space was behind the brothel. He slogged across. The black mud sucked at his shoes, and broken roof tiles clacked underfoot.

The burned and broken posts and debris tapered off. Oscar reached what he guessed had been the rear of the building and turned in a slow circle, running the light across the black, glossy ground. He picked up a length of steel pipe and began methodically jabbing it through the pitchy sediment. The pipe caught regularly on strands of electrical cable crusted with melted insulation, cold bricks, more pipe. Under a slight hillock, it caught the corner of something hard. He knelt and felt cold wetness seep through his trousers. He carefully balanced the flashlight on a blackened tile and forced his hands down into the muddy ash, tracing the object's shape. He found another corner—it was metal, about the size of a domestic clothes dryer. The kiln.

Oscar straightened, and his damp arms grew instantly cold in the chill air. This was a thin lead: a fortune-teller who'd pinned stars to her walls. He shivered in the cold. "Go home," he told himself. His flashlight had rolled a few feet away. He reached out for it, putting all his weight on one arm. Suddenly, the ground beneath let out a wet, splintery crack and gave way, and his arm plunged into the ash to his shoulder; his chest and face connected with wet slurry, and a sharp corner of broken tile nipped at his cheek. His arm was underground and hanging in empty space. He must have pushed through a charcoaled table.

Something crawled on his fingers and up his wrist.

He yanked his hand up and out of the ground. Three cockroaches rode it, each as long as his thumb. He shook them off, and they flung away like nasty black comets.

Oscar carefully circumvented the hole, reached for the flashlight, and shined it down into the darkness. In the circle of light at the bottom of the hole, the ground flexed and shifted, a rustling pelt not of black fur but of two-inch wings, shiny and hard as black-lacquered fingernails.

Cockroaches. Thousands of them. And they were crawling over something.

Christ, he thought. What if that's *her* down there? What if she'd died in the blaze and those ten thousand sly-feelered, black-mandibled *things* are feeding on her? If he pushed his hand through their shifting mass, what would his fingers touch? A twisted arm—a root of charred bone and loose, spoiled flesh?

He gingerly put his weight on the unsteady hillock and slid his hand into the hole. First, just cold, damp air on the skin of his sensitized fingertips, palm, wrist. Then something jumped onto the back of his hand and whispered there. His hand flexed. Don't squeeze, he thought, that might be worse. He willed his hand to stay steady as he pushed it down. More and more tiny, flickering weights jumped onto his hand and began to crawl up his wrist and burrow beneath his sleeve.

"Oh, man," he whispered.

A dozen more cockroaches skittered over themselves to feed on his fingers. His stomach began to tighten and quiver. But beneath the scuttling mass he felt something hard. Oscar brushed the insects aside, but the spiny little legs kept returning; one had burrowed its way up his sleeve to his elbow and was crawling steadily up his biceps toward his armpit. He ignored it, hunting for a place to grab the object. Whatever he'd found was cold; not smooth like metal but rough like brick or stone. It felt about a foot and a half long; its shape was irregular and impossible to guess under the shifting veneer of seething insect flesh.

The cockroach in his sleeve was now near his underarm—it felt as big as a matchbook, and its sharp little feet nipped into his skin for purchase. A dozen more were making their way steadily up his forearm.

His hand found a hole in the object, and he slipped his fingers inside. The cockroach in his armpit began to nibble.

He yanked upward.

The object exploded up through the crust of ash, bringing with it a contrail of cockroaches that scratched at the air and took lazy flight. Oscar dumped the object on the ground and shook his arm like a dog gripping a snake—tiny black sparks flew off in all directions. Then he drove his fist into his armpit and felt a wet pop against the skin. The roach there scritch-scratched twice, then stopped moving. He squeezed his forearm all the way from the elbow to the wrist and felt cockroaches squash and explode. Stomach heaving, he plucked open his sleeve and shook his arm wildly. A dozen dead and dying insects tumbled out.

Oscar's heart hammered, and he tasted bitter adrenaline. He forced himself to take slower breaths.

He stooped and picked up the flashlight and returned to the object he had unearthed. As the beam of light played over it, he felt something tighten in his chest. His mouth grew dry, and the hairs on his neck rose like parade-ground bayonets.

The thing was earthenware—fired clay—and was the length of a man's thigh and the diameter of a dinner plate. Even with all the ashen slurry and mud and resistant cockroaches still playing over it, he could make out its disturbing shape. At first, he thought it was a clay monkey, then a gargoyle, then a hunched woman, then an owl. Then he realized it was all of those. Horns topped its head, not feathered but actual horns, caprine and twisted. It had wings, but instead of feathers at its wing tips it had clutching, skeletal fingers that reached down between squat, avian legs and held open a wide, vaginal gash. The idol's eyes were round and staring. Its beak was alien and deformed: both upper and lower beaks had split sideways, and the mouth was open unnaturally wide, as if to feed on something that would otherwise be too large.

I have parted the curtain of bone.

Again, the thought came from nowhere, but was as clear in his mind as a lover's whisper. Oscar had the sudden urge to drop the idol back in the hole. Instead, he leaned closer and shined the flashlight carefully over it. Its surface was scratched to approximate feathers or scales. Up one wing was a large flaw, a fissure that must have occurred during the firing. He reached down to set the idol upright. Instantly, a wave of cockroaches vomited from the thing's quartered mouth and the ugly cleft between its legs. He dropped it again with a start, and the idol rolled, waving its spread legs at the dark sky before stopping on its split-beaked face. Oscar waited, then gave it a few sharp raps with the flashlight to unsettle the last scuttling roaches—the vessel rang tunelessly and hollow.

Oscar stared.

On the idol's back was marked a seven-pointed star.

Chapter 15

The car jostled on the drive back through the city. Oscar's head swam, aching behind his eyes and stinging where the girl had hit him with the bottle. He suspected that he should go to the hospital, but he didn't relish the idea of a six-hour wait in Emergency. He wound the window down, and cold, wet air blustered in. On the passenger seat, the garbage bag around the pottery idol fluttered with the sound of wings.

A star. An idol. A fortune-teller. A fire.

A star. A dead girl. An auger. A robbed womb.

Another rumble, this time his stomach. Oscar tried to remember the last time he'd eaten properly, then the thought of the swarming cockroaches made his gut spasm. He could still feel them scuttling like black crabs up his arms.

Crabs. River.

Purden. Murder.

Haig.

Haig—his smiling, polished face was everywhere and nowhere.

At a stop sign, Oscar glanced in the side mirror. Twenty paces behind, the dead boy stood on the footpath, watching. There was no other traffic.

Oscar turned and called to him, "Do you know?"

The boy's hands waited, hovering at his waist like a pianist's at a keyboard, wondering what to play.

"No," Oscar said after a pause. "I didn't think so."

The rain started again. First, light drops, then a steady, cold downpour. The dead boy didn't seem to notice.

A patrol car roared past, lights strobing and siren wailing. Oscar's heart jolted stupidly in his chest. His head throbbed.

Five minutes later, he turned the wheel and stopped the car in front of the graffitied shutter. Out of habit, he killed the engine, left the headlights on, and stepped out into the rain. He shivered and knelt at the padlock.

He froze.

It's in there.

The dog's head, wrenched from its body and crushed like an egg under a man's boot heel, was just a warning.

Whatever did that is in there. Waiting.

Oscar's heart pumped hard in his chest.

He shook his head, trying to dislodge the thought. It was ridiculous. In the last hour he'd had a bottle smashed over his head and been arm-deep in a nest of cockroaches. He was tired, he was hungry, he needed to sleep, that was all. He'd locked the window with the chain. There was nothing inside.

He steadied his breathing, slid the key into the padlock, and pulled it clear of the staple. The shutter clattered loudly as it rose.

The two cones of white light speared through the empty garage, onto moldy boxes and empty oilcans. No dark gods. No dismembered dogs. Just dust and silence.

"Idiot," he said aloud, and got back in the car. He restarted the engine and rolled the car into the garage. The worn engine and tired exhaust rattled and echoed off the musty timber walls. Oscar twisted the key, and the engine coughed once and silenced. The nose of the car was centimeters away from the stack of oilcans, and the headlights reflected bright flares off the grimy tins. He flicked off the headlights, and the garage fell into darkness. He quickly opened the door, and the dome in the car's hood lining sputtered on, a weak light not much brighter than a candle. He got out, retrieved the bag holding the idol, and closed the car door. Oscar put the key in the door lock and twist-jiggle-twisted until it locked.

A drop of water fell on the back of his neck.

He turned around and looked up.

High overhead, all the hopper windows were wide open.

Oscar looked behind him at the chains that should be fastening them. They hung loose.

The shutter rattled down hard and fast, hitting the ground with a loud bang. Oscar jumped. He was suddenly in pitch darkness.

He dropped into a hunch on the concrete floor.

He listened. Each rapid pump of his heart rocked his body.

"Who's there?" he said loudly.

Silence.

All he could see was the imprint on his retinas of those damned oilcans. He was blind. The bag rustled in one hand. With the other, he reached out and found the cold steel sides of the car.

"Police!" he said. His voice echoed emptily.

High overhead, a loose window frame tapped. Just once.

The garage was quiet.

He stood.

Scratch. Something moved in the darkness on the other side of the car. A tiny shuffle. A sly, faint rubbing. Enough for Oscar to know that he wasn't alone.

He silently cursed the empty gun in its holster and placed the plastic bag on the ground: its crinkling rustle was loud in the dark silence; the pottery idol inside it clack-clacked as it rocked on the hard concrete slab.

Scraaatch. A little closer. Whatever was in here was coming around the car.

Oscar's eyes were wide but blind, still seeing ghostly imprints left by the headlights. His heart banged in his chest. He bit his lip and reached into a pocket. His fingers closed on the metal cylinder of a small flashlight.

And if you do see something, he wondered, what then?

Oscar listened.

Nothing. Or maybe it was just a rat.

Scratch-flick—from beside him at the nose of the car. He whirled and pointed the flashlight like a weapon, thumbing the switch on. The circle of light seemed stunningly bright: a dazzling reflection in the rear-vision mirror. As Oscar squinted, something huge and gray flurried like a cape and—*Bang!*—struck him in the face. He whirled instinctively as wind rushed about him, smelling of dry soil and old rot. Dust flurried up into his eyes, stinging and dry. His feet danced to stay upright and one came down on the plastic bag—there was a quick crunch of pottery breaking, then his foot slid away from under him. His knee came down hard on the concrete, sending a white bolt of pain up his leg. The flashlight landed near the shutter, casting a tiny, useless crescent of light into the corner of the garage.

He was on all fours, blinking to clear his eyes of the dust. *Bang!* He was knocked to the ground, and his forehead smacked into the cold cement. His vision swirled with bright spirals.

The car, he thought. *Get inside the car.* His fingers scrabbled on the cold metal and found the handle. Locked. He'd locked it himself.

The air pulsed above him, like two mighty breaths, and something large beat the car door like heavy curtains. The car shuddered under his fingers. And he heard grinding scratches in the dark, like bone on stone.

It had landed on the ground in front of him.

He snatched his hand away and ducked just as something large punched through the space where his head had been and speared hard into the glass of the door's window, shaking the car on its springs.

Oscar dropped to his stomach as a shape swooped above him, slicing the air he'd just occupied. Sharp shards of broken pottery bit through his ash-damp trousers into his thighs. He dared to twist his head and look up. All he could see was the twin, blurred rectangles of the high windows, dark gray against black—then something above him, blocking out all light. It descended.

He yelled and rolled under the car. Behind him, something hard as horn struck the concrete with an angry snap.

He squirmed deeper under the car, palms scraping on the concrete. His heart ran inside his chest like a trapped cat, and his breaths came in snatched, panicked bursts. He could see nothing: darkness, shadow in shadow.

But it was out there. He knew it. It was close, waiting at the sill of the car. And he could smell it. The scent filled his nostrils: an unpleasant stink, like old fur or an abandoned nest. Or dry dead things.

Scriiiiitch-scratch.

Oscar stared through wide eyes. The flashlight still shone from the ground into the garage corner. And into that tiny arc of light he saw it move. It stepped slyly with a bony clack, cast into silhouette. A dark crescent as long as a man's finger and shining like polished granite. A claw. A talon. Then a second. And a third. A foot. The weak light revealed only the very edges of its long, fingerlike toes, ridged in scutes as rough as crocodile skin, and those three long, old talons. Then he heard the thing shift. The whisper of feathers upon feathers; a hushed rustling like an old crinoline dress unfolding itself from an empty wardrobe. The foot silently placed down again, toes first, on the plastic bag that held the cracked idol. The weight of the creature pressed down, and Oscar heard the already broken pottery shatter into smaller pieces. Then, with sudden violence, the foot swiped the bag away as a rooster might scrape away a clod of dirt, and the bag smacked against the oilcans with a shockingly loud bang.

Oscar gasped.

And the creature went still.

Slowly, silently, the thing lowered itself to the floor. Oscar's mouth went as dry as a tomb. He saw from under the car, just an arm's length from him, the glint of an orb: a disk twice the size of a poker chip, as black as oil but rimmed in glistening bile yellow. An unblinking eye, watching him.

Then it struck.

Bang! The creature's head hit the sill of the car and the vehicle rocked. Oscar jolted backward, and his own head struck the cold, hard steel of the drive shaft.

He had just a moment of swimming, sliding vision—seeing the huge gray avian head twisting, looking for a way under. Then dark stars swallowed his sight, and he slid into unconsciousness.

Chapter **16**

The girl was dreaming of custard. She liked custard. She could eat it all day. She hated green vegetables and tried to say so, but the words always came out as a grunt or a groan. But this dream was happy. In this dream, she could speak. She'd asked for custard, and had received a clean white bowl that was sooo big—

"Taryn?"

—and the custard was soooo yellow, and in this dream she didn't need Miss Zo-zo to feed her, she was feeding herself! And then—

"Taryn?"

She blinked awake. Someone was touching her shoulder. She opened her mouth to ask who was there, and a noise came out.

"It's okay, Taryn. Sorry to wake you."

There were two people standing in her room. It was night. Night was for sleeping. Everything was blurry. She didn't think she knew these people. She couldn't see them, because they were blurry.

Taryn asked, *Who are you?* but another noise came out.

Then one of the someones put her glasses on her face and all the blurry vanished. Two men. The man who had put her glasses on her face was small and wrinkly. Like the pixie from the book that Miss Lucy read. In the book, he was a nice pixie, and this man looked just like him. When he turned, Taryn saw that he had a silver tail on the back of his head, just like a pony's! Taryn looked across the dark room to see if Becky was awake, because Becky liked ponies. She called out to Becky—

"No, Taryn. No," the pixie-man whispered, and put a warm finger on her wet lips. "Don't wake her. We just want you."

Taryn liked his voice.

The pixie-man smiled. "And we have something for you. Look."

She followed his long, thin arm and looked at the other man. This man wasn't small. He smiled and held up a big pink jacket.

"Wa?" Taryn thought it was the most beautiful jacket she had ever seen. "My!"

"Shh, yes. It's yours. But you have to be nice and quiet. Will you be nice and quiet?"

Taryn nodded hard. She couldn't take her eyes off it.

"Then let's put it on," he whispered.

Taryn wanted to jump and hoot, but she was good. Nice and quiet. She put one arm in, then the other. Outside the window, she could see, up up, some stars.

"Nigh-time!" she said.

"Yes," agreed the pixie-man. His hands were soft as he slipped her shoes on her feet. "We're going on a nighttime trip."

The jacket was warm. Taryn smiled. She was going to see the stars.

Chapter 17

S tars were diamonds, the moon a fingernail. The air was ice-cold. "How do we kill a rabbit?"

The sun had not yet risen, and the sky in the east was a smudge of light no particular color. His new daddy was in a good mood. Oscar followed the man as he walked over tufts of grass that tinkled and snapped under their gum boots. Oscar could not remember ever having been so cold. Frost covered the paddocks, and loops of frozen dew hung from fence wires like dark-gray pearls. The air was so still that the man's voice, only a whisper, was almost shockingly loud. Oscar's six-year-old heart pounded, because he carried a gun.

It was heavy, the rifle, very heavy, and his small bare fingers felt numb. But he refused to let the weapon slip or drop. The man carried a similar rifle. Both had scopes. The man's was a Weatherby, he'd explained yesterday after they arrived at the farm, "And yours is a Marlin. Like the fish." They'd gone to the shed behind the farmhouse and the man had shown Oscar how to load the magazine, how to screw on the silencer made by a "friend of a friend," how to unfold the two legs of the bipod, how to lie on the ground and tuck the stock into his right shoulder with his left hand, work the bolt, and sight through the scope. Satisfied, the man had said, "Tomorrow we hunt *conigli*." This morning he'd been pulled up from sleep like a fish hauled from a deep sea, disoriented and a bit fearful. Daddy helped him dress, tucked two magazines into his pockets, and handed the black-and-silver rifle to him. Shivering and excited, Oscar had followed him out into darkness.

"How do we kill a rabbit?" Daddy repeated, whispering as they walked. The farm was in drought, Oscar learned last night, and the rabbits were fearless and numberless. A plague.

The night before, from his sleeping bag in the spare room, he'd heard his new parents sitting with Uncle Andino. There had been the loud pop of a cork from a bottle. More talking: something about a trial finally over. Corks and drinking usually meant good news, Oscar had thought, but the voices weren't happy, so he wasn't sure. But today the man's talkative mood was impossible to ignore. Maybe he just had a funny way of showing happiness.

"He is no fool, rabbit. And nature has given him lots of help. Big ears for hearing. He is brown, like the grass is brown. And he is fast. His eyes work better than yours or mine at the dawn and the dusk. He knows these paddocks better even than your Uncle Andino, much better than you or me. Where rabbit comes from, far across the seas, everything eats him. Hawks, wolves, owls. So he has eyes each side of the head"—the man touched each temple—"to see all round. But we don't have eyes like the owl, or sharp teeth like the stoat. No? So what is our advantage?"

Oscar thought, and said, "We have guns."

Sandro shrugged, a satisfactory answer. He took Oscar's gun and held fence wires down with one foot and up with his hand, letting the boy climb into a new paddock. He handed back the rifle.

"Guns, yes. That's part of it. Guns and scopes, so if we do it right we can kill the little fellows before they even know we're there. That's good. Nothing likes to die feeling afraid. But people have been eating *conigli* for thousands of years, long before guns. Do we just eat rabbit?"

Oscar thought about this. "No."

The man looked at him from the corner of an eye, and nodded again. "What other animals do we eat?"

Oscar saw shapes shifting on the glowing horizon.

"Cows."

"Cattle," Sandro agreed.

"Sheep. Chickens. Fish."

"Yes."

Oscar fell silent, thinking. He willed his frozen fingers to grip the gun tight. He knew the man wanted an answer, and Oscar wanted to please him. He was a policeman, and made Oscar a little afraid.

"Ducks?"

Sandro smiled. "Yes. Lots of things. What do we do before we eat them?"

"Cook them?"

The man laughed. "And before that?"

"Kill them?"

The man nodded. "We kill them. We kill everything. Rabbit, cattle, fish, seals, ducks, insects, little tiny bacteria, giant whales. Everything. Even each other." The man fell quiet for so long that Oscar wondered if he'd forgotten his new son was even there. Then he whispered, "The difference between us and the other animals is we kill even when we're not hungry. That's our advantage. We are good at killing, because we enjoy it."

Oscar frowned. "Do you enjoy it?"

"Every man does," Sandro replied after a long moment. "You just have to decide how much. Shh, now."

The man motioned for Oscar to follow quietly, then stopped at a large tuft of grass and nodded ahead. Oscar looked. Beneath the fence line was a cutaway of dirt and a dark, almond-shaped hole. The burrow entrance. The east was behind them, and the stars overhead were fading. The man nodded. Oscar lay down. The ground beneath his belly was cold. He felt his heart tripping fast in his chest as he set up the gun. He did what they'd practiced yesterday afternoon: tucking the butt tight against his shoulder, steadying it with his left hand, gently lifting the bolt, drawing it back, and locking it forward with an oiled click. The man leaned over and peered through Oscar's scope, checking. Oscar could smell the oil in the man's hair, and the pleasant scents of soap and tobacco. The man leaned back and nodded.

Oscar squeezed one eye shut. The view through the scope juddered with every heartbeat. In this half-light, the crosshairs were barely visible over the black eye of the set entrance. Oscar's small index finger slipped over the cold metal of the trigger. Thoughts and instructions swirled in his head like bright embers above a bonfire, impossible to control. *Gun, recoil, rabbit, gun, I'm going to shoot a rabbit, steady, breathe in, hold my breath shoot a gun, rabbit—*

"Remember," the man whispered in his ear. "Don't jerk. *Squeeze.*"

Then the man made a noise that sounded like a cartoon kiss, a squeaking through the lips that sounded like an enormous mouse. Silence. Another kiss-squeak.

It arrived. It moved silently into the circle of the scope, the glow in the eastern sky just enough to pick its bark-brown fur out from the dirt behind it. Its ears were tall and its dark eyes glittered as it turned its head this way and that, looking for another rabbit. The man kiss-squeaked again, and the curious hare took another half hop forward.

Oscar hesitated. The crosshairs willed themselves down over the animal's body, dancing wildly.

"So?" came a whisper in his ear.

He squeezed. The gun suddenly coughed—*Ptap!*—and kicked back into his shoulder.

Oscar blinked in surprise, then made himself look through the scope. The rabbit was lying at the mouth of the set, motionless.

He felt his face break into a wide smile, and he turned to the man.

He was nodding, but not smiling.

"You're a natural," he said. "Fun, yes?"

Oscar wondered if he should lie, but he knew the man would see right through it.

"Yes," he said.

"Another?" the man asked.

"Yes."

He watched Daddy retrieve the body, return, then kiss the air again. Another curious animal crept from the burrow. Click-click— Oscar loaded. *Ptap!* The animal fell. This time he did not feel elation.

"Good shot," Sandro said. He fetched that dead rabbit and laid its limp, blood-furred body next to Oscar. Its eyes were dull. "Another?"

"Can we go back now?" Oscar asked.

The man shook his head and pulled something from his pocket. It was a box of cartridges.

"Not till you're sick of killing them."

He made Oscar chamber round after round, kissing the freezing air again and again, and the little brown bodies fell down.

———

Click-clicketty.

Click-clicketty . . . Click-clicketty

Get up.

But he was so cold.

. . . Click-clicketty . . . Click-clicketty . . .

Get up. Got to get up.

Shivering. Lying on the frozen earth, wondering why he could no longer see through the scope. He was so ashamed about crying.

. . . Click-clicketty . . .

Up! Awake!

Through the red sea of his lids, shapes waved like seaweed, or drowned men's arms.

Oscar forced his eyes to grind open.

A skull lay beside him, staring.

Oscar yelled. He flailed and tried to roll away, and struck his nose against the cold metal of the exhaust pipe and rolled back.

It was not a skull but a face. A face with no eyes. Behind each lid was a black, depthless well that fell into nothing. The dead boy's empty eyes widened and he, too, skittered backward, away from the underside of the car and out of sight.

. . . Click-clicketty. On the cold concrete, Oscar's phone buzzed and skittered on tiny grains of dirt. He fumbled for it, grabbing with numb fingers. He saw blood on his nails. His head throbbed, and he was so damned cold.

"Hello?"

"Where are you?" Neve sounded annoyed.

"Uh," he said. "Under the car."

"Broken down?"

He suddenly remembered the sight of that huge, scaly, taloned foot stepping carefully on the concrete, and his skin crawled. He looked around, turning his head carefully so that he wouldn't scrape his raw scalp on the ground. Daylight coming through the high windows showed the walls of the garage, the collection of oil tins and boxes, the twisted curls of the garbage bag that held the broken idol. But there was no sign of the creature.

"I'm okay," he said, and slid toward the side of the car, wincing at the thick, pulsing ache in his head.

Neve continued, "Moechtar came looking for you. Something about a request for a DNA sample from the Roths."

Oscar carefully poked his head out from the underside of the car.

Above him, the high hopper windows were all shut. The chains that secured them closed were tight, each linked securely over its hook. He blinked. "Did Moechtar sound receptive?" he asked.

"No. He wants to know what's going on."

Oscar rolled out from under the car. Everything hurt. As he moved, the scabbed wound on the back of his head opened up and he felt blood creep on his scalp. He stood, and the edges of his vision turned a fragile, sparkling white and a wave of nausea rose from his belly. *Concussion.* His shaking breaths plumed in the cold garage. No giant bird. No scent of dry, dead rot.

"I'll come in later," he said.

"Oscar—"

He ended the call.

He leaned down to look in the car's side mirror. A rivulet of blood crusted on his forehead, and a scratch across one cheek had freshly reopened and wept ruby pearls of blood. He walked painfully to the front of the car and knelt over the formless rumple of the garbage bag. He picked it up.

Shards of terra-cotta tinkled inside. Dream or no dream, the idol had been destroyed.

———

Gelareh Barirani squinted in the doorway. Her hair was an electric frizz, and a little spot of dried saliva rode the corner of her mouth.

"I'm sorry," Oscar said. He'd forgotten that she was a shift worker. "I'll come back."

"It's okay," she replied, pulling her hair back from her face. He watched her eyes rove over his cut and bruised face. He had washed and changed, but combing his blood-matted hair had hurt like hell, and he was sure the job looked less than half done.

"Rough night?"

"Interesting night," he replied.

She stood aside and let him in. "Tea?"

His stomach was still a precarious tightrope, but he nodded. She went to the kitchen and put water on the gas flame.

"I got your better photos," she said. "But I haven't had much time to work on them."

"I have something else, aside from those," he said. "Quite a tricky thing." He lifted the clanking plastic bag and pointed to her tabletop. "May I?"

She nodded.

Oscar set aside the candlesticks and placed the bag in the middle of the table. He folded it down, revealing the dozens of earthenware fragments.

Gelareh sauntered over. "This is not old pottery," she said, inspecting the edges. "Contemporary. Brand-new, I think. Recently broken."

"Yes," Oscar agreed.

She looked at him archly.

"An accident," he said, shivering at the memory of the leathery, sharp-clawed foot that had flung the bag with such purpose into the oilcans.

Gelareh began picking over the potsherds with careful fingers. "So, what was it?"

"I'm not sure. Some kind of idol. About yea high; this round. That's a horn there. It has two horns."

"A bull?" She began sliding pieces together.

"A demon, I think. An owl. Wings. But it's a she."

Gelareh's eyebrows rose a little.

"Breasts?" she asked. "Sex organs?"

"Both. Quite exposed. And a seven-pointed star on her back."

The corners of the researcher's mouth turned down. And suddenly her fingers stopped moving. She leaned closer.

"This is writing." Her fingers traced the patterns that Oscar had mistaken for feathers or scales. She looked up at Oscar. She was smiling. "I can read this," she said.

"You can put it back together? Translate?"

"Transliterate," she murmured, excited. "Again, it's not just one language." She leaned close. "Wait."

"What is it?"

She headed over to the shelves at the side of the room.

"I found something like this on your photographs." She returned with the blowups and tracings. "From the girl. I didn't know if I was reading right, but now I think I am. So, here."

On the paper were small traced ligatures that looked like arrowheads and staves. She pointed.

"This here, it looked to me very much like Akkadian cuneiform."

"Arcadia?"

"Akkadia. The empire before Assyria and Babylonia. About 2400 BC. Akkadian has a small alphabet—fourteen consonants, four vowel sounds." She picked up a shard of pottery and her fingers traced over the wedge-shaped symbols.

"What does it say?"

"*Door*," she replied, delighted. "And that ties in with the vévés, don't you think? And this, I'm almost sure it's Assyrian cuneiform. I could be wrong, but I don't think I am. It says, *Li-lit. Lilith.*"

"*Lilith?*"

"*Lilith*, the first wife of Adam. From the Babylonian Talmud. She bore him devils and spirits."

The water bubbled on the stove. Gelareh handed Oscar the shard and went to carefully measure tea into a pot. He recognized the leaves he had given her.

"The Catholic Church removed references to Lilith when they decided the canon in the fourth century," she continued. "*Lilitû*, in Akkadian, means 'female spirit.' A demon. It also means 'black,' or 'night bird.' Or 'evil,' depending on context. Some scholars interpret the *lilitû* to have come from the desert, like jinni, envious of human women, particularly women giving birth. They commanded disease and lions, fed on children, fucked men in their sleep."

She handed Oscar a steaming cup of tea.

"What does that all have to do with this?" Oscar waved his fingers at the broken idol.

Gelareh shrugged. "At least one scholar believes Lilitû was a single entity, and she was the handmaiden of Inanna. You remember Inanna?"

Oscar nodded. "The queen of heaven."

"Yes, and sister of Ereshkigal." Gelareh sipped her tea, thinking. "So you could draw a connection—a loose one—between Ereshkigal and Lilith. Early depictions were certainly similar."

They fell silent, drinking their tea. Oscar looked at the dozens of broken pieces of pottery, each marked with tiny symbols and arcane letters. And suddenly he knew where he had to go.

He stood. "Will you keep track of how long it takes you?"

She nodded, running a careful finger through the patterned pot-sherds, already lost in the mystery.

He hurried to his car.

————

The late-morning sky looked as fragile and colorless as a dusty lightbulb. Under its dull gray curve, the market tents were like a field of flowers—some fragrantly bright, others faded and drooping, some poisonous-looking. Vendors shouted, children laughed, charcoal fires sizzled, a stricken fiddle stitched the air with notes. Oscar dodged hawkers and the fingers of beggars, and wound his way to the row of tents where the fortune-tellers plied their trade.

Mother Mim had her back to the stall front and was humming an old Rolling Stones song while she made herself a cress sandwich on hard bread. Oscar approached quietly and looked over the items she had laid out on bright-colored cloth. Among the broken watches, the pencil stubs, the incomplete decks of playing cards and dusty Christmas baubles were some small terra-cotta figures, none larger than a sardine tin. Three represented signs of the zodiac—the maiden, the archer, the scorpion; each had been carefully inscribed with words and sigils. Oscar recognized Florica's handiwork.

"The man in the hat," Mim said, her back still to Oscar. "You're back."

"I'm back," he said, impressed.

She turned; again, she wore sunglasses. "You have a distinctive walk," she said, chewing. "A bit slumpy. And you're still wearing your hat," she chided. "Are you looking up, like I told you to?"

Oscar's mouth suddenly went dry as he remembered the rustle of feathers, the tick-tick of sharp claws, the smell of ancient rot. He changed the subject.

"Florica," he said.

Mother Mim stopped chewing.

"These were hers," he said, and rocked the fired-clay scorpion with his fingertip.

"I didn't steal them," she said.

"She had the stall next to yours."

Mim fell quiet, as if trying to divine where this conversation was going. When she spoke again, her voice had a harder edge.

"You're police," she said.

"Yes."

She was silent a long moment.

"Fine, that was her stall. Florica and I looked after each other's things sometimes. When I had to duck off for a wee, et cetera and so on, she'd look after my gear. And I'd look after hers. And sometimes we'd sell each other's stuff. But one day she left"—she took the figure from under Oscar's finger—"and she never came back."

"Did she ever meet someone here?"

"She met lots of someones here—this is a market."

"You know what I'm talking about," Oscar said. "Someone you've connected in your mind to her disappearance."

Emotions played across the blind woman's face, as tiny as pond skaters. Then she nodded. "There was a man here. The day before she never came back. An older man—I didn't care for his voice. It was worn. Worn and tight."

"How old?"

"I didn't see," Mim said tartly. "He was either sixty or more, or he'd done sixty years' worth of nasty."

"What did he talk with her about?"

"Chitchat about these figurines and how she made them."

"And then?"

"Then she asked me to mind her shopfront, and they went into her tent to talk business. I didn't hear, and when they came out and he was gone she went all mum and wouldn't say anything. But she was excited. Money excited."

"And?"

The blind woman shrugged. "And the next market day she didn't come. Haven't heard from her since."

Oscar thought. An older man talking business. Was he the important client that the prostitute Dalmar had been shuffled out Florica's door for—the man who'd commissioned the hideous idol now in pieces on Gelareh's kitchen table? He was sure they were the same man, but his only eyewitness was a blind woman.

"She's dead, isn't she?" Mim asked.

"I think so. Is there anything about him you can tell me?"

Mim grinned. "Like the color of his eyes? Gold tooth and polka-dot pants?"

Oscar nodded. "Thanks."

He turned away.

"He had a ponytail," the woman said.

Oscar hesitated.

"I heard him," she continued. "When he was first talking to Florrie. I heard his shirt wrinkle as his arms went up, and I heard the twing-twang of a rubber band." She mimed pulling back her hair and stretching elastic on opening fingers. "Ponytail."

"Thank you," Oscar repeated.

"Nothing for nothing," Mother Mim said loudly.

Oscar sighed and dug into his pocket. All he had was a gold two-dollar coin. He dropped it on the counter. Her speedy fingers plucked it up.

"For that you get info plus."

"Plus what?"

"Plus more info."

She reached into the fish tank full of skinks and plucked a little brown lizard from the branch in the tank.

"Touch it," she commanded Oscar. "On the head."

He could see the small lizard's pulse throbbing in its neck. He touched its hard, cool skin.

Mim nodded and produced a brass tray and a small, very sharp knife. With practiced fingers she flipped the lizard onto its back and ran the knife from its throat to its anus, just deep enough to penetrate skin and muscle. Then she peeled the creature open and ran a careful finger over its still beating heart, across its tiny pink liver, and through its intestines. Oscar suddenly felt unwell. He saw the animal's heart stop. The woman looked up.

"You'll be dead soon," she said softly.

He left.

———

Back at his car, he jiggled his keys in the door lock. He noticed that his fingers were trembling. When his phone rang, he dropped it. He picked it up, but didn't recognize the number.

He answered, "Mariani."

"Oscar Mariani?"

"Yes."

"This is the Emergency Department at the Royal Hospital. Your father's been brought in. It looks like he's had a heart attack."

ndocarditis. There's an infection in the valve of his heart."
The doctor had a strong South African accent, and "heart"
came out "haaht." She stood beside Oscar at the foot of Sandro Mariani's bed in the crowded Emergency Department cubicle. She
looked very tired. The ED was a quiet storm of subdued panic—the
power was out and the backup generator was giving trouble. Fluorescent lights would gutter and wink out, then surge brightly again; monitors would blank out, then startle awake with warning beeps. Nurses
moved as quickly as Olympic walkers; doctors called for manual sphyg-
momanometers and ran worried fingers through their hair. The corridors were lined with patients on gurneys. Someone was crying loudly
in pain, and a man nursing a bandaged arm soaked in blood yelled that
he'd been left alone here Three Fucking Hours Now.

In contrast to the chaos, Sandro Mariani was still, his papery eyelids
closed. On one thin biceps a pressure cuff hung limply. In the other arm
was a cannula that led to an IV bag. The hairs on Sandro's chest were
nearly white, and among them diagnostic electrodes stuck to his skin
sprouted wires that tentacled back to a monitor where colorful lines
moved as sluggishly as drying creeks. His face was a sickly oyster-gray.
The only sign of life was a light fogging inside the clear plastic oxygen
mask over his mouth and nose.

"We think a piece of the vegetative mass broke off, and that was the
cause of the infarction, not a clot," the doctor continued. "We've put
him on intravenous antibiotics."

"So, a couple of days?" Oscar asked.

"Well, no. Normally, that's a six-week course. But the Doppler scan
wasn't encouraging. To be frank, we don't think his heart will keep

going six weeks, not as it is. It looks like he also has stenosis of the mitral valve, so his heart is having to work very hard to push blood through a narrow gate. There's a risk of heart failure."

"So, surgery," Oscar said.

The doctor nodded. "The cardio surgeon wants to see another CT of the chest, but we're looking at a valve replacement as soon as possible."

"Three Fucking Godless Fucking Hours!" the unseen patient yelled. Nothing wrong with that guy's heart, Oscar thought.

"How bad was the heart attack?" he asked.

"Well, time will tell." She nodded down at Sandro's hands. "We were initially worried about that, thought it might have been some kind of Parkinsonian symptom presenting."

Oscar saw that both of Sandro's thin-fingered, big-knuckled hands cupped empty air, as if they were holding something. Something the size of an infant.

"That's nothing to fix," Oscar said quietly. He glanced up and saw that the doctor was looking at him.

"Would you like us to check you over?" she asked, her eyes roaming over his bruised face and the clots of blood still in his hair.

Oscar shook his head. "When will surgery be scheduled?"

"The medical team will meet tomorrow."

"I'll check in later, then."

The doctor nodded good-bye and then headed toward the glassed-off central offices for another patient file.

———

He stepped out into a long corridor punctuated by overhead signs. Every second strip light was off, so the effect of light and shadow was like being inside a tiger's tail. Far down the corridor, two doctors conversed, and an orderly wheeled a canvas cart full of laundry. Nearer, a large man and a thin woman sat silently on plastic chairs. The dead boy stood beside the stairwell, watching Oscar expectantly.

Oscar didn't move. Something was awry. He didn't know what, but he felt it: something had changed the instant he stepped into the passageway, something subtle. Not the dead boy, something else. He'd missed it, but he felt its tiny wake.

Oscar stood still and forced his eyes to relax. He stopped himself from probing the corners and the shadows and simply let his eyes flow over the hallway. It was a trick he'd learned hunting rabbits—they were nearly impossible to spot in the semidarkness of morning, their brown fur almost invisible in the dry grass. He had taught himself to lie still and simply wait for an ear to twitch or a tiny, glossy eye to suddenly appear between the grass leaves. He watched and waited. The doctors parted and went separate ways. The orderly went through double doors. An orderly wheeled a man wearing an oxygen mask out of Outpatients. A flicker of movement, reflected in a framed print twenty paces down.

Oscar's eyes fixed on the picture.

It was a print of stylized flowers and hung on the passage wall next to a map of the wing and a fire alarm and nearly opposite an adjoining corridor.

Oscar walked toward it. The overhead sign at the junction read ATRIUM—CRITICAL CARE—MEDICAL IMAGING. He walked faster. More movement in the reflecting glass, diminishing now.

Down the adjoining passage, a figure was walking away. It was a girl. She wore a baggy jumper, a skirt, black stockings, green boots. Her hair was short. It was the young woman from Elverly, the caregiver who had calmed Megan.

"Zoe," Oscar called, remembering her name.

She didn't seem to hear. Her shoulders hunched and she walked faster.

"Zoe!"

She turned a corner.

Oscar jogged. By the time he reached the corridor she was halfway down the adjoining passage, walking even faster. Oscar ran. She cast a glimpse behind her but didn't slow. Her boot steps were sharp on the vinyl floor. Beside her, two plastic sheet doors opened and a woman with a catering trolley backed into the corridor. Zoe slipped through the open doors. Oscar blundered into the cart and the caterer swore in a language he didn't understand.

The kitchen staff, in white aprons and puffed plastic caps, turned only bored glances toward the darting, slim woman and the puffing, untidy man slowly gaining on her. Zoe's boots had inch-thick soles and were not made for running. She slammed through another set of translucent plastic doors into gloom. Oscar lifted his knees into a sprint. His head throbbed with every footfall.

This murkier passage was choked like a diseased artery with dusty IV stands, broken gurneys, dull-eyed monitors, and lame wheelchairs. A single light flickered over a patch of floor before a service lift; opposite the elevator were two doors: a stairwell and an electrical service room. Oscar opened the stairwell door and listened. Boot steps echoed, but it was impossible to tell whether from above or below.

A door slammed, definitely below him. He took the stairs three at a time, passing one door and reaching a second one at the bottom of the stairwell. He looked down at a puddle of dank, oily water there—faint ripples were dying on its surface. He pulled open the door.

Another passageway. A door on the left, MAINTENANCE STAFF ONLY, locked. Two doors on the right: one unsigned, the other labeled HYDRO-THERAPY. He opened it.

She was on the opposite side of a small, empty swimming pool with wide steps and stainless-steel rails. A single downlight shone on the circular cavity and bounced up off gray tiles. Twin doors were behind her, and through the tiny gap between them he caught a glimpse of chain. She held a small sharp knife in front of her, as an angler would hold his rod. Her chest rose and fell as she panted between set teeth. Her pale, sharp cheeks were coloring pink and her eyes sparked green.

"You followed me," Oscar said. He, too, was panting.

She said nothing, but looked left and right. As long as he stood there at the door, she could not leave. Not without using the knife.

"Put it away," he said. "I'm not going to hurt you."

She took a step to her left, to see if he would take one to his right. When he didn't move, she retreated, keeping the pool between them.

"I said, I won't hurt you."

She laughed, a harsh and bitter gallop in the tiled room.

"You're awesome, Mariani," she whispered. "You sound just like a real cop."

Zoe stepped to her right again, but this time the knife led the way. When Oscar didn't move, she stopped.

"How long have you been trailing me? Since Elverly?"

She licked her lips. They were painted pale pink to match her skin. He could see her hands shaking.

"Cops never think they can be followed," she said.

"Congratulations."

Oscar looked her over. The baggy sweater hid a slight figure. The boots were almost comically large. Her nails were short but clean. Clever hands. The blade was a double-edged boot knife, a serious little thing that could stab and slice. He thought he could defend himself, but in this half-light a scuffle could easily lead to a lost eye. At least he was in a hospital.

"I don't get it," he said. "You follow me, then you pull a knife on me. What do you want?"

She inclined her head—let's not be children about this.

He continued, "You're not leaving till you talk."

She took a step toward him. Her pupils were wide, and he could see the pulse racing on the side of her white throat.

"Sides," she said. "I want to know the sides."

He frowned. He had no idea what she was talking about. She took another step toward him. "Look," he said, "if you know something—"

The knife slit the air just a centimeter in front of his face.

"You stay away," she hissed. "I'm not ending up like Penny and the others."

Oscar felt strings pull tight in his stomach.

"Others? What others?"

Zoe froze. Her eyes narrowed, then the corners of her mouth turned down.

"Don't fucking bullshit me."

"What others, Zoe? Other children?"

Every pore of her pretty face seemed to tighten, and her eyes flickered over him with the intensity of a surgical light. And widened, just a little.

"Oh, God," she whispered, her voice trembling. "You really don't know." She pushed past him.

"Wait." He grabbed at her arm.

The knife whipped down and a bee sting of pain fired on his knuckle; a ruby pearl welled. As he pulled back his hand, she kicked the flesh of his left calf and bright agony flared like the mother of all cramps. He bent to the pain.

She opened the door and ran.

Now he knew why she wore boots.

———

He limped quickly to his car. This case was waging a war of attrition on his body. So far, he had a lot of wounds in exchange for very few leads. He phoned his own office desk, ready to ask Neve for help.

A male voice answered. "Yo?"

"Foley?" Oscar said. "Why are you answering our phone?"

"Neve's in the loo."

Oscar frowned. "But it only rang once. Are you in her chair?" There was a long, awkward silence. "Never mind," Oscar continued. "Can you log on to Prophet?"

"I'll try," Foley said. There was a tapping of fat fingers. "Hey, you know Moechtar's looking for you?"

"I heard."

On the street, Oscar saw a parking officer keying his car's license plate into a handheld device. He limped faster.

Foley whistled, waiting for Prophet. "So are you investigating something?"

"Yes."

"So me looking now, this is part of an investigation?"

"Yes."

"Sweet. Okay, we're on. Better hurry while Loss is playing ball."

"Missing Persons."

More tapping. Oscar arrived at his car. He cleared his throat. When the parking officer turned, Oscar showed his ID. The parking officer inspected the badge, nodded, and put the ticket under his wiper.

"Hey," Oscar said. "I'm a cop."

The officer pointed to the sign. "Emergency Vehicles Only. Sorry."

"It's a cop car!"

The officer gave Oscar's tired sedan a sympathetic look, then went to the next vehicle.

"I'm on," Foley said.

"Look up Elverly House."

"Elderly?"

Oscar pulled the ticket out from under his wiper and walked back to the parking officer.

"Elverly. With a *v*."

"Dates?"

"Let's try the last eight weeks."

The parking officer looked up, annoyed. "No returns, mate."

Oscar took his phone from his ear and snapped a photograph of the parking officer and his name badge.

"Hey, Jesus, what the hell?"

"If I get pinged," Oscar said, tucking the ticket in the officer's shirt pocket, "I'm coming to find you."

"Mariani!" Foley called.

Oscar left the parking officer holding the ticket, the scales in the man's mind teetering unpleasantly. "What?"

"Ah, fucksticks, Prophet's just crashed," Foley said. "But there were three kids missing."

Oscar felt his throat tighten. Three?

"Did you write them down?" he asked. Another awkward silence. "Okay, listen—"

"Wait, no, wait!" Foley said, and Oscar could almost hear him concentrating. "Three, all girls. One was Penelope. Penelope something. And one's surname was White, something White. Fiona? Faye?"

"And the third?"

"Tara something. No, not Tara. Taryn."

———

What drew Oscar's attention was Taryn Lymbery's shoes. Sneakers, scuffed but neat, matching in style but one notably smaller than the other. They sat at the bottom of the small wardrobe under a hanging bouquet of dresses.

"Intellectually disabled," Oscar said.

"That's right," Leslie Chalk said softly. She stood in the doorway, stiffly upright and motionless. Her hair and clothes were impeccably neat, but the shadows under her eyes were as dark as bruises. "From birth. Fetal alcohol syndrome, we think, though Taryn never knew her mother."

Oscar closed the wardrobe. "When did you notice she was gone?"

"This morning." Chalk's smile was tense and fragile. "Breakfast time. Taryn would never miss breakfast. She loved breakfast."

On a chest of drawers as compact as the wardrobe was a photo of Taryn Lymbery holding a lamb at a zoo. She looked about twelve in the photograph, which, Chalk had told him, was a little more than three years old. Taryn's hair was a dirty blonde, her glasses thick, her eyes a little closely set, her smile wide and genuine. In the photograph, she cuddled the lamb with unreserved delight. Oscar looked over the rest of the room. Her bed was rumpled, but the single bed opposite was neatly made.

"And her roommate?"

"Becky sleeps like the dead." Chalk rubbed her hands together. "We searched the grounds. I went to the train station and showed the stationmaster her photo. Her backpack is gone. Underwear. Her good pair of shoes."

Oscar opened the top drawer. A tiny harvest of balled socks and underpants, a threadbare training bra. "Have you contacted her family?" he asked.

Chalk nodded. "I rang her aunt in Perth. She's never visited. She needed some reminding that Taryn even existed."

Oscar went to the barred window.

"How did she get out?"

Chalk sighed. "Every child here with mental capacity knows the keypad code for the front door. We change it each week, but as soon as one spies a staff member using it, the jungle drums get it around."

In the next drawer, summer clothes, mostly untouched. In the bottommost he found a small wooden box. Inside was a broken seashell and a small floral printed envelope with no card or letter inside. A treasure box without treasure.

"Do you think she ran away?" Oscar asked.

Chalk shrugged. "I thought she was happy enough. Of all the girls here, she seemed most content. But when they reach an age, they all get notions, to visit a boyfriend or girlfriend or the movies or the beach."

"Tell me about Frances White."

He opened the other file he'd requested from Chalk's office. The single photograph attached was of a tall, unnaturally thin girl with long features and a toothy, awkward smile.

"Frances." Chalk smiled fondly at the picture. "What a lovely girl. A hair-trigger temper, but a dear thing."

"Same deal?"

"Absconded in the night? Yes."

Oscar looked between the bars out onto the gloomy greenery. He couldn't blame anyone for wanting to escape these small rooms and shadowy halls.

"Three kids in a month?"

He turned back to Chalk. All her muscles were tight with tension.

"I don't like it any more than you do, Detective."

As he watched her, she folded her arms tightly around herself. It was clear that she wanted him to go. Yet she waved anxious fingers at the window. "Can you get someone here to take fingerprints, all that stuff? The officers this morning weren't too enthusiastic."

Oscar shook his head. "Scenes of Crime won't come out for a run-away that's only just logged with Missing Persons. Unless there are signs of abduction, no one will do anything till Taryn's been gone twenty-four hours."

"Can't you pull some strings?"

Oscar felt a blush of embarrassment crawl up his neck. "Not really."

"Oh," Chalk said. "I see." He saw something flicker behind her eyes, but it was gone in an instant. She frowned at him. "Are you the only officer taking these disappearances seriously?"

Oscar didn't want to tell her the truth. He met her stare until she looked away.

"I'm sorry," she said. She didn't sound sorry, though.

"Who was on shift last night?" he asked.

The answer came as no surprise. "Lauralie Kenny was in here—it was Lauralie who did the head count this morning. And over in B-Block was Zoe. Zoe Trucek."

————

Lauralie Kenny was a big girl whose whole soft body shook as she cried. Elverly's break room was a section of side-entry vestibule that had been sheeted in with fibrous cement and frosted glass. There were two chairs, a round timber table, and a sink with a bench just wide enough for a toaster and a breadbox. A row of timber lockers ran along the old wall to the far end of the room, where tall windows looked out onto the rambling grounds.

"I couldn't help it," Lauralie said, sniffing back snot. "I din' mean to. I come in here just for a tea. It was late. I just put my head down for a second, I swear."

She dissolved into another silent quake of tears.

Oscar put away his notebook. "How long were you asleep?"

Lauralie wiped her eyes and licked her large, formless lips. "Two and a ha . . . two and a ha-ha . . ."

Oscar nodded; he got the picture. Two and a half hours: a wide window of opportunity for any would-be abductors. If every coherent child in the place knew the access code, it wouldn't have been hard to bribe it out of one with a little gift. He rubbed his hand—of all the wounds on his head and body, the one that hurt most was the spot where Zoe had nicked him with her knife. Why a knife? What was she afraid of?

He looked over his shoulder at Chalk.

"I need Zoe Trucek's home address."

———

The house was empty: a gutted shell with broken windows, no furniture, strange unsavory stains, and reeking of urine from a dozen species. Ceilings sagged and wall sheeting had been kicked in. The toilet pedestal had been smashed off its moorings and sat like a broken tooth in a room that smelled of shit and dead things.

Walking back outside, Oscar called Elverly. He got the crying girl, Lauralie, and asked when Zoe Trucek was next on shift. The day after tomorrow. Was there a phone number for her on file? No. He ended the call.

A false address, and no phone number. His most interesting lead could be anywhere in this city of a million citizens.

Chapter 19

Three disabled girls gone from Elverly in a month.

Oscar walked up the fire-escape stairs from the headquarters basement garage against a nearly silent tide of public servants all taking the quickest route down to the ground floor and out into the late afternoon.

Three. He could almost believe it was a sad coincidence were he not convinced that the remains in Kannis's cold room were one of the missing, and were one of Elverly's caregivers not following him. He had to find Zoe.

He climbed straight up to the ninth floor and along the plush carpets to Moechtar's office, then pulled off his hat and knocked.

The inspector was behind his large desk, packing up papers, ready to go home. He looked up at Oscar through doll-like eyes, with no hint of emotion.

"Detective. You've been out."

"Yes, sir."

Moechtar checked his watch and decided he had a moment. He sat and flipped through the contents of his in-tray. "I have your request for DNA samples."

"Yes, sir. Carole and Paul Roth. I believe the Jane Doe we pulled from the sewage plant is their daughter."

Moechtar nodded. "This requires the signature of the coroner or an acting coroner."

Oscar wasn't sure where this was going. "I believe so, sir."

"When I couldn't raise you, I took the liberty of ringing Forensic Services to see if we couldn't find a"—Moechtar paused—"less intrusive way of identifying the cadaver. Forensic Services said they don't have that cadaver."

"Someone fast-tracked it to the crematorium," Oscar said. "I have it."

Moechtar watched Oscar with a more fixed attention now. Not exactly interested but with a distinct lack of uninterest.

"Someone at the morgue made a mistake?"

"I don't think so, sir. The body was signed for destruction by a state pathologist named Tetlow. He left town the same morning. Bribed or threatened, I don't know, but that's why I didn't return the body to the morgue."

Moechtar stared at him for an unsettlingly long time. "Why haven't you told me any of this?"

"I wanted to have something firmer for you first, sir."

Moechtar rubbed a manicured thumbnail thoughtfully.

"You say you have the girl's body."

"Yes, sir. Quite safe."

"And it's against this body you want to compare samples from the Roths?"

"Just to identify her, sir. They're not suspects yet."

Moechtar nodded and fixed his eyes on Oscar. "The cadaver has to go back."

Oscar blinked. "I don't trust—"

"It *has* to go back. I can't approach the coroner and ask for his name on a court order if proper process isn't being observed." A light frown line appeared on Moechtar's smooth forehead. "Already this is messy. Very, very messy."

"Sir—"

"We'll have to look into what happened, how that body was released prematurely. But, Oscar, I want you to return that body. I'm not actioning this until you do."

Moechtar put the form back in his in-tray and looked up at him, as if inviting argument.

"Yes, sir," Oscar said quietly.

Moechtar checked his watch and stood to put on his coat. He kept his back to Oscar, who realized that he had been dismissed.

———

Oscar returned to the Industrial Relations floor. Neve had tidied most of the files away into an archive box. Only a handful of folders remained on the desk. She was typing, and didn't look up when he sat beside her.

"Finished?" he asked.

"Almost. Another hour."

"How does it look?"

Neve stopped typing. She stared at the screen a long moment before turning to look at him. "Have you signed my transfer?"

Oscar opened his mouth, ready with another excuse, but he simply nodded and reached into his pocket. He pulled the form from the envelope, flattened it, and signed and dated the bottom corner.

"Thank you," she said quietly, taking the form.

They sat in silence a while. On the far side of the room, the last of the public servants was collecting her lunchbox from a fridge. At the door, the woman caught Oscar's eye and signaled whether she should turn off the lights. Oscar nodded, and two-thirds of the lights flicked off.

"You'll miss your mate Foley," he said. "Leaving will disrupt his plans to get you on a trans-Asia love holiday."

Neve smiled, but it was a sad expression. She looked up at Oscar. "You look like a hatful of shit, boss. If you're getting into fights, I wish you'd let me know. What have you done here?"

She gently took his fingers and turned the cut knuckle to the light. Her hands were warm.

"New interrogation technique," he said. "I let people cut me and see what they have to say about it."

She clicked her tongue disapprovingly. "You should look after these."

She fell silent, and let go of his fingers.

He thought about telling her about the idol he'd found in the ashes of the old brothel, and about the clawed creature in the garage. But she was leaving. The Barelies' days were numbered. Neve had her transfer.

She's safe now.

Neve chewed the inside of her cheek, and they both fell silent again. Then she looked up.

"You see Moechtar?"

Oscar nodded. "Wants me to take the body back."

"What if she goes missing again?"

He shrugged. "I don't think I'm going to get this solved before Friday.

And if that report"—he nodded at the document on her screen—"is as bad as your face says it is . . ."

His shoulders rose and fell again. He didn't need to finish: *it will never get solved.*

Neve frowned. "Is there another way to identify her?"

Oscar rubbed his face. It hurt, so he stopped. "I checked Elverly's records—she doesn't seem to have had a dental visit for years. And her teeth look fine, so I think no joy there."

"Cerebral palsy?" Neve murmured. Oscar nodded, and she asked, "Where did they diagnose that?"

Oscar blinked. Then he jumped forward. Neve jerked back, but he still managed to land a kiss on her cheek. "Brilliant."

He picked up the phone and gestured for the White Pages. Neve handed him the book while he got an outside line. He dialed the hospital.

"Patient Records, police inquiry."

A few minutes later, he had a promise from the records department that they would send through a summary sheet for Penelope Adeline Roth to the Barelies' fax number.

He hung up the phone and grinned at Neve, but there were no words in his mouth.

"Fancy this," she said eventually, and touched the transfer request with a tentative finger. "Just as you're getting into fights and I'm coming up with decent ideas."

He grinned.

Neve bit her lip and fiddled nervously with the mouse. A new expression slid across her face like a soft shadow. She spoke quietly: "Things have changed a lot. You know. In the last three years."

"Yes," he agreed.

"With the church, I mean," she continued. "The Catholic Church." Her ears started to color. "You know?"

"Sure," he said, a little confused.

"Divorce. In these new times. We're not so bad."

Oscar frowned, lost. "But you're not married."

Neve's blush deepened. "I'm not talking about me." She swiveled in her chair, back to the monitor. "I have to finish this."

He stared, stock-still, unsure.

She nodded for him to leave. "Go on. I'll call you if the fax comes."

"Okay."

He left, baffled.

———

Oscar drove home through traffic that was unsettlingly light. The western horizon had a fireside glow and, for the second night in a row, clear skies rode above him. Waiting at a working set of lights, he stopped and thumbed in the number of the hospital's cardiology wing. The medical team had seen his father, but there was nothing on the chart about surgery time. The ward receptionist took his number and promised to call straight back. The light changed, and he accelerated.

Above the dead streetlights, the stars shone. Among the winking dots of ice white, a regular flash of red—a passenger jet. Its blink-blink-blink reminded Oscar of a task left unfinished, but he couldn't think what. He watched the plane's silent passage through the sky. For a moment, it seemed as if the world could return to normal. Could *be* normal.

Oscar's phone rang. He didn't recognize the number and assumed it was the hospital calling with the surgery details.

"Mariani," he answered. "When will it be?"

A woman responded, "When will what be, Detective?"

It took him a moment to recognize the voice.

"Ms. Chaume," he said. "I was expecting someone else."

She was silent for such a long moment that he wondered if she was, too.

"We parted in quite a hurry the other day," she said. "Odd circumstances."

"The parting? Or the meeting?" he asked. He wondered why she was calling him. If she was after a favor, she'd soon discover—as Leslie Chalk had—how small his sphere of influence was.

"Both, perhaps," Chaume said, and he could hear a smile in her voice. "What are you doing tonight?"

Oscar felt his jaw tighten. He wasn't about to turn around and go back into the office to run some trivial errand for a rich girl who'd just met her first policeman. Still, there was a part of him that would do so eagerly. He remembered her slow, promising smile.

"I'm quite busy," he said.

"Ah." Again, he wondered if he'd lost her. Then she spoke and again he heard that smile in her voice. "Well, if you become less busy I'm having a get-together at my house this evening. It is black tie, I'm afraid, and rather short notice. Still, if you find yourself at a loose end . . ."

It was Oscar's turn to fall momentarily silent.

"Chislehurst is the property name," Chaume continued. "On Connaught Road."

"I know it."

"From eight."

Oscar found himself nodding. "Right."

He was left holding a silent phone.

No. The world was not normal at all.

———————

The front porch of his house was purple shadow, the sky above the house the color of cold, dark wine. He opened the door and called for Sisyphus. The cat didn't appear. He went inside, took off his jacket and holster, lit the lantern and put water on the stove. He found himself wondering what sort of a state his suit was in.

Oscar opened the window and heard the sounds of digging in his backyard.

He loosened his pistol from his holster and slipped quietly out the front door and down the narrow side of the house through shadows pitch-black and cave-cold.

A figure was in his vegetable patch, driving a pitchfork into the soil with an expert gardener's easy strokes: levering, loosening clumps of rogue grass, batting them against the metal tines to reclaim the soil, and tossing the weeds into a stack. Sisyphus sat watching the man curiously. Oscar approached silently and thumbed back the hammer of the semiauto with a distinctive click.

"Now that's hardly necessary, Mariani," Haig said, pushing the fork in again. "I'm freeing your okra beans, not stealing them."

Oscar moved forward, his finger still on the trigger guard. Haig had created a prodigious pile of grass and weeds. His jacket hung on a spade driven into the ground three feet or so away.

"Besides," Haig continued, "what are you going to do with an empty pistol? Beat me?" He stopped and straightened. Despite the work he'd done, he looked hardly strained. "Me, I'd put my money on the man with the pitchfork. Or the man with the friend."

Oscar looked around.

Under the shadow of the pawpaw tree near the back fence, Detective Kace leaned against the bricks of the old incinerator. All he could see of her face was the two bright glints of her eyes.

Oscar felt his heart hammer faster. He looked back to Haig. "What are you doing here?"

"Helping." Haig grinned, and stepped easily out of the garden. He dusted his hands together and grabbed the pitchfork again. "Always helping."

With no tie and rolled sleeves, Haig still seemed polished and impregnable. It wasn't the uniform that made him this way; it was the man himself. Haig made the plain clothes look lean and efficient, as if they weren't clothes at all but a pelt. He lowered himself easily to sit on the garden bed's edge; when Sissy came up to him, he scratched behind the cat's ragged ears. His other hand rested lightly on the haft of the fork. He looked up at the sky.

" 'I come into a region where is nothing that can give light.' Do you know Dante?" he asked. *Il Sommo Poeta*. Am I saying that right?"

Oscar noticed that Kace hadn't moved. Business was yet to be done.

"I wouldn't know. I'm not Italian."

Haig rolled his eyes. "Oh, I know. You were adopted. I know you ran away from home at fifteen to try and find your real parents, then slunk home to Sandro and Vedetta, poor things. They did have a child, did you know? A boy. Only lived two days."

Oscar was shaken. His mother had told him that she and Sandro had been unable to conceive. There was no grave for an infant. Yet into his mind sprang the recent memory of his father's sleeping hands clutching an invisible infant. "You're a wealth of information," he said, fighting to keep his voice even.

Haig shrugged. "You know, you remind me of Dante, Mariani. He was a journeyman, like you. A soldier, a poet, a diplomat—"

"And an exile," Oscar finished.

Haig gave a pleased nod. "Yes! Poor Dante. Never seemed to know which side to choose."

Oscar's heart cantered. This was the second mention today of sides, and for the second time he felt lost and stupid.

"What are you doing here?" Oscar repeated.

Haig leaned, picked a sprig of mint, rolled it between a tough thumb and fingers and sniffed them. "I know you don't think much of me, Mariani."

"Why do you care what I think?" Oscar asked.

Haig seemed to consider this. Overhead, a silent armada of black-winged flying foxes arced through the evening sky. "There are times I am doing something, and suddenly, of all the people I know or have known, who comes into my mind? Oscar Mariani!" Haig laughed. "And I wonder: what have I done to upset him? I mean, Mariani knows me so *well*. He and I are closer than most friends. He's been inside my personnel folder, inside my house, even inside my telephone. Why doesn't he like me?" Haig turned to the female detective. "You like me, don't you, Kace?"

Kace was silent a moment, then replied, "You have your moments."

"See?" Haig said. "And I treat her like shit. Much worse than I ever treated you."

Oscar could see that despite Haig's cheerful demeanor his stare was hard: it was focused on Oscar like a gem cutter's, about to strike a blow that would save or destroy a rough diamond.

"You're corrupt," Oscar said. "You have people killed. And you don't answer questions."

Haig became silent and still. "You could only prove one of those," he said quietly.

Oscar could see that the knuckles of Haig's hand that gripped the pitchfork had become almost white. A man as strong as Haig could throw the tool like a javelin. There was no need for Kace.

"There's a party tonight, Mariani. You've been invited."

Oscar blinked.

"What's it to you?"

"Don't go."

With that, Haig stood. In one easy move, he lifted the fork and threw it into the ground just a handspan from Oscar's toes. He pulled on his jacket.

"Remember your Dante," Haig said, walking up the side of the house and disappearing into shadow. "'No one thinks of how much blood it costs.'"

Kace pushed gracefully off the incinerator to follow Haig. As she passed Oscar, she leaned toward him and whispered, "Better load your gun."

Then Oscar was alone.

His legs were trembling.

————

The water on the gas ring was steaming. Oscar washed. Then, naked and shivering, he paced.

Don't go.

Fucking Haig. In his own backyard!

Don't go.

Warning him off. Telling him what to do.

Don't go.

Oscar went to the bedroom and flung open his wardrobe to look for his suit.

Chapter 20

Chislehurst was a beacon, a sarsen placed high to touch the sky, and lit from within by a thousand warm lights. It perched at the very top of the Heights, its five manicured acres commanding views in all directions—or perhaps commanding all its surrounds to look upon it. Oscar steered the car between massive bluestone gateposts. The driveway was a silver river twinkling with pleasure craft—two dozen limousines and a similar number of sports cars. At its terminus, the drive opened and curved under a wide portico with white columns that glistened like icicles.

Chislehurst was built when the state itself had been just five years old and boasted a mere sixty thousand citizens. The building, commissioned by an English auctioneer who had made his fortune selling land for the growing river city, was neither an Edwardian triumph nor a bastard child; it was its own unique self. It looked from the outside like a strong stone beast, its tower complete with crenellations and narrow, arched windows.

Oscar parked the old sedan behind a long dark-blue Mercedes, locked it, and chuckled at the prospect of a thief choosing it over anything else parked on the drive. He buttoned his black suit jacket against the cold and stepped onto a path of neatly swept flagstones that climbed alongside the drive toward the mansion's entrance.

If driving into the Heights had been a step back in time for Oscar, walking into the wide marble hallway of Chislehurst was a plunging leap. He felt as if he had suddenly stepped from a long, wearying train trip onto a platform as solid as rock, at once alien and familiar and utterly, achingly beautiful. The floors of the hallway were marble in burnished white and warm black. The walls were paneled in silky oak and walnut, and were so high and set so far apart they gave the sense not of walking within a house but of strolling through a wooded glade across a forest floor dappled with new snow and shadow.

Oscar stopped in the entry vestibule. On one wall was a hall stand big enough for King's College, and two dozen umbrellas were slotted neatly into it like carbines.

"Yes, sir?"

A tuxedoed man, as wide as a commercial oven, stood behind a timber lectern that looked perilously threatened by the weight of his well-manicured hands.

"Oscar Mariani."

The giant opened the leather-bound book and checked names on the cream pages.

"Very good, Mr. Mariani. May I offer you a tie?"

The man placed on the lectern a small wooden box, which he opened. Inside were several bow ties—fixed-length blacks and ready-tieds.

Oscar took one of the ready-tieds and clipped it under his white collar. He wondered if the tie detracted from the scabbing wounds on his face. The giant was no guide: he nodded as if he'd never seen a more pleasing example of the urbane gentleman and opened one of the beveled-glass-and-waxed-timber doors leading within. Music swelled, riding on waves of laughter and a drawing undertow of warm conversation. Oscar stepped inside.

The ballroom was a huge oval a hundred and thirty feet long. Chandeliers depended from vertiginously high ceilings, and a thousand tiny flames set in candelabra of silver and crystal glowed like new copper coins tossed into the air of summer sunlight. This shifting light, born a thousand times and reflected a thousand times more in crystal and cut glass and polished silver, seemed to move with the music. The ballroom's circumference was twelve sections of thirteen-foot-high folding doors, now neatly stacked away in banks retained by rods of polished brass. Above this perimeter and the mezzanine and an oval balcony floor was the delicate white sky of the vaulting domed ceiling. Twin staircases, set on opposite sides of the vast room, rose like the living curves of ox horns to a mezzanine floor held aloft, it seemed, by delicately curling balustrades as fine as wire. And through this forest hall of marble and wood and the shifting, golden air moved people. Men in black tuxedos and crisp white shirts moved at ease, looked for all the world like the marble floor had sprung upward into mirror-shiny shoes and sharply creased trousers; women glided in gowns of silk charmeuse, satin more liquid than water, velvet so dark and rich it drew the light and held it like a warm secret.

Oscar moved through the crowd like a ghost. He tried to catalog the faces but was quickly overwhelmed. A pretty girl in a black-and-white waiter's uniform offered a tray of drinks, and he took a glass of scotch. He followed the lush patterns in the mosaic marble floor to the broad master staircase. Guests parked in groups on the maroon carpet. He followed the smooth rail up to the next floor and spotted a gap near Nouveau balusters that gave him a vantage from which to watch the elegantly moving sea of people below. In the center of the room hung a chandelier as large and brilliant as a firework frozen in ice.

He sipped the excellent scotch, and the alcohol bloomed in his stomach. His phone rang. It was his own desk number.

"Neve?"

"Where are you?" she asked. "I hear music."

"Party."

Her tone cooled. "Really." Then her words came quickly, eagerly. "The fax came through. From the hospital. Penny Roth's record."

"And?"

Neve couldn't hide the grin in her voice. "She had a tenotomy when she was eleven. Some people with cerebral palsy, their muscles tighten and shrink. The tendons are cut to allow the muscles to stretch. That's the surgery she had."

"Where?"

"Both hips."

Oscar felt stupidly excited. "Scars?"

"Yes," Neve said. "It should leave a tiny scar."

Oscar felt himself smile. The distinct scar from this kind of specific surgery would eliminate almost all doubt that the Jane Doe in Kannis's cold room was Penny Roth. Something very solid to present to Moechtar.

Neve was animated. "I know her right hip was messed up, but we should go look at her left."

"We'll go in the morning."

"Kannis's isn't far, I can go tonight—"

"No," Oscar warned. The thought of Haig making himself at home in Oscar's backyard chilled him. Haig had known about this party, and Oscar's invitation. Maybe he had the Barelies' line tapped, too. "Just do nothing. We'll go in the morning."

He slipped the phone into his pocket. He felt the smile still on his face. There was hope yet. He drained his scotch and took another off a passing tray.

He moored himself to the balcony rail. Chaume wanted him here. Haig wanted him to stay away. Neither made sense. His eyes, adjusting to the height and to the impossible, golden light, began to work and he started to search for her tall form and dark hair. Among the crowd, he began to recognize faces: local celebrities, entrepreneurs, high-level public servants, patrons of the arts.

There was the state treasurer, his smile as glossy as his scalp, laughing with the minister for economic development. And there was a former fashion model who had risen from the ashes of a universally maligned music career to marry a newspaper proprietor who owned half of Cadogan Square, London. And there, behind a fountain of lilies, was the daughter of a mining magnate who had inherited her father's figure and his ruthlessness, yet had several journalists trapped in orbit. There alone was the jaundice-yellow owner of an island resort pouring a doleful stare at his much younger wife as she chatted with a catwalk-handsome waiter. And there, in a far corner near a marble bust that might have been Hadrian or Nellie Melba, were three figures that caught and held Oscar's eye. One because Oscar passed his portrait every time he used the toilets on the fourth floor at police headquarters; the other two because he'd met them two days ago: the police commissioner was talking with Paul and Carole Roth.

Paul was laughing at something the commissioner said, while Carole stared into her wineglass as if it held a drowned spider. Still, she downed its contents in a swallow, whispered something to Paul that killed his smile like a bullet, and walked away through the crowd. Roth watched her go for a tenuous moment, then returned his attention to the commissioner.

Oscar threaded quickly among the guests, excusing himself, moving as quickly as he could toward the stairs. Carole drifted like a boat pushed and drawn on flood currents. On the ballroom level, visibility dropped to a few arm's lengths. Ahead, he caught a glimpse of blue that might be Carole Roth or two dozen other women. Guests eddied around a table as long as a yacht holding bowl upon bowl of ice dotted with crystal punnets of glossy black caviar and blood-red Ikura. Ahead, he heard Carole's voice, but her words were indistinct. He followed it like a scent. He did a short two-step with a stout man heading for the food, then slipped past the folded doors and into the hall. And stopped, eyes scanning.

"Oscar?"

Another familiar voice, directly behind him. He turned.

Sabine was frowning, inspecting him with the careful stare of a dog owner whose pet has suddenly revealed that he can play "Chopsticks."

"What are you doing here?" she asked.

"I couldn't say," he replied, and cast his gaze through the tight press of black wool and satin.

"Do you know Anne Chaume?" Sabine's eyes narrowed.

"She invited me."

"Huh." Sabine's frown deepened, and her eyes ran over his beaten face. "Are you okay?"

"I'm sorry, Sabby, but I really have to—"

"Hi, Oscar."

Another voice. Oscar turned. Lambert Powter arrived holding two drinks.

"Lambert. Fantastic. I'll catch you both soon."

Oscar swiveled and slid away, leaving Sabine's disconcerted stare behind him.

He walked, riding crisscrossing streams of strangers' words and laughter, listening for Carole Roth's voice. The hallway rounded a corner, became narrower. Groups thinned to couples, couples gave way to waiters.

Oscar gritted his teeth. He'd lost her.

"Psst."

Oscar turned.

Off the hallway was a boothlike alcove, half paneled in modesty glass and holding two leather-padded bench seats. An old hand-crank telephone with a brass-edged receiver hung on the wall. Carole Roth sat primly out of sight, with just her legs visible.

He slipped in and sat opposite her.

"No one actually says, 'Psst,' Mrs. Roth."

"Don't sit down," she hissed. "I saw you following me. I'm sure other people could, too."

"Relax," he said. "We're just guests, chatting."

"You dress like a detective, not a guest." In the two days since he'd seen her, Carole Roth's eyes had sunk farther back into her skull. Her cheekbones seemed more angular, the skin over them disturbingly thin. The addled confusion she had been in at her house was gone, replaced by something fevered and manic. Her eyes darted over Oscar's face. "I've seen you before."

"I came to your house."

Without breaking her stare, she reached into a purse as small as a medallion, pulled out a white pill, and swallowed it dry.

"Paul," she said.

"Penny," he corrected.

At her daughter's name, she flinched. Then she shook her head once and repeated, "Paul."

Oscar felt a shot of excitement.

"What about Paul?"

Carole Roth's eyes grew wide. Tears welled above her lower lids, threatening to spill. "I don't know." She leaned over to him, closer and closer until her lips touched his ear; he could feel the heat radiating from her. Her voice was barely louder than a breath: "But I suspect." Then she jerked back and stood in a sudden flurry. Oscar found himself on his feet, too. "Tomorrow morning," she said. "Nine. Come to the house."

Then she was gone, lost in the colorful tide.

Oscar slowly sat. He thought for a moment, then reached for his cell phone to call Neve. This was good.

A man nearby coughed politely, and Oscar looked up.

Standing at the doorway to the booth was Karl, the tall, razor-thin driver who had led Oscar to Anne Chaume at the Roths' house. Close up, his colorless face and platinum hair seemed unnaturally smooth and fine; he might have been twenty-five years old or fifty. Oscar saw that the man's eyes, like Anne Chaume's, were ice blue. Then he was surprised to see that he was only half right: one eye was blue, the other brown. The driver was a heterochromiac.

"Karl, isn't it?" Oscar asked.

Karl smiled and nodded, and indicated the crank-handle phone on the booth's wall.

"It's Chislehurst's original. 1880. This was only the second house in the country to have a telephone."

"Very sensible to wait till there was someone else to call."

"Would you mind?" Karl motioned for Oscar to follow.

Oscar trailed the thin man through the crowd. "You look like you've had quite the day or two, Detective." Karl glanced over his narrow shoulder at Oscar; the effect of the mismatched stare was unsettling. "Help yourself to another drink if you'd like."

Oscar did. It was good scotch. "Do you know why I was invited?"

"This is a birthday party, Detective. Not a crime scene." Karl smiled. "Not everything has sinister reasons. I expect you took Ms. Chaume's fancy."

Oscar followed Karl past a wide fireplace, through a heavy door, and into a quiet hallway. On its tall walls hung a series of matching blackwood timber frames: photographs of Chislehurst through the decades, from its present-day garb, with verandas enclosed with glass and a dainty pavilion berthed alongside, dating back one hundred and fifty years, to a black-and-white picture of a treeless hilltop studded with workmen, barrows, and drays.

"What did you get her?" Oscar asked.

Karl stopped at a door. Oscar saw mild interest on the man's strange face. "Such a personal question."

"Is it?" Oscar said.

Karl watched him for a moment. "Nothing," he said. "Ms. Chaume doesn't need anything from the likes of me."

He held Oscar's gaze—and his expression said clearly, "Or the likes of you." Then Karl rapped at the door, waited a few heartbeats, then pushed the door open to allow Oscar inside.

The door closed silently behind him, and Oscar was alone in a powder room—green tiles the color of rain-forest frogs, enamel the color of good cream, a second door opposite the one he entered through. Oscar caught sight of a man at the far wall and was about to apologize for intruding when he recognized the flop of coppery hair and the poorly shaved face with its crusty scabs and bruises. He looked thin. The room was silent. Oscar wondered if a mistake had been made.

Near the vanity, the second door opened, and Anne Chaume stepped inside. Once again she wore gray—a sheath of silk that ran like liquid pewter down her length to spread into petals that exactly kissed the floor. Her shoulders, arms, and neck were bare, and her pale skin was as striking as a camera flash: as unsettling a surprise as seeing marble brought to life. She wore jewelry this time—four pieces of polished jet that caught the light and gleamed: earrings, a hairpin, and a ring. Dark points of a strange compass. But it was the pale oval of her face that captured and held Oscar's eyes. Her red lipstick was as shocking as a wound, yet somehow perfect and full—an ideal balance to her ice-blue eyes that roved over Oscar's face and chest and legs. Again, the sense of being physically touched by that forthright stare was an unnerving, pleasant shock.

"Detective Mariani." Her voice inflected quiet wonder, as if she had not been told that he was waiting here and had stumbled upon him by coincidence. But her eyes showed no surprise. She had known he would come the moment she asked him to. She took a step closer and narrowed her eyes. "I'm hoping like hell you have a cigarette."

He checked his trouser pockets. A small miracle: he found a rumpled, nearly empty pack of Jilu.

When he looked up, she had moved closer still, as if by some silent magic. Maybe because the dress hides her feet, he thought, and suddenly imagined tracing fingertips from those feet up slender, milk-white calves.

He lit her cigarette, and she inhaled greedily.

"Thank you."

"Happy birthday," he said.

She watched him light another for himself. "I got the sense you didn't go for these things."

"Cigarettes?"

"Parties."

"I'm trying to quit both."

"Ah." She studied him, as if calculating his weight or guessing his star sign. "I'm not helping."

"There are probably better cigarettes out there," he suggested, indicating the corridor outside that led back to the ballroom.

"Better cigarettes, beastlier people." Her eyebrows arched. "You saw Paul."

The way she said her barrister's name made it sound a little diseased. It wasn't a question.

"Saw," he agreed.

Chaume leaned against the vanity and tilted her head back as she exhaled again. She was dressed as finely as any of Europe's princesses, but he could imagine her same stance in jeans and tank top, eased against the rails of a country fence. A smile toyed with the corners of her lips.

"I hope you won't use my party as an opportunity to interrogate my guests." She drew in more smoke. "I thought you were here for fun."

Oscar thought about it. "I'm really not sure why I'm here."

They smoked in silence a while, and she stubbed out her cigarette on porcelain.

He offered her another.

"Two in one night? Aren't you the accommodating man."

He watched her slide the cigarette out of the box. The gesture was at once perfectly innocent and supremely erotic. He saw the artery on the side of her pale neck pulse. And those startling eyes, as pale as windows, inscrutable and sparkling. She seemed so alive, more alive than anyone he'd seen in months. Maybe years. She watched his fingers as he held the lighter to her cigarette. She made a small, approving sound. Oscar felt his own blood pulse harder. He knew what she was doing. And the moment that thought took his mind, she smiled, as if they were sharing a good, playful joke. She was beautiful, and despite the hundreds of guests outside she seemed in no hurry to leave him.

"Why are we doing this in private?" he asked.

She stepped closer, no magic now, a deliberate approach.

"You don't fit in out there." She smiled. "Don't take that badly. It's a compliment."

"Why did you invite me?"

Her smile disappeared slowly into another, deeper expression.

"That's a very good question," she said, but didn't answer it.

Under the scent of tobacco, he could smell her: a slow, warm fragrance of sandalwood, vetiver, and clean skin. "Karl told me you looked tired." Her voice was softer now. "But Karl is very polite."

"I've had an interesting week," Oscar admitted.

"Can I help?"

"How could you help me?"

Her gaze didn't shift. It was frank and ready, as if nothing he said would surprise her. "Lots of things are possible."

He looked at her long throat. He wanted badly to lick it.

"Your father is Sandro Mariani," she said.

He was surprised. "That's right."

"My father owned the Fenhurst Hotel—do you remember it? In Alice Street?"

He nodded, recalling an elegant building that was sold for a small fortune to a French chain.

"There was a murder once, in one of the penthouses," she said. "This was a while ago, I was nine or ten. I remember, the phone rang in the middle of the night, it woke us all. A plastic surgeon had plastered his suite with cocaine and then beaten a call girl to death with the alarm clock." She smiled sourly. "My father insisted on good-quality appliances. Everyone panicked. The floor staff, the duty manager, the general manager. They rang my father. 'What will the press say? What do *we* say?' He asked if the police had arrived, and then asked who the investigating officer was. It took them a few minutes to find out, and they said, 'Sandro Mariani.' And my father said, 'Don't worry,' and he went back to bed. Apparently Sandro Mariani didn't like the press, didn't take bribes, and understood that scandal died in a vacuum."

"Dad believed in letting the job speak for itself."

She looked him up and down. This time she made no pretense about the gaze. It was a gourmet's stare. Hungry.

"And did he pass that on to you?" she asked quietly. "Discretion?"

"No." He found he was whispering, too, they were that close. His blood pumped hard. "I had to learn that on my own."

She nodded, watching him. Her eyes glittered. "Mariani." She said his name very softly, as if it puzzled her. "Are you happy?"

"No," he found himself answering.

She was so close now. Close enough for him to see that those pale-blue eyes held the faintest motes of gold. "Unhappy, because of your wife?" she whispered. "Or your job?" Her breath was sweet, her lips red. "Or your ghost?"

His phone rang, a sound so loud in the small room that he jumped.

He looked up at Chaume. Her eyes said, "Don't answer."

"I'm sorry." He pulled out the cell. "Mariani," he answered.

It was the night desk. "There's been gunfire at a meat trader's in Red Hill. Detective de Rossa and a man named Kannis are dead."

moke twisted in coils of orange and black, a choking, madly capricious serpent that swayed to its own crackling rhythm, breathing down choking gasps of arsenic, hot metal, and burned flesh. The underside of the black, pregnant billows reflected winking sapphires and rubies from the emergency vehicles below. This is what a dragon would look like, Oscar thought. Gluttonous and venomous and glittering with unreachable riches.

More earthly, more tangible treasures were being beaten from the hands of looters stealing meat from the only cold room not yet ablaze, the one farthest from where he'd placed Penny Roth. A unit of firefighters, exhausted already from a night's worth of work, stood in a ragged line like soldiers who'd arrived too late for the battle.

Despite the heat that struck his face and chest and legs, Oscar felt frozen.

"What started it?" he asked quietly.

"Gunfight," said a firefighter from a face as stage-blacked as a vaudeville minstrel's. "Loose shot hit a propane tank."

"Can't you put it out?"

The firefighter shook his head. "It's the polystyrene. It's sandwiched between sheet metal, so the water can't reach it, and it goes up like . . ."

"Like polystyrene," offered another firefighter, and the rest nodded sagely. "Poisonous. And there's more gas bottles. We're not going in there."

"Bodies?" Oscar asked.

"They got the shooters out."

Oscar found the sergeant in charge of the scene. He led Oscar to a small white tent that had been set up in the adjoining lot. Inside was a Scenes of Crime officer texting on his phone, and pathologist Dianne Hyde wearing a lab coat over her pajamas. When she saw Oscar, her face tightened. She looked as if she wanted to be anywhere but here.

"They called me out," she explained. "Busy night. I'm so sorry, Oscar."

Two bodies lay on a small tarpaulin.

Kannis's face was red, and his hair had been burned from his head. One bullet had smashed into his cheek, raising the corner of his mouth into a roguish grin. Burned skin had begun to split and peel from the back of his skull. Neve's hair had been singed, and one side of her face was a blush so deep she might have been caught praising herself. Her shirt was open, and Oscar saw between her breasts a tiny hole—dark and red, like the world's smallest volcano.

The icy weight in Oscar's chest dragged him down, and he knelt clumsily. He wanted to grab Neve by the chin and shout in her face that she should have listened, should have *waited*. Instead, he softly touched her neck. It was cold. He forced himself to breathe. He didn't want to.

"They shot each other," the sergeant said. "We're waiting for Homicide, of course. Two rounds from hers, one from his."

"Maybe he thought she was trespassing," Hyde offered.

Oscar looked at the bodies. "The weapons?"

The Scenes of Crime officer uncovered two evidence bags—Neve's service semiauto, and the little silver pistol with which Kannis had killed the horse.

"Where did you find her pistol?"

The sergeant looked at Oscar as if it was a trick question. "Next to the body."

"Underneath? Left? Right?"

The sergeant sighed, closed his eyes momentarily. "She was on her left side, and it was near her right hand."

"Photos?"

"No time. The fire. We didn't know if they were alive or dead, we got them straight out. Why?"

"She was left-handed." Oscar stood. "No witnesses?"

The sergeant shook his head.

Hyde tried to touch his arm. "Oscar—"

He pushed past her, followed by the sergeant.

Outside, the roar of the flames had grown louder. A crowd was gathering around the titanic bonfire.

"Has she got family?" the uniformed officer asked.

"Her parents are dead. No siblings." Oscar took a deep breath and regretted it—the air this close to the fire was bitter. He coughed. The roof of a cold room fell in and flames jetted up like red spines. Onlookers cheered.

"What was she doing here?" the sergeant asked.

"There's another body in there," Oscar replied.

He pointed to the remains of the cold room that held Penny Roth. The roof had fallen in, and the leaning walls buckled and jigged as if something inside was trying to kick its way out of the inferno.

"Seriously?" the sergeant said.

"The morgue was snowed under. Neve got a fax from Health about hospital records pertaining to the cadaver. I guess she came up here to check them herself."

Oscar stared at the flames. While Neve was being murdered he was in a lavish powder room, flirting with a rich woman.

He noticed the sergeant taking notes. "And who was the cadaver?" the sergeant asked.

Oscar watched the cold room containing the remains of Penelope Roth collapse in a fountain of sparks that birthed a billowing crown of tall orange flames. More cheering.

"A Jane Doe."

———

Fifteen minutes later, rain arrived, and with it came the Homicide branch: a fat detective sergeant and young Detective Constable Bazley. When Bazley saw Oscar, he instinctively flinched, then composed himself and put on a vulpine grin. Oscar knew from the smile what Homicide's finding would be.

Oscar crossed the street and headed for his car. He slowed when he saw a sleek white patrol cruiser parked behind it. Its driver silently wound down the window.

"How was your party, Mariani?"

Oscar walked over to Haig's car. The ice in his chest spread into his skull; he felt untied and cold. A pendulum had swung a full arc, from the brilliant sense of aliveness looking into Anne Chaume's eyes to feeling numbed and emptied now. His hands were white fists. From under the bandage on his cut knuckle, fresh blood wept.

"You did this," Oscar whispered.

Haig looked up at him, impassive. "You're a fool, Mariani."

Oscar's fist struck forward. But Haig was quicker. He caught the blow and firmly pressed Oscar's wrist down on the doorsill. Oscar knew the man could break it.

"A fool," Haig repeated. "I asked you to give me this case. A good cop's dead now. A waste."

Flames reflected in Haig's eyes. Kace was a shadow in the backseat.

Oscar slowly twisted his wrist. Haig didn't release the pressure, so the pain was searing. Oscar wondered, with every heartbeat, when his bones would snap—he realized he didn't care if they did. Skin tore on the rubber of the sill, and blood trickled, lubricating Haig's grasp. Oscar's eyes and Haig's were locked. Oscar pulled his hand free.

"Too far, Haig."

Bleeding, he went to his car, got in, and drove off. His hands on the steering wheel felt disconnected, not his own, and the view through the windscreen could have been a movie projection. He wondered with a little curiosity whether those remote hands might jerk the wheel and steer him into a power pole or another vehicle or over a bridge. They didn't. They took him to Neve's apartment building.

He went up the stairs slowly and knocked at the door.

Alex's face was wet and her eyes were red. She took aim and slapped Oscar as hard as she could.

lood and fire.

She smelled them, even from afar.

They roused her from her slumber, made her listen.

Voices. They were faint, but the words were right. The air was right. And the smell—the scents on the air of tender flesh and clean fire were *more* than right.

She rolled, stretched her claws. No. She did not want to be bidden. The howling of the dying dumb thing repulsed her.

Oh, but the smells! Her mouth watered.

The words, the asking, the call, the pull, the—

Flesh.

Sweet, clean blood. *Sweet, clean* flesh.

She was displeased. She could come and go as she wished now. Why should she listen to these requests? But her stomach growled. She was still hungry.

She rose and called her favored pets.

Chapter 23

The city straddled the river like a wide saddle hung over a thin crooked spine. But this morning the city was erased, hidden in fog, and the snaking river was invisible under a cobweb-white shroud.

Oscar drove slowly; he'd had less than two hours' sleep. He followed his headlights away from the city, along the river, then across one of its many bridges to a suburb where picket fences were bared like teeth through the dreamy fog and the trunks of old trees lined the quiet streets in rows, gray as the shins of bony gods. He checked the address, parked, and entered a neatly painted gate. At the front door hung a brass ship's bell. He rang it and waited.

A man makes assumptions that, when proven false, surprise him with their shortsightedness. A man hardened to major crime has no problem believing that a mother could choke the life from her infant, that a clergyman could be caught with a suitcase full of church money and a dead transsexual in the trunk of his car; that a ten-year-old could be found with twists of licorice in one hand, twists of iron bar in the other, and the pulped head of the shopkeeper he'd robbed at his feet. But to discover that Benjamin Moechtar lived not in some strange, dry little storeroom among pinned hexapods but in a pleasant house with an attractive family and an Airedale terrier made Oscar wonder what a poor judge of character he was.

Moechtar answered the door, held back his excited dog, and led Oscar through his home. The two children, a girl and boy, smiled at Oscar, then went back to the toy castle she was building and he was destroying. The boy giggled as he knocked over a tower of colored blocks, and looked over to an empty chair in the corner for approval, and giggled more. Children had ghosts, too, Oscar knew. Back when he could afford newspapers he'd read a theory that children born after Gray Wednesday would grow up without fear or wonder at their invisible playmates. Their ghosts would be no more remarkable than shadows, and when these children were middle-aged the world would speculate what an unhaunted life could have been like. With Neve's family all gone, Oscar wondered who would get her. He hoped it would be a little girl.

"And my wife, Susan," Moechtar said as they walked through a kitchen of clean lines and tall windows.

Oscar shook hands—Susan Moechtar looked ill, and he noted a box of cold-and-flu tablets near the kettle. But her husband seemed unconcerned. "Have you had breakfast?" Susan asked.

"I'm fine," Oscar replied.

"Coffee?" Moechtar offered. "I've just made some."

"There should be a law against Ben's coffee," Susan said, waving them out. "Go talk, I'll bring you some fresh."

Moechtar motioned Oscar toward the back door, and he could see the tension in his inspector's shoulders.

The yard was a subtle watercolor in grays and greens: trees and hedges wrapped lush arms around puddles of grass the color of wet jade. Rising from the mist was the prow of a boat carved from crystal: a greenhouse, its glass fogged. Oscar followed Moechtar across mossy flagstones to the glass door. Stepping into the warm, wet air was like blinking awake in a jungle—a sudden assault of color and scent. Hundreds of beautiful, strange flowers. Orchids, Oscar realized. Not so far from bugs.

"You read my report?" Oscar said.

"Hold these."

Moechtar put into Oscar's hands two plastic spray bottles and reached for a box of fertilizer.

"Neve and Kannis were murdered," Oscar continued. "Someone knew Penny Roth's body was there and went to destroy it. They were seen by Neve and Kannis and had to kill them."

"Keep still." Moechtar took a tiny measure and scooped crystals into each bottle. "With their own guns? How did the killer convince Detective de Rossa to surrender her firearm?"

Oscar held the bottles steady while Moechtar topped them with water.

"Or killers," Oscar said. "They put a gun to Kannis's head and said to Neve, 'Drop your weapon or we kill this guy.' What would she do?"

Moechtar twisted spray heads onto the bottles. He handed one to Oscar and pointed to the lower row of broad-leafed, whip-stalked orchids, then turned his back and began to spray the opposite row.

Oscar continued, "I want their deaths to be part of my investigation."

"Detective Bazley from Homicide has the case," Moechtar said after a long moment. "He's treating it as a double manslaughter. Detective de Rossa failed to identify herself to Gregos Kannis, who shot her as a trespasser. She returned fire in self-defense."

Oscar saw how tightly he was gripping his own bottle and forced his fingers to relax. "That's bullshit. Least-resistance, no-class bullshit."

"I'm not sure a magistrate would agree with you." Moechtar adjusted his nozzle, getting a finer mist. "Inspector Haig also wants you to hand your Jane Doe file over to Homicide."

Oscar laughed.

Moechtar remained silent. The puff-puff of his spray bottle sounded like the hissing of a tropical snake.

Oscar continued, "We had a very solid ID on Penny Roth. Distinctive scars from surgery when she was a child. She's not a Jane Doe."

Moechtar cupped a leaf as delicate as rice paper and sprayed it. "There were several propane and liquid-petroleum gas bottles at the scene. Forensic Services agree the body is probably a girl's, but it's burned bone. The attending pathologist doesn't think she can determine cause of death from the remains."

Oscar remembered the worried strain on Dianne Hyde's face. No doubt she was shitting herself that this charred little boomerang had come back to her morgue.

He asked, "What about DNA? Is there tissue they can sample? Bone marrow?"

"They're going to try."

A glimmer of hope flickered in Oscar's mind. He checked his watch. Still an hour before his meeting with Carole Roth. "If the coroner lets us take a DNA swab from Carole Roth, we can make a match—"

"Carole Roth died this morning," Moechtar interrupted. "An overdose of imipramine."

Oscar blinked as if slapped. He tried to corral his thoughts, but they had bolted in all directions.

"Dead?"

"Oscar." Moechtar had stopped spraying and was staring at him. Oscar suddenly registered the anger pouring off his inspector. It was an odd sensation, like seeing a butterfly suddenly present a stinger dripping with venom. "Take just a moment to see how this looks from my shoes. My detective refuses to give a murder case to Homicide. Fair enough, she *did* have some occult mutilation. But when the cadaver is released from the state mortuary because of a paperwork slipup—"

"There's no way—"

"—does he tell me, his inspector? No. He takes the body and hides it in a blackmarket butcher's cold room. Was it even the same cadaver that left the morgue?" Oscar opened his mouth to protest, but Moechtar held up a hand. "*I* believe you. But a skeptic—a defense lawyer doing his job, for instance—could argue it could have been *any* girl's body you had in that cold room. You say the dead girl was disabled. Do you have any reliable witnesses?"

Oscar thought about Teddy Gillin, a disbarred doctor who spent his days half-shot at the racetrack. "No."

"Then you tag the deceased as the stepdaughter of a prominent, well-respected barrister."

"A DNA test—"

"And let's for argument's sake say Mr. Roth did agree to that, and you did get a DNA sample from the deceased Mrs. Roth, and it did match. So the burned skeleton we have back at Forensic Services is Penelope Roth. We can't determine cause of death, let alone pursue a murder investigation. Now Detective de Rossa and a member of the public are dead as well. To say we're worse off than we were two days ago is an understatement."

Moechtar's eyes were small, unblinking chips of stone.

He continued, "An inspector under pressure would be tempted to place the responsibility for those awful, avoidable deaths squarely at the feet of the supervising detective who should not have let his partner go out of hours to the premises of a man suspected of dealing contraband. An inspector who didn't know better might ask, Why didn't she have backup?"

The door opened and Susan Moechtar entered with coffee cups, milk, and sugar. Sensing the tension, she quickly left.

The greenhouse fell silent. The fog outside killed all noise. They could have been in a capsule under a white, careless sea. Moechtar sprayed the last plants in the row; the white and pink flowers of a dendrobium looked like fleshy fish disappearing into white supernovae. He put down his sprayer.

"Have you made any other headway?"

Oscar thought about it. Some speculation on the symbol, which itself was now no more than unofficial photographs that could have come from any body, anywhere, and a shattered piece of clayware that had no clear link to the charred bones now back where they started, at Forensic Services.

"Not really."

"Motive?"

Oscar shook his head. "Something ritualistic, but I still don't know."

"Suspects?"

Oscar considered: Who had the authority to cow Neve into submission and relieve her of her firearm? Who could have made Dr. Tetlow disappear, and dump Lucas Purden's tortured body in the river? He said, "I'd like to know where Geoffrey Haig was last night."

Moechtar looked up. "Why?"

Oscar thought for a long moment. Haig had covered his trail; there was nothing more than veiled threats and shadows. Finally, he shook his head. He had nothing.

"Have you done your operational summary?"

"Neve finished it."

"And how does it look?"

Oscar hadn't read it. But he'd read Neve's face.

"Let me ask it another way," Moechtar said. "If you were me, would you allow the Nine-Ten Unit to continue?"

"No."

Moechtar held out his hand for the return of his spray bottle. This informal meeting was nearing its conclusion.

"I expect to face quite a bit of insistence to stand you down, Oscar. The annoying thing is"—he removed his glasses to wipe them, and turned his unblinking gaze on Oscar—"I believe you were actually getting somewhere. I believe you saved the cadaver with good reason. And I believe you're right—she was Penelope Roth. Identifying her was no mean feat. And I'm sure there's more you're not saying. And don't tell me; I don't want to know. I listen too much, I get caught up in the thrill of policing." He smiled at his own foolishness and replaced his glasses. "I received a report, an informal report, about your disturbance at a party recently. Apparently you were quite distressed, believing you'd witnessed a suicide."

Oscar felt his stomach tighten. "Oh?"

"The gentleman involved spoke to me off the record, as I'm speaking to you. He was genuinely concerned about your well-being."

Oscar pictured the counterterrorism sergeant who had been at Jon and Leonie's apartment.

"That's nice."

"I've booked you in for a psychological assessment on Monday." Moechtar watched him. "I trust you don't object."

Oscar said nothing.

"You have two days. Take them as bereavement leave. I hear your father's sick, so you could take them as family leave. It's up to you. I'd be grateful, before you do, if you get that summary report onto my desk. Remember that I'm the one who signs your transfer to wherever you go."

———

At his desk, he felt Foley's stare and the eyes of a dozen public servants. He ignored them all and read the report that Neve had prepared—the operational summary of the Nine-Ten Unit's activities over the past twelve months. It was a gallows confession. The tens of suspects he'd let off on Clause Seventeen rang a resounding knell of failure. He'd acted like some frontier judge, holding court for thirty minutes before deciding whether the accused should face the judicial system or all but go free. And he'd let off so many. He might try to shift them around like the three cups in the short con, but they kept delivering the same result: he'd screwed up. The numbers didn't lie, and in these days of tight belts with new holes, numbers were everything. If he was lucky, he'd be demoted and shipped to a flyspeck town in the middle of nowhere. More likely, he'd be cashiered for negligence—and a stain like that would prevent him from getting even a forestry job like the one Jon had tried to help him with.

Neve's dead.

The thought steamrolled any concern he had for himself.

If only he'd signed that fucking transfer slip in the first instance, she could be settling into a new, dull job checking requisition forms for the Fleet Management Branch, or cross-checking the serial numbers of stolen Blu-ray players in Property Crime, instead of lying cold in a steel drawer.

Dead.

His phone rang. It was Jon.

"I heard," Jon said, softly.

"Yes."

"Not your fault, mate."

There was a hint of a lie in Jon's voice. It *was* his fault. All his fault.

"Thank you."

"We should talk. Grab a beer. My shout."

"Yes."

He hung up. It would have to be Jon's shout. Oscar had no money at all. He'd be lucky if he was just pensioned off; more likely he'd be fired and charged with negligence, maybe even with interfering with a corpse.

And who will pay for Megan's care?

The thought suddenly chilled him.

Megan.

Elverly.

He had to talk to Zoe Trucek.

———

The fog persisted. It closed the gravel drive to Elverly House down to a strip of gravel bounded by unkempt hedges and silvery willow leaves wrapped in gray, steamy silk. If Oscar let himself, he could imagine he was on a bridge, or on a mountain pass, or driving down a tunnel of different silk, heading toward something poisonous and hungry. Then Elverly House appeared through the fog. While the gauzy air made most things seem light and weightless, Elverly instead looked dusky and laden, like some ancient clipper lost and adrift—but not empty.

It was still early. A portly girl rocked from foot to foot, unsure whether to let him enter before visiting hours. He decided for her and gently pushed past.

He took off his hat and asked, "Is Zoe Trucek on?"

The girl nodded.

"Where?"

"I'll look," the girl said, and cast a glance inside the office. "She's just due to start. Try the break room—our lockers are there."

As he headed up the tiled hall, he saw in a mirror that the girl was reaching for the telephone.

Mist glowed outside the tall windows of the break room. Zoe Trucek leaned against the windowsill, arms folded as she watched him. As Oscar stepped closer, Zoe's face appeared in the exact opposite way that Elverly House had emerged from the fog: not dark from light but white from shadow. Her sharp jaw was clenched and her green eyes glittered. She took in Oscar's face, the grazed skin and the bruises, and her eyebrows rose impatiently.

"Three girls missing," he said.

"I don't know what you're talking about." Zoe's eyes slid to check the doorway.

"You wanted to know whose side I'm on. Why?"

Zoe tried to push past him. He slammed an arm across the doorway. It was like their dance in the hydrotherapy room, only no knife.

"What do you know about Frances White, Penny Roth, and Taryn Lymbery?"

"I know Penny Roth is charcoal."

"You followed me again?"

"You shouldn't flatter yourself."

He grabbed her shoulders. "What did you see?"

Zoe dug her nails into his hands. "Do you know how long it took me to get this job?" she hissed. "Chalk will be here soon. If she sees a cop interrogating me, she'll think I'm a thief."

His grip tightened. "My partner was killed," he said. "Her name was Neve."

"You should take better care of the people you're responsible for."

"What did you see?"

"Nothing."

"What did you see the morning Taryn Lymbery went missing?"

"*Nothing.*"

He didn't loosen his grip. "We can do this at headquarters."

"We can do it on the moon; you'll hear exactly the same thing."

Her eyes were hard. Scared. From up the corridor came voices and the stopwatch clicking of approaching footsteps.

Zoe shook off his grip.

"I followed you," she hissed. "But you can't even keep your own people safe." She vanished behind the dimpled glass. A moment later, Leslie Chalk appeared in the doorway.

"Detective Mariani?"

Chalk looked as if she'd rushed the last leg of her makeup and was not pleased about the fact.

"Mrs. Chalk. How are you, after that death in your family?"

The question threw her, and she took a half step back. "I'm fine. Thank you."

"Unexpected deaths are the worst ones."

She nodded curtly, and then shook her head as if to dislodge this unsettling line of questioning.

"Did you interview Zoe all right?" she asked.

"She didn't have anything useful."

Oscar watched her. She took another barely perceptible step back, as if she was regretting blustering in on him. She nodded. "Yes. The same when I asked her. The help around here is half-blind, I swear." She raised her chin. "Can we call Missing Persons again?"

"I guess."

An uncomfortable silence fell on the break room. Realizing that Oscar wasn't going to leave in a hurry, Chalk inclined her head.

"Would you like to see Megan? She has a visitor."

———

The inquest into the accident that had crippled Megan McAuliffe had been a hurried affair, one of thousands backlogged after Gray Wednesday. When he was let off with a small fine and a warning, Oscar had felt a flutter of relief that still disgusted him. Anthony McAuliffe had shouted for more. In the courtroom, McAuliffe had looked his age, just over forty. Now, three years later, the man was old. His hair had gone gray and his skin had an unhealthy tan with a crosscurrent of jaundiced yellow. He wore a dirty orange shirt with reflective strips across the back and baggy blue pants that were more patch than trouser. Council work was hard to get and poorly paid, but when the universities pinched their belts or closed their doors the literacy level of road crews climbed dramatically as liberal-arts graduates and journalism lecturers joined their poorly paid ranks. McAuliffe had been a humanities professor; now he looked like a criminal. He held Megan's hand while she snored. His eyes were red.

"You," McAuliffe said when he saw Oscar.

"Me," Oscar said. "Can I come in?"

McAuliffe ran his eyes over Oscar, taking in the wounds on his face, the bags under his eyes, his own patched clothes. He grimaced and shrugged. Oscar stepped into the room.

In sleep, Megan's face had lost its angry, frustrated twist, and she looked almost like any other teenage girl. But the air around her smelled sour. It was her father; from McAuliffe's skin rose an invisible cloud of sweat and alcohol. Oscar felt a flurry of anger. How much of the cash that Oscar slipped into McAuliffe's letterbox was he blowing on home-distilled ethanol? He bit his tongue.

"How is she?" Oscar asked.

"Destroyed," McAuliffe said.

If the word was aimed to hurt, it was a bull's-eye.

"Are you coping?"

McAuliffe returned his eyes to his daughter and watched her for a long moment. He slowly shook his head.

Oscar wondered if he should put his hand on the man's shoulder. He didn't want to, and he hesitated so long that the moment passed. They sat and stood there, watching Megan's chest rise and fall under the blankets.

"Contraception," McAuliffe said at last. "They say she's got periods and they need to put her on the pill." He looked up at Oscar. "It'll cost."

Oscar tasted bile. But he nodded.

He wasn't sure how many minutes passed, but eventually he slipped silently from the room.

Chapter 24

The Bordeaux was the color of ox blood. Oscar filled his only wineglass to the middle, lifted it, toasted Neve, and drank.

Outside, sunshine was burning off the fog and setting the sky into a white blaze so bright that it made eyes so used to rain and gloom sting and water. So he'd drawn the curtains. Besides, drinking was always easier in the dark.

"Sissy!" he suddenly called.

The cat didn't come. Maybe it had smelled failure and madness on him, and had gone to find more reliable lodgings. Smart cat.

Oscar drained the glass. Refilled it. Drank. The Bordeaux was good. He'd heard that the French police had also experimented with units similar to the Barelies; they'd shut them down nearly eighteen months ago after it became apparent that some officers had not only drawn up a price list outlining the costs involved for a suspect wishing to be relieved of his murder charge but had also value-added by offering citizens advice on how to commit murder and blame it on ghost-driven insanity. Oscar toasted that enterprise.

He refilled the glass again.

Halfway down it, he dialed the hospital. The line rang a dozen times before it was answered. The reception nurse said valve-replacement surgery was scheduled for that afternoon. What time? They would let him know. You were supposed to call back yesterday. We're very busy. Could he call back later? He could please himself about that. He ended the call, exhausted. His empty stomach was absorbing the alcohol like a sponge.

He rose unsteadily and fetched from his fireplace cache a packet of cigarettes and a box of matches. He broke two matches lighting his smoke; he got it fired on the third. He dropped the match on the clear cellophane cigarette wrapper and watched it shrivel and twist. Is that how little Penny's lifeless body had shifted and shrugged as the cold room became an oven? He caught sight of the nasty welts on his wrist, the cuts from Haig's car door.

Haig. Haig. Haig. He was never far away.

Haig knew if he said to stay away from Chaume's party, you would go. He played you like a marionette, pulled all the right strings to keep you out of the way while Kannis's was torched.

Neve was at the wrong place at the wrong time.

It should have been you, Oscar thought. It *would* have been. He drank.

Three dead matches. Three missing girls. Frances White, missing almost a month, surely dead. Penny Roth, a stack of black bones back at Forensic Services. Taryn Lymbery, missing.

The thought of Taryn's photograph made his throat go tight—a beautiful, simple thing with thick glasses and a trusting smile. Would she turn up, like Penny Roth, with a hideous symbol carved with an artist's hand into her belly? No. Penny's discovery in the auger was a mistake. Haig wouldn't let that happen again. Taryn's body would simply disappear.

And Paul Roth? Even Chaume, his richest client, disliked him.

Haig had means. Roth had money. Yet neither had motive. He could picture neither researching the gods of ancient Persia that birthed the foul symbol carved on Penny Roth's belly. And neither fitted the description of the old man with the ponytail who commissioned the sculptress Florica to make the grotesque idol. With Penny Roth's flesh now crisped and cindered, the hideous clay idol—now broken just as thoroughly as Penny had been—was the last, tenuous link bearing the symbol.

He thought about the studio behind the incinerated brothel. There had to be more clues. There had to be something he'd missed.

Oscar stubbed out the cigarette, poured his unfinished wine back into the bottle, and grabbed his keys.

———

It took imagination and some stubborn staring to picture the street as an exclusive row of doctors' offices and boutique art galleries. In crisp daylight, the narrow lane looked smaller than it had at night, its buildings more conspiratorial, the rubbish slumped on its footpaths and caught in rusting fence wires more rotted and offensive. Even the sodden pile of ash mud where he'd found the idol seemed unremarkable—just another building, like hundreds in the city, that had burned to the ground.

He parked his car and found curved triangles of glass at the spot where Dalmar had smashed the bottle into his head. He walked slowly to the middle of the lane and looked around, squinting against the rare sunlight. He felt like a man in a small canyon, flanked by gully walls and washes. He turned slowly, a full circle. Nothing moved. Windows were closed or boarded up. No one came out to ask him for money.

Oscar knocked on half a dozen doors. No answer.

He went back to the car and leaned, his arms resting on the roof and his chin nestled on his hands. He cleared his mind and let his eyes roam where they wished.

Just a narrow street. Dark buildings, dirty fences. He forced his body to remain still, his mind to fall quiet. Just look.

Details began to become clear. Someone had jammed a rock up the storm-water pipe in the gutter, and leaves and twigs had accreted behind it. A nail had been driven into the mortar of a nearby building, and a bottle cap hung off it. Tiny white bones, maybe a rat's, lay picked clean near a sooty patch tucked in a doorway—someone's fire spot, out of the wind, where they'd cooked dinner.

Blink.

Oscar felt his heart skip.

He looked up. Something at the top of his vision had blinked red.

He stared, forcing himself to be patient.

Blink.

And there it was.

Twenty-five feet off the ground, a galvanized-steel arm struck out from a light pole. At its end was, of course, a streetlamp—its Perspex cover hung loose, its bulb gone. But there was something else attached to the galvanized arm: a tiny inverted dome, tinted a dark gray. A CCTV camera. Oscar stared at the dome.

Blink. A tiny red light.

Most of the cameras in the city had been taken down—there were simply no municipal funds to monitor or service them.

Blink.

It was working.

A nearby terrace house had a window nearly the same level as the camera. He went to that building's front door. It had a frosted-glass panel, etched with the logo of a now defunct graphic-design company. He knocked on the glass and waited. No answer. He knelt and peered through the letterbox slot in the door. It looked directly onto a set of carpeted stairs rising into semidarkness. On the stairs was the shadowed form of a large dog.

"Hello, puppy," he called nervously.

The dog didn't move.

Oscar found his flashlight in his jacket and shined it through the brass slot. The light glistered off the glazed surface of the ceramic Doberman. He imagined a dozen would-be thieves doing just as he'd done, only without the flashlight, and being dissuaded from entering by the shape of the guard dog.

Oscar pulled out his plastic library card, leaned his weight against the door, and jiggled the bent plastic against the lock tongue, hoping the owner hadn't deadbolted the door. With a satisfying click, the lock tongue cleared the mortise and the door opened.

Oscar stepped onto a pile of letters, the bottommost yellow and curled with age. The ground floor was office space: two desks, a small meeting table. Bars on the windows. Oscar climbed the stairs and went through a blue door. A narrow living room; flat-screen TV; bookshelves with brassware, including a sextant and a diving helmet; a ghost-faint tang of spoilage coming from the kitchen, where a puddle in front of the fridge had crusted and peeled. He climbed an even narrower set of stairs to the third floor. A bathroom, a linen press, and a bedroom overlooking the street. The bed was unmade: a rumpled mess of sheets that were once white but were now cobweb-gray under fine dust. A drinking glass on the floor, and three empty blister packs of tablets. Ahead was the window Oscar had seen from the street. A pair of curtains hung lank, parted just enough to allow light to fall on the mummified remains of a woman. She sat in a chair, her hands on her lap. Her hair cascaded over her shoulder, and her sunken, dry face peered up at a water stain on the ceiling. Her legs were thin leather over dangling bone. As Oscar got closer, he saw something that made his heart sag. Off the bedroom was a walk-in wardrobe; on its doorway architrave hung a baby bouncer: a clamp from which suspended a lightweight chain, a spring, and a harness. In the harness was a tiny little skeleton, dressed in pink.

Oscar went to the window and drew wide the curtain.

From here he had an almost clear view of the lot. The light pole was only a few yards away, and the window was almost level with the lamp arm and its gray teardrop camera housing, shiny as mica.

Blink.

Oscar hurried downstairs to the bookshelves. Among the nautical bric-a-brac was a replica ship's telescope. He held it to his eye and saw a disorienting, enlarged view of the reversed window logo. He returned to the bedroom window, extended the eyepiece, and focused on the security camera.

Tiny print was wrapped around the top of the Perspex dome: "Astor Security Pty Ltd. For service or repair . . ."

Oscar wrote down the address.

matter-of-fact chrome plaque declared this to be the address of Astor Security. The gray building was squeezed between a boarded-up nightclub and a boarded-up electrical wholesaler. There were two doors: a painted steel entry door and a closed shutter just wide enough to admit a car. Oscar ran a shoe sole over the doorstep. It made no mark. Compared with the patina of dust on the nightclub's step, Astor's front stoop was spotless. Someone was going in and out. Beside the plaque was an intercom panel with a glass lens. He pressed the button.

There was a long pause. Then a deep voice: "Astor Security."

Oscar showed his badge to the glass lens.

Another pause.

A buzz. A click. He pushed inside.

———

"Oh, God, please don't tell anyone."

The man's name was Stuart. He was short, had a melon belly, and his hair had been dyed an unnaturally vigorous brown and was frozen by mousse into an architectural cantilever over his round face. Stuart's eyes were a freakish violet—contact lenses, Oscar realized—and were wide with apprehension so sharp that it bordered on terror.

"Why not?" Oscar said. "You answered the door."

"Yes, but no one's rung the door in years." Stuart waddled along rich, charcoal carpet through a reception paneled in brushed stainless steel and granite and into a control room that smelled of good coffee. A bank of LCD monitors surrounded the desk. In a far corner was a very comfortable-looking single bed.

"Well, *idiots* have rung," Stuart corrected himself. "At first, all the religious nuts. Then the *anti*-religious nuts. Then the looters. I'm not worried, the door is steel. But if I *am* worried—" He leaned into a microphone and hit a switch; his voice boomed out of hidden speakers in a gravelly basso: "Leave right now or I'm authorized to remove you from the premises." Stuart switched off the mic. "And if I'm *really* worried, I have this." He opened a drawer and let Oscar peek inside. Beside a set of keys and a small box of tissues was a huge chromed revolver.

"Forty-four Taurus," Oscar said. "Very Clint of you."

Stuart shrugged, pleased. "Coffee?"

"Real coffee?"

"Of course."

While Stuart poured, Oscar studied the security-camera monitors. There were five large screens, and each was divided into quadrants showing views from different cameras. The images scrolled through, sometimes coming up with black rectangles where, Oscar guessed, the camera had broken down or been ripped out.

"So, Stuart," Oscar said, "does Astor Security know you're here?"

The small man laughed nervously.

"Well, you could say they do. You could *argue* it." He handed Oscar coffee. It smelled divine. Stuart sat in his Herman Miller chair, and Oscar noted that the fellow wore expensive trousers, Italian boots, and a pinkie ring.

"They keep paying you," Oscar said. They didn't just keep paying him: they kept paying him *well*. "An oversight?"

Stuart's neck grew red. "I'm doing my job. It's not my fault if they can't keep their paperwork straight."

The average wage fell by more than seventy percent over the six months following Gray Wednesday, and never recovered. If slip-through-the-cracks Stuart was being paid at his old rate, he was raking in a small fortune.

"And what happens if you see a crime?"

Stuart reached for a telephone. "I dial the Mobile Support Team."

"And do they answer?"

Stuart blushed and slurped his coffee.

Oscar pulled out his notepad and showed Stuart the number he'd transcribed from the side of the CCTV camera overlooking the burned-down brothel. "Is this camera still up?"

Stuart flicked a switch and a tiny beam of light shone down onto his keyboard. He moved the notepad into the light and typed in the number.

On the center monitor appeared the streetlamp's view of the street Oscar had not long left. The camera was framed primarily on the auction house but also captured a good view of the cinder-covered block next door.

"Oh, yeah." Stuart nodded, recognizing the image. "I used to like this one."

Because it had afforded the occasional licentious glimpse of call girls, Oscar guessed.

"How long do you keep the tapes?"

Stuart shook his head. "No tapes. All digital." He cracked tiny knuckles. "The whole system has a capacity of about four months. Then the oldest files are overwritten automatically."

Oscar said, "Let's go back five weeks."

Stuart glanced at Oscar. "I hope you don't expect hi-res goodness. Our cameras' default sample rate is one frame every three seconds."

Stuart pressed buttons, and suddenly the image onscreen changed. Where before there had been black mud and burned posts, there now stood a two-story Colonial building with a set of stairs, filigree iron tracework on an upper balcony, and a narrow lane running down one side. To Florica's workshop, Oscar thought. A red glowing sign above the brothel door proclaimed: 1001 NIGHTS. The shop window next to that door was whitewashed, but Oscar could still read the word "Gallery."

"Now what?" Stuart asked.

"Play it through a bit."

Stuart's fingers moved. The image onscreen shifted, and figures moved even faster than the black-and-white jerkings of an old silent movie. Men sauntered at comic speed, some arriving, some loitering, some leaving. The footpath would fall empty, then someone might run through like a flash. Car headlights came and went like tiny meteors. The door to the brothel would wink, revealing a ruby glow inside and the curved shapes of women in short dresses and high heels.

"Remember the fire?" Oscar asked.

Stuart nodded morosely. "That was a shame."

"Take us forward to it."

The image changed speed, time lapse now: the figures whirred as quickly as dragonflies, little more than blurs. Night brightened to day, and shadows stretched one way, shortened, then lengthened the other. Night. Day. Night. Day. Night. And a sudden furnace flare of brilliant orange.

The image froze. The pretty little two-story building now resembled a black mask with billowing orange ribbons gouting from the eyes of its windows and the door of its mouth. It was night, but the camera automatically adjusted for flames as bright as daylight.

"Back it up," Oscar said.

Stuart pressed more keys, and the flames began to suck back into the building, getting smaller. Soon there was just a glow coming from inside the top right window, and women in dressing gowns and scanty clothes and next to no clothes ran in odd, crane-awkward steps back up the stairs and into the building. The glow of fire stopped. The red-lit sign came back on.

"Slow it," Oscar instructed.

Keys tapped. The images slowed.

A man reversed into the brothel doorway, head down. Cars reversed up the street. One reversed up, disgorged a fat man with a walking stick, then kept reversing. A large woman with short-cropped hair rolled with a docker's gait back up the stairs and into the red glow. A dark sedan reversed up, slightly forward of the brothel entrance, and its headlights extinguished.

"Slower now," Oscar said.

The passenger-side door of the sedan opened and a small figure eased himself back out of the car. He walked backward across the footpath, carrying something carefully with both hands. His head was down. He stepped backward not up the stairs to the brothel but down the lane beside it. Oscar felt a strange shiver of certainty wash over him.

That's him.

"Play it forward," Oscar said. "Real speed."

Stuart hit a key.

Each frame lasted three seconds. An empty lane, all shadows. Then a shadow within the shadows. The man emerged onto the street, backlit by the brothel's lights. Onto the footpath—he wore a pea jacket and dark pants, his face turned to the dark sedan parked at the curb. At the car door, he lifted the object gingerly onto the car roof and looked up the street, presenting the camera with his profile and his silver ponytail.

"Stop," Osar said.

Stuart hit a key.

Oscar leaned in toward the screen.

The object on the car roof was wrapped in string and brown paper, but its vaguely humanoid form was clear. The idol.

"Can you zoom in?" he said.

Stuart waggled his round head. "About fifty percent."

He reached for a mouse and clicked it on the face of the man with the ponytail. Another click, and the image zoomed instantly in.

The picture was pixelated; the light was low, the man's face was lit mostly by reflection from the brothel's sign in the car's glossy flanks. But Oscar could make out his face. An older man, sixty or sixty-five but trim and well kept. A small goatee. Dark pixels suggested lines up each cheek. Eyes level and looking carefully up the street as he kept a grip on his precious idol. It was a face that Oscar had never seen in the flesh, and yet it was familiar. He'd seen it before.

He turned to Stuart. "Can you print that?"

Stuart nodded. "It'll take a few minutes to warm up."

He hit a couple of keys, and somewhere in the dark room machinery hummed alive.

Oscar watched the screen, eyes locked on the ponytailed man.

"Can we move while it's printing?" Oscar asked.

"Sure."

"Reverse us, please. Triple speed."

The ponytailed man walked his disturbing parcel backward down the lane. A girl in a puffy pink anorak and bare legs reversed her way back into the brothel. A thin young man in stovepipe jeans emerged from the brothel door and chicken-walked back down the street. A dog wandered into the corner of the frame, sniffed around, wandered out. Then the man with the ponytail emerged back-first from the alley and reversed, empty-handed, to the black car. He hesitated, looked up and down the street, then eased himself into the sedan. Its lights blazed and the car reversed out of frame. Two girls, arm in arm, walked back into the brothel. Another figure emerged from the lane, walking backward into the street.

"Slow."

The procession of images went to normal speed, a frame every three seconds. The woman reversed to the footpath, then started to move in slow circles, looking up and down the street, waiting for someone. She had long hair in cornrow braids, black lipstick, a silver necklace, and the biggest earrings Oscar had ever seen.

Florica, Oscar thought.

She checked her watch, then reversed back down the lane. Unless she'd disappeared through a back entrance, she'd never come out; her burned bones were somewhere under the ash.

The printer began a staccato zip-zipping.

"Thank you," Oscar said.

He heard a metallic click and turned to face Stuart.

The little man was holding the big pistol. Its hammer was cocked back. Oscar was unsurprised.

"How do I know you won't tell anyone I'm here?" Stuart said.

Oscar watched him. "You don't."

The gun shook a little in Stuart's hand. Large-caliber revolvers were, Oscar knew, quite heavy.

"I don't want to lose all this," Stuart said.

"I love what you've done with the place."

"I think I could keep this going for years."

"Could do."

"So why should I take the risk and let you go?"

Oscar shrugged. "I might be missed."

Stuart shook his head. "You don't look like the kind of guy people miss. In fact"—his little mind was ticking—"I'd be surprised if anyone knows you're here."

Oscar nodded and stood. "Then I'll go about my business, and you can make up your mind." Oscar turned his back on the other man and went across to the AV rack where the printer was. He felt the eye of that enormous pistol staring, and his skin crawled. "Killing's not like you see in the movies, Stuart. It's messy, especially with a rhino gun like that. Slug's as wide as your thumb. No matter where you shoot me, it's going to punch through and take a whole lot of cargo with it. Hit me in the head and you'll be picking skull and teeth out of your ceiling all weekend." He picked up the print of the ponytailed man from the printer tray. He turned and faced Stuart. "Hit me in the chest and you'll be finding bits of spine in the room next door. Either way, you'll need new carpet; there's a good six liters of blood in a man my size, and that cannon there would let most of it out. And then you have to get rid of the body."

Oscar stepped forward. The little man's stubby finger was on the trigger. The gun remained aimed at Oscar's chest but was shaking: the huge muzzle wavered an inch side to side. Oscar slowly reached and took the big pistol and uncocked the hammer.

"Don't feel bad," Oscar said as he tucked it into the small of his back. "I don't know if I could shoot a man, either."

"Are you going to arrest me?" Stuart asked quietly.

Oscar clapped him on the shoulder. "Stuart, you only pointed a gun at me. You're one of the nicest people I know."

———

Oscar hurried to his car, excited.

Stuart had spoken about being arrested.

Now Oscar remembered where he'd seen the ponytailed man.

———

The key was where it had been hidden for the past thirty years: beneath a potted maidenhair fern beside the newel post of the back stairs. Oscar unlocked the downstairs door and smelled damp rot and mold. Most of the water had drained away, leaving only dark puddles around the concrete washtubs and in a low corner. Out of habit, Oscar flicked on the bare suspended lightbulb. It remained dead. He went to the workbench and carefully lifted the box of newspaper clippings outside into the sunlight.

In a few moments, he held the clipping he was looking for.

The yellowed newsprint had a halftone photograph of Sandro Mariani leading away in handcuffs a laughing young man. There was no caption, no body copy—only the headline reading "Killer Remanded. Full Story Page 5." In the black-and-white picture, Sandro Mariani was Oscar's age now, making the clipping around thirty years old. Although the crim's hair was short and dark, and the hair of the man who carried the wrapped idol from the fortune-teller's door was ponytailed and gray, one thing was clear: they were the same man.

Chapter **26**

ntravenous tubes, catheter tubes, oxygen tubes. Looms of wires.
Spots of blood on bandages holding cannulas and on the white
sheets near the elbows. Despite the web of conduits, Sandro was
asleep. It seemed strange to Oscar that this withered person, this barely
alive thing, had dominated his mind for nearly thirty years. Quietly terrifying; terrifyingly quiet—then explosive.

Oscar had seen his father in action only once. At sixteen, Oscar
knew Sandro's work shifts, and had caught the late-afternoon train into
the city and crossed Roma Street to police headquarters. By then the
desk sergeants knew him well enough to wave Oscar through the back
corridors to the adjoining watchhouse. In the watchhouse drive, a standard unmarked cop sedan was parked, engine running, and he recognized Sandro's partner, Vic Pascoe, a man with features so rough and
hard you were glad to look away from them. Pascoe was helping out of
the car a young man whose huge arms and bare back were a forest of
tattoos: grinning skulls and nude women and wolves. The felon's wrists
were handcuffed, and Oscar could just glimpse Sandro through the
sedan's rear window, his face seemingly suspended in reflected orange
clouds. Suddenly, Vic Pascoe was on the ground and the tattooed man
was running. Where he thought he'd get to, Oscar didn't know—the
gates at the top of the drive were ten feet high and frosted with razor
wire. Oscar was standing between the escaping felon and the gate.
Then the felon's eyes turned to him. Oscar could see the difference
machine in the man's head take him in, add him up, and spit out an
answer: if Oscar got in his way, he'd kill him. Oscar was so startled that
he froze. An instant later, the tattooed man's eyes widened in surprise
as his feet left the ground. Sandro Mariani had moved so quickly that

Oscar hadn't seen him. He pulled the bigger man down and put his knee on the felon's blueprinted neck. Sandro's open hand waited in the air above the man's nose like a hawk on a thermal, ready to strike. He regarded the tattooed felon with an expression that looked to Oscar like mere curiosity.

"Take me home."

The dry voice pulled Oscar back into the present.

Behind the clear plastic mask, Sandro's mouth was a hyphen. He opened one eye. Oscar was shocked at how sunken it looked: a dull thing held loosely in ash-gray flesh.

"How are you, Dad?"

Sandro licked dry lips. "Take me home."

Oscar shook his head.

"Your mother would take me home," Sandro whispered. His eye roved over Oscar's face, disappointed.

"She'd tell you to grow up," Oscar said.

Sandro took a few breaths. Each was short and laborious.

"They want to cut me open," he said. Every word was an effort. He drew an unsteady finger down his sternum. "*Fft.* Like a corpse."

"They're going to fix your heart."

"Henh. What's the point?"

Oscar looked at the lines on the heart monitor: weak ripples, like misty raindrops on a pond. "We want you to get better."

"Who's we?"

"Me."

Sandro rolled his head a little and opened the other eye, too, fixing Oscar with a stare. A cynical, unhappy stare. "Don't"—he caught a breath—"lie."

Oscar blinked. "It's not a lie."

Sandro's eyes closed, and his breathing steadied. Slow, shallow breaths. Just as Oscar was convinced that he was asleep, he spoke again. "Did you. Find them?"

"Who?"

The old man's eyes remained closed. "Your. Real. Parents."

Oscar stared.

He'd run away at fifteen. He tracked down the foster homes he'd lived in ten and more years earlier. He visited maternity hospitals, psychiatric hospitals, cemeteries. At every turn, he was stymied by the same thing. He was only fifteen. His legal parents were Sandro and Vedetta Mariani. Come back when you're eighteen. Oscar slunk home, penniless, thin, smelly. Despite Oscar's overtures over the next twenty years, despite Vedetta's whispers in her husband's ears, Sandro never forgave him for this act of betrayal.

"I never tried again," Oscar said quietly.

Sandro's eyes opened a little. They hunted for a moment, then found Oscar's. Oscar could see they were exhausted.

"You're ashamed," Sandro whispered.

"What?"

Sandro grunted. "I've . . . heard you. Say you're not . . . Italian. Ashamed." Sandro swiveled his eye to Oscar. "Of me."

Oscar was stunned. Yes, he had said that, but he hadn't meant . . . and he realized that he wasn't sure *what* he'd meant. With those words he had been trying to hold tight to something intangible, to some sense of self that had no foundation and no currency. Oscar felt water drop on his hand. His cheeks were wet.

"No, Dad."

Sandro's breath shuffled, caught. He looked away from Oscar, and his eyes began to flutter closed.

"Dad." Oscar wiped his face and reached into a pocket; he unfolded the old clipping of Sandro and the laughing man. He squeezed Sandro's wrist. "Dad? Who's this?"

Sandro blinked, and his eye took a long time to focus on the newsprint. But when it did, a hard glint appeared there.

"Naville. Bert . . . Naville." Sandro's eyes narrowed, and they shifted to Oscar's face. "Dead. A jail fire."

Oscar frowned. Burned. He remembered Sandro and his empty bottle of grappa and Sandro's toast to a dead man.

"When was that?" Oscar asked. "Dad?" Sandro's eyes were drifting shut. Oscar squeezed his hand. "Dad? Where did they send him up?"

"Road." Sandro's voice was an arid whisper. "Boggo."

Then his old mouth was ajar, and the breaths came shallow and even.

Boggo Road. Maximum Security.

Chapter 27

"Yes, they sent Mr. Naville here when they began winding down The Road."

The deputy manager's name was Hamblin, and considering his girth he set a fast pace. Oscar kept up as Hamblin strode along the wire-shrouded walkway between concrete yards. He had apologized to Oscar for the rush, but he was about to head a weekly management-team meeting; their boardroom was being remodeled, so they had to use a garage on the far side of the compound. A uniformed correctional officer trailed ten paces behind. Dark, jade-hued clouds prowled the horizons like a dog pack, but right now the jail was in sunlight, and a thousand tinier suns sparkled off chain-link fencing and the sharp blades of the razor wire. Cell blocks were low affairs with silvery roofs. The place glittered like a town woven from metal. This was the maximum-security complex built more than twenty years ago to replace the nineteenth-century Boggo Road Gaol.

Hamblin chuckled and his large body jiggled. "Yes, coming here after The Road, Naville musta thought he'd landed in Club Med. Cunning little rock spider."

Naville had earned the title of "rock spider" after being convicted of the deprivation of liberty and murder of a fifteen-year-old schoolgirl. Her dismembered body had been found in a weighted suitcase at the bottom of a dam. Naville's molestation of the girl included carving what the prosecution described as "occult markings" into her breasts, buttocks, and inner thighs. At trial, Naville had not said a word.

"I had to hand it to him. He survived thirty years in max. Not bad."

"More like a cockroach than a spider," Oscar observed.

"Touché." The deputy manager pointed a fat finger pistol at Oscar and clicked his tongue.

They passed a yard overlooked by watchtowers where two hundred or more inmates moved in bored discontent. There was barely room for each to sit or stand, yet they'd somehow made space in the middle of the yard for a compressed game of football. Those not in the game played cards or chess; or smoked; or watched Oscar, the deputy manager, and the screw stride past.

"So, Naville's dead?" Oscar asked.

"I'm afraid so." Hamblin's tone became somber. "A good six weeks ago—right, Tom?" He glanced behind at the stone-faced officer, who nodded once.

Hamblin explained that Albert Naville was working in the prison laundry when one of the industrial dryers caught fire; no doubt the prisoner's own fault: he should have been checking the machines' filters for dangerous buildup of flammable lint. "The fool had managed to hand-truck a bag of soiled linen in front of the fire doors. A bag so-high." The man's fat fingers hovered at his shoulder. "No one could get in, and he couldn't get out."

"He was in there alone?"

"Naville was a longtime man. Earned the right to work alone."

They passed another yard as empty as the first was full. In the middle, a gang of three prisoners was constructing a podium from which struck tall posts supporting a stout crossbeam.

"A gallows?" Oscar asked.

The fat man wagged his head and laughed. "I know, I know. Legislation's not even through Parliament yet. But we both know it will be, right?" He winked at Oscar. "And it doesn't hurt to keep the boys busy. Busy with their hands, and busy with their heads. Sight like that gets them thinking about behaving."

"May I see the laundry room?" Oscar asked.

"Of course." Hamblin slowed like a liner coming in to dock. "That's it right there. Or it was."

They were at a bend in the walkway, and dead ahead was a section of yard enclosed in temporary fencing lined with green shade cloth stenciled with an oval logo: THATCH CONSTRUCTION. Behind, it was easy for Oscar to see the yellow arm of a back-end loader knocking down the last part of a brick wall, its inner face black with soot. Burned brothel. Burned butchery. Burned prison laundry. Coincidences? He felt Hamblin's attention turned on him like a radar dish, listening in, waiting.

Oscar asked, "What happened to his body?"

"Seared, then baked." Hamblin chuckled. "I don't know what they do with the ashes. I'm sure you can find out."

"Was there an investigation into Naville's death?"

"Naturally."

"And?"

"And the tribunal decided we shouldn't leave men, even longtimers, to work alone in any prison industry. Rap on the knuckles, my bad." He tapped one fat hand with another and grinned.

"Were there any other deaths on the same day Naville died?"

Hamblin looked back. Despite the jolly grin, Oscar could see careful intelligence in the narrow eyes. "You know, I'd have to look into that."

"Could you?"

"It will take time. Leave me your contact details; I'll call you when I've dug through the records."

Time was one thing Oscar could not afford, but he pulled out his business card and handed it over.

"One last thing and I'll get out of your hair," Oscar said. "I need a photograph of Albert Naville. Right away, if I could."

The deputy manager watched him, smiling. Oscar could almost see the scales in the man's mind shifting, finding their level.

"Yes, sir, we can manage that," he said carefully. "Might be a few years old. We only snap them when they shift complex or get themselves injured." He looked over Oscar's shoulder at the correctional officer. "Tom, would you be a treasure and zip to the office, fetch a copy of the latest photograph of the late inmate Naville? Get Detective Marino here what he needs?"

Oscar watched the officer retreat along the walkway. Alone, the officer collected a hailstorm of catcalls from the prisoners. Oscar glanced at the sky. Heavy, greenish clouds rolled over the sun, painting the prison with a palette of gray. Even above the hydraulic digger, Oscar could hear the hammering of men working on the gallows. He saw Hamblin watching the timber construction with a sparkle in his eye.

"They worry about overcrowding here. Don't know why they do. Everything's going to work out fine."

————

At the correction center's reception, Oscar stared at the color photograph of Albert John Naville. The inmate was looking at the camera. Although he was smiling, not laughing as he'd been in the photograph with Sandro, Oscar could see the same gleam of mad delight. His hair was gray, and a profile shot showed a red rubber band holding it back in a ponytail.

"That all?" asked the correctional officer; the man's face was stone.

"Naville's belongings, from his cell," Oscar said. "Did anyone claim them?"

"I don't know." The officer didn't move.

"Could you check?"

The officer gave Oscar a stare as cold and dangerous as a ski jump, then retreated into the back office. He returned a few minutes later and dropped a small plastic bag onto the counter.

Inside were half a dozen items. A safety razor. A plastic comb. Roll-on deodorant. A toothbrush. A stub of a pencil, and a small spiral notepad—just the front and back cards: every page in between had been torn out, leaving just their confetti remainders trapped in the spiral spring. Oscar held the gray-brown cardboard of the back card on an angle to the light. The ghostly impressions of words intersected and blurred; only three were legible: "charcoal" and "cinnamon incense."

Oscar looked up to thank the officer, but he was gone.

————

Oscar's car accelerated onto the highway. The clouds were now rolling over the sky like Titan's chariots, as green as a storm sea and dropping hailstones that clanged on the hood and shattered on the asphalt like tiny bombs. Cars and motorcycles began to race for the cover of underpasses and bridges. An ice stone the size of a golf ball smashed onto Oscar's windscreen.

He was determined to get back to the city, though what his next step would be he didn't know. Oscar was leaning forward as he drove, his left foot tapping with nervous energy. Naville hadn't died in that laundry fire. He'd escaped. He'd found a way out and was killing again.

Sandro had arrested Naville in 1983 for homicide. Now Naville was out again, and young people were dying once more. Someone had spirited the killer out of prison, leaving another inmate to burn in the prison laundry in Naville's place. Once out, Naville had found Florica at the markets, commissioned her to make him an idol, and then incinerated her. Naville had been jailed for mutilating and murdering a teenage girl. Penny Roth had been mutilated and murdered.

Symbols. Rituals. Murder.

Burn, burn, burn.

The hailstorm crescendoed to a cannonade, smashing down on the car and dimpling the metal. Oscar slowed to thirty miles per hour, then twenty. His view of the highway was now more white than black. He could see no cars in front or behind.

The image of Naville's belongings stuck in his mind. The pencil. The notepad. *Charcoal. Cinnamon incense.* The latter was unusual, and tugged at a hidden, recent memory . . . but it eluded him.

The car's engine hiccuped, and Oscar frowned. It coughed again, then sputtered and fell silent. The car coasted, decelerating. He looked at the fuel gauge. Empty. It had been half-full when he drove into the jail.

He rolled to the side of the highway, parking as tightly as he could against the high concrete barrier, and flicked on the hazard lights. Hailstones smashed on the roof, blows sounding like a madman with a hammer. A tiny crack appeared in the windscreen. Oscar pulled out his phone to call the police breakdown service, wondering if they still regarded this vehicle as breaking down or broken. Before he dialed, he noticed a sedan pull up behind him. He leaned back and waved through the rear glass, hoping the good Samaritan had the sense to stay in his car; going out in this weather could result in a broken skull.

Then Oscar's car rocked as a third vehicle hit it and scraped hard up its side, smashing off the driver's side mirror before halting directly alongside. Oscar jumped reflexively; through the smeared glass, he could just make out a man in the other vehicle's driver's seat pulling on what looked like a white hat. The man got out of his car and hurried around in front of Oscar's hood. Despite the downpour of hail, Oscar could see that he wore a heavy jacket, a construction hard hat and, underneath it, a balaclava. Something shimmered in his hand. A bottle with a flaming neck. The man threw the Molotov cocktail hard at Oscar's hood, which erupted into a sheet of flame. The man reappeared in the corner of Oscar's side mirror and threw a second flaming bottle at the asphalt near the rear wheel of his car. A crash of glass, and more flames erupted with a mighty gush of hot gas. Over the hail, Oscar heard a car door open and close, and the vehicle behind him reversed a few feet, then sped away, vanishing in the storm.

Oscar tried opening his car door, but it wouldn't budge against the abandoned car alongside. The roar of flames outside was loud. He shut the door. He'd parked himself against the tall barrier, so neither passenger door would open. He was trapped. Flames were now turning the windscreen soot-black. There was a loud bang as a rear tire blew.

Oscar grabbed the photograph of Naville, tucked it into his jacket, and threw open the glove box. He grabbed a polishing chamois (that, to his knowledge, had never been used) and quickly wrapped it around one hand. He snatched up his hat and climbed into the backseat. The air in the car was already growing hot and thinned of oxygen. Yellow flames obscured the view out the side glass and half the rear window. He wondered what would happen if the tank blew now. It was empty, but the residual fumes could still blow like a bomb. He didn't need to speculate much; he'd seen the remains of a woman caught in a burning car—a large splinter of ruptured fuel tank had driven right through her rib cage and severed her spine like a scythe. Quicker, at least, than burning alive. Sweat began to pour from his skin. He lay back on the rear seat like an amorous teenager at a drive-in and swung his feet up toward the rear glass. He drew his knees down to his chest, then kicked upward. The shock jolted through his body, and he bit his tongue. The glass held. There was another ominous pop from somewhere underneath the car. He drew down his legs and kicked again, harder. The rear glass crazed into a jellied sheet of ten thousand crystals, and the sound of flames became as loud as storm surf. Oscar pushed the glass aside with his chamois-wrapped hand, held his hat over his face, and climbed out onto the trunk lid, keeping as close to the barrier and as far from the flames as he could. Melting ice made the metal slick. Hailstones pummeled his scalp and shoulders, and a heavy ice stone struck him hard on the back of the skull—his vision blurred.

Don't pass out now.

Fire licked at his hair and loose strands shriveled. Another pop, louder this time. Oscar scrambled off the trunk and fell onto the road. He smelled the acrid reeks of melting plastic and burning paint. He staggered to his feet and ran, slipping on ice balls and wet tarmac, away from the vehicles. There was a third, very loud pop, followed by an even louder metallic clap, and Oscar was shoved to his knees by an enormous warm slap of air. Something whizzed by his right ear and clattered on the roadway far in front of him.

His car was now a lantern, burning brightly on the inside. He skittered backward on his behind as the other car, a plain white utility, suddenly jumped up as if stung from beneath. A fireball rose sixty feet into the air, and the utility landed on bursting tires.

Hail continued to fall. Oscar pulled his hat over his head, his collar over his hat, curled into a ball, and gritted his teeth against the pain. As the hail thundered down, ice stones hitting his body and exploding on the asphalt, Oscar peered between his elbows. The dead boy was sitting beside him, his ghostly hand resting on Oscar's arm.

Chapter 28

"Ow."

"Baby."

Oscar tried not to wince while Denna Lovering inspected his scalp. He sat in front of a kerosene heater with a towel around his waist, teeth gritting whenever she found tender spots. Paz fidgeted in the kitchen doorway.

"Only you could get yourself next to murdered in a hailstorm," Lovering muttered. "Selfish, I call it. You going to pay for the panel-beating on my car?"

"Pazel Hadasse," Denna warned.

"What?" Lovering said. "Look at it now. Dented everywhere. Seriously devalued."

"It was seriously devalued in 1989 when you drove it drunk into my mother's pear tree."

"It's a classic."

"It's a Toyota."

Denna rubbed ointment onto Oscar's cheek. "I can't tell which cuts are from today, or two days ago, or whenever," she said to Oscar. "You need a holiday."

"That's coming," Oscar said.

"I think you should take it now," Paz said softly.

Denna excused herself and left to get some bandages.

Oscar looked around the room. The dead boy was nowhere to be seen. When the hail had eased and Oscar saw blue-and-red flashing lights coming toward him, the boy had retreated. Lovering, whom Oscar had called after the police, arrived not long after. The uniformed officers had run the plates on the white utility: it had been reported stolen from a nearby railway station that morning.

"How much trouble are you in?" Lovering asked quietly.

Oscar shrugged. "I don't know."

"Is this all about the dead girl?" He drew a star shape over his belly.

"Yes." Oscar felt the older man watching him. "What?"

Lovering frowned. "This thing you're involved in, you need to get uninvolved."

"I can't."

Lovering shook his head. Oscar could see that he was anxious. "We filmed stuff in Iraq, Oscar. Back in '05. Stories about the reconstruction. We were out in the desert, way out nowhere, northwest of Ash Shabakah. Dangerous spot. Our transport broke down, and we were stuck waiting for parts. We heard rumors that we were near an old pre-Christian town, so we decided to shoot some overlay footage. What the hell, we were bored. We went out on donkeys. Two hours, and we were there. A whole fucking deserted city. A ghost town. There was one building, I remember. Our guide wouldn't go in. He said the city was cursed by God, and that building was the reason. In its heyday, it had been filled to the ceiling with the bones of children."

Oscar looked at his friend. He could see that the old man was scared.

"We're a long way from the Middle East, Paz."

Lovering shook his head, eyes locked on Oscar. "Don't mess around with this shit. You don't know what the fuck it is."

"They're killing children here."

"Well," Lovering said. "Judging from today, they'll soon be killing you."

"Here, now." Denna returned with a small box of butterfly bandages and used two to close a gash on the back of Oscar's hand. She straightened. "There. Best I can do."

He stood and kissed Denna's head. "You're a mensch."

She squeezed his chin. "And you are a schlimazel. I'll make coffee. Is Pazel driving you home?"

"No," Oscar said, turning to look at Lovering. "He said he'd lend me his motorbike."

Lovering's eyes widened.

Denna's eyebrows rose. "Really?" She looked at her husband as if he'd made a very significant breakthrough and gave him a kiss on the lips. "Finally, my husband's growing up."

Lovering glared at Oscar, who stared back evenly.

"I'll get the keys," he said glumly.

———

Everything hurt, but the wind in his face felt good. After the storm, the air was crisp and smelled clean, and blew coldly against his skin.

Lovering had taken him to the Triumph Triple like a prelate leading a novice to a holy sepulchre, spouting a monologue of remonstrations and instructions, then reluctantly handed Oscar the keys.

Without knowing where else to go, Oscar rode to headquarters. The outflux of public servants had finished, and Oscar had the stairwell to himself. He exited on the third floor and went to the Department of Civic Prosecutions. There was no one on reception, and he walked through to the offices. Jon had a gray cubicle in the middle of the floor and was shutting down his computer. When he saw Oscar, his eyes widened.

"What the fuck happened to you?"

Oscar sat heavily and told him about the attack on the freeway. When he finished, Jon sat quietly for a long while, his face tightly drawn.

"Are you sure they were after you?"

"It was a deliberate attack," Oscar said. "Someone siphoned most of the gas out of my car. They knew I'd run out on the freeway."

"Someone siphoned your gas," Jon agreed. "That happens five thousand times a day across the city."

"They jammed me in and tried to burn me."

"Okay," Jon conceded. "But because you have state secrets? Or just because you were an easy target on the side of the road? You know there are plenty of young turks out there who get their jollies setting things on fire. People included."

"It was planned," Oscar insisted. "Something happened at the jail."

"Something," Jon said. "What?"

Oscar unfolded Albert Naville's prison photograph. "They say this guy died. I say he escaped." He then unfolded the security-camera printout from Stuart, showing a shadow-faced, ponytailed man carrying a large cardboard box toward a car.

"You think these are the same guy?" Jon asked. Oscar heard skepticism undercurrent in his friend's voice.

"You think I'm making this up?"

Jon shook his head slowly. "I don't know. No. But I do know conspiracies are fucking hard to organize."

"I didn't say conspiracy."

"You said the jail has him down as a death-in-custody but you think he's out. No one escapes from jail on their Pat Malone."

"Look at the photos."

Jon tapped hard on the security-camera printout. "I work with prosecutions. This could be anyone. It's a likeness, but it's a crap image taken at night. I could make a jury believe this was Pope Benedict if I wanted to." Jon's voice had risen. He toned it down. "Who is this guy supposed to be?"

"Dad put him away for mutilating a girl. I had a young Jane Doe with a similar mutilation."

"Jesus!" Jon whispered.

But it wasn't the tone that Oscar wanted to hear. "Jesus, what?"

"Your *father* put him away? You know what a defense-appointed psychologist would do with *that*?"

Oscar blinked. "I don't have issues with my father."

"*Everyone* knows you have issues with your father! *Everyone* knows you had an episode at Leonie's party. *Everyone* has heard that your partner was killed by a bootlegger and you're really upset."

"Kannis didn't kill her." Oscar was silenced by the look in Jon's eyes. "You think I'm going nuts," he said quietly.

Jon shook his head slowly but didn't deny it. "I'm worried about you."

"I'm not fucking crazy." Oscar stood. "These are the same guy. He's abducting disabled kids and cutting them up."

"And I suppose Geoff Haig is helping him out."

Oscar said nothing.

"Oh, for fuck's sake, Oscar."

Oscar turned and stalked out of the room, fists clenched.

———

Foley's computer was on, but his chair was empty. Oscar sat at his own desolately empty desk. He rang Jon's extension but hung up after twelve rings and stared out the window.

They tried to kill me, he thought.

That was encouraging; it meant he was on the right track.

"Heya, Mariani."

Foley waddled into the room, tucking his shirt into his vast trousers. When he saw Oscar's face, his eyebrows rose an inch. "Fuck me, what've you been doing? Buggering crocodiles?"

"How are you, Foley?"

Foley inspected Oscar's head, face, neck like a plumber looking over a badly blocked toilet. "Dear oh fucking dear. I *heard* you totaled a car."

"Not me. I was there, though."

"Hmm. How's your dad?"

"Operation's tonight."

Foley sat heavily and his chair wailed a protest. "Good luck there." He swiveled to his computer and opened up a spreadsheet. "Get your message?"

"What message?"

Foley turned back to face Oscar. "There." Foley stared, and frowned. "Hmm. I left it on your desk."

Oscar's desk was empty.

"From Moechtar?" Oscar asked.

"Nah, from a chick. Not the chick with dick from the other night, another chick. Zoe! I remember that. Zoe."

Oscar cocked his head. "What did she want?"

"To talk to you. I said give me a number. She said she didn't have one." Foley turned back to his monitor. "Left an address. I guess she'll call back."

Oscar frowned. "She left an address?"

"Yep."

"And you left it on my desk."

"Yuh-huh."

And now it was gone.

"When did she call?"

Foley was typing, two-fingered. "Oh, hour or so ago."

Zoe had called him. Zoe, who was scared of cops. She'd left her address, and it had been stolen off his desk.

"Who's been to my desk?"

"Christ, Mariani, who the fuck would come to your desk? No offense."

"Foley." The urgent tone of Oscar's voice brought Foley back around, blinking. "What was her address?"

"Man, you really got to get a secretary."

Oscar took two fast steps forward, and Foley's eyes widened. "Whoa-whoa!"

"Seriously," Oscar said.

"Okay!" Foley said. "Fucksticks. Jeezjeezjeez."

Foley opened his drawer and pulled out a notepad, ripped out a page and handed it to Oscar.

"You copied it?"

"She sounded cute."

Oscar ran for the door.

———

The motorbike's exhaust echoed against the concrete balusters of the bridge. Oscar sped across the river, into West End. Two-story shopfronts, shuttered restaurants, blocklike apartments, and tin-roofed houses in dark narrow streets crooked in an arm of the river.

An hour. Someone had come looking for Oscar and found the address of the girl from Elverly on his desk. Haig? Kace? It didn't matter. Time did.

He slowed, looking for street signs, but few sign posts had escaped thieves' wrenches. He hoped his memory served him. He leaned the bike and twisted the throttle.

Workers' cottages were purposeful as miners jammed in a lift, each house an arm's width from its neighbor. Weatherboard faces under corrugated hats, all dark. A dog barked. Oscar let the motorcycle roll to a stop outside a rusted chain-link fence guarding the skeletal, weed-choked remains of rosebushes. Out front was a glossy black sedan with no plates.

The house was a pinched-looking timber building on dark stumps: two windows, a faded set of Buddhist prayer flags under a sagging awning, a set of dangerously listing stairs. Oscar dismounted the bike, listening.

He stepped over the fence, avoiding the rusted gate, and hurried up the stairs.

The front door was locked. He went down the side of the house, squeezing between the dark, warped battens and the side fence, his boot soles slipping on the mossy concrete.

The backyard was a long, narrow pit of tall grass smelling of jungle rot. The thin light leaking from the evening sky picked out the aerial-like wires and struts of clothesline; a sheet hung like a limp sail, and a second trailed one end through the grass, still clipped to the line by a single peg. Dark paths had been beaten through the grass toward a hunched toolshed in the yard's far corner. From behind the shed came sounds of struggle.

Oscar ran. Two figures grappled silently in the black corner; the grass around them was beaten down by their fighting. Zoe Trucek was pinned to the ground by a dark figure who was trying to wrap a third bedsheet like a noose around her neck. Zoe was kicking hard, but the makeshift rope was finding purchase, and her legs swung weakly. The man had his back to Oscar, who was halfway across the yard.

"Hey!" Oscar ran, reaching for Stuart's gun tucked in the small of his back.

The attacker's shoulders froze momentarily, then he renewed his work with greater urgency. He twisted hard on the sheet around Zoe's neck, and Oscar heard a strangled croak.

Oscar thumbed back the .44's hammer.

The attacker hesitated no more than a second, then pushed powerfully onto both feet, ran three light steps to the fence, and vaulted it into the neighboring property.

Oscar let his momentum carry him into the corner, feet sliding on the wet grass. He looked over the fence.

The neighboring yard was a dark clot of shadows: a maze of vegetable gardens, compost bins, and fruit trees covered in nets. There was no sign of the man.

Oscar dropped to his knees and pulled the sheet from around Zoe's neck. She had a weak pulse but wasn't breathing. He quickly felt the skin of her throat—the thyroid cartilage and the structure of the larynx felt whole. He pinched her nostrils closed, put his mouth over hers, and inflated her lungs. Listened. Inflated. Listened. Felt her pulse, weaker.

"Zoe," he said sharply in her ear, and clamped his mouth over hers, exhaled.

A choking gasp, a rattling suck of air.

She rolled away from him, pulled her hands to her neck and her knees to her chest. She coughed harshly, and he heard a liquid spill and smelled the tang of vomit. From the front of the house, Oscar heard a car start—and, a moment later, the heavy clatter of Lovering's motorcycle falling on its side.

"We have to go," he said.

She rolled back. In her hand was a tiny wink of silver. He ducked back as the knife sliced the air. He clamped his hand over hers.

"You sent them," she said. Her voice was a croak, her breaths harsh.

He simply shook his head.

Her wrist vibrated in his hand. He let her look at him.

"We have to go."

Her green eyes were dark, shining.

"You sent them," she repeated. But he could hear the doubt in her voice. She let him lift her.

———

Oscar raised Paz's bike. It had a dented tank and a huge gouge through the chrome of the gearbox housing. He put the key in and twisted the throttle. It started. He looked back at Zoe.

"You can't stay here," he said.

She watched him for a long moment. Then she climbed on behind him.

———

He stopped the bike at the top of his street and scanned the shadows under the trees. Then he switched off the headlight and did a loop of the block. No dark cars, no one surveilling his house. He parked the bike down the side of the house and helped Zoe up the stairs. She walked on weak legs, most of her weight on his shoulders. He winced with every step. She was sleepy, a natural aftereffect of shock.

He took her inside and put her on the couch. She curled her knees to her chest and in moments was breathing deeply. He lit the kerosene lamp and saw the bruising starting to rise on her long, thin neck. He went to the fireplace, placed the .44 on the tiled hearth, opened his cache, and pulled out a box of cartridges. Slowly, carefully, he loaded his service pistol.

———

He boiled water, opened one of his few remaining packets of tea, and made a pot. He drank slowly, cup after cup, feeling the caffeine sparkle in his blood. He pulled a chair close to the front window and watched the street.

In the empty bus shelter opposite, the dead boy stood, watching. He raised his fingers to his chin. Oscar licked his lips and looked up the street. No cars came. Nothing else moved.

———

When she began to stir, he checked his watch. It was after nine. He poured her a cup of tea from the pot—it was still warm. When he went to her, she was sitting up, watching with green eyes tinted bronze by the orange lantern glow. He handed her the cup. She didn't take her eyes off him.

"I don't trust you," she said quietly.

He nodded. "But you have to."

A long moment later, she took the cup and sipped.

On the roof, a tick. Tick-tick. The first drops of rain.

"Why did you want to talk to me?" he asked.

She watched him over the rim of her cup.

"Someone needs to know."

"Know what?" he asked.

She watched him with catlike eyes and shook her head. "I don't trust you."

———

They sat in silence as hard and fragile as glass. He reached into his jacket and pulled out his service revolver. She lifted her chin, and he saw her shoulders tense. He handed the gun to her, grip first.

"The safety's on," he said.

She slid it off with a practiced thumb, pulled back the slide, and chambered a round. The semiauto's hammer remained cocked. She raised the muzzle level with his belly.

"Did you send him?"

"No."

"Who is he?"

"I don't know."

"What happened to Penny Roth?"

"They cut her, a symbol. A ritual killing. We found her. Someone on the inside tried to destroy her body. I saved it, for a while. But they got to it again. Like you said, she's burned."

The gun pointed at him didn't waver.

"Someone on the inside," she said. "You don't know who?"

He shook his head. Her eyes traced over every square centimeter of his face. The cuts, the bruises, the singed hair, the plasters. With every flick of the eyes, she connected mental dots.

———

She had him place down the Taurus and she put it in her pocket. She made him take off his jacket. She checked the pockets. She patted him down. Then she clicked the semiauto's safety back on, took the lantern and went around the room, looking in the dusty vases, under the tabletop, in the kitchen cupboards.

"What are you looking for?" he asked.

"Bugs. Recording devices."

It made Oscar wonder. He let her go.

Maybe we'll both discover something, he thought.

———

She sat on the table, cross-legged.

"You should sleep," he said. "I'll keep watch."

She laughed. Her teeth were white; her eyes were sharp.

"You're alone, aren't you?" she asked.

"I told you. My partner was killed."

"Why doesn't anyone else trust you?"

He watched her carefully. "I think they think I'm going mad."

"Are you?"

He thought about that a long time—about the creature in the garage, its claws and the smell of the dead.

"I hope so."

Her eyes narrowed.

———

It was after ten. He watched her while he lit candles and disconnected the gas cylinder from the lantern and screwed it to a heater element. The space between them warmed.

"What did you see at Elverly?" he asked. "Tell me about Frances White and Taryn Lymbery."

She held his pistol in her lap but said nothing. Growing warmer, she undid her jacket. Beneath, she was thin, but not as thin as he'd thought.

He found the phone and called the hospital.

"He's just gone in for surgery," the cardiology nurse said. "Call back in a few hours."

Zoe watched him.

———

She returned to the couch, and he to the window. He watched the street. Rain fell softly, a whisper. No cars. The dead boy stood under the bus shelter across the road. When he raised a hand, Oscar tentatively raised his own. Then he turned around and saw that Zoe was asleep.

He went to his room and found a blanket, returned, and put it over her. She didn't stir.

He heard the sound of a motor. A car was turning into the street. Oscar froze and listened. The vehicle went slowly past. He hurried to the candles and puffed them out. The room was lit only by a warm, red glow of the heater. He went to the window.

The car had gone. He watched for a long moment. The rain was almost silent. Across the road, the dead boy was still beneath the bus shelter, but he wasn't looking at Oscar; he was staring down the street. The boy seemed to feel Oscar's gaze and glanced across the road to him. Slowly, the dead boy raised an arm and pointed down the street to a deep pool of shadow under a large satinash tree.

Oscar went to Zoe and carefully pulled the Taurus from her pocket.

He crept down the back stairs and into the rain. He climbed his neighbors' fences and cut across their backyards, traveling parallel with the street, through spiny pumpkin vines and gardens and spiderwebs. He was ashamedly grateful that Terry/Derek was dead. In a backyard six houses down from his own, he turned and struck up toward the street, holding the silver Taurus in one hand.

On the footpath, the dead boy was waiting. When he saw Oscar he nodded and pointed again. Behind the boy, under the satinash, was a dark sedan. This one had plates. Oscar could make out a figure behind the wheel of the car, staring up the street toward his house. The figure shifted, and Oscar felt his feet and hands tingle. The driver held a shotgun.

Oscar licked dry lips. He wiped one hand on his trousers, got a better grip on the Taurus, and strode across the footpath. He flung open the passenger door, darted inside, grabbed the stock of the shotgun, and pressed the silver pistol's muzzle against the stranger's neck.

"Fuck!" called the figure.

The car's dome light was bright, and Oscar blinked. The man behind the wheel was Anthony McAuliffe.

Emotions wrestled on McAuliffe's gray, unshaved face. Fear, embarrassment, anger, and his dirty teeth chattered. The air in the car stank of cheap alcohol.

"Mariani," he said.

"What are you doing?" Oscar asked.

McAuliffe looked from Oscar to the pistol to the shotgun. "I'm leaving," he said.

Oscar saw a taped-up cardboard box and a patched, fraying suitcase on the backseat. He watched the former professor.

"And what did you want to say to me?"

McAuliffe said nothing, but his thin hands still gripped the barrel of the shotgun.

"What about Megan?" Oscar asked.

"You're losing your job," McAuliffe said. "I rang, asked for your unit. It's closed. You have no job. Megan's screwed anyway."

Oscar stared, his heart beginning to pound harder. "And after me? Was she your next visit?"

McAuliffe tried to pull the shotgun away. His two hands were stronger than Oscar's one. Oscar thumbed back the Taurus's hammer.

"What are you going to do, Mariani? Kill me like you killed her?"

The men stared at each other. Rain tapped on the roof.

"Mr. McAuliffe?"

Zoe stepped up to the driver-side window, into the glow of the car's inner light.

Oscar looked up and watched her green eyes take in the pistol, the shotgun, the two men.

McAuliffe looked from Zoe to Oscar.

"You two?" McAuliffe asked.

Oscar yanked the shotgun away. The man seemed to deflate without it—he sagged against the steering wheel.

"Hurt your daughter and I will kill you, McAuliffe."

The man shook, and Oscar could see that his cheeks were wet.

"Get out," McAuliffe whispered.

Oscar did.

McAuliffe's car started loudly, and a moment later it disappeared up the street.

Chapter 29

Oscar lay on one side of the bed, clothed, holding the shotgun and listening to the house shift and creak. When he felt Zoe's weight press on the other side of the bed, he didn't move. He listened.

For a long time, they were both silent and still.

Finally, she spoke so softly that Oscar wondered if he was dreaming her voice.

"Franky," she said.

"Franky?"

"Frances White. But she liked to be called Franky. She had Fragile X syndrome. Learning-impaired; she had lots of trouble with remembering things. Little problems would get her upset. But such a sweet girl. Tall, but not very strong, always anxious. But so sweet. She *loved* her pencils. Loved to line them up, just so. Very shy. She had agoraphobia. She wouldn't run away." As she spoke, he heard her fingers move on the grip of the pistol she held. "It was five in the morning. Pretty dark. I'd just finished work and was outside on the street, about to walk to the train when I saw a car come by. Big black car, dark windows. I stepped into the shadows till it went past. And I saw it switch off its headlights and drive into Elverly. My next shift, I was told Franky had run away."

Oscar waited.

"And Penny?" he asked finally.

Zoe let a breath out through pursed lips.

"I was on shift. I was supposed to be in B-Block, at the back. Everyone was asleep. I went across the lawn to A-Block, the old building, and broke into the kitchen. I was in the pantry. They don't pay us very well, you know?"

"I know."

She nodded. "Elverly is on a slope, and the kitchen is half-underground, yeah?"

"Like a basement."

"Only with some windows, high up, so you can just see out of them. They're level with the drive almost. Well, I saw a little flash of light outside, out those windows. And I climbed up on the bench and looked out. And there was a car. The light I saw was the one that comes on inside when the door opens. I just saw the door close, and the car drove off. No headlights. I checked all my kids in B; they were fine. But the next morning Penny was missing."

"You told Chalk?"

"I told her I thought I heard a car in the night. I didn't tell her where I was when I saw it." He felt her roll toward him. "It was a cop car," she said.

Oscar felt a chill ride up his neck.

"How do you know?" he asked.

"It had the little lights on the back parcel shelf. The red and blue lights. It was an unmarked cop car."

Oscar rolled and looked at her. Her face was a carved mask in white and black: pale skin and shadow.

"Come with me," he said. "Come into headquarters; I'll take a formal statement."

"No."

"We can subpoena vehicle records for the last month—"

"No." She shook her head. Unrushed. "You knew a cop was involved."

"I have no proof," he said.

"Neither do I. But they know we know."

Oscar shifted, and he felt the muzzle of the gun she held against his ribs. Then the metal pulled away.

They lay still for a long time. Eventually, he heard her breathing become slow and deep. It was hours, though, before he slept.

———

Wind rushed like a foaming ocean in his ears, and the world beneath charged up at him like a crushing wave. Then he was caught—great fingers wrapped around his head, and iron spikes drove into his spine and through his cheek. The momentum of his body swung it through and his neck snapped like celery, and the last thing he heard, as the mighty fingers squeezed his head and ground bone against bone and his skull crushed like an egg, was the steady beating of monstrous wings.

———

He jolted awake, covered in cold sweat. In another room, his phone had beeped. He felt her eyes on him as he padded out of the room.

Crossing into the kitchen, he checked his watch. It was nearly three in the morning.

The message was from Gelareh. She had finished repairing the idol.

Chapter 30

S he answered the door wearing a robe; her hair was wet.

"I didn't expect you to come straight over," Gelareh said.

"I was up," he replied. "Sorry to intrude."

"Not a problem." She stood aside and let him in. "We can eat together."

He closed the door behind him and wandered into the apartment. In the kitchen, soup simmered over a flame. Her cleaner's uniform hung over the back of a chair.

"A minute?" she asked.

He nodded, and she went into her bedroom to dress.

On the table was a gas lantern, and a shape covered by a cloth. Oscar turned on the gas and lit the lamp's mantle. When it was glowing white, he dropped the shielding glass and lifted the satin cloth off the form. He'd seen the idol whole only by flashlight while he was ankle-deep in ashy slop. Now it was rebuilt, and in the white glow of the gas lamp he could see it in awful detail. It was spiderwebbed with cracks, and some small missing fragments left dark triangular or rhomboid holes—but it was whole. It stood about two feet tall and was half that in diameter. Its legs were spread obscenely wide, exposing a gash two-thirds the width of its body and traveling a third of the way up its bloated abdomen. Its feet were avian, with horned plates and long talons. Its breasts were small, goatlike teats. Its mouth was an alien chasm: the upper and lower beaks divided horizontally so the orifice was opened like a quartered orange, exposing a split tongue that led to a flat disk of woven metal—a tiny grille separating the mouth from the belly space below. The demon thing's eyes were wide-set and owl-like. Even though this was merely clay, the eyes conveyed unsettling intelligence and ruthless hunger. From its head sprouted two horns, curled and mismatching. Its wings were more like a bat's than a bird's: like the rest of the idol, they were covered with markings that Oscar had first taken to represent feathers or scales but which he could now clearly see were the letters of a strange language. On the idol's back was the seven-pointed star, and the fissured flaw where an air bubble in the clay had exploded during its firing.

Oscar was drawn back to the idol's eyes and the mouth. Wide eyes, predator's eyes, round and unblinking and as rapacious as its gawping mouth, split widely not once but twice, so eager to consume some kind of special flesh.

"She's no oil painting, is she?"

Gelareh's voice startled Oscar. She now wore tracksuit pants and a woolen cardigan, and was pulling her hair back into a band. He saw by the way she looked at the totem that she found it both intriguing and repulsive.

"And every time I see you, you look worse," she added, taking in his fresh batch of wounds. "Next time I see you, you'll be dead."

He smiled, but felt an ominous chill. Mother Mim had said something all too similar. He nodded down at the idol. "How did you go?"

She crossed to the table. "It was interesting. Whoever made this had spent quite some time getting it right. The languages, I mean."

"There's more than one?"

"I can make out three. Soup?"

He realized he was hungry. "Please."

"Sit," she said. While she ladled, she continued: "The Aztec glyphs, like I said before, I really can't help you with. But the rest, yes. Some are Akkadian, but just single terms. The majority of the writing is Sumerian. Some of the cuneiform were ruined by the flaw here"—she touched the ragged hole on the idol's side—"and some when it was broken."

She handed him the bowl of soup. It smelled delicious: spiced and hot. She returned the pot to the flame.

"And?" he said.

Gelareh sat beside him and opened a notebook. There were twenty pages filled with the wedgelike symbols scrawled into the pottery, accompanied by words in Hebrew and English. There were tables of letters and symbols, and dozens of instances where words had been scratched through and new interpretations written above them. There were sketches of the idol from four angles, highlighting spots where key phrases of ancient text were written.

"Good Lord, you've been busy."

"They cut some of my work shifts," she explained. "And fortunately I'm fairly familiar with those two languages." She unfolded a pair of reading glasses and looked at Oscar. "Yes?"

"Please," he said.

She smiled. "That is, in fact, what it says here. And here, and here." She touched the birdlike totem on its shoulders and on the top of its horned head. "'Please.' Messages of supplication. And here, there, and there it says, effectively, 'We beg you' or 'We beseech you.' But here, around the star, we see the main message."

Oscar leaned forward. "And what is that?"

The room was still. The light in the lantern flickered and made the shadows on the idol's gruesome, hungry face shift. It was as if the idol were listening.

Gelareh licked her lips, and read, "'Queen, our Queen. You, behind the darkness. You, behind death. You, behind the curtain of bone.'"

Oscar felt the skin on his arms and neck prickle with goose bumps. His eyes were drawn to the wide, gluttonous mouth of the totem, its grossly spread legs, its unblinking stare.

"'Accept this gift we bring with joy. Ereshkigal, Queen of Queens, the gate is open. Come as you will and grant us your favor.'"

She looked up at Oscar and raised her thin eyebrows.

"Eresh—?" he began.

"Ereshkigal."

"You mentioned her last time. The sister."

Gelareh nodded and left the room. Oscar looked out to the dark courtyard. The tiny bleed of light from the lantern made the wider darkness look enormous, holding infinite secrets. Gelareh returned with a heavy book entitled *Artworks of Mesopotamia*. She placed it on the table and flipped expertly through it.

"Here." She turned the open book down so that Oscar could see the color plate. "This is what's called the Burney Relief."

When he saw the image, he felt his face suddenly tighten, as if someone had dashed ice water across it. The photograph was of a bas-relief carving. It depicted a naked woman. Her breasts were high, and her hands were raised, each holding a ringlike amulet. Large, feathered wings descended from her shoulders, and her legs ended not in feet but in powerful three-toed talons. Her eyes held no orbs but were dark, hollow pits.

"We don't know where she came from," Gelareh said softly. "But she is, many believe, Ereshkigal."

The winged woman seemed to float above two lions—not restful beasts but carnivores alert and watching, lean-flanked and hungry. Beside each big cat was an owl. They looked as large as the lions, with talons as long as the big cats' claws; each feathered head was as broad as the winged woman's hips. These monstrous owls were wide-eyed, staring obediently from the stone, as if waiting for their mistress's command to fly or to hunt. Oscar remembered the childlike form falling from the apartment building opposite Jon and Leonie's apartment, plunging earthward, but leaving no trace below. And the dog's head, ripped from its body and crushed, as if in a vise, or by those long, powerful claws. And the talons that had tick-ticked on the garage concrete just inches from his face. It was no dream, he was sure now.

His mouth was as dry as sand.

"Owls," he said.

Gelareh's eyes were on the photograph of the relief. "Owls and lions." She smiled. "But you see her wings? Her talons? She is closest to the owls. They're her messengers, her ambassadors. Her soldiers." Gelareh looked at Oscar. "Are you all right?"

"Thirsty," Oscar whispered.

She went to the kitchen and he heard a glass filling. "She was painted red originally." She handed him the water. "But she faded over time."

"Red?"

"Red ocher." Gelareh smiled grimly. "For blood."

Oscar stared at Ereshkigal's sculpted head. Rings of horns held her hair above a face that was serene, almost smiling, beauteous but for the almond-shaped black hollows she stared from.

"And what does she do?" Oscar asked.

Gelareh shrugged. "Whatever she pleases. She is the Queen of the Night. Goddess of the underworld."

Three years ago, such things would have raised wry smiles. Today, there was no joking about death. The door to it had already been opened. The curtain of bone had been parted.

"And this"—he touched the idol, and the skin of his fingertips seemed to recoil—"is to please her?"

"To please her," Gelareh said, staring at the idol she'd rebuilt. "To feed her. To summon her."

The room fell silent again. Oscar watched Gelareh. She looked paler, as if she, too, felt the listening, waiting stillness.

"*Masha' Allah*," she whispered, and went to the kitchen. She moved the soup saucepan and slipped a disk of woven metal over the flame. She reached into an earthenware pot and threw a handful of seeds onto the hot wire grill. He heard her say softly, "*Aspand bla band Barakati Shah Naqshband Jashmi . . .*" Her whispered words were obscured by the popping of the heated seeds.

She returned, wiping her hands and smiling self-consciously.

"Aspand," she explained. "Syrian rue. I know: I'm a superstitious fool. But this thing . . ." She shook her head at the reconstructed idol. "I haven't enjoyed cohabiting with it."

Oscar noted the similarity between the grill Gelareh had just thrown the rue seeds upon and the circular grillwork in the throat of the idol.

"Is that how she is summoned as well? Seeds on the hot grill?"

"You're right, hot coals go in here." She indicated the vaginal gape between the idol's legs. "But this is an altar for holocaust. The offering goes, of course, into the mouth, where it burns away. I'm not sure what the offering would be. In traditional holocausts, a whole animal or person would be burned. The priests would check it, to make sure it was unblemished. If it had a coat, it would be flayed, and its blood sprinkled about the altar. But this is quite small. The mouth here is big enough to accept maybe a bird or a rodent or a handful of flesh."

Oscar pictured the gash in Penny Roth's abdomen, and Teddy Gillin pointing out the rude cuts where her ovaries had been excised. "A handful of flesh," he repeated.

Gelareh nodded. "At least we can say this has never been used. This crack here ruined it. The dark queen has not been summoned."

She smiled, but it was a forced expression. Oscar didn't tell her about the ponytailed man who'd carried this idol's wrapped twin from Florica's.

They sat in silence for a long moment.

"Will you have more soup?" she asked, and they both smiled at how startling her sudden words were in the quiet.

"No," he replied. "Thank you."

She nodded, and went to the bedroom again. She returned with a cotton shopping bag and placed the idol in it.

"If you want to break it again," she said softly, "be my guest."

A bang startled them both. The French door to the courtyard swung loose on its hinge. Outside, the cold wind hissed in the climbing jasmine. The flames under Gelareh's soup danced, and the aromas of herbs rode inside on the shifting air: basil, Jafari, star anise. Gelareh apologized and hurried to bolt the door shut.

"This weather," she complained. "Everything has gone mad."

Oscar let his nostrils drink in the last, delicate tendrils of fragrance. An idea jumped into his head.

"Do you have any cinnamon incense?"

Gelareh's dark eyes fixed on him and narrowed. Without a word, she turned to the pantry and returned with a small earthenware jar that she placed in front of him. She opened it to reveal short, sticklike curls of brown bark.

"Just the bark," she replied at last. "Some people burn it as incense."

Oscar inhaled, and with the strong scent returned the memory of exactly where he'd smelled it last.

Chapter **31**

The wind battered the motorcycle with invisible fists. Leaves and scraps of paper swirled through the white cone of the headlight. He could smell rain coming, and in the east, lightning flashed in the clouds over the ocean. He raced north, ignoring traffic signals and hunching his shoulders as he sped through intersections.

Oscar stopped the bike not far from where he'd parked to visit Tanta and stepped onto the footpath where he'd paced waiting for her to finish with a client. Music played somewhere, an angry and shrill tune. The wind preceding the storm flung past a mixture of scents that combined into an unpleasant greasy ensemble. From a doorway, two boys in rags watched him with the attention of hungry rats.

"Two bucks?" asked one.

Oscar showed his badge, and the boys retreated into shadow.

He went to the head of a narrow alleyway. It was here, two days ago, that he'd smelled fish and coal smoke and incense. Cinnamon incense. The buildings' old downpipes whistled low and tunelessly. He stepped into the alley, and the wind diminished. It was dark, and he paused to let his eyes adjust. As he waited, his nostrils flared. He smelled spoiling potato, diesel oil, fish heads and, so faint that he wondered if he was imagining it, the earthy smell of burned cinnamon.

He took the Taurus from his pocket and walked carefully down the damp alley.

The walls were lined with old bins that leaked puddles of noisome liquids, and plastic milk crates and yawning old refrigerators that stank of piss. In shadows as thick as velvet, he heard tiny things scurry away. He inhaled. The herbal tang grew stronger.

He stopped and looked up.

A dozen feet overhead was a tiny window, hardly two handspans wide. Behind it, the orange light of a candle flame fluttered like a handkerchief in a breeze. Oscar didn't dare turn on his flashlight, so he stepped toward the black wall beneath the window, one arm outstretched. His fingers touched cold brick, slick with mossy growths of who-knew-what. His fingers went left and right, feeling for an architrave. A wooden door. Its paint was peeling. He found the doorknob. Beneath it a keyhole.

It was an old single-lever mortise lock. Of all the locks he'd picked in the locksmithing course at the academy, the single levers were the oldest and easiest to corrupt—a bent piece of wire would open them, as would most keys of the same type. Oscar pocketed the Taurus and quietly pulled out his own house keys, careful not to let them jingle, and found the one for his own home's back door. He slid it slowly into the keyhole; it fitted and turned easily.

Now was the test. If the resident within had so much as a single barrel bolt inside the door, he was stymied. He gently twisted the doorknob.

The door creaked just a little and opened in its jamb.

Inside was darkness, but the chorus of smells was much stronger: fresh flowers and tobacco and cinnamon incense. Oscar pulled out the pistol again and felt his way forward, left arm swinging in the dark like a blind man's. It found something round and small as a child's skull. His fingers traced across it, and he smiled to himself. It was a small sphere of timber, the cap of a newel post. Stairs.

He kept as close to the wall as he could, slowly pressing and releasing his weight with each rising step. As he climbed, the smells grew stronger yet, and he became aware of vague shapes: an edge here and there, a rail, banisters. As his head grew level with the next story's floor, a strip of light appeared: a line of candlelight from under a closed door.

Oscar stood still. Now was the time to call the controller to send support units, Code One. But if he dialed now Naville might hear him and take another way out of his hidey-hole. But that wasn't the real reason Oscar didn't call. He wanted to catch the man himself.

He padded softly toward the closed door.

And something crinkled underfoot.

He stood stock-still, cursing his luck. He listened, and felt his heart pushing hard behind his ribs. No sound from behind the door.

Oscar slowly raised his boot.

Beneath it was a bottle cap.

And the light beneath the door went out.

Oscar swore under his breath. If Naville slipped away, he would never be found. A rock spider who had survived three decades in maximum security knew how to keep a low profile. It was now or never.

Oscar reached into his pocket for his pencil flashlight, held it beneath the grip of the Taurus, and stopped in front of the door, bracing for a shotgun blast through the thin timber. He raised one boot and kicked hard just below the lock. The door burst inward with a crash of splintering timber and snapping metal. He flicked on the flashlight, stepped quickly inside, and ducked.

His heart raced as the light swept left to right, up and down, picking out details of an utterly unremarkable room: two wooden chairs at a tiny lopsided table; the curved arm of a tattered sofa with a blanket neatly folded at one end; a plant stand holding a jar of wildflowers; an unlit kerosene lamp; a small transistor radio on a sagging chipboard bookshelf that held only half a dozen westerns; a kitchenette that was merely a sink and a gas hot plate, with a breadbox and a small Tupperware container of spreads and cereals. Oscar fixed the beam on something noteworthy: a large mortar and pestle, flanked by a dozen jars of seeds and stalks. A large earthenware bowl covered with chicken wire. From the ashes on the mesh came the powerful, smoky kick of burned cinnamon.

"Albert?" Oscar said. "Albert Naville?"

Across the room, in an indented nub of a hallway, clustered three narrow doors. One was wide, showing an old porcelain toilet. A second was ajar, and through the gap Oscar saw a single towel hanging on a glimmer of flaky chrome rail. The third door remained closed.

Oscar crept to the bathroom door and carefully pushed it all the way in, keeping the gun barrel back and ready. The bathroom was empty.

He went to the closed door and listened. From behind came a soft but insistent sound, a whispered rustling like a dozen small birds trapped in a box. The thought of wings made Oscar's heart gallop faster.

"Albert?"

No answer.

He put the pencil flashlight between his teeth, took the cold brass handle in his left hand, and in one move twisted the knob and threw wide the door. In the same instant, he dropped low, grabbed the flashlight, and swept it across the room.

There was no one in it. In the far wall was set the small, single window Oscar had seen from the alley. It was wide open. Cold air rushed in on a stiff breeze, and the busy, winglike flutter grew louder. Oscar looked up.

"Fuck," he hissed.

Every square inch of the ceiling was covered with papers. Hundreds of sheets were pinned by thumbtacks to the ceiling, and they jittered and flapped in the wind. And every page was filled, either with words or with drawings or symbols. Some were English, some Latin, some French; hundreds more were covered with the rune-like cuneiform Oscar had seen on the idol, and on Penny Roth. Pictographs and hieroglyphs: Egyptian, Chinese, Mesoamerican. And symbols: vévés, crosses, swastikas, ankhs, eyes of Horus, signs of the zodiac, and stars. Dozens and dozens of seven-pointed stars.

Oscar shined the flashlight around the rest of the room. Leaning against one wall was an old aluminum stepladder and, beside it, a small wooden footlocker. The room was otherwise empty except for a woven sea-grass mattress in the center of the floor, and a notebook and pen.

Oscar heard a distinctive metallic click behind him.

The voice that followed was calm and unhurried.

"You never looked behind the couch."

Oscar felt adrenaline flood up his chest and neck. "My ex-wife used to say the same thing when I lost my keys."

He went to turn, but the voice froze him. "No, no," said the man behind him. "Turn off your flashlight and put that cannon down."

Oscar flicked off the flashlight, and realized that a softer, warmer light came from behind him. Naville was holding a candle. He slowly bent and placed the Taurus on the wooden floor, not far from a notebook and an open cardboard box of thumbtacks.

"Kick it away."

Oscar nudged the heavy pistol across the floorboards with his boot. And at last turned to face Albert Naville.

Naville was more than a head shorter than Oscar, a spare man with no spare flesh. Despite the cold, he wore just a singlet and shorts; his limbs looked ropy and strong. Although he was in his sixties, Naville's face was strangely youthful; he was clean-shaved, and his eyes and lips shared an odd, detached smile, as if he were remembering an unfunny joke told by someone pleasant but witless. His feet were bare, and his long silver hair was loose about his shoulders. It seemed that Oscar had disturbed him at his work. No time to dress, but time enough to find his pistol: a tiny derringer, but with two big holes in twin barrels. It looked to Oscar like a Noris Twinny—a nine-millimeter next to useless over more than twelve feet or in nervous fingers, but Naville was only six feet away and seemed eerily relaxed.

He noticed Oscar looking at the small gun, and his eyes twinkled. "Yes, beware the little things."

He gestured for Oscar to remove his jacket. Oscar dropped it to the floor, revealing the empty holster under his left arm.

"You know, I was in two minds about you," Naville continued, and motioned for Oscar to lift his arms and turn full circle. "I am a student of behaviorism as well as innatism. I said to myself, don't underestimate Oscar Mariani. He may yet be his father's son." He nodded at Oscar's trouser cuffs. Oscar lifted them, revealing no ankle holsters, no more weapons. Naville seemed satisfied and grinned, showing a hint of the wild smile that Oscar had seen in the newspaper clipping. "And here you are."

Oscar wondered if he could close the distance between him and Naville before a lead slug smashed into his heart, and decided there wasn't a hope in hell.

"Where's Taryn Lymbery?" Oscar asked.

Naville tutted. "Straight into it, Detective. Where's the foreplay?"

"It's not too late, Albert. You can go back to your cell, no need to extend your sentence. You just have to tell me—"

"Cut it," Naville said, glancing at his watch. "And kick me your jacket."

He kicked the jacket to the old man.

Naville knelt. "Now, which pocket do you keep your cuffs in?"

"I don't remember," Oscar said.

Naville shook his head, disappointed. He kept the Twinny trained on Oscar and began to search the jacket pockets. Oscar saw something small catch the flickering light on the floor behind Naville. Two thumb-tacks had escaped their box.

He said, "Who are you working with, Albert?"

Naville pulled out Oscar's key ring, a cigarette lighter, and his bribery stash of condoms, tea bags, and Viagra tablets. "I'm a solo flyer, Mariani. Didn't your father teach you anything?" He looked up at Oscar and affected a frown. "Or maybe he couldn't be bothered."

He grinned and kept searching.

"You screwed up dumping Penny in the sewage plant, didn't you, Albert? Bet they weren't happy with you then."

Something flashed behind Naville's eyes. "You're a shithouse guesser," he said. "I'm amazed you found me at all."

The old man glanced again at his watch.

"When are they getting here?" Oscar asked.

Naville hesitated as he emptied pockets. "There's no 'they,' Mariani."

"They're coming, aren't they? You keep checking your watch. That's what you did when you heard me outside. You grabbed your phone and you called your betters."

"They're not my—" Again, a flash behind the old man's eyes: something twisting and reasonless as fire. Oscar realized that Naville was, indeed, almost mad. "Things will be easier if you just tell me where your cuffs are."

"Did they let you kill Taryn Lymbery? Or were you only allowed to mark her, since you screwed up so badly with Penny Roth?"

"*I* didn't screw up." Naville bit down on his next words. This time his sharklike smile had to thrash harder to beat down the madness in his eyes. He lifted the pistol. "Keep stalling and I'll shoot you right here and burn it all down. I've done it before. Handcuffs, please. Now."

Oscar could see the snub barrel of the Twinny shaking. The knuckle of Naville's trigger finger was turning white. Oscar swallowed down his fear and shrugged.

"So now they're freezing you out. They don't need you anymore. They've got the altar, so now they can get rid of Bert Naville before he fucks up again."

"I didn't fuck up!" Naville snapped, stabbing the pistol toward Oscar's chest. His wild grin was unmoderated now: it was the same savage smile Oscar had seen in the photograph of Naville cuffed to Sandro. Naville's hand was shaking. His blood was up. "Cuntish Marianis," he whispered. "Cuntish guessers."

Naville looked at his watch, did a calculation in his head, then kicked Oscar's jacket away. He was done searching for the cuffs. "I wanted to keep this place. Too bad."

He aimed the pistol at the center of Oscar's chest.

Oscar clapped his hands together and shouted in his best approximation of a correctional officer: "Inmate Naville!"

The old man jerked instinctively. The Twinny barked, and Oscar felt hot air brush his cheek like a salamander's lick as Naville took a startled step backward and suddenly howled, reflexively grabbing at the thumbtack in his bare heel.

Oscar dropped and jumped for the Taurus.

Naville, unbalanced on one foot, spun as he tried to follow Oscar with the Twinny.

The trigger pull on the .44 was heavy, but there was no time to cock it first. He aimed for Naville's thighs, and squeezed. The boom of the large gun shook the cold air in the room. A hole the size of a softball appeared in the wall behind Naville. The old man bleated and aimed the derringer at Oscar's face.

Another thunderclap, and a large part of Naville's upper leg disappeared, and a violent fountain flumed out behind it. The old man twisted and collapsed like a breaking chair. The Twinny yacked again, but Naville's second shot went wide, high into the wall.

"Naville!"

The old man dropped the Twinny and grabbed at his spouting leg. He was spasming, his mad eyes wide and searching.

Oscar could see that a fistful of flesh was gone from the upper thigh. Shattered bone protruded and blood gushed. He scurried over and clamped both hands down and into the deep wound. Blood simply squeezed out between his fingers, under his palm.

"Where is Taryn Lymbery?" Oscar said. "Albert? Where is Taryn? Is she dead?"

Naville's face grew white, and suddenly all the years flowed back onto it. His other leg began jolting like a dog's in sleep.

Oscar squeezed harder, fingers probing and catching on sharp bone, trying to find the artery and stop the tide. "Who were you doing this for, Albert? Is it Haig? Albert!"

Naville's eyes lost focus and his jaw suddenly jerked wide.

"Naville!"

The old man went still, and breath slid out of him in a soft sigh.

Oscar looked around. A puddle the width of a child's wading pool had flowed from the body.

"Fuck. Fuck. Fuck."

And he glimpsed Naville's watch.

A car was coming. Naville's accomplices.

Oscar grabbed the Taurus and his flashlight and hurried through the lounge room, looking around wildly. No sign of Naville's phone. He ran down the stairs and into the alley. The loud reports of the pistols had roused residents of nearby buildings, and shadowed figures appeared from dark doorways. "It's all right," Oscar said, running and trying to hide the bloody .44. "Police! Go back inside."

It had no effect; more figures began to arrive, murmuring and shouting over the wind: What happened? What's down there? Who shot who?

Oscar ran to the head of the alley, where a small but growing crowd had gathered. "Move away!" he called. "Police!"

Someone flicked on a bright flashlight and shined it down the alley.

"No!" Oscar shouted, and pushed through the onlookers to try to stifle the beam.

"Fucking cops," someone said.

"Put in a complaint," suggested another, and there was a burst of laughter.

Oscar saw the headlights of a dark car appear at the far end of the street.

"Back *inside*!" he hissed.

"Fuck you," someone said.

The dark sedan stopped, too distant for Oscar to read its license plate. Men and women and children milled at the head of the alley. A group of boys squeezed past and ran down into darkness, tiny flashlight beams winking like fireflies. Oscar saw the car reverse, perform a quarter turn, and speed away.

He swore, his voice bouncing off the hard brick. Then three or four copycats of both genders contributed their own echoes. Peals of laughter rode over the wind.

———

Oscar returned to Naville's flat and was almost knocked aside by the two young boys from the shadowy doorway; they scampered out carrying armfuls of food from Naville's kitchenette.

"Hey!"

Oscar hurried back inside.

Naville's body remained where it had fallen, but footsteps radiated from the blood puddle like crimson petals. The ladder was gone. Naville's wooden footlocker had been upended and pawed through; paper and notepads were strewn across the floor, and a dozen old books were scattered. Nothing there had interested the thieves. Oscar heard footsteps behind him. A pasty-limbed girl of ten or eleven appeared in the doorway—she regarded the body without interest, then looked over the rest of the room.

"Anythin' left?"

Oscar showed his badge and she slumped away, disappointed.

In the distance, the faint, tweezing pinch of approaching sirens.

He returned his attention to the wooden footlocker and its contents. It was old, and three letters had been carved in its base: A.J.N. Oscar hunched on his heels and peered at the books and papers. He pulled out a handkerchief, wrapped it around an extended finger, and began picking through the papers. There were titles on the occult, Mesopotamia, Aztec religions, African vodun. All were published before 1983.

The sirens grew louder. Overhead, the papers rustled louder in the stiffening wind.

One book stood out from titles on lost civilizations and diabolism: a King James Bible. Its cover was a dark-blue fabric, worn through at the corners, and the exposed edges of its pages were the color of brass. This book looked more than a century old. Oscar carefully picked it up. Why would an occultist keep a Bible?

The inscription in the front read, "For Elliot Naville, with gratitude and regard, the Mgt. & staff of Gowe & Smith & Co." On the next page was a list of family names and significant dates: births and marriages, deaths and divorces. A family tree.

The sirens pulled up outside as Oscar found Albert Naville's name and birth date. And, next to his, his sister's: "Leslie Naville." Only her surname had been bracketed in ink of a different color and prefaced with "nee"; next to it was written a wedding date, and Leslie's married name.

"Chalk."

————

The bike slewed dangerously, throwing a rooster tail of gravel as he raced up Elverly's drive. The windblown branches of willow trees whipped at his hunched back. He dropped the bike and ran up the stone steps.

The front doors were locked.

She's not here, he told himself. *She'd be at home, tucked in bed.*

But the tight knot in his belly told him that wasn't so.

As he rang the buzzer he smelled gasoline.

Oscar ran down the side of the old building, his boots crunching on twigs, and overgrowth catching at his cold, bloodied trousers. Somewhere a loose metal door banged loudly. Despite the rushing air, the dry-swallow stench of petrol fumes grew stronger.

The back of the building had a concrete pad, large bins, propane tanks with heavy chains, and a utility shed. The shed's door was loose and it clanged monotonously against the metal sides. Oscar tried the back door. It opened.

The reek of fumes inside made him cough and gag. Children were crying. It was dark. As he stepped onto the old polished-tile floors, he slipped. His fingers came away wet.

Gas.

"Chalk!" he yelled, and his voice echoed off the dark timber.

He flicked on his flashlight, and the circle of light reflected off a wet trail running up the hall. He played his light on the timber walls but saw no fire alarms to sound. He ran as quickly as he could without slipping, and the cries of frightened children grew louder. Some banged on their walls. Two girls appeared, arms upraised against the light, the larger with crutches, the other a mute limpet on the older one's side.

"What happen? What happen?"

"Outside!" he yelled as he ran. "Get outside!"

He followed the fumes, expecting any moment to see a sunlike puff of yellow ahead, followed by a rolling wave of red fire.

He rounded the corner into reception. He stopped, his feet sliding treacherously on the wet floor.

Leslie Chalk hung from a rope threaded through the carved fretwork breezeway above the office door. Her slippered feet twisted lifelessly above a red plastic jerry can. The fingertips of one hand were purple, trapped between the choking rope and her pinched neck. Her other hand hung like the bob of a stopped pendulum; directly beneath it, on the gas-soaked floor, was a yellow plastic cigarette lighter.

The lights of emergency vehicles made the glossy leaves of Elverly's trees and bushes flicker like the facets of great gems—jumping forward when the strobing lights hit them, then retreating into darkness. Three patrol cruisers were parked on the gravel near the entrance. Behind a LaFrance fire truck and two ambulances, the Scenes of Crime van was packing up. Even out here in the cold air, the smell of petrol wafting from the main doors made Oscar's tongue curl to the roof of his mouth. He watched as undertakers loaded a small covered body into the back of their hearse.

He sat on the front steps, rocking gently and humming. His knees stung from kneeling in the gasoline attempting to revive Chalk, and he wanted badly to wash from his mouth the taste of her dead lips, but he didn't want to let go of the girl sleeping in his lap. Megan was crying when he found her. He simply lifted her and carried her outside as he made all the phone calls. Summoned from the other buildings and roused from sleep in their homes, caregivers shepherded the children from the old main building into B-Block; some pushed wheelchairs, some carried small mattresses and blankets. Every time one of the caregivers came to get Megan, the look in Oscar's eyes sent them away. The tears had dried on her face, and he'd wiped away most of the mucus from under her nose. He stroked her hair and hummed.

As the Scenes of Crime van went past him, the officer in the passenger seat sent Oscar a cold, superior stare. A fourth cruiser was coming up the drive. Oscar watched the van stop halfway down the drive beside another patrol car arriving. The drivers talked for a moment, then the van continued and the glossy cruiser parked near Oscar. Haig alighted and walked toward him, the gravel under his highly polished shoes grinding like worried teeth.

Oscar stopped humming. He felt Haig's stare.

"Is this the girl you hit?" Haig asked.

For a long moment Oscar said nothing. "Back, are you?" he asked finally.

Haig sniffed the air and pulled his cigarillo tin from his jacket. "What makes you think I've been here before?"

"There were no prints on the jerry can," Oscar said. "And no prints on the cigarette lighter. Kinda weird, don't you think?"

"Gasoline's a solvent," Haig said. "Dissolves body fats."

"And Chalk's car isn't here. How did she arrive?"

Haig's eyes glittered, reflecting his lighter's busy little flame. "Murder, you think?"

"Yes," Oscar replied. He felt drained. "I do."

"Someone was covering their tracks, then."

"That's my thinking," Oscar agreed.

"And you *say*"—Haig produced a clear plastic evidence bag from a pocket and held it open in front of Oscar—"the woman was dead when you arrived?"

Oscar snorted a laugh and pulled the silver Taurus from his jacket pocket. He quite liked the way the Taurus felt in his hand. Solid. And he knew it worked. He let the muzzle aim loosely at Haig's belly.

"Neat thought, Geoffrey. I killed Chalk. And what would be my motive?"

The inspector shrugged. "I really don't know. You're an odd fish. Not money."

"No. That's your game."

Haig inhaled and the cigarillo's end glowed brightly. His face was as impassive as firelit stone, yet his eyes sparkled smugly. He knows I won't shoot him, Oscar thought. He thumbed back the hammer of the pistol.

Haig's eyes widened the tiniest bit.

"What are you thinking, Mariani?"

"We both know Naville and Chalk weren't working alone," Oscar said.

Haig exhaled smoke. A dozen possible futures raced through Oscar's mind like the dogs at Gillin's track, bounding in colorful streaks. Shooting Haig, and being gunned down before he reached the bike. Shooting Haig, and going on the run. Shooting Haig, being arrested and led to the holding cells while wondering what would happen to Megan and Zoe. He thumbed down the hammer and dropped the pistol into the evidence bag. Haig slowly zipped it shut.

Oscar realized that his career was over. Megan wriggled in her sleep, and he stroked her face.

"You're the wrong man for the job," Haig said. He walked past Oscar up the stairs into Elverly. "Always have been."

A few feet away, two caregivers hovered nervously with an empty wheelchair. Oscar nodded, and the girls came to get Megan. He watched them wheel her away.

He stood and walked on stiff legs toward the motorcycle. His partner was dead. He'd run out of leads: two perpetrators were dead, but he still knew nothing of their motive, nothing of their collaborators, nothing about where Taryn Lymbery was.

And Haig. Something told him that Haig was implying the truth, that he really had never been here before.

Oscar lifted the Triumph from the gravel, and every muscle hurt.

Haig was right. He was the wrong man for the job. Always had been.

Chapter 32

The cold chicory water swirled in a pleasingly hypnotic rhythm. Oscar watched the oily rainbow slick shift and break on its black surface. As long as he swirled, he didn't think. As long as he didn't think, he was okay.

From the far end of the corridor came a carillon trill of laughter. Two nurses joked. The predawn sky out the window was pewter-gray. By habit he glanced up at the hospital corridor clock. It was nearly six in the morning. Behind him were the double doors leading back into Cardiac Care. He'd moved out here at around four, after he'd caught himself watching the blips on Sandro's cardiac monitor with the intensity of a doomsday scryer. At some point, a nurse had brought him a pair of trousers from Lost Property and spirited his old pair away, but he still smelled faintly of gas and blood.

A door opened somewhere, and he heard footsteps approaching.

Moechtar's suit and face matched—businesslike and bland. He carried a leather document folder. Oscar nodded to himself. Only dazzling promotions and embarrassing departures arrived out of the office at six in the morning, and there was no fanfare accompanying his inspector.

Moechtar sat beside him. They were both silent for a long while.

"How is your father?" Moechtar asked eventually.

"Surgery went well. But he's had a reaction to the antibiotic. They've changed it. We'll see."

Moechtar rested his hands on the document folder.

Oscar asked, "Did anyone find Naville's phone?"

Moechtar pulled off his glasses and wiped them with a white handkerchief. "No. Detective Bazley suspects there probably was no phone, given that one must present photo ID to purchase a SIM card, and Naville, having left prison unlawfully, couldn't have ID."

Oscar nodded. Of course, one could go to any market and buy a stolen phone complete with SIM card and a bunch of credit for twenty bucks. Oscar wondered why he wasn't angrier. Tired, he supposed.

"Inspector Haig has a different view," Moechtar continued. "He thinks Naville may have had a phone, but it was stolen while you were out on the street instead of keeping the crime scene secure."

Oscar smiled. That was tidy: Bazley with one approach, his boss with another. Homicide's own double-barreled Twinny, a bob each way.

"Me, though"—Moechtar unzipped the leather binder—"I was quite impressed. You identified Penny Roth's body and you found her killer. The coroner is prepared to accept your photographs of her body and the evidence found on Naville's ceiling with a view to declaring her legally dead and Naville as her killer."

"And Leslie Chalk's death?" Oscar asked, already knowing the answer.

"Suicide."

Oscar nodded, unsurprised.

Moechtar handed Oscar a sheet of paper. He tried to focus on the words printed there but was simply too tired.

"What's this?"

"Your resignation," Moechtar replied. "I did the math. By resigning now, your payout will, in fact, exceed your earnings should you continue in another department at a considerably lower pay scale."

Oscar stared at the paper.

"Where would that other department be?"

Moechtar thought about that, then spoke in a tone reserved for far-fetched theorems: "Well, in light of the performance record of the Nine-Ten Unit and the fact that you recklessly abandoned a crime scene, your demotion would be significant, and any reposting would be a long way from here."

An orderly wheeled past a cart of soiled laundry, dragging sad and unpleasant smells.

"Naville's place was searched," Oscar said. "Did anyone find the altar I described in my report?"

Moechtar sighed. "No."

"And the images of Naville leaving the building that burned down?"

"There is no clear connection between those and Penelope Roth." Moechtar's voice was growing tighter, as if wound by invisible ratchets. "If you found something on-site there, you should have formally logged it. Honestly, Oscar, how did you expect me to help you when you do everything outside the system? What did you think would happen?"

"I thought that whoever got Penny Roth's body to the crematory and Naville out of jail would get rid of my evidence, too."

"I've requested permission from the commissioner to investigate those anomalies and I'm pleased to say he's agreed."

"And Taryn Lymbery? And Frances White?"

Oscar noticed that Moechtar was watching him with an expression that took a moment to identify. It was pity.

"They're missing, Oscar, and Albert Naville is dead." He reached into his pocket for a pen and slid the folder and paper onto Oscar's lap. "Here."

Oscar heard light footsteps, and one of the swinging doors behind him opened.

"Mr. Mariani?"

It was one of the cardiac nurses. Oscar stood and handed the folder and the unsigned letter back to Moechtar.

"I'm sorry."

Moechtar nodded. "I'll need your identification," he said. "The suspension's temporary."

Oscar reached into his wallet and slipped the badge out.

"And you'll have to surrender your service weapon."

"It's at home," Oscar said.

"Bring it in later." Moechtar stood and offered his hand. Oscar looked at it, then shook it. "I'll push to find you something decent in a town as close as possible."

Moechtar left, and Oscar followed the nurse into the ward.

———

Sandro Mariani was as pale as paper. Tubes and wires seemed to have him suspended in an electric spider's web. He looked worn and diminished, attrited by the years; the stubble on his chin and cheeks was no longer gray but the dead yellow of old grass. The clear plastic mask over his nose and mouth clouded as he muttered in his sleep.

"I'm sorry," the nurse said. "He was awake. A bit disoriented, but he asked for you."

Oscar nodded and pulled a chair beside the bed to sit. Nurses moved as silently as ghosts. Sandro's sleeping hands searched for a small bundle to hold. Oscar reached and gently took hold of the arthritic fingers. They closed around his hand.

———

He was five, and nervous. He couldn't stop thinking about his pants. He didn't want to wet them. Mrs. Waislitz had helped him pack the night before, and her daughter Bethy—who was older than Oscar and liked to give Indian burns—had cried a lot, even though he'd been with the Waislitzes only a month or so. "How long will I be with these ones?" Oscar had asked.

"Always," Mrs. Waislitz had replied.

It didn't make sense.

And now a policeman. He was quiet, but he looked scary and angry. He gave Oscar strange little looks as he drove. Up through the windscreen, Oscar could see clouds of brilliant purple pass overhead.

"Jacaranda," the policeman said. "From South America."

Oscar crossed his legs and said nothing.

"Here." The policeman turned the wheel and nodded to himself. "We're home."

The car stopped, and the policeman got out. There were voices, the policeman's and a woman's. Oscar looked at the window; the sun was shining on its dust and making it almost too bright to look at. He didn't know if he should get out or wait. His bladder felt ready to burst and he wanted to cry.

Then the door opened and warm air rolled in.

The sun was behind her, and it lit her brown hair gold. He had to squint to make out her face. She was pretty and smiling. Then she laughed. "Oscar," she said. "Welcome, Oscar." And she laughed some more. It was such a pretty sound, and from then on he heard it whenever he saw the lavender bells of jacaranda flowers.

The woman helped him out of the car, and the world became a swirl of sunlight and purple and green grass. It didn't make sense.

"Big boy," she said, although Oscar knew he was little. "Such a big boy."

Her hands were warm and dry. And as she turned him—sun to shadow, sun to shadow—he saw the policeman looking at his wife and smiling at her delight.

He was woken by a coded alarm and the padding of soft-soled shoes. Sandro's eyes were open and sightless, and his grip was soft. His vitals monitor flashed panicked red rectangles.

"You'll have to go," said one nurse, and another began to whip a curtain closed around Sandro's bed. A doctor rushed in.

Oscar nodded as gentle hands urged him out, and the curtain swished shut behind him.

It was afternoon when the undertakers came for the body. "You don't have to wait for them," the nurse told him, but Oscar said he would stay, and she offered him sandwiches.

The doctor had come and explained about how Sandro's reaction to antibiotics had weakened an already weak system, and how he had not been a candidate for further surgery while the infection remained so severe. Oscar tried to think of questions to ask, but he couldn't come up with any. The doctor smiled kindly, squeezed his shoulder, and left. A nurse had come, patted his hand, checked her watch, and was gone. Then another nurse arrived with more sandwiches and ersatz tea. A wardsman asked if it was okay to take the body now, and Oscar watched as they rolled Sandro away under a sheet, down the corridor, toward the service lift.

He followed it, and was allowed to wait in the small visitor section of the hospital morgue. When the funeral director arrived, Oscar saw that it was the same bald man from whom he'd taken Penny Roth's body. Oscar barked a laugh, signed several forms, and then went home.

Chapter 33

He tried to sleep but couldn't. The sunlight was hatefully bright. When he got home from the hospital, Zoe was gone. He washed, called for Sisyphus, waited, then crawled into bed.

He lay awake, wondering what he should be thinking about. His father. His career. The missing idol. Taryn Lymbery. Megan McAuliffe. How much a funeral cost. Who would perform the eulogy. His brain shucked off every suggestion, refusing to engage.

He rose and pulled on work clothes.

The backyard had the sweet, pleasant smell of rotting fruit. A possum-ravaged pawpaw sat beneath the tree, and around a few tomatoes buzzed fruit flies. The basil had gone to seed, and the grass had grown almost to his knees. The only sign of neatness was the patch of vegetable garden Haig had weeded. There was irony in that, somewhere, Oscar thought.

Near the fence stood the dead boy. Oscar forced himself to look at him. He was small. Maybe fifteen. His skin was pale. Sheaves of grass protruded through his legs. His eye sockets, even in the sunlight, were as black as Whitby jet.

"How is my father?" Oscar asked.

The boy bit a thin, pale lip. He shrugged.

Oscar nodded. "Useless," he said, and looked away.

He bent to work, pulling weeds and tossing them, as Haig had done, into neat piles.

His phone rang. It was Jon. He offered condolences. Oscar realized how pointless they were, but thanked him nevertheless.

"Sandro was one of the old guard," Jon said. "One of the good ones."

"Yes."

A silence. Jon cleared his throat. "And I heard about your suspension. Bullshit, utter bullshit."

While Jon railed, Oscar muddled about pulling clumps of wiry asparagus fern from the spinach patch and snaking Madeira vine from the trellis. Maybe he should resign. Take the money. Garden.

He realized that Jon had asked a question and was waiting for a reply.

"Sorry?"

"What are you going to do?"

Oscar stared at the overgrown garden. "I don't know."

"Have you got a copy of his will?"

Oscar had no idea.

They made loose arrangements to catch up for a drink.

Oscar fetched the push mower. As the sun warmed his back, the mower clattered and sprayed showers of green. He had to run over each patch of ground twice to clear the stubble. He assumed there was a will. Vedetta had a sister somewhere in Melbourne. He supposed the house could go to her. But if the house went to him, he could sell it. Or he could move there, sell this house, and pay for a live-in caregiver for Megan. Maybe Zoe would agree to move in.

The mower wheel caught.

Oscar stopped. He knelt and parted the tall fronds.

It was roughly cylindrical, about as long as a large eggplant; a twisted mass of gray fur and white bone. It smelled leathery and faintly acidic. Oscar tilted the huge pellet with his shoe, and little white grubs crawled away from the light. At one end, he could just make out a blank white eye socket, and a jawbone with sharp, feline teeth.

Sissy.

A wild panic overtook him, and he checked the sky. He suddenly wanted to be indoors. He quickly buried the wadded remains, and hurried into the house.

———

The afternoon brought clouds, and rain. The bedroom became dark, and Oscar curled naked in bed, half listening as the drops hit the roof and rattled down the pipes. He felt light, so light that he might rise through the sheets, through the ceiling, and drift away, so he gripped the sheets and listened. The room was silent. He kept thinking of wings and claws.

I'm going mad, he thought.

In the house, he heard something shift. A tiny, careful rustle. He felt under the pillow for the service pistol that wasn't there; Zoe still had it. Another rustle. A click of something hard bumping the tabletop.

He had the sudden, childlike desire to pull the sheets over his head and curl tighter. Instead, he quietly stepped out of bed. His foot touched cold steel, and he was surprised to see McAuliffe's shotgun on the floor. He quietly picked it up and stepped on bare feet into the hall.

Rustle. Click. Something was just around the corner.

He stepped in, raised the shotgun to his shoulder.

Zoe flinched at the sight of the weapon, then frowned at Oscar's nakedness. On the table, she'd placed plastic bags containing her belongings from the house she'd fled: shampoos, clothes, a few books. He could see that the skin around her neck had darkened in a bruised band.

"Are you all right?" she asked.

He nodded, lowered the gun, and padded back to the bedroom to dress.

———

It was dark, and they drank tea, dressed warmly against the cold. Rain drummed overhead and dribbled down the window glass. She said that after she'd gone home to get her things she'd gone to Elverly.

"They're going to shut it down," she said. "Distribute the kids around the city."

He nodded slowly. "When?"

"No one knows."

The silences between words were strange and delicate. He wanted to stand and light a lantern, but he was afraid that if he moved she would, too. She might go and not come back.

"Maybe I could bring Megan back here," he said quietly.

She watched him.

"Maybe," she said. "Yeah."

"You don't think it's a good idea?" he asked.

"I think it's a great idea," she replied. "It's just weird hearing it come from you."

He stood, finally, and lit a candle. As the yellow flame squirmed alive, something pale shifted at the side of the room. The dead boy stood beside the curtains. He gave Oscar a small smile.

Oscar turned back and saw that Zoe was watching him.

"Who is it?" she asked quietly. "Your ghost?"

Oscar hesitated.

"A boy," he said. "I don't know who he is."

"You don't know him?" She frowned a little. "Have you never tried to find out?"

Oscar returned to the table and sat opposite her. He felt the dead boy's stare on his back and was sure he was listening. "I did. I checked the deaths registry, and Missing Persons. I didn't find him."

"You're a detective," she said. There was admonishment in her voice.

Oscar spoke carefully. "When he appeared, the first time, he was in the middle of the road. I was driving. I swerved to miss him. I hit Megan."

Zoe said nothing for a long time. "And you think that was his fault?"

Oscar opened his mouth to protest, but there was no energy in him for it.

"No," he said. "Not anymore."

She watched him for a long moment, then stood and walked around to him. Her frown deepened and her lips parted, but she didn't speak. She reached down and took the hem of his sweater and lifted it off him. Cold air pressed against his arms. He watched her. She lifted his T-shirt. He braced for more cold, but heat came from inside him. Her green eyes followed her fingers as they swept back his coppery hair, stroked down his neck, to a dusting of russet hairs across his sternum. She placed one palm across his chest and felt his heart. It beat quickly.

As he reached up, she took his hands, curling his fingers in hers.

"Cold," she whispered, and lifted his hands under her own jumper onto the skin of her belly and slowly up to her breasts. Her nipples hardened when his cold fingers touched them. He saw her mouth open just a little wider.

He slid one hand around her back and pulled her closer. Her pupils were large, her lips were warm, her breath was hot and clean. Her tongue found his, and then he was on his feet. His hands moved down and unbuttoned her jeans; they pooled around her ankles, and he placed her on the table. He went to his knees, and she pulled his face in toward her. She was wet skin, warm silk. She took a handful of his hair and raised his head, lifting him with one hand, unzipping his pants with the other. He pulled her to the edge of the table and entered her. She watched his eyes and nodded.

"Good," she whispered, and wrapped herself tightly around him.

———

In bed, she nestled behind him. He felt her breasts beneath his shoulder blades. Her hands on his ribs felt as delicate as small birds, ready to fly. There was no light in the room.

He thought she was asleep until she said softly, "I'm sorry about your father."

Outside, the rain was easing. They listened to the drops slowing.

"Who is yours?" he asked.

He felt her narrow chin lift against the flesh of his shoulder. "Mine?"

"Your ghost."

"Oh," she said. "A boy, too." She fell quiet for so long that he thought she'd drifted off to sleep. But then she spoke again. "I was sixteen. And he was five weeks old. I hadn't hardly slept since he was born, not more than two hours at a stretch. Mum had married a—" She went silent again for a moment. "Home was no good, so I lived underneath a friend's house, with Will. Little Will."

Raindrops rolled off the awning and dripped softly on the grass below.

"I was so tired," she continued. "He rolled. Or I rolled, I don't know. I must have rolled in my sleep, and I woke up and he was all still." Her hand on his ribs had gone hard. Angry. "They kept asking if I resented him. If I missed my old life. Saying I was only sixteen and I must have missed being single and carefree. Police."

Oscar said nothing. He hardly breathed.

She seemed poised like a tightrope walker.

"He was little," she said. "And I was young. But I loved him."

Oscar heard her roll away.

She whispered, "But why did he have to come back?"

———

He woke. The rain had stopped. Water dripped in the downpipe outside, a slow and mournful tocking like a distant, broken bell. Deeper in the house something moved.

Zoe was not in bed. He rose. The air was cold.

She sat at the kitchen table, her pale face painted orange by a single candle's light. The cotton bag Gelareh had given him was folded on the kitchen table, and Zoe was staring at the reconstructed altar. She didn't look up as he approached. The idol seemed to watch her with those wide-set, strangely sentient eyes and to reach for her breasts with its ugly, doubly split beak. He had the sudden urge to shout a warning, smash the thing again, and wrench her away. But her stillness stopped him.

"What's this?" she asked, not looking up.

He told her. He told her about the dog's head in his garage and the creature that had crushed the idol there, Sisyphus dead in the backyard. He told her about Albert Naville, his arrest by Sandro thirty years ago for defiling and murdering a girl, his escape by fire, and his destruction by flames of the occultist he employed to make this profane idol and its twin. He told her about the writing on the totem, its ancient symbols and its sister glyphs carved into Penny Roth's abdomen before her uterus was cut out and fed into the obscene, flaming brazier.

Zoe stared at the clay thing's malformed face.

"It's because they're virgins," Zoe said quietly. "Virgins make the best sacrifices."

Of course, Oscar thought. Adolescent girls, away from their parents, untouched because of their afflictions.

Zoe turned to look at Oscar. In the candlelight, her green eyes were black. "What are they trying to raise?"

"The Queen of the Dead," he replied.

The room fell silent.

Oscar's telephone rang and they both jumped. He looked at the screen. The number was blocked. Zoe watched him carefully.

"Mariani," he answered.

"Detective." The voice at the other end was smooth; apologetic without sounding the least bit sorry. "I realize it's late. Commiserations about your father."

Oscar put a face to the voice.

"Thank you, Karl. What can I do for you?"

"I was wondering if you had a moment."

Chapter **34**

Oscar stepped onto the porch and drew the front door closed with a loud click.

Across the street was Chaume's long, gull-gray Bentley Karl stood inspecting the street with the repose of a man admiring a well-executed landscape painting. He didn't seem to notice the drips of rain that fell from trees and beaded on his tailored wool suit. As Oscar crossed the road, he unhurriedly opened the car's rear door.

The deep leather seats were empty.

"Where is Ms. Chaume?"

"Not far," Karl replied. "Inspecting a property."

The big car rode in near-silence, up the street to the ridge road. It sailed like a ghost ship past dark shuttered shopfronts, blank-eyed houses, and rambling, tangled gardens to the road's highest point, where Karl slowed and stopped.

The back door opened again, and a gust of cool air tossed Oscar's hair. He stepped out. Karl pointed, then got back behind the wheel, leaving Oscar to make his own way.

The Church of St. Brigid speared like a sharp-knuckled fist of red brick from the peak of the hill. Here were the buttressed walls where Delete addicts hovered around fires, where deep shadows held the gruntings of sex or violence close under tall spires and narrow windows. Oscar walked past the black cavities between the buttresses, and his fingers instinctively hunted under his jacket for a pistol that wasn't there. But he heard none of the rough sounds. The place seemed deserted. The parasites had fled. High above, something flapped, and his eyes jerked upward. Tied to the crenellated wall was a large sign:

THATCH CONSTRUCTION. He walked past the building across the asphalt church grounds. At their edge was a parking lot bordered by a short brick wall that dropped away sharply, and beyond it was the panorama of the city: a grounded galaxy of weak stars. The suburbs far to the east, near the ocean, were obscured by an invisible curtain of rain that swept like the train of some goddess's black dress, trailing behind her as she stepped out to sea.

Oscar didn't see Chaume; rather, he noticed an absence of light. Like some distant, unknowable planet, she caused the space around her to shift. As he came closer, he made out her shape against the winking lights below. She stood on the edge of the brick wall, her back to him, staring out at the city.

"Detective," Anne Chaume said, not turning.

She wore a coat of dark fur, and her jet-black hair fluttered like a wing. He stopped below her.

"You're not scared?" he asked.

Chaume's eyebrows rose. "Of?"

She took a step along the wall edge. Oscar could see the sheer drop an inch from her shoe, and the soles of his own feet twitched vertiginously. She watched not the ground but him. Her pale eyes shone like polished metal.

"I don't really get scared," she said. "I thought we had that much in common."

"I seem to be scared a lot lately."

"Ah." She turned her face back toward the view. "Don't you love the city?"

"I used to," he admitted.

Her long fingers swept a length of silken hair behind a tiny ear. "I do. There's so *much* of it."

"You've bought this?" he asked, indicating the church.

She turned and smiled.

"Have you ever noticed that Catholic churches are always on the high ground? Nearer to God? Or, simply, most valuable? They knew what they were doing. What do you think I should do with it?"

Oscar looked up at the brick church.

"Keep it," he said, thinking of Neve. "Religion's not dead. People will rally."

Chaume watched him for a moment. "I'm counting on it."

She stepped catlike down from the wall. Her face was china pale and seemed almost to glow. He'd forgotten how beautiful she was.

She smiled at him. "You left in a hurry the other night."

"My partner was murdered."

"I was sorry to hear it. And to learn about your father."

Oscar nodded.

"I read that your husband died," he said. "Sometime back."

Chaume nodded. "He did. Went and got himself a parasitic infection, poor silly fellow."

"I'm sorry."

Her eyes didn't leave him. "Not quite so tall. A bit tidier."

She put out her hand. He crooked an elbow, and she slid her arm through it. His heart beat a bit faster. He felt foolish, and foolishly proud, and traitorous all at once. They walked beside the wall.

"You don't seem a very happy man, Detective Mariani," she said.

"I'm working on it."

She was silent a long, easy moment. "What could make you happier?"

He could smell her scents: French creams and verbena and immaculately clean clothes. She walked lightly, and he could feel her arm shift under the expensive fur. He imagined her skin bare and struggled to change the thought.

"I've considered becoming a multimillionaire," he said. "It seems to agree with you."

She made a noise, unimpressed.

"No? Are the rumors true, then?" he continued. "Money can't buy happiness?"

"Oh, money is like milk in the fridge," she said. "Handy to have, but you can live perfectly well without it."

"So you've tried living without milk?"

She smiled. "I did, once. I went through a phase where I despised my father, and everything he supposedly stood for, and I ran away from home. Do you know what that's like?"

She seemed already to know his answer.

"Yes," he replied. "Where did you run away to?"

"To be with a man I thought I loved. I was sixteen. It's easy to love men when you're sixteen. Every year after that, it gets just a little bit harder. Or maybe men just get a little bit duller. More scared."

Oscar realized that she had pulled his arm closer to her own body. Beneath the fur, he could feel the swell of her breast against his triceps.

"Let me ask you something," he said. "I've seen these all over the city." He indicated the Thatch Construction banner behind him. "What happens if those projects fail?"

She inclined her head. "They won't."

"Are you that rich?"

She turned her profile to him as she considered this. "Money gets you so far, but then its influence runs out. Beyond that, you have to offer something else. Power. Sex." She looked at him. "Serenity."

"Serenity," he said. "Hence the church?"

"Fuck the church." Her voice was soft. "I want the high ground."

They reached the end of the wall, and stopped. The view of the city was uninterrupted, horizon to horizon. She turned to him. "What do you want?"

"I'll take the serenity," he said.

Chaume leaned closer. And, as she did, her ice-blue eyes appeared like bubbles from a dark pond. Her breath was sweet. Her lips glistened, reflecting the faint light.

"I can help. What are you going to do? Now that your case is closed, I mean. Now you're on the market."

Her words were simple but rich with promise.

"I'm suspended," he said with effort. "Not unemployed. And I don't think the case is closed."

"Really?" she said softly. "I heard you got your bad guy."

"I got a cog," Oscar said. "I want the whole clock. And the guy who wound it. That would give me some serenity, Ms. Chaume."

Someone moaned, high up behind him. Oscar turned sharply, only to realize that it was the wind through the bell tower. The tops of the buttress walls were peaked and looked like massive teeth. When he turned back, Chaume's face was shadowed.

"Does that mean you're unavailable?" she asked.

"For what?"

"Does it matter?"

He hesitated. "Yes," he said. "Unavailable."

"Your father's son." She reached up, just the little she needed to, and kissed him softly on the lips. She backed away and became once more a strange planet. "Another time, perhaps."

She climbed again onto the low wall and turned to the vista—ten thousand yellow diamonds on a wide black silk. "This *city*!"

When she didn't turn back, he left.

———

Karl said nothing on the drive back home. He pulled up outside Oscar's house and left the engine rumbling while he opened the back door.

"Goodbye, Detective."

The Bentley did a smooth U-turn, became a pair of taillights in the dark, then was gone.

———

Zoe was in bed. He lay beside her, listening to her breaths, thinking of Anne Chaume's lips.

"Who was that?" Zoe asked.

"No one."

He heard her inhale, smelling the air around him.

They both stayed awake a long time.

———

He woke and looked at his watch; it was early afternoon. He went through the house on bare feet. Zoe had left. Her bags of toiletries and books were gone. His semiautomatic service pistol was nowhere to be found. He found some biscuits and ate them with water and went back to bed.

———

When he woke again, the bedroom was dark. He wondered why his phone hadn't rung and checked it. The battery had plenty of charge. Then memories returned, tapping into each other like falling dominoes.

Oscar went to the kitchen, heated water, washed, and dressed. He used more of his precious tea and finished the biscuits he'd found earlier. He wondered what to do with the cat food that was left. Into his mind flashed the picture of that foul and horrible casting he'd found in the garden—the football-size, acrid lump of fur and gristle and bone.

He paced the hall.

He went to the kitchen, found his phone, and texted Jon, rain-checking their catch-up.

He pulled on his jacket and grabbed Lovering's motorcycle key.

Chapter 35

He parked at the back of his father's house and let himself in with the key under the maidenhair fern. The basement floor was wet again, a patchwork of brackish puddles. The beam of his flashlight bounced off them and reflected onto the joists overhead, the jittery light picking out strands of dusty cobweb and little oases of mold. Sandro would never have tolerated it, not in his prime; his kitchen and workshop had always been fastidiously neat. In one respect, it was a good thing that Vedetta had succumbed before Gray Wednesday and its consequent power outages; she would have spent her last years bent over a copper boiler and scrubbing floors on her hands and knees before letting her house go to ruin.

At the bottom of the stairs, Oscar took off his damp-soled boots and set them neatly aside. He followed the flashlight beam upstairs, into the kitchen, and lit a hurricane lamp. Something smelled. The kerosene fridge had run out of fuel. He opened it and sour air puffed out at him. He emptied the milk carton down the sink and ran the tap, and threw the greening cheese and oily salami knob into the bin. He stared. In the plastic bag was the crust of a half-eaten sandwich, curled and drying. He picked it out and ran a finger along the sandpapery bread. His father's last meal here. On the drainer, a knife, breadboard, spoon, plate, and teacup. Sandro had tidied up before heading out to the street where he had collapsed. The island bench had been wiped clean. Oscar stared at the space where his parents had spent so many hours, weeks, years of their lives, kneading dough and stuffing meats and pickling vegetables, talking and arguing, singing and silent. The spot where Oscar had seen Sandro stare lovingly down at his empty, nesting hands. Only they hadn't been empty to him.

A boy, Haig had said. An infant boy. He'd lived two days.

Oscar felt eyes on him and looked up.

Across the room, the dead youth stood beneath a painting of Monreale Cathedral and its asymmetrical towers. The house was silent.

"Do you ever sleep?" Oscar asked. "Do you get time off?"

The boy licked dry, pale lips. The holes where his eyes should be seemed to shift and curl. Oscar looked away. How did it work? he wondered. Did Sandro now find himself standing over a newborn infant? Would that child—maybe a little boy—grow up with a proud, stern-faced man watching over him?

Oscar looked across the shadowy room to the dead boy.

"What happens when I die?" Oscar asked. "Are you freed then?"

The boy gave Oscar a small shrug, and his dark nylon coat lifted silently, too big on his narrow shoulders. He put his hand to his chest.

Something tapped the window behind Oscar and he turned.

There was nothing outside. He lifted the lantern to the window and stared at his own ghostly reflection. A moth, perhaps, drawn to the light.

He carried the lantern down a hall lined with vibrant wallpaper to a set of stairs and climbed.

His parents' bedroom was small. "Big enough for sleeping," they had said. Vedetta's duchess was beneath the window where it had always been, and her crystal perfume bottles were neatly dusted. Oscar opened the wardrobe and looked at his father's clothes, hanging ironed and neat on hangers. He'd have to decide what to do with them: which to sell, which to gift, which to keep. At the back, crinkled plastic reflected the lantern glow. Sandro's police uniform. On the shelf above the rail was a cardboard box. Oscar pulled it down and put it on the bed. Inside were his father's visored officer's cap, a neatly curled belt, and a set of epaulettes sealed in cling wrap. And one more item. A little key ring, with two mismatching keys.

Movement in the doorway made him jump.

The dead boy stood there. He wasn't watching Oscar. He was looking across the bed and out the window.

Oscar followed his sightless gaze.

The window was a blank eye behind floral curtains. Nothing moved.

"What?" Oscar asked, looking at the boy.

He bit his pale lips and raised a hand—a signal for attention.

Oscar picked the keys from the box. He knew what they were for.

In the upstairs hallway was a polished mahogany writing desk: turned legs, two drawer stays with brass handles on the front, a large inlaid drop lid that would swing down to reveal a green leather writing pad, a clever stack of pigeonholes, stationery shelves, and miniature drawers. But from the moment he set foot in this house Oscar had been forbidden to touch the desk, which was kept locked by the smaller of the two keys now in his hand.

Oscar set the lantern on the floor and slid the key into the desk's brass lockplate. He looked behind him. The dead boy stood at the top of the stairs. His feet shifted silently. Seeing that Oscar was looking at him, he sharply raised both pale hands and waved them anxiously.

"I'm busy," Oscar said. He'd been waiting thirty years for this.

He pulled out the desk's two velvet-topped stays, turned the key, and dropped the lid down.

There were surprisingly few items. Good paper for thank-you notes. A fountain pen and a silver letter opener. A small brass abacus that Sandro had actually used. And a dozen envelopes of various sizes, stacked on their ends in one of the pigeonholes. Half were unsealed; half had been neatly sliced open along their top edge. Oscar flicked through them. The largest was marked "Wills, Copy." He opened it. Inside were two nearly identical four-page documents: one his mother's, one Sandro's. It took Oscar just a moment to find the clause that said if both his parents were dead the estate was to go to him. He felt hollow.

Marriage certificate. The death certificates of Vedetta's parents and Sandro's parents. On a yellowing police-service letterhead, Sandro's formal letter of appointment as a sworn officer. Another death certificate: Primo Alessandro Mariani. Age at death: two days. In the same envelope, a receipt from a funeral home, including payment in advance for reinterment upon his mother's death. The infant was buried with Vedetta.

They hadn't told him.

The last envelope was marked in Sandro's hand: "Adoption."

Oscar held it loosely in his fingers and slipped it back among the others.

The air shifted.

He looked across to the dead boy. He was still at the top of the stairs, staring down into darkness. A stronger breeze tugged from the stairwell.

A door had been opened down there.

Oscar felt the hairs on his neck rise. The boy's jaw was set tight, his slight frame tense. He suddenly lifted his colorless, narrow face to Oscar and pointed down the stairs.

Oscar carefully removed the key from the desk and quietly screwed down the wick of the lantern. Darkness squeezed in with every turn until the lantern was out. Then he remembered that he had no weapon.

But he had the key ring. The second key was for Sandro's gun safe, in the basement.

To get there he had to go downstairs.

The light coming in through the windows was gossamer thin. He could make out the rectangles of doorframes, the vertical teeth of banisters, the sallow triangle of the dead boy's face. He was mouthing something, but Oscar couldn't tell what.

Oscar went to the top of the carpeted stairs and looked down into the living room. Oblongs of faint gray light fell over the furniture, picking out the curves of chair arms and the angles of bookshelves but leaving most of the room in pitch darkness. The shadows moved. Curtains were blowing. A door banged, and Oscar dropped to a crouch. He watched. The shadows stopped moving. Whatever door had opened was now shut.

The dead boy was no longer behind him. He was downstairs, his back to Oscar, looking.

Oscar crept down one tread at a time, willing his irises to open wider to counter the heavy darkness. The stairs creaked under their carpet pelt, and Oscar grimaced. Across the lounge room was the dining room, the kitchen, and on the far wall the stairs to the basement. Thirty feet through darkness.

Oscar felt the hairs on his scalp and arms rise. How long would it take to cross to the kitchen? Six seconds? Five? If he ran fast enough and didn't hit any furniture, maybe—

Scrape.

Something moved in the deep shadows below.

The dead boy whirled and turned his white face to Oscar, raised his arms, and dropped them hard.

Without thinking, Oscar ducked.

Something huge streaked over his head and smashed into the wall. Air flumed around his head and a charnel-house stink assaulted his nostrils.

"Fuck!"

Oscar lost his footing and tumbled down the remaining stairs. He fell on his face, sprawled on the carpet runner.

Foul wind poured like a wave over his face, and a huge mass punched through the air above him. Something sharp nicked into his shoulder, tracing a bright line of pain. There was a gigantic whuffing of air, then ahead of him the brass chandelier dropped to the dining table with a deafening crash.

Oscar got to hands and knees and scrambled to the dining table, hurling chairs out of his way. Behind him, the air shook again, and something weighty landed on the floor. He turned to see between the table and chair legs a large hunch of darkness, shifting and moving inhumanly toward him. Then a leathery scrape as it gripped timber, and one of the chairs was flung across the room, shattering on a wall.

Oscar glanced ahead and saw the dead boy crouched in front of him, frantically waving him foward. Oscar felt the air pulse behind him and heard a mighty suck of wind. He fumbled between the table's end legs and felt a razor nick in his ankle. He jerked his leg away and heard hard, sharp things tear carpet.

There were two creatures. Into his mind flashed the Burney Relief and the winged, clawfooted woman flanked by lean cats and two huge, death-eyed owls.

Oscar got to his stockinged feet and ran toward the dead boy.

A great shadow detached from the darkness above and barreled down at him. He had just a moment to see it grow as two enormous capelike wings arced high. He threw himself behind the island bench as a great chunk of painted wood exploded from its corner, splintering out across the floor. Air buffeted Oscar as he flung his hands over his head and curled; the massive shape swept past him, and he heard the crackle of dry feathers slapping the laminated bench top. A graveyard stench dusted the air, and the creature's momentum carried it on into darkness. Furniture was tossed aside, torn and snapped.

Oscar looked behind him. The boy stood at the top of the basement stairs, gesturing urgently for Oscar to follow. Oscar didn't want to move—there was no cover between the bench and the stairs. He could feel warm liquid dripping down inside his shirt—the cuts stung like razor slashes. The dead boy waved sharply—now! Oscar rolled to his feet and ran in a crouch, his eyes on the boy's wan face. Glass splinters stabbed through his socks and into his feet. He ignored the pain.

The boy's black, blank eyes seemed to widen, and he threw his hands to the floor. Oscar let himself drop and felt fetid air blast past him. Hair was torn from his head, and new strips of ice-sharp pain flared across his rib cage. The crockery cupboard above him burst apart as a huge gray shadow slammed into it—glass and shards of timber flew like shrapnel, and the air was thrashed in huge, violent scoops.

Oscar dived through the door and down the basement stairs. His knee twisted painfully as he whirled to the door—he took its painted edge and slammed it shut just as something smashed at the other side, and Oscar heard the timbers of the jamb squeal in protest. He reached up and rammed the barrel bolt home. *Smash!* The timber in the middle of the door began to splinter. He turned and felt his bad knee fail, and he slid on his backside down the stairs, each tread punching painfully into the small of his back. He landed in a heap at the bottom just as a third blow smashed at the door, and he heard the screws that secured the barrel bolt ping away into the darkness like bullets.

And bullets were what he needed. He limped across the wet floor toward the workbench. Above it was the padlocked metal gun cabinet. He fumbled in his pocket for the key.

Smash! The door at the top of the stairs shook on its hinges and more strained metal squealed. Oscar looked around but couldn't see the dead boy. He felt with one hand for the padlock and jabbed at it with the key. It wouldn't go in.

Smash-smash! Twin blows against the door, and a loud crackle of failing, splitting timber.

Oscar flipped the key, and it slipped into the lock. He twisted hard and the hasp snapped out. He wrenched the metal door open. He knew what was in there: the two .22 rifles that he and Sandro used to take rabbit-shooting—the Weatherby and the Marlin. Scopes. Magazines. Cardboard boxes of cartridges.

SMASH! CRASH! The door flung open, and the air in the basement shuddered. Oscar's fingers closed on a rifle, a magazine, a box of shells. He felt rather than saw what was coming and dropped to the floor just as everything on the workbench was swept aside by a vicious wave, and there was a piercing shriek as sharp claws scraped across metal and the gun cabinet was wrenched from the wall to clang loudly on the floor.

As Oscar ran across the basement, he realized with dismay that the box of cartridges he clutched in his hand seemed to be getting lighter, and he heard the brassy tinkle as shells fell to the floor. He gripped it harder and sprinted for the tiny bathroom on the other side. The dead boy was beside its door, pinwheeling his arms. Oscar felt the air behind him charge with a building rush as things gathered momentum and streaked toward him. He dived into the tiny cubicle, smacking his head painfully on the porcelain—a dazzling white cloud of sparks roiled behind his eyes. He swung one leg and kicked the door closed behind him, then braced it shut with the other just as the creature smashed into it.

CRASH! A powerful shock of impact jolted up Oscar's leg. He put his bleeding shoulder against the porcelain pedestal and braced both feet on the door.

CRASH! Splinters of wood struck his face; his legs shuddered and fresh pain erupted from his twisted knee. He rolled the rifle onto his chest and fumbled for the magazine, and with shaking fingers began to feed in cartridges. He realized that from the whole box he had only six in his palm.

CRASH! An ugly nova of gray half-light appeared in the middle of the door. Oscar fed two more shells into the clip. His shoulder was growing ice-cold.

The crashing stopped. Silence. His trembling fingers slipped the last cartridge into the magazine.

BANG! The timber of the door quaked under a massive impact, and the whole toilet room shuddered. Grenades of pain went off in Oscar's knees, shoulder, neck. And by the murky trickle of light coming through the new hole in the door he saw three claws as large as daggers spear through the timber and begin to tear.

"Fuck off!" Oscar shouted.

The claw wrenched away a chunk of door paneling as large as a bread plate and Oscar saw a curve of horn as large as a man's shoe slide slyly into the new gap. Its beak. Oscar felt his stomach go to water. The room went black and the door timber screamed and splintered as the beak bit and twisted.

Oscar slammed the magazine home, chambered a round, pointed

the barrel at the widening hole, and pulled the trigger. The shot was deafening in the small space, but not as loud as the awful, alien howl from the other side—a piercing sound like a thousand fingernails across blackboards. He chambered another round and fired again. Another shriek, as shrill as shearing metal. His ears rang. He chambered another round.

An eye appeared in the hole—a sulfur-yellow disk with a black and lifeless oil pool at its center. Oscar aimed from the hip and fired. He heard the creature's head snap to the side. He slid the bolt and fired one more time through the door. There was a final, frustrated screech as loud as a braking train. A massive flurry of air. Silence.

Oscar lay on the cold, damp concrete, listening.

There was no sound except the ringing in his ears and the harsh, fast gasps of his own breaths. His heart pumped pain around his body. He had only one round left in the gun.

He held it tight on his chest, pointed at the door, for a long, long time.

———

Over the shaking barrel of the .22, he peered carefully out the ugly hole wrenched in the toilet door. Misty gray light of early morning shone through the basement windows. He could see the damp floor, the workbench with its scattered mess, the twisted crumple of the gun cabinet. In the middle of the room was the dead boy. He gave a small smile and raised his thumb.

———

Jon found him seated at the dining table, drinking from a bottle of cooking sherry he'd discovered at the back of the pantry.

The big man looked around at the smashed chairs, the shattered cupboards, the loaded rifle in front of Oscar.

"Oscar," Jon said carefully. "What the fuck?"

Oscar shrugged stiffly.

"What happened?" Jon asked. "I couldn't get you on your phone. You weren't home. What the *fuck*?"

Oscar watched Jon turn slowly, surveying the damage. He didn't know what to say. In the basement, he had found the rest of the .22 cartridges, fully loaded the magazine, and gone through the house. There were no feathers. There was no lingering smell of the crypt. No sign of forced entry. Only a drunk, distraught man who'd just lost his father and his partner and his job, and a trail of destruction.

"You're bleeding," Jon said, looking at Oscar's shoulder, shirt, bare feet.

Oscar nodded again and offered the grappa bottle to Jon, who batted it away.

"What happened, man?"

Oscar wondered if he should tell him. Tell him about the symbol, about Haig, about the missing children and the altar and the Burney Relief and the owls as big as Alsatians.

But he knew how it would sound.

"I drank too much," he whispered. "It's nothing."

Jon lifted him. "I'm taking you to Emergency."

Oscar shook his head, and nausea swelled in his gut.

"I'll call you later."

———

Oscar tidied the house. Straightened the chairs. Swept up the broken glass and the splintered wood. And shivered the whole time. He sobered quickly and rode home.

———

He was sprinkling salt into a shallow saucepan of water over the gas ring when he realized that she was behind him. He could almost feel her eyes wandering over the puncture wounds and shallow slices in his bare shoulders.

"What have you done now?" she asked.

He turned around.

Zoe stood in the doorway, her bags in her hands, undecided. Four paces behind her, the dead boy stood watching, too. The sunlight was harsh.

"You should go," he said quietly.

Her eyes narrowed, and she stepped into the kitchen, putting down the bags.

"What happened?" she asked.

He shook his head. She made him sit. She poured some salt water into a bowl, dipped a cloth in it, blew gently to cool it, and dabbed at the wounds. He gritted his teeth.

"What did this?" she asked.

"You have to leave the city, I think," he said.

Her pursed lips seemed to say that she was considering the same thing. She dipped again, and the water stained pink.

Oscar looked up. The dead boy was closer. He was looking not at Oscar but at Zoe. He extended a finger and cut a Z into the air. He made an O with fingers and thumb, then pulled their tips tight toward his pale palm.

Oscar stopped her hands and looked at her.

"Do you have any deaf kids at Elverly?" he asked.

"Why?"

"Do you sign?"

"A little."

Oscar repeated the three letters the dead boy had made.

Zoe raised an eyebrow. "Cute. I didn't know you signed."

Oscar felt like a fool. "I don't," he said, and looked at the dead boy. "Who are you?"

The dead boy's wormhole eyes seemed to fix on Oscar's moving lips, reading them. He frowned, and Oscar could see his chin tremble. Then his head jerked and his hands rose and began to move. Oscar awkwardly emulated every movement: he patted his chest, tapped two fingers of each hand together, then held up crossed fingers.

Zoe watched and spoke. "My. Name. Is . . ."

The dead boy licked his lips and signed each letter. Oscar copied.

"J-a-m-y. B-r-u-m."

Oscar stared. "Hello, Jamy," he whispered. "Thank you."

The dead boy nodded and gave a small smile.

"You were deaf?" he asked the boy. "You read lips?"

Jamy nodded shyly. Then his hands rose again.

Oscar copied; Zoe interpreted.

"I. Am. S-o-r-r-y."

Jamy turned his empty eyes to the floor. Outside, sunlight made the windows bright and the boy seemed to glow. Motes passed through him.

"Sorry for what?" Oscar asked.

The dead boy's hands rose and performed a graceful, simple pantomime. One hand was a car. The other a person. The car swerved. The person fell.

Oscar felt a strange lightness in his chest. He felt empty, almost weightless. He looked at the boy with the downcast, horrible eyes.

"That wasn't your fault," he said.

The boy shrugged.

Then he seemed to steel himself. He raised his hands and signed again.

"And," Zoe interpreted.

Jamy's hands fell mute at his waist.

"And? And what, Jamy?"

The dead boy pursed his lips. Chin still low and narrow shoulders hanging, he signed some more.

Zoe said, "Let. Me. Show. You."

Chapter 36

Zoe's arms tightened around him as he took each corner. Every pothole caused the bike to shudder and pain to spark in his body. Steam rose from the wet asphalt, and the sun flared on the glass towers of the city. Every time Oscar rounded a corner, Jamy would be on the side of the road or at the lights ahead, standing still, one hand pointing the way. Oscar would see Jamy retreat in the rear-vision mirror and the next moment when he looked ahead, there the boy would be again.

Traffic was sparse, and thinned further as they wound past the light-industrial buildings of the Valley down into the riverside suburbs. The sun was a harsh but heatless winter light that made him squint.

Jamy appeared on a corner near a smashed telephone box. He raised a hand and gestured for Oscar to slow and turn down into a side street. As he passed the boy, Oscar could see his thin, pale fingers shaking.

They stopped on the verge of an overgrown park. Oscar knew it, though he'd not been here for years. He, Sabine, Jon, and Leonie had visited once for a boozy Sunday picnic. Above the thigh-high grass rode the blackened tips of children's play equipment, scorched by a long-ago fire. Oscar and Zoe dismounted. Jamy waited in the grass and gestured for Oscar to follow. Oscar looked at Zoe; she nodded.

The boy's passage didn't disturb the grass as he led the way. Oscar plowed through it, feeling his feet squelch as the sodden ground let cold liquid run into his shoes. Zoe followed.

Ahead, on the far side of the lake of grass, was a row of massive fig trees. Oscar recalled how inviting they had once looked, their wide canopies offering cool shade under which picnickers could lounge while their children climbed the friendly limbs. But now the trees were untended and wild: their domelike canopies were lushly dark, and their lowest branches hung down almost to the tips of the thigh-high grass. Beyond them, the river.

Jamy walked toward the third tree and cast a look back to be sure Oscar was following. The boy neither rushed nor tarried, a condemned man's pace. The ground smelled spoiled, overrich with moisture and rot. Oscar glanced back toward the road. There were no cars.

Jamy didn't duck but passed through the low-hanging coins of leaves into shadow. Oscar stooped. As he moved into the tree's dark shadow, the lush grass gave way to stragglier yellow blades and eventually a mulchy floor of damp twigs, spongy rotten leaves, and stands of mushrooms. They were now in a private semidarkness that smelled of woody damp. Massive branches as gray as slate rose into a nightlike canopy; the few tiny glimpses of sky became the stars. Out of the sunlight, the air was cold. Jamy waited.

The trunk rose from the ground like a giant, fluted wrist twelve feet wide; from it struck a wild spiral of huge roots, each emerging from the trunk at shoulder height, writhing and curling out to a good ten paces from the trunk before plunging down into the black carpet of leaves. These buttress walls of live wood were covered with graffiti, a thousand carved initials, but none was fresh. In toward the trunk, the tall roots formed twisting trenches that seemed to descend to burrows and secret places.

Jamy led them toward the trunk.

"It smells," Zoe said quietly.

It was worse than that. The air was becoming thick with sweet rot. Somewhere, flies buzzed.

Jamy stepped into one of the tunnel-like alcoves between the roots and waited.

Oscar reached into a pocket and found his flashlight. Its circle of light was shockingly bright in the gloom. He looked up at Zoe.

"I'm coming with you," she said.

They went into the strange tunnel, crouching where a loop of root as thick as his thigh curled over its sisters. Oscar played the flashlight down the slick passage of wood, but it curled away into darkness. He touched the smooth bark to steady himself; it had the uncomfortable feel of animal hide. The buzzing grew louder, like the hum from a midnight hive. They stooped lower, duck-walking into the twist and downward into the earth. The smell grew stronger: spoiled meat.

The roots now rode in all directions, forming a warped, slick shaft that was almost erotic yet utterly repulsive and claustrophobic. Things with many legs scuttled away from Oscar's flashlight beam. They were forced to crawl. Finally, the tunnel stopped. A metal dinner tray blocked the way; on it was printed a sketch of Melbourne's Carlton Gardens. The stench was almost overpowering in the clogged air. Oscar's stomach spasmed. He looked around at Zoe; she nodded grimly—do it. He gritted his teeth and pulled aside the tray.

A cloud of flies buzzed past, lighting on his face and crawling into his hair and ears. Oscar felt his traitorous stomach give way—he turned aside and let loose a thin soup of brine and sherry. He reached into a pocket and found a latex glove and turned the flashlight back into the gloom.

"Oh, Jesus!" Zoe whispered.

Two bodies were crammed into the tiny space. The topmost was a girl's, and she had been dead a few days. Flies—lethargic in the cold—crawled in and out her nostrils and open mouth. Her skin had sagged and was an unpleasant waxy yellow. She was naked, jammed into the cramped space, her legs folded pathetically one over the other. Oscar could see a patch of ugly black above the faint nest of pubic hair. He reached in and shooed the flies away. Crusted black, and peeling away, the skin was incised. He could just make out the points of a star. Above it was a gash right across her belly. In this, tiny white things wriggled. Maggots.

He'd found Taryn Lymbery.

The body below Taryn's was clothed; where the girl had been shoved in headfirst, the corpse beneath had been thrust in the other way round. Oscar recognized the black jacket. He'd seen it every day for the past three years. The lank hair was still there, perched precariously on a skull that had begun to sink into the stained earth. There were patches of dry, leathery skin on the cheeks, and his shirt was visible. It was a dark rust brown. Blood. Oscar knelt in and shined his flashlight on the boy's neck bones. His throat had been cut so deeply that the blade had scored the vertebra.

Oscar turned. Jamy's ghost was behind Zoe, staring sadly through worm-pit eyes at his own body.

"Let's go," Oscar whispered.

Zoe nodded, but Jamy didn't move. He held up one hand. Stop.

"I have to call Homicide," Oscar said.

Jamy shook his head. He waited to be sure he had Oscar's attention, then, very deliberately, put one hand down into the left pocket of his black jacket.

Oscar turned back to the grave. He gently eased aside one of Taryn Lymbery's naked legs and reached. His cheek rubbed against the dead girl's cold, naked skin, and his vision swam. Flies began to probe the corner of his eyes. He blinked hard and reached deeper, his gloved hand running down the slick nylon of Jamy's jacket. The cheap fabric was falling apart, its stitches almost rotten. The pocket began to tear as his fingers slid in, groping. They closed on something frail and fine.

He pulled back from the darkness into the gloomy half-light and waved away the dozens of flies. He held a slip of paper: it was damp and had begun to tear in two. The writing, in ballpoint pen, was childlike and simple and faded to a sky-blue.

But it was clear.

It showed a date from just over three years ago. An address that Oscar recognized as an alley behind a bar in Fortitude Valley. And the time: 9 P.M. The time, date, and place of the meeting that Jon Gest had arranged with an informer who supposedly had new information about Geoffrey Haig; the meeting that Oscar had arrived too late for, discovering Jon in the alley gutter, stabbed and bleeding.

Oscar looked at Jamy.

"You stabbed Jon?"

The dead boy nodded.

"What is it?" Zoe asked.

Oscar didn't take his eyes off Jamy. "You're the informant? You knew about Haig?"

Jamy's stare was unsettling. He shook his head, no.

"Then why were you there?"

Jamy looked at the ground and swallowed. His hands began to move. Oscar awkwardly repeated the movements to Zoe.

"To. Stab. You," she translated.

"But you stabbed Jon instead," Oscar said.

Jamy nodded, and lifted his face up to Oscar. The holes where his eyes should be seemed to twist into darkness.

"He. Told. Me. To." Zoe's voice was barely a whisper as Jamy's hands moved and Oscar's mimicked. "You were late. He was scared. He said, 'Stab me here, here, here.'"

The dead boy pointed to the places where Jon claimed he'd been stabbed by an attacker who'd struck him from behind. Oscar stared, stunned.

"Jon set it up?" Understanding came quickly, then, and he felt cold hands squeeze his heart. "There was no informant. He wanted you to attack me, hospitalize me, get me out of the way long enough to shut down the Haig investigation." He looked up at Jamy. "What did he offer you?"

The dead boy smiled sourly and rubbed his fingers and thumb together.

"Instead . . ." began Oscar.

Jamy looked down at his body.

Oscar's mind began to whirr. When Oscar hadn't shown up, Jon had the boy stab him, to get himself off the investigation. Had he been scared of Haig? Or bought by him? Whichever, it had worked: a week later, the investigation was put on ice. "You were a loose end."

Jamy nodded and signed.

"After he left the hospital, he found me."

"And hid you here."

Jamy nodded.

And then Gray Wednesday. The boy had been murdered just in time to appear in front of Oscar's car. And after the auger screws at the sewage plant had failed to get rid of Penny Roth, Jon had reverted to this old hiding place to stow Taryn Lymbery's body.

The strength left Oscar's limbs and he folded quietly against the hard timber, slumping on wet knees.

Jon was a murderer. Jon had stolen the children from Elverly.

———

As they emerged from the dark curtain of leaves, Oscar heard a motor start on the far side of the park. He saw sunlight glint off a rear windshield as a dark sedan drove away.

Chapter 37

Oscar slowed at the top corner of his street and looked down. No squad cars. No new cars hiding under the trees. He idled down and did a U-turn to park in front of his house.

He dismounted and helped Zoe off.

"Have you still got the gun?" he asked.

She nodded.

"There are more cartridges in a cupboard behind the fireplace." He gave her the key to the front door.

"I'm coming with you," she began.

"Don't answer the door."

He revved the motorcycle and sped away.

———

Moechtar's office door was closed and locked. Oscar ran down the fire-escape stairwell to his own floor and jogged between the workstations of the Industrial Relations branch toward his desk.

"Christ on a cracker, Mariani. What are you fucking doing?"

Foley's large face was a mask of shock. He rose from his chair with surprising speed. Oscar realized that a number of the public servants were turning to look at him, some whispering to others.

"Come here," Foley whispered, taking Oscar by the arm and leading him toward a set of doors.

"What is it?" Oscar asked.

"Exactly!" Foley said loudly, clapping Oscar on the shoulder and making him gasp in pain. "Wow, what a misunderstanding!"

He led Oscar into the side corridor and put his bulk against the doors, and pulled Oscar close, his fat cheeks wobbling.

"What are you doing here, are you crazy? There's a warrant out for your arrest."

Oscar stared. "What charge?"

"They found some bodies in a park at New Farm." Foley blinked nervously. "Murder."

Oscar found himself smiling. Jon hadn't wasted any time.

"Well, it's your sworn duty to arrest me."

"Screw that. It's a setup one-oh-one. But fuck." Foley took his arm again, heading toward the fire escape. "Gotta get you outta here."

Oscar stopped. "I need to get a message to Moechtar."

The loose flesh under Foley's chin quivered. "I really don't want to get involved."

"Just tell him that Jon Gest took the kids. Okay?"

Foley stared. "Gest? Seriously? Because he's who I've wanted to talk to you about. He's been appointed to the board of the Thatch Group. A copper, to the board of the biggest construction company in the state. Fishy fucking fishfood, I thought. Fuck me."

Oscar felt an idiot. If he'd just listened to Foley.

He put out his hand. Foley looked at it, then took it.

"Get out from behind that desk," Oscar said. "You're wasted there."

Foley grinned. "Ah, I'm too fat for street work." His smile faded. "Moechtar, huh?"

Oscar nodded. This time he did listen to Foley, and hurried to the fire escape.

———

As he rode, thoughts clicked together, connecting inevitably, joining faster. No wonder Jon had tried to get him out of town with a job offer. No wonder Jon had seemed unimpressed by Oscar's discovery of Albert Naville's escape from jail. Thatch Construction: its banners were everywhere around the city, the one company that continued to build when its rivals had failed and fallen. The Thatch Group was Anne Chaume's inheritance. And now Jon was on its board. His reward for stealing children for Naville to mark up and gut? Oscar had taunted

Naville, saying he'd failed with Penny Roth. But Naville protested that he hadn't failed. The birds that had stalked Oscar through Sandro's house were proof. *Her messengers. Her soldiers.*

What was it Gelareh had translated off the flawed idol? *The gate is open. Come as you will and grant us your favor.*

Naville had opened the gate.

Naville was dead, but that didn't mean the killings would stop. The second altar, the one Naville carried away from the brothel in the security footage, hadn't been found. Carved patterns could be learned. More favors could be asked if the right flesh was offered.

Oscar parked the bike outside Jon and Leonie's apartment building, right beside the spot where he'd thought a child had plunged to its death from the neighboring rooftop. A breeze messed with the trees; slate-gray clouds closed in on the sun. The main gate was locked. Oscar's shoulders screamed as he climbed the fence.

He stopped at the bottom of the stairs and changed direction. He went below the building to the shuttered carports, and found the one with Jon's apartment number. He picked a rock from the garden and slammed it down on the handle. The door swung loose and he lifted it. The single-car garage was very neat. An old plant stand, a disused oil heater. At the back was a small workbench with a Peg-Board. On the board were two dozen tools, neatly hanging in front of their assigned silhouettes. Only one tool was missing. The hammer. He remembered the distinctive, almost circular impression in the back of Lucas Purden's skull.

Oscar looked beneath the bench. Nothing. He pulled out its sole drawer. Inside was a collection of tools: screwdrivers, a hacksaw, electrical tape, emery paper, pencils, and tape measures. All were new and unused, and their seeming haphazardness looked staged. He drew the drawer back until it reached the end of its travel. It didn't look as deep as it should. He scooped the tools out and tapped the rear panel of the drawer. It rang hollow. He put a knee to the bench and strained. Something snapped and the drawer came out. Oscar put it on the bench. At its back was a false panel with a slyly hidden hinge. Inside the small cache were three neat stacks of fifty- and hundred-dollar bills.

Oscar took the money, went back outside, closed the shutter, and climbed the stairs. He knocked sharply on the apartment door. The breeze stiffened, hushing softly as it ran along the exposed balcony, ruffling his trousers.

The door opened. Leonie's red eyes widened a little when she saw Oscar, then she smiled sadly and stepped aside to let him in.

The apartment was as neatly furnished as ever, but it felt oddly empty. On the kitchen bench was a soda siphon, an almost empty bottle of Pimm's, and a glass bowl of melting ice.

"Is he here?" Oscar asked, although he could feel Jon's absence.

Leonie padded unsteadily on small, bare feet to the kitchen and found another glass. Without asking, she filled it with ice.

"'Scuse fingers," she said, and poured the fruity liquor over the cubes and topped it with the siphon. She held out the drink to Oscar. "No? Willful waste, woeful want." She sat and crossed her ankles demurely, raised the glass, and drank deeply.

Oscar placed the wad of money on the bench. Leonie glanced at it and returned to her drink. "Ah," she said. "That."

"Where is he, Lee?"

She shrugged theatrically, giggled a little, then sobered. "Oh, Oscar. He wanted to invite you in, he did. But he knew you wouldn't."

"In to what?"

She gave him a scolding look—*As if I'd tell.* "I wish he'd thought the same of me. I do."

Oscar could see that her eyes were unable to focus. Then she saw something behind Oscar and pointed accusingly, "Fuck *you*. Just you wait." She drank again, long swallows, swaying on the chair.

"Lee. He needs to turn himself in."

Leonie watched him over the glass, then burst into laughter, bubbles exploding in the drink and spilling down her blouse. Oscar could see now that she wore nothing beneath the white shirt. She saw him notice that and raised an eyebrow.

"Remember that beach holiday we went on? Jon went down to the water, Sabine went into town. We were alone." She undid a button. "I thought you might try to seduce me then. You have such nice hands."

As she reached for the next button, Oscar took her wrist and squeezed it.

"You're hurting me," she said through a smile. "I deserve it."

"Kids, Leonie. Children. Why?"

She shook her head. "You never did understand the rules. Nothing for nothing. Poor Oscar."

She lifted his hand around her wrist and kissed his fingers. Oscar pulled his arm away, and Leonie's face crumbled. She sat hunched for a moment, then wiped her mouth and took another drink.

He strode away.

But at the door he heard her whisper, "Elverly."

The storm arrived, blindfolding the sky and wailing. At its front was a shockingly cold wind that made power lines whip and whistle and stripped malingering leaves from trees in panicked clouds of green. It buffeted cars and made trucks on the highway shift lanes against their will. As Oscar flicked on the headlight, he felt like a cork on wild rapids. It was all he could do to keep the Triumph somewhere in the middle of the road, praying that he wouldn't be shoved by the gusts into the oncoming traffic.

Then came the rain. It came almost horizontal, stinging like bird shot. He passed an SUV on its side, with an upended caravan still attached, like a fallen chariot. The sky was almost black.

One of the gates to Elverly House was pinned open; the other was swatted by the air, its hinges moaning as it swung loose on the mossy gatepost. Oscar pushed it aside with a foot and rode up the drive. He was lashed by the flaying leaves of the willow trees and his front tire shook unsteadily in the wet gravel.

The rain reduced Elverly House to a clifflike, looming mass. Parked at the main building's stone steps were two charter buses. The windows of the front bus were fogged and dark, and spindly patterns of dripping condensation ran down inside them. Oscar could see the bobbing heads of children and the blonde hair of a caregiver moving about.

Elverly's reception was a crush of bodies; children cried and laughed and howled. Several caregivers cuddled the frailer ones. Wheelchairs and walking frames were everywhere, and to one side was a large pile of packed suitcases, backpacks, and boxes. In a corner, two stout bus drivers in shorts and knee socks compared grievances. Two nights had passed since he cut down Chalk's body here, but the air still had the nasty back-of-the-throat acridity of gasoline. Oscar pushed his way gently through the bodies, but couldn't see Megan. He went toward a large girl who held a clipboard and was calling out for everyone to just relax.

"Lauralie?"

She recognized Oscar. "Detective. We're moving today. Well, we've started."

"Storm?" Oscar asked.

The girl nodded. "We had to stop loading."

"Where's Megan?"

Lauralie blinked.

"She's gone."

Oscar felt his chest tighten.

"Gone where?"

"On the first bus. On the minibus."

"What minibus?"

"Gone," she repeated, going paler. "It left already. Before the storm."

"Who organized it? Show me the list."

She held the clipboard protectively against her chest, but something in his expression made her hand it over. Two dozen names had ticks beside them—the children outside on the charter bus, Oscar guessed. But the names of four girls had been run through with a pencil. One was Megan McAuliffe.

"How old are these girls?"

"Thirteen, fourteen." Lauralie looked at the names.

He took her arm, and she winced. "Tell me about the minibus," he said. "Who took them?"

"It looked all organized." Her voice was pleading. "They said they were taking the girls to Clayfield." An awful realization appeared on the girl's rounded face. "It looked really organized! I mean, they had a minibus."

"Tell me about the driver."

"I didn't really see," she blurted. "Who looks at bus drivers? He carried Megan onto the bus. He was big."

———

He ran out into the downpour. The rain found every bruise and cut on his face and scalp. Jon had taken them. But where? Where had he taken Frances White and Penny Roth and Taryn Lymbery?

The Thatch Group.

Anne Chaume.

Chislehurst.

Chapter 38

The guard booth was a little cube of green light under a sky as dark as night. The squall made the raindrops under the halogen light above the boom gate twist and curl like schools of silver minnows.

He stopped at the boom gate. A guard came out under an umbrella. Oscar showed his police photo ID and hoped the guard didn't ask to see his badge, too. He didn't; the gate rose and Oscar was waved through.

Oscar rode up zigzagging streets, climbing, slowing only to ease the bike around hairpin turns and fallen branches. Thunder cracked with the sound of rocks splitting.

The tall black gates of Chislehurst were closed. Oscar rode around a corner and pulled the bike up beside the ten-foot-high brick wall. He lifted the bike onto the center stand. He climbed onto the seat and reached. He could just hook an elbow over the wall. He jumped and pulled, and sparks of pain ran from his reopened wounds. He slid both legs over and dropped into a garden bed, his boots disappearing into mulch. He picked his way out and onto a wide lawn that skated away into darkness as thick as night.

Lightning scratched wildly across the sky, striking Chislehurst into bold relief, making its wet stone haunches twitch. Yellow lights shone from its tower. Again, there were a number of European coupes and dark limousines parked in the large circular driveway, but, this time, no fairy-tale path of sparkling lights, no inviting party hubbub or glow of orchestra music. Only a single light at the driveway and the howl of cold wind around stone.

Oscar ran a plodding pace, pushing against the wind. With every step his legs became heavier and heavier, millstones hanging from his tired hips. He gave the castlelike building a wide berth and jogged around a long arbor, where he had to stop in the pitch darkness and wait for the lightning to help him navigate thorned hedges and hissing stands of trees.

At the rear of Chislehurst was a smaller carriageway where catering vans and cleaners' vehicles could park. In shadow, under the low roof, was a white minibus.

Oscar's legs burned, and he dropped to his knees. He pulled his jacket over his head, pulled out his telephone, and dialed Moechtar.

"Hello?"

Oscar was so surprised by the inspector's immediate answer that it took him a moment to recover. "It's Mariani."

"Oscar? Where are you?"

"I didn't kill those kids."

Oscar turned his back against the wind so that he could hear better.

Over the line came the clink of crockery; he'd disturbed his inspector's tea. He heard Moechtar stop chewing, a thoughtful pause. "Then you should turn yourself in."

"Did Foley find you?"

Another pause. "Yes, I got his message. About Jon Gest."

"He took four girls from Elverly."

"That's quite an accusation, Oscar."

"I think he's brought them to Anne Chaume. On the Heights."

For a moment, all Oscar could hear was the wavelike roar of heavy rain, and he was sure he'd lost the connection. Then Moechtar said, "That's also quite an accusation."

"Jon is on the board of the Thatch Group."

Another pause.

"The minibus he took them in is at Chislehurst right now."

Lightning spiked the sky, and Oscar's fingers reflexively clutched into wet grass and cold soil as thunder boomed.

" . . . there now?" came Moechtar's voice.

"Sorry?"

"Are you there now?" Moechtar repeated.

"Yes."

Moechtar sounded disappointed. "For God's sake, Oscar."

"Call Tactical Response. I'm going inside."

"No! No, no—you wait. I'll get some backup—"

Oscar ended the call. He crept closer to the van. He turned the phone on its side and aimed it at the vehicle. He pressed a button, and a silent flash made the minibus seem to leap forward. He sent the image to Moechtar's number, then backed up for a wider shot.

"Detective?"

The voice came from behind Oscar.

He recognized it and turned.

A thin, ghostly figure emerged from darkness under a large black umbrella that strained in the wind.

"Hello, Karl," Oscar said.

The pale man had a towel draped over the arm that held the umbrella and a SIG pistol in his other hand. Oscar gauged the distance and realized that even a poor shot would have three slugs in him before he'd moved five feet. And his legs didn't feel cooperative.

"Quite the bit of weather," Karl said.

"Yes."

"Have your handcuffs? Slowly, please."

Oscar wondered if he should stall as he did with Naville but realized that with Karl it would be a mistake. He reached into a pocket of his jacket and withdrew the hinged cuffs.

Karl said, "On one wrist, if you would."

Lightning flared. Thunder seemed to shake the ground.

Oscar clicked the cuff around his left wrist.

Karl finished, "And you can imagine."

Oscar got down on his knees and put both hands behind his back. He felt the steel of the muzzle against the back of his head while a skillful hand snapped the other cuff closed. Then a towel draped over his head and shoulders. He felt stupidly grateful.

"Before you get up," Karl said, and stepped around in front of Oscar. He had the umbrella tucked in the crook of one arm, crouched, and with his free hand reached into Oscar's jacket. He felt the empty holster and looked unsurprised. He found Oscar's phone and threw it into the darkness. Then his long fingers went into Oscar's right inner pocket and withdrew his wallet. In the coin section, Karl found the shining nickel handcuff key. He pocketed it, replaced the wallet, and stood. When lightning flashed again, his strange, mismatched eyes sparkled.

"Welcome back to Chislehurst."

Chapter **39**

Sconces high on the timber walls cupped tiny gas flames that really only made the darkness seem deeper. Oscar walked with Karl behind him. Their footsteps echoed on the marble tiles and high up into the invisible ceilings. Chislehurst folded around them.

Oscar said, "Did anyone ever tell you that you've got eyes like a husky?"

The thin man didn't break stride.

"In middle school," Karl replied. "A boy named Dean Abernethy said it. He thought he was very clever."

"How did you take it?"

"I told him huskies were obedient, hardworking dogs of moderate intelligence with no body odor. He said something to the effect that in that case I couldn't be a husky because I stank like a faggot." Karl nodded for Oscar to take a door on his right. "I seem to recall his house burning down the following night."

Oscar felt the skin on his stomach crawl. That was not the sort of information you gave a policeman you expected would live. How long would it take Moechtar to get patrol cruisers here? Fifteen minutes? Ten?

"You're quite good with fires, then?"

"Not bad."

"You taught Naville?"

Karl paused while he held open a timber door, and Oscar stepped into a wide hallway that smelled of wax and flowers.

"There was fair exchange of information."

Jon must have delivered the girls less than an hour ago. Oscar listened, but all he could hear was his and Karl's echoing footfalls, and the muted moan of the storm.

They reached a pair of glass-paneled doors. Oscar's own reflection looked back at him, pale and scared. Karl's thin white face was smaller, farther behind. Smaller still was a third face that remained unmoving even as Karl pushed the door open. Jamy waited ahead, less substantial even than the thin gaslight, watching anxiously. He gave Oscar a small nod.

"You could have spared the boy at school," Oscar said as they moved through the larger space. His voice echoed, and it sounded stretched and thin. "You could have told him many great people also had hetero-chromia. Alexander the Great. Michael Flatley."

Oscar heard the smile in his captor's voice: "If only I'd known you sooner, Detective, what a different life I might have led."

"What was it Alexander said?" Oscar asked, slowing. " 'Were I not Alexander, I would be Diogenes.' Who would you be, Karl?"

"Why, Detective," Karl prodded him with the pistol muzzle, "I'd be you."

Oscar tried to hide his surprise. "Oh?"

"A less foolish version, of course. But Ms. Chaume is quite taken with you."

"She tried to have me killed."

"I find that hard to believe." Karl smiled. "Given how you're alive."

Oscar's clothes were drenched, and he realized that he was shaking. He willed himself to be warm. He was losing track of where they were in the building.

"Well, Diogenes was a cynic," Oscar said. "Do you love her?"

"Ms. Chaume? Very much. She is a visionary. If anything, she is the one more like Alexander."

"She wants to conquer the world?"

"No. Just the city."

Ahead, half the hallway was taken up by two adjoining sets of car-peted timber stairs: one set rose; the other descended. Jamy stood anx-iously at the central newel post. As they came closer, Jamy moved: he ascended three steps, then looked anxiously back at Oscar.

"Up or down?" Oscar asked, keeping his voice light, and turned his head a little to listen.

"Down, please."

Oscar judged that he was about three feet ahead of Karl. Enough.

He dropped to the ground, lifted a knee, and spun. Karl was too surprised to use the gun and instinctively tried to hop over the approaching leg. As he did, Oscar brought his other leg down and hooked the thin man behind the knees and rolled. Karl's eyes opened wider and his mouth became a surprised O as he fell and began to tumble down the stairs, grabbing wildly at the brass stair rods and banisters. He kept a firm grip on the gun.

Oscar scrambled to his feet and ran up the adjoining staircase, taking the treads two at a time. Jamy nodded briskly and ran silently ahead of him.

"Detective?" called Karl, a warning.

Oscar lifted his elbows high behind him, the handcuffs to the small of his back. He heard the wispy sounds of Karl getting to his feet in the darkness below. Jamy reached the top of the dark stairs and waited. When Oscar got closer, the dead boy ran along the top corridor, glancing backward to check that Oscar was keeping up. He came to a closed door. Oscar awkwardly twisted his wrists and turned the brass knob.

"Detective!" Karl called from the darkness behind.

Oscar followed Jamy down another, narrower hallway. This one was more brightly lit, with several gas sconces flickering at its far end, and a doorway with glass inserts admitted a warm glow. By its light, Oscar saw framed portraits of Anne Chaume, her father, and her grandfather. And at the very end of the corridor was a tiny semicircular side table: a half-moon no more than six inches deep. On it was a single vase and, in it, an orchid.

Which Oscar recognized.

He'd seen it growing in a greenhouse.

He slowed, his feet suddenly feeling disconnected. Jamy waited beside the door.

"Detective!" Karl snapped, his running footsteps ringing on the tiles.

Oscar dropped his weight onto the lever handle and stepped inside.

The sitting room smelled of pine smoke, tobacco, and flowers. A pleasant fire crackled in the large tiled fireplace; from the ceiling depended a long chandelier that reflected the warm flames in its facets. On a low coffee table were decanters of water, whiskey, and port wine. Six faces looked up from leather chairs, startled. Oscar recognized them all. Five he'd seen at the party here just a few nights ago: Paul Roth, the state minister for economic development, the director of the Department of Public Works, a judge from the Supreme Court, and the commissioner of police. But it was the last face that made Oscar's chest hollow and his legs as weak as traitors.

Inspector Benjamin Moechtar slowly got to his feet.

"Who is this?" the judge asked from under white planks of eyebrows.

"Nobody," Moechtar said. "No one at all."

Chapter 40

Oscar walked numbly, escorted by Karl and Moechtar, hardly aware as Karl's thin, strong hands guided him down stairs, through doorways, along corridors. At some point, Oscar heard the expert snick of a semiauto's safety coming off. At another, he thought he heard the sounds of girls laughing.

His mind clicked like an old combination lock as all its rust-flecked wheels finally came into alignment, the fence fell into its notches, and a heavy door swung wide revealing a stupidly obvious truth. Of course it was Moechtar. Moechtar, who'd kept the least influential detective assigned to the Jane Doe case. Moechtar, who had urged him to return the body. Moechtar, who had no doubt buried Oscar's request for a DNA sample. Moechtar, who tried to have Oscar resign once his questions about the second altar became too dangerous.

"Why?" Oscar asked. His voice sounded like a doomed man's. "I don't understand."

Oscar felt his inspector's hand on his shoulder. "Never mind." As it touched, thunder cannoned, and Oscar jumped.

There was no sign of Jamy.

———

This staircase was narrower, lined with brick on both sides. At the bottom of the stairs, the three men stepped into a utilitarian hallway with lower ceilings, painted brick walls, and chipped skirting boards. The air down here was cooler and still.

"I don't mind doing this," Karl said.

Moechtar shook his head. "It should be me."

"It *should* be Gest. But I'll do it."

Moechtar grunted.

They stopped at swinging doors with porthole windows, and inside Oscar saw a single cook working over a blue gas flame. Karl went in, spoke briefly, and the cook turned off the gas and hurried away. Karl nodded through the glass, and Moechtar held the door open for Oscar.

"In here."

Oscar stepped inside, leaving Moechtar in the corridor. The kitchen was whitewashed brick walls, stainless-steel benches, and cold slate floors. The blue-white light of gas lamps glittered off dozens of hard edges. A high line of windows was set in one wall; like Elverly's, this kitchen was a basement room, almost underground. When lightning flashed, trees were frozen in mid-twist, cast silver, and wrenched by the wind. Oscar smelled blood. There was meat on the bench. His heart pounded behind his ribs, and he knew now how the horse in Kannis's killing floor had felt. When he looked down, he saw that he stood over a drain grate in the floor. Karl had stepped quietly back. Karl was going to kill him here, and he didn't want to die. Oscar's mind reared like that horse, mad in a panic, wanting to kick out and find a weapon, but he couldn't take his eyes off the pistol.

"Thank you, Karl."

Oscar turned to the familiar voice.

Anne Chaume stepped into the room. Her skin was as pale as ice, and her blue eyes seemed electric. Her hair fell like black water. Her red dress was fitted and ended just above her bare feet; her lips were the same shade of bloodlike carmine. White, black, red. She frowned deeply as she walked up to him. Oscar heard the shuffle of retreating footsteps and glanced around; Karl had performed his magic and was out of sight. Something dripped and echoed. Oscar realized that his sodden clothes were leaking into the drain, cold drops falling into subterranean darkness.

Chaume stopped just out of the range of any lunges or kicks. Oscar wondered if he had the strength to do anything. It didn't feel like it.

"Where are the girls?" he asked.

Chaume looked him up and down, taking in his drenched clothes and wet hair, his battered face.

"You should be more worried about yourself," she said.

Lightning flared again, turning the room into a flash pan of white and silver, and making her red dress spark like a slap. Red lips. Ice-blue eyes.

"Have you figured, Detective, what it's all about?"

"Ereshkigal," he said.

"Yes." She smiled, pleased.

"But why?" Oscar said. "Three girls dead already. And four more for four other—"

"People of influence?" she finished for him. "Yes."

"Why?" he repeated.

The beautiful woman was staring at his face as if it were a puzzle. "To take their ghosts away."

He shook his head. "I don't understand," he said.

Chaume's voice was soft. "The world's a mess, Oscar. These ghosts. People can't work. They can't think, they can't fuck, can't buy, can't sell. These dead things are sea anchors, dragging at the world. Slowing commerce. I can't afford them. So I found a way to get rid of them."

Oscar smiled wryly. All this killing, for fool's gold.

"You don't believe me?" Chaume asked.

The nearest gas lamp flared suddenly, then its mantle cooled to a candle-flame orange, guttered, and went out. Chaume's face was now lit from one side only, and her eyes became strange yellow disks that reminded him of the owls. "Have you seen the change in Paul Roth, now he's lost the albatross round his neck? He's a new man." Lightning flashed, and Oscar could see Chaume's alabaster face beaming proudly. "I can unburden people. I can free them of their ghosts."

Oscar watched her. "And all you need to do is torture and murder girls."

Her eyes went hard, like stones in a winter stream.

"It's not murder, not for these girls. It's a mercy."

"Strapped down while they're cut open? You have a strange sense of mercy."

Chaume moved a step closer to Oscar. Her dress moved lightly on her body. Oscar could see the points of her breasts, a smooth curve of hip. He smelled her skin; for the first time, it repulsed him. "You have a broken one, here. Your Megan. Do you think she loves the life you gave her, Oscar?"

He hated the truth. He hated her for telling it.

"It's not for me to know," he said.

"*I* know," Chaume said, stepping closer still. "I know that for the cost of candles already spent, we can get back the sunlight. That's a good trade."

"Why are you telling me?"

She was close enough for him to reach her with a kick or to strike at her with his head. But she knew he wouldn't move while Karl was hovering in the shadows with his steady hands and his gun.

"Because I despise waste." She smiled and continued, "Gest is a brute. Useful, but an opportunist. Untrustworthy. You are a stranger thing. You're an honest man."

A horrible feeling slid into Oscar's chest. Hope. Hope that he might live.

"And what would I have to do?"

Chaume's voice was sweet and gentle. "Turn a blind eye. That's all. What will that cost you? Nothing. You haven't got a job. You haven't got a wife or children. You do have a burden, though. But she'll be freed, whether you accept or not. I'd just rather keep you."

"Whatever you called up, you asked to send its creatures after me," he said.

"Just warnings," Chaume said. "But I like that they didn't stop you."

"You had Naville sacrifice Frances White to get rid of whose ghost?" Suddenly, he knew. "Karl's."

Chaume nodded.

Oscar stared into Chaume's tourmaline eyes. Maybe he was, after all this, still a Nine-Ten detective. He felt a cold smile on his face. It all made sense now. He continued, "When you knew it worked, you had Penny killed for her stepfather, your barrister. Another good man to have onside. Pity her mother found out. And then"—Oscar nodded to the house above them—"you had all your guests upstairs here the other night. At your party. You wanted me to stay, too. For your dem-onstration. Whose ghost did you get Ereshkigal to remove with Taryn Lymbery's death? Yours?"

Chaume shook her head, and her long hair whispered on her dress. "Why would I want to get rid of my husband?" She sent a fond look to an empty space in front of the industrial refrigerator, then returned her cool eyes to Oscar. They glittered. "No, the Lymbery girl was for your inspector. And tonight . . . well, you saw our guests upstairs. Including your commissioner. I think you should come with us."

Oscar felt a cold ball in his gut.

"And I think you can go to hell, Ms. Chaume."

She stayed there, though, just inches from his face, looking into his eyes. A puzzle, but no time left to solve it. She kissed him lightly on the lips.

"Good-bye, Detective."

She stepped back lightly, and by the same strange magic Karl reappeared with his pistol. Chaume turned, a silent twirl of red and black, and was gone.

Karl remained, head cocked, listening to ensure his mistress's departure.

"I'm unsurprised, Detective. If that's any consolation."

He waved the pistol for Oscar to step out away from the bench, back over the grate. Karl stood between him and the door. The only other way out was through the windows behind him. There was no escape.

Does it matter, Oscar wondered, whether I die here or a foot to my left? He stepped out. And as he did a form appeared behind Karl's shoulders. Jamy Brum held up three fingers.

"Thank you," Karl said, and leveled the pistol.

Jamy curled a finger, still held up two.

"Would you like to turn around?" Karl asked.

"No."

The thin man nodded—as you wish. Jamy dropped another finger, holding up just one.

Karl raised the pistol.

Jamy flapped both hands down and crouched.

Oscar threw himself to the ground as lightning flashed as bright as day. Thunder smashed at the building, shaking the windows and making the hanging pots ring like bells. A bullet whined into darkness.

Oscar waited for the shock and the pain, wondering where the misaimed slug had hit him.

The pain didn't come. He straightened.

Jamy stood over Karl's body, which twitched a little, then was still. In the light of the single lamp, Oscar could see that the dead man's right eye was gone, a wormhole, a bullet hole. A puddle of oil-dark blood spread behind him. Oscar became aware that the sound of rain was louder. He turned.

The window behind him was broken. Zoe Trucek lay on the ground, Oscar's service pistol in her shaking hand. Her green eyes were wide.

"Cops never think they can be followed," she said.

———

They ran. She had his service pistol, and he held Karl's SIG.

"Where are they?" Zoe whispered. She was shivering; her short hair was plastered flat against her skull, and her clothes were soaked.

Oscar shook his head, trying to clear it of all the thoughts and images racing through it: Karl's shattered skull; the elation of being alive; the feeling of hugging Zoe so hard that she complained it hurt. The corridors were a maze, and to Oscar they looked identical in their deep shadows and burnished opulence. He searched for Jamy, but the dead boy was gone.

He slowed and stopped, and gestured for Zoe to halt as well.

He waved for quiet and closed his eyes, trying to remember where he had heard girls laughing, not knowing what was waiting for them. How long did they have? The intricate pattern he'd seen sliced into the abdomens of Penny Roth and Taryn Lymbery would take time to inscribe. Twenty minutes, maybe thirty. Time was running out fast.

"Okay," he said, and started up a set of stairs.

She followed as he retraced the route he'd taken flanked by Karl and Moechtar.

They reached a juncture where two hallways converged and a central staircase rose. Oscar grinned. Jamy was waiting at the end of one corridor.

"This way," Oscar said.

Off the hallway were four doors in two opposing pairs, and copper mirrors between each. They walked up, listening.

"No!" a girl's voice protested. Others shushed her. "I *want* to go *home*."

Oscar tried the door. It was locked. He looked at Zoe. She nodded. He raised a boot and waited for lightning to flash through distant windows. When thunder rumbled, he kicked hard and the door flew open.

The girls looked up: a little blonde girl with walking sticks; a tall, horsey girl with thick glasses and stains of blue and orange around her mouth; and a third, broad-faced freckled thing who lay on the bed, her close-set eyes red from crying—when she saw Oscar, she began to cry again. Dresses were scattered around the bedroom—some frilled and a century old, others new and pretty—as were hatboxes and costume jewelry from a small wooden chest. On a bedside table sat a tray with a few colored lollies left in a bowl and a nearly empty bottle of soft drink. A wheelchair was in the corner. Megan wasn't there.

"Miss Zoe!" cried the blonde girl, delighted. She wore a batiste blouse that was too large for her, and a velvet hat with a faded gray ostrich plume that made Oscar's skin go cold. The girl on the bed looked at Zoe and wailed, "I wanna go *home*!"

Zoe shushed them. "It's okay," she said, opening her arms.

"He broke the door."

"Shh, now."

"Did you see my hat?"

And Oscar heard a faint, distant scream.

Chapter **41**

he air felt potent, charged with something more than the power of the storm. He'd left Zoe with the girls, told her to try and find a way to get them out. His footsteps clapped and echoed on marble and polished wood. Another scream: a girl's voice raised in terrified pain.

Ahead was the grand staircase. At the bottom were sets of tall glass doors as dark as windows to the sea floor; beyond them, the great ballroom. Where else more appropriate to invite a goddess?

Oscar started down the stairs.

The shot took him in the calf. The lower limb went numb and he lost balance, clutching at the dark wood banisters. He rolled halfway down the carpeted staircase before halting his fall. He realized that Karl's pistol was no longer in his hand.

"Oscar?"

Jon's voice was low and easy.

"Yeah," Oscar said.

"Ah."

The sky lit white through a skylight high overhead, and thunder followed. Jon's giant form stood at the top of the staircase. "You okay?" His large hand made his pistol look comically small. "Where'd I get you?"

"Leg," Oscar replied.

He lay sprawled on the stairs. He tried to rise, but a feeling like ice water was spreading around the gunshot wound. His hand felt below his knee; it came back very wet and sticky.

"I was aiming higher," Jon said apologetically, descending. "Light's not good."

Oscar's hands probed the dark stairs. Where was the fucking gun? Lightning flashed again, and Oscar looked wildly around in the split second. No sign of it. Thunder roared like rapids, and as it faded Megan's screams from the ballroom grew louder. The air coming from below seemed colder.

Jon arrived, his bulk a presence more felt than seen. His knees cracked as he knelt.

"Oh, getting old," Jon said. "You gave Karl some trouble."

Oscar nodded.

Thunder pealed again. "I can't stay long," Jon continued. "I have to take care of those crips. Your squeeze won't get far. I had enough trouble getting the little bitches up there."

Oscar's lower leg felt frozen now, and his head felt perilously light. He began to feel the bird-wing flurry of panic around his mind. *Bleeding,* his mind shouted. *You're bleeding out.*

"I tried to help you." Jon's words were a gentle reproof. "Stubborn motherfucker."

"You tried to have me stabbed," Oscar said. "I was your partner."

Jon was quiet for a long moment. "You just couldn't let Haig go. So he paid me to help you along."

Oscar groped along the treads, hunting for Karl's gun. It could be anywhere between here and the top of the stairs.

"Haig paid you then. Moechtar and Anne Chaume now," Oscar said. "That's why you do this? The money?"

Jon laughed, a self-deprecating chuckle. "I just need more than you do. I guess I always have. You know, none of this might have happened if the service just paid us a bit better."

"And Neve?" Oscar said.

"Ah, Neve." Jon nodded regretfully. "What could I do? Naville and I were just about to set the fire, and up she comes with Kannis in tow. Pity."

Oscar saw silvery mist invade his vision. His fingers shook. Where was the goddamned *pistol?*

"Turn yourself in, Jon," he whispered.

Jon laughed again. "Not that I would, but to who? Everyone's coming over. Moechtar. The commissioner." Oscar felt Jon's hand on his shoulder. A soft touch. "I told Anne you'd never sell out, that you were screwed together too tight."

In the darkness, Megan's screams grew louder. "They're just kids," Oscar said.

"I know," Jon said gently. "But it's a different world, Oscar."

Oscar's fingers closed around metal. The pistol. He was lying on it. If he could just lift himself, but his body felt detached. All he wanted to do was sleep.

Jon's hand left Oscar's shoulder and held the back of his head. Oscar felt the gun muzzle touch the top of his skull. No. There was no more time. He took a shuddering breath.

"You're a good man, Oscar," Jon said. "I'll see you."

Oscar rolled and pulled the trigger. Through the corner of his eye, he saw Jon's chin lift a little. The big man jerked, as if feeling a sudden chill, and collapsed. Jon rolled down the stairs. Near the bottom, there was a muffled report as his pistol went off, then he became a still mass, knees tucked, quiet.

A shriek from the darkness below. Oscar could see something through the glass. A gleam, shifting in the old glass like moonlight reflected in a dark pond.

Oscar forced himself to move. His leg felt as if it were carved of frozen wood. He willed his wet fingers to clutch a banister, put his weight on the hand pressing on the gun, and pushed himself up. Bright gray fireflies swarmed in his vision, and he teetered. He jammed the gun into a pocket and grabbed the rail before he fell.

Lightning flared again, a halogen flash, and he saw that his pants were soaked red.

Bad, he thought. That's pretty bad.

He knew he should put a tourniquet around the leg, but Megan was howling now: a horrible, almost endless scream. He hopped down one stair at a time, and as he descended the air became colder and colder. His breaths began to condense and fog. He passed Jon's body and hobbled to the nearest of the doors.

———

As the door swung shut behind him, frigid air struck his face and chilled the blood on his neck. Megan's sobbing rose and fell like the wind: choking back a moment, then redoubling in awful terror.

The ballroom felt as large as a canyon. The very air seemed to promise a long, terrifying fall, as if it yawned not only up to high ceilings but down into fatal, endless depths. The feeling of emptiness was so palpable that it took all his will to keep moving forward; every step threatened a cliff edge. Where a few nights ago the room had sparkled with constellations of candles, now there was just one light; a greenish glow, tiny at the end of the darkness.

My dream, Oscar thought. I am shuffling in my dream.

His heart began to rock behind his ribs. The light was the same, unearthly green glow at the end of the tunnel, the glow that would become a tapestry larger than a sail, clattering with bones and skulls. And behind it waited something ready and hungry.

He didn't want to go up there.

She'll be waiting. Behind the curtain of bone.

Megan howled again, an awful, pleading noise that became the simplest of words. "No! No, no, no!"

The glow shifted like green firelight. Sixty feet away, in the middle of the room.

Four figures.

Megan, naked on a table, her eyes staring at nothing, her chest rising and falling. Anne Chaume, in her tight red dress, bent over the girl, working a scalpel and whispering. Moechtar in glasses, standing beside Chaume, holding a dark cloth as a surgical nurse will hold ready a swab. And the police commissioner, leaning unsteadily on the table, his shoulders shaking. None looked up; they had not heard the gunshots above the storm.

The source of the light, the flickering green, had its back to Oscar. It sat at the end of the table, between Megan's bound ankles, shining its awful glow up her spread legs and over the four of them. Oscar could just make out the idol's silhouette. Hunched and horned. It was hard to see; its outline seemed to shift and flicker, to pulse. The air was as cold as a snow peak's, dry and dead.

Oscar stumbled. His leg was a lump of numb flesh now, a liability to drag around. His vision doubled and darkened. A bit longer, he pleaded in his mind, just a bit longer. He bit his cheek and tasted blood. His eyes cleared a little. He pulled the gun from his pocket.

"No, no, no," Megan wailed, squirming against straps, her pale flesh shaking, her face wet with tears and mucus.

Thirty more feet, but it might have been a hundred. The pistol in Oscar's hand felt as heavy as a suitcase. He knew he needed to halve the distance if he had a chance of hitting anything. Just a few more steps.

Chaume's red dress looked almost black, and her black hair was so glossy it reflected jade. Silver glinted in her hand, also reflecting the greenish flames. Copper, Oscar realized: it was the copper grate that burned green. There was blood all over Megan's quaking belly. Moechtar wiped it off while Chaume cut. The commissioner looked ready to faint. The frigid air was tainted by coal fire, vomit, and urine. Oscar felt so *tired*. Sleep.

Then he heard her voice. The words Chaume spoke were alien, rolling and hushed, like Arabic, but no Arabic he'd ever heard, mixed with Germanic fricatives, *zh, zh, zh*. Lulling. Urging. Only one word Oscar recognized. *Ereshkigal*.

The strange, horned altar seemed to swell as Chaume chanted. It seemed to expand, to *grow*.

Still, they hadn't seen him. The idol, the only light source, was between them and him. Twenty-five feet. Twenty. His cold leg was turning to black ice, spreading a choking dark frost up his body and neck, over his eyes. His vision was cloaked in black, and the three bodies around Megan seemed to be at the end of a tunnel. Fifteen feet but it looked fifty. They were tiny figures, little puppets on a diorama.

Megan screamed again, and her soft body arched. Chaume put down the scalpel and picked up a long, shining knife. Its triangular blade reflected the eldritch green light.

Oscar forced another shuffle forward. The air was so cold that his breaths formed veils of mist in front of him, tinged green. The room was at once a bell tower of noise—thunder; Megan's wailing; Chaume's imploring, rising voice—and oddly muffled, as if they were characters on a screen while he watched from the bunkered distance of the projection booth. He lifted the gun, but his arm wouldn't move. The pistol was so heavy it might have been an anvil, a cannon, the moon. *God*, he pleaded. *Please*. His arm slowly rose.

Chaume, a tiny thing, lifted the knife to the flame. Moechtar, now the doll he always seemed to Oscar, watched through glasses that were shining emerald ovals. The commissioner closed his eyes. Megan's belly was a small patch of red and white. The foggy air shimmered like a soft green curtain.

"Stop now," Oscar croaked. The pistol at the end of his arm looked small and shortened, like a coracle at the end of a long, thin jetty.

Chaume looked up. Moechtar turned and reached into his jacket. The knife moved down. Oscar told his finger to squeeze the trigger. Something shifted at the end of his arm, but it might have been the tremor of a pulse or a puff of breeze. *Don't jerk. Squeeze.* A flicker, but it might have been lightning. A sister flash, from Moechtar, as small as a firefly in a distant willow grove. People were moving, and then they were gone.

All was green. Soft as moss. Dark. A curtain. Something tinkled, like bones on a butcher's block.

Tick-tap-tick.

Or dice in a wooden bowl.

Or . . .

Chapter 42

He pushed aside the curtain, a simple thing of loosely woven wool threaded with tiny beads of colored pottery.

Green.

Color filled his mind like wind through a suddenly opened window. *Green. This room is so beautifully green.*

And yet, as he stepped in he realized that it was not the room itself that was green; the walls were mud bricks rendered with a plaster. It was the light that seemed green.

Tick-tap-tick.

Oscar stepped onto a flagstone floor, and found himself in an alcove. The sound of ticking, tapping wood grew louder. He followed the noise around the corner and saw the kitchen. At first, he thought he was back in Gelareh's apartment: warm afternoon sunlight filtered through vines and herbs in the courtyard outside and struck the room a thousand shades of emerald, peacock, jade, and lime. Smells arrived like a fresh dash of water—frying onion, simmering rice, apricots, saffron, bread, mint, walnuts, tarragon.

Tick-tap-crack.

But this was not Gelareh's flat. This house was older, much older. Its ceiling was domed and rendered. The courtyard was too bright to look at directly—the light poured in from the west, cooled by the winking sea of grapevines and honeysuckle and jasmine, but still dazzling. A breeze played at another curtain: more strands of thick, rough wool seeded with pottery beads. A figure was passing through it and out into the courtyard and the last of the day. From outside came the sounds of children laughing and playing.

"You'll see," said a woman beside the curtain, and she drew the beaded strands closed again. She smoothed her hands on the cloth she had tied about her loose dress. Then she seemed to realize that Oscar was behind her and she turned.

Her hair was black, held back by a worked-leather clip. She was tall and slim but luxuriantly curved; the makeshift apron knotted about her waist accentuated her hips. She was not young, but certainly not old—Oscar would have said she was his own age, in her mid-thirties, but any number refused to stick. Her beauty was timeless. A long, straight nose, narrow and in perfect proportion to her high forehead. Her lips were full; high cheekbones dropped sleekly to a strong jaw and a long neck. The skin of her arms and neck was the color of almond meal; her face was a shade paler. Her eyes were wide-set and almost black, outlined by kohl and long lashes.

She gazed at Oscar, and her eyes sparkled. She was either delighted or furious; amused or disappointed; lustful or chaste. All he was sure of was that she recognized him. Her lips drew upward in a pleasant smile.

"Well, well," she said. "Here you are."

Only she didn't say that. The words she said were older, curled with accents from a land Oscar had never seen, but, somehow, he knew them.

"I was asked to keep an eye on you," the woman said. She scrutinized his face a little longer, then she gestured with long, slender hands toward the kitchen. "Help us with the walnuts."

Tick-tick.

The kitchen was part of the same vaulted room, and as he approached the cooking smells grew stronger. Everything was set at knee height, so one could work while sitting on the flagstone floor. The wide bench of the same whitewashed handmade brick was two feet high, and its top was polished stone almost invisible under vases spilling with basil, baskets of plums and apricots, smaller vessels of fragrant seeds, tiny open sacks of orange, brown, and yellow herbs. White cloth sacks were suspended in an alcove pantry, and Oscar could see the pink curves of garlic bulbs and the serrated leaves of angelica. Two little brown cockatiels stirred in their head-tucked sleep in a carefully wrought bronze cage. Sweet woodsmoke rose to a hole in the ceiling from a waist-high fire pit upon which was a hot stone and, on it, a circle of flatbread cooking. A girl knelt on a reed mat beside the fireplace, attending the bread.

"Turn that before it burns," the woman suggested.

The girl nodded—*I know, I know!*—and reached for the bread, tweezing it between her fingers and flipping its uncooked side onto the stone. The girl turned and grinned at her achievement. It was Megan. She saw Oscar, and her eyes widened just a little in pleased surprise.

"Don't be so cocky. Take it off now," the woman said, and Megan plucked the flatbread off, put it onto a wooden platter, then reached for a ball of dough that she began teasing out into a flat disk. "Easy, don't poke holes in it."

"I won't," Megan said, and rolled her eyes conspiratorially at Oscar. There was no sign of her crippling brain damage. She was again the normal young girl, pretty with the freshness of youth, that she had been before Oscar's car hit her. Except she was older. Three years older. She grinned as a sleek cat rubbed itself against her thigh.

A dream, Oscar realized. *I am having a beautiful dream.*

The woman led Oscar to the other side of the low bench, and he saw a third figure who had been hidden behind a flourish of sweet basil. He sat cross-legged with a bowl of walnuts on his lap and was cracking them open with a wooden mallet—*tick-tick-tap*. Jamy wore a plain white shirt and dark-brown trousers. He looked up at Oscar and smiled. His eyes were hazel and reflected the rectangles of warm light pouring through the windows and courtyard door. Oscar felt the woman's hand gently press on his shoulder. He sat beside Jamy, who handed him a second mallet and moved a small basket of husked nuts closer. Oscar sat, and realized that his pains were gone.

A very pleasant dream.

No, said another voice in his head. A soberer voice. *You're dying.*

"So," the woman said, but didn't say. "We need to decide if you're staying for dinner. We have plenty, but we need to plan." Her voice was as refined and lovely as her face. It reminded Oscar of desert dunes—tight ripples on long curves, with sharp edges between light and shadow.

Oscar felt a warm nuzzle on his buttock and looked around to see another cat rub itself against him. He scratched behind its bony shoulders, and its purr vibrated through his fingers. He realized that he was hungry. He couldn't remember the last time he had eaten. The aromas of rice and herbs and yogurt and fresh flatbread made his mouth water.

"I don't know," Oscar replied. He looked at Jamy and Megan. "Are you staying?"

"I'd like to," Jamy said. He had a soft, pleasant voice.

Megan frowned, but Oscar couldn't tell if it was at the question or the hot bread she pulled off the cooking stone.

The woman took a small tuck of skirt on each thigh, lifted, and sat in a graceful descent that allowed Oscar to see, very clearly with the afternoon sun shining through the thin cotton, the shape of her strong, slim legs. She sensed his stare and raised her black eyes to meet his. Again, they sparkled, either with displeasure or delight. She patted her hands with flour and began to roll more dough.

"Well, the day is fading and you need to decide." She looked at Jamy. "Is he quick at decisions?"

Jamy shrugged. "Some," he said. "Others . . ." He looked at Oscar, a small reproach, vanished with a grin. *Tap-tick-crack.*

The four of them fell pleasantly silent for a moment, preparing their foods in the glow of late day. A breeze brought in the smells of sorghum and dates, cows, distant sand, and the more distant sea. Outside, in the brilliant afternoon light, Oscar could make out the forms of children laughing as they ran after a ball, or chased one another for the sheer delight of it.

The sunlight gleamed off something near Oscar's knee.

Glass. Two circles. And metal. Moechtar's glasses.

"He doesn't need them anymore," the woman said, and whisked them away.

Oscar nodded and shelled walnuts, pleased by the simple feelings of their smooth wood and yielding nut flesh under his fingers.

I might stay, he thought. *This is nice. Yes, I think I will—*

Knocking interrupted. Knuckles on a door somewhere out of sight.

The woman sighed and kept rolling her dough.

More knocking. Insistent now.

The birds in the bronze-wire cage stirred again and looked up. Oscar could see that they weren't cockatiels; they were too full and fluffed, their heads more flattened. They were tiny owls. One of them looked at Oscar, and he was sure its amber eyes narrowed in recognition. Then it yawned and showed its gray, dry tongue.

The knocking grew sharper. And a new scent arrived on the air. Not the bread, not the spices—something farther away but growing stronger. Meat cooking.

The woman rose to her bare feet, and Oscar found himself watching her breasts move as she stood.

"Why is it," she said, "that when you sit down to do something someone decides that *now* is the time to disturb?" She looked down at Oscar and smiled. It was beautiful but dangerously hard. Her nostrils flared, and she licked her lips. "What would you do?"

Oscar suddenly knew who was knocking at the door. He knew what the smell was.

"Send them away."

The woman's dark eyebrows arched, as if she found his answer obvious. "Regardless?" she asked.

"Of?"

The woman shrugged her slim brown shoulders. "Manners. Obligation. Gifts. Appetite."

Megan coughed conspicuously and dropped a disk of dough onto the hot stone with a sizzle.

"This is your house, isn't it?" Oscar asked.

The woman lifted her chin. "Do you not like it?"

"I love it," he answered, honestly.

This seemed to content her, and Oscar realized that he would not like to displease this woman. Her cats rubbed at her shins and calves. He envied them. "So?" she asked.

"Do you want what she brings?"

The woman shrugged, but it was a knowing gesture. Megan studiously poked at the bread.

"Then it depends on what pleases you most," Oscar continued. "Receiving gifts. Or doing as you will."

The woman kept her gaze on Oscar. The sun was dropping in the sky, and the greens in the room were being supplanted by warmer tones: coppers, dark golds, reds. Her eyes were lost in the shadows of her sculpted cheeks. It seemed as if he were staring into two dark wells. The hairs on the back of his neck rose.

The woman went to the cage, and the tiny owls stretched their wings and landed on her finger. Oscar could see their needle-sharp talons bite into the woman's skin, but they drew no blood.

"Come on, you lot," she said, and the cats trailed their mistress as she walked with her own catlike grace out of sight.

Tick-tick, crack.

Oscar looked at Jamy. The boy seemed to feel his stare and blushed, embarrassed. Oscar leaned over, kissed the boy's cheek, and roughed his hair. Jamy grinned and batted away Oscar's show of affection.

"Hey," Oscar called to Megan.

She looked up from her bread. She smiled, but her cheeks were wet.

Oscar rose, dusted walnut shell off his pants, and knelt beside her. There must be words, he thought. There must be words that can express a thousand sorrows and a thousand regrets. But none came. He felt her hand on his own head, much softer than the way he had just touched Jamy.

"An accident," Megan said softly. "That's all."

He looked up, and his eyes swam with tears.

"I'm so sorry," he said.

The girl wiped his cheeks with a thumb and gave him a piece of bread. "No complaints," she insisted.

The room was becoming cooler now. In contrast, its hues grew warmer with the setting sun. Coral pinks. Ember reds.

The hallway the woman had gone down was dark. And from the direction of the door came the sudden sound of a woman's scream.

Out in the courtyard, the children's laughter stalled for a moment, then redoubled. Such things were drops in the ocean, sand grains in the desert. And Oscar realized that he didn't want to stay. Not yet.

The door clicked open.

Oscar stood.

The woman was returning through the dark hallway—a black form in a gray, nestlike tunnel. It was perhaps a trick of the half-light, but the tunnel itself looked wider, higher, darker. The birds looked as large as mastiffs, and the cats as long as crocodiles . . . and the woman herself was tall, so much taller, filling the hallway. Her feet did not pad but clacked on the flagstones, and from her back spread not shadows but dark and powerful wings. But it was her face that trapped Oscar's eyes. It was beautiful still, but beautiful in the way an eagle in flight is beautiful. Inhuman. Her eyes were wide and large and the color of liquid copper. Her nose was long, hard, curved over her mouth. It dripped.

Then the woman stepped into the pleasant, brass-warm glow of sunset and the owls were small and fluffed, and the cats petite and remotely curious, the woman just a woman. But in the late light her face and skin and dress were red. Red, the color of fresh, thick blood.

Her eyes rested on Oscar for a long moment.

"You're leaving," she said. It was not a question.

Oscar nodded. "If I can."

Her hands rose, and Oscar flinched. Then she touched him. And her skin was warm. She pressed herself to him, and he felt her firm flesh through thin cloth. Her breath, as she kissed both cheeks, was warm, and smelled of blood.

"I shall see you soon."

She looked over Oscar's shoulder and nodded. Jamy stood, brushed off his own trousers, and came to Oscar's side. He sighed.

"Can't he stay?" Oscar asked.

"He does stay," the woman said, leading Oscar to the alcove he arrived through. "He is playing outside. But he goes with you, too."

She smiled and drew aside the curtain of wood and tiny beads. As she held the strands aside, he saw that the beads were not pottery at all. They were tiny, carefully painted knuckle bones.

Then the screaming started.

Chapter 43

t was Zoe. She was shouting at him to come on, to come *on*, Oscar!

Jesus, but it was cold. Why had he left that warm, lovely kitchen? *Come on! Breathe!*

He rocked on the ground. Her face was on his.

Cold. And beneath it, pain, awful pain, like a layer of acid bound in ice. His heart lay still in his chest, waiting for his decision.

Oscar!

Hell.

Beat, he said. Go on, and beat.

So it did.

————

He struggled like a fish thrown back into water, gasping and thrashing.

And with the air, rushing in through throat and nostrils, the tang of gunpowder and the salty stench of blood.

Somewhere behind the rumble of thunder, sirens wailed.

N̲o rain today. Oscar watched the sky with a cynical gaze. The clouds were as delicate as tiny fish scales, and so high and thin that they seemed themselves a pale blue. Nearby, the small leaves of pepper trees sighed in the breeze. Closer still, a deliberate cough.

Oscar looked down from the sky.

The clergyman caught his eye and nodded at the little silver pail of soil. Oscar stepped forward to the graveside. He took a little dirt in the scoop and tossed it down onto the casket. The soil tapped on the lid like fingers on a door. Oscar gave it no mind. He knew there was no one inside. Not really.

———

Oscar adjusted a crutch under one arm. He hovered in the background while the other mourners drifted away; he felt conspicuous in his dress uniform, although no one had given him a second glance except Jamy, who looked amused, and Zoe, who did not.

There weren't many people at Sandro's funeral. Vic Pascoe was in a wheelchair, his senile eyes staring vacantly as his nephew pushed him toward the parked cars. The commissioner had been unable to come: he was on remand, and on suicide watch. But the deputy commissioner had attended, in blues so richly ornamented that he looked like a flag come to life; he'd shaken Oscar's hand and said that they just didn't make detectives like Sandro Mariani anymore, all the while looking Oscar up and down very cautiously and no doubt thinking, So *this* is the one.

Foley came, after confirming that there would be a wake with a bar tab, and was chatting salaciously to the deputy commissioner's buxom aide-de-camp, whose watch needed a lot of checking. It was Foley who'd spirited to Oscar the Scenes of Crime photos from Chislehurst. They showed a large pool of blood where Oscar had lain while Zoe resuscitated him. He'd bled from the leg and the chest: the slug from Moechtar's gun had collapsed a lung, shattered two ribs, and missed his liver by less than a centimeter. Jon's body was photographed lumped like a wheat sack at the bottom of the stairs. Moechtar had been shot cleanly through the left temple and was slumped over Megan as if listening for a pulse. There was none: Megan had been opened up like Penny Roth. "They found her bits in that thing," Foley had explained with disgust. "In that clay thing. Chaume, that fucking butcher bitch."

It was Anne Chaume's body that was most interesting, and most unpleasant to look at. There was sufficient skin left on one finger to print and match with items in her bedroom, and thus confirm that the body was hers. The corpse had been flayed: her face and breasts and the skin of her arms and legs had been ripped from her body. The gouges in the bones of her skull and anterior rib cage were, in places, a quarter inch deep. Her eyes had been plucked out, and her soft organs torn and savaged. Many chunks, Foley said, were just plain missing. He'd looked at Oscar, wanting more, but Oscar had said nothing.

In the hospital, Oscar learned that the commissioner was being charged as an accessory to murder, and had, by all accounts, gone quite mad. In his bed, Oscar had been asked a lot of questions. He'd answered them all but said nothing of his trip into the kitchen where he shelled walnuts with Jamy Brum and watched Megan smile as she turned flatbreads on a hot stone. Anthony McAuliffe could not be found, so Oscar arranged Megan's funeral from the hospital. Hers had been yesterday, his father's today, Neve's tomorrow. The minister was now talking to the funeral director. The mourners were gone; time to wrap it up. Sandro's headstone, next to Vedetta's, looked good. Oscar had paid to add a boy's name below his mother's.

Oscar shifted on his crutches and started back to the parking lot alone, wincing at the pressure of the crutch pad in his armpit.

Zoe waited on the footpath, a scowling sprite. She found funerals unpleasant, she claimed, but he knew that she simply didn't like the look of him in uniform. Up the road, something caught Oscar's eye. Parked under a wide Moreton Bay chestnut tree was a sleek white patrol car. Haig leaned on its hood, admiring the lawns.

Oscar looked at Zoe. "Give me another few minutes?"

"I have to work today," she said.

He nodded and shuffled stiffly toward Haig, who was lighting a cigarillo.

"I didn't see you at the service," Oscar said.

"Well," Haig said, clicking his lighter shut. "We both know you don't notice the obvious."

Haig gestured toward a nearby open rotunda, and Oscar nodded.

"Not a bad stick, your father." Haig walked with his hands in his pockets. "Incorruptible. We had a fight once. An actual fight. I can't even remember what it was over."

"Ethics, I expect."

Haig shrugged. "He won. I was drunk, and he fought dirty. Dirty little Italian. Just like you."

Oscar didn't mind the sound of that. They reached the shade of the rotunda, and Oscar sat stiffly.

"You warned me off Chislehurst," he said. "You knew something was up."

"Like I said," Haig said through smoke, "I didn't know which side you were on."

"You knew Moechtar was crooked."

Haig stared out across the headstones. "Not crooked," he replied. "Guilty." He looked at Oscar. His eyes were as bright and hard as ever. "I just didn't know what of."

They sat in silence. Oscar watched as the last of the mourners got into their cars. Foley saw Oscar, and took a step toward the rotunda; then he noticed Haig and stopped dead before awkwardly changing direction.

Oscar sighed and signaled for a cigarillo. Haig's eyes narrowed, then he handed over his silver tin. Oscar took a smoke and waited for Haig to light it.

"You had Jon try to get me out of the picture. Way back when."

Haig nodded. "I did. You really were pissing me off." Haig rubbed his chin thoughtfully. "Inexcusable, though, what he did to that boy. Damned unprofessional."

Jamy sat a few yards away, under a tree, looking down at an ants' nest or a twig or nothing at all.

Oscar nodded. Through the trees, he could see a little orange backhoe trundling down a path, heading toward Sandro's grave.

"I could bring that up again," Oscar suggested. "Implicate you."

"Ah, yes. You could." Haig stubbed out his cigarillo on the painted timber and looked at Oscar. "But not a lot of evidence. Besides"—he pushed himself up off the seat and stepped into the brilliant sunlight—"you're no longer pissing me off. Sorry to hear about the Barelies. When you're up to it, drop by."

Oscar watched Haig walk back to his car, unsure what it all meant. He was alive. He was wearing his uniform, and no one had asked him to take it off. It was a strange world.

He looked up at the mackerel clouds skating silently high overhead. No rain today.

Acknowledgments

I owe great debts of thanks to many people who helped this novel arrive. I'm certain I've missed some, and to them I apologize.

As ever, I want to express my gratitude to my tireless and inspiring agent, Selwa Anthony.

My publisher, Vanessa Radnidge, at Hachette Australia, possesses amazing insight and endless patience—her skill, ideas, and deep care for her books and her authors are treasures I value enormously.

Heartfelt thanks go to my editor at Doubleday, Robert Bloom, whose love for good storytelling is infectious, and whose abilities are priceless.

Huge thanks must go to the rest of the Hachette team and Michael Windsor, Joe Gallagher, John Jenkinson, and everyone else at Doubleday for the hard work and great faith they've put in this book.

Copy editors Carol Anderson and Claire de Medici helped elevate the text to a new level and made countless wise suggestions.

It's important to both thank and congratulate Karina Machado, whose brilliant nonfiction book *Spirit Sisters* opened my mind to what ghosts might be and mean.

I'd like to thank Tania and Nicole Brancato for their invaluable thoughts.

Sharon and Malcolm Hinton deserve special thanks both for checking details against their own experiences and for their precious friendship.

My deepest thanks are for my family, who tolerated my long absences while this book came to be: my divine children, Max and

Poppy, and my beautiful wife, Sarah, who makes everything easy—I adore you.

Finally, I'd like to thank you, the reader, for taking the time to pick up this book. I hope you've forgiven its flaws (they are all mine!) and enjoyed it.